Praise for *The Tragedy of Arthur*

"Splendidly devious."
— *The New York Times Book Review* (cover review)

"Sparkling and imaginative . . . Shakespeare would applaud a man who does him so proud. Readers, too, may well praise Phillips for crafting so wily and witty an excursion into the ties that bind fiction and life."
— *The Boston Globe*

"His wildest and funniest yet, at once homage to Nabokov's *Pale Fire*, satire of literary hagiography in general and Shakespeare scholarship in particular, and a hilarious yet trenchant riff on memoirs."
— NPR.org

"Devious and exhilarating . . . such a wonderful con job."
— *The Wall Street Journal*

"A brilliant piece of literary criticism masquerading as a novel . . . the most ambitious book on Shakespeare I've come across in many years . . . a compulsively fascinating read."
— JAMES SHAPIRO, The Daily Beast

"There are few limits to Mr. Phillips's imagination."
— *The Guardian*

"Wily and wonderful . . . a shape-shifting stunner . . . diabolically merry."
— *Cleveland Plain Dealer*

"A literary treasure . . . shows off a writer at the top of his game."
— *The Washington Post*

"[Phillips] writes beautifully. His prose crackles with wit, and tough but shrewd observations. . . . Certainly, it contains literary echoes of Nabokov, Stoppard and even the Thomas Pynchon of *The Crying of Lot 49*. . . . I don't think these comparisons are unmerited. This is the real deal: You just can't fake this stuff. . . . Ultimately, this is a book about authenticity, not only of literary texts but also of people and filial relationships. . . . Serious and emotionally rich material, and Phillips handles it skillfully and sympathetically."
—*San Francisco Chronicle* (cover review)

"Phillips invests the metafictional gamesmanship with bracing intelligence and genuine heart. . . . The energy never flags as the book develops into both a literary mystery and a surprisingly effective critique of the Bard." —*Entertainment Weekly*

"The novel is, indeed, a tragedy of authorship, but it is also the story of a man whose self-inflicted, tragicomic woes are as affecting and wincingly believable as those endured by the hero of any conventional fiction. That Arthur's spectacular crash-and-burn comes nestled in a web of ingenious and very funny literary allusions only makes it that much more of a treat." —Salon

"Witty, touching, intricate." —St. Paul *Pioneer Press*

"As a concept, *The Tragedy of Arthur* is ingenious. As a novel, it is affecting. . . . A concoction of such amusing erudition, obvious Bard worship and hilarious footnotes you sort of wish it were real. What is real is Phillips' ongoing work as one of our most original writers."
—*Newsday*

"Like his spiritual brother, David Mitchell, Phillips not only kicks postmodernism awake but encourages it to shoot crystal meth."
—*The Village Voice*

"A long-lost Shakespeare play surfaces in Phillips's wily fifth novel, a sublime faux memoir framed as the introduction to the play's first printing—a Modern Library edition, of course. . . . Then there's the play itself, which reads not unlike something written by the man from Stratford-upon-Avon. It's a tricky project, funny and brazen, smart and playful." —*Publishers Weekly* (starred review)

"What a great idea. For his fifth novel, *The Tragedy of Arthur*, Arthur Phillips has created—or discovered, to go along with the conceit of his fiction—a lost Shakespeare play, *The Most Excellent and Tragical Historie of Arthur, King of Britain*, purportedly written in 1597. Or has he? That's part of the point of this audacious novel, to blur the lines between reality and imagination, to use the play as a starting point for a meditation on the nature of family, identity, deception and literary heritage. . . . How fun to watch a writer be so discursive and irreverent, producing a story within a story that cannot help but comment on itself." —*Los Angeles Times* (Faces to Watch in 2011)

"A memoir and a Shakespearean play wrapped into a novel? Who could pull this off but the prolific Phillips? . . . Highly recommended for all who enjoy inspired, original, entertaining writing—deftly delivered here by one of our most talented arthurs, uh, authors." —*Library Journal* (starred review)

THE TRAGEDY OF ARTHUR

THE TRAGEDY OF A
NOVEL BY ARTHUR
PHILLIPS RANDOM
HOUSE TRADE PAPER
BACKS ⬠ NEW YORK

2012 Random House Trade Paperback Edition

Published in the United States by Random House Trade Paperbacks,
an imprint of The Random House Publishing Group, a division of
Random House, Inc., New York.

RANDOM HOUSE TRADE PAPERBACKS and colophon are trademarks
of Random House, Inc.
RANDOM HOUSE READER'S CIRCLE & Design is a registered trademark
of Random House Inc.

Originally published in hardcover in the United States by Random House,
an imprint of The Random House Publishing Group, a division of
Random House, Inc., in 2011.

LIBRARY OF CONGRESS CATALOGING-IN-PUBLICATION DATA

Phillips, Arthur.
The tragedy of Arthur: a novel / by Arthur Phillips.
p.   cm.
ISBN 978-0-8129-7792-9
eBook ISBN 978-0-679-60506-5
I. Title.
PS3616.H45T73 2011
813'.6—dc22   2010021192

Printed in the United States of America

www.randomhousereaderscircle.com

2 4 6 8 9 7 5 3 1

Book design by Simon M. Sullivan

PREFACE

Random House is proud to present this first modern edition of *The Tragedy of Arthur* by William Shakespeare.

Until now, Shakespeare's dramatic canon consisted of thirty-eight or thirty-nine plays, depending on whose scholarship one trusted and whose edition of the *Complete Works* one owned. Thirty-six plays were included in the so-called First Folio of 1623, published seven years after the playwright's death. Two more—collaborations, likely delayed for copyright reasons—were added to subsequent seventeenth-century collections. A thirty-ninth play, *Edward III*, has over the last two decades garnered increasing academic support as having been written, at least in part, by Shakespeare, but it was published only anonymously in his lifetime and is by no means universally acknowledged as a Shakespeare play. A further two works—*Cardenio* and *Love's Labour's Won*—are referred to in historical documents, but no copies of either have survived. Another dozen or so plays—the so-called Apocrypha—do exist and are debated, but none have acquired anything approaching scholarly consensus as being the work of Shakespeare.

The Tragedy of Arthur was published as a quarto in 1597. Its cover's claim that the text is "newly corrected and augmented" implies a previous version now lost, but this 1597 edition was, as far as we now know, the first play to be printed with Shakespeare's name on the title page, pre-dating *Love's Labour's Lost* by one year. Likely banned, or at least judged politically dangerous and therefore excluded from the 1623 folio, the play apparently fell into disfavor, and only one copy of that 1597 quarto has so far been discovered. It was not found until the 1950s, and has been held in a private collection until now. *The Tragedy of Arthur* is, therefore, the first certain addition to Shakespeare's canon since the seventeenth century.

The story it tells is not the legend of Camelot most readers know. There is no sword in the stone, no Lancelot, no Round Table, no Merlin or magic. Instead, Shakespeare seems to have worked from his usual source for history plays, Raphael Holinshed's 1587 *Chronicles of England, Scotland, and Ireland*. The resulting plot is something more like *King Lear*, a violent argument of succession in Dark Ages Britain. But, like *Lear*, it is about so very much more, and the white heat that courses through the whole structure is Shakespeare's unmistakable imagination and language.

Many people have worked with great dedication to make this book possible. It could not have come to pass without the academic leadership of Professor Roland Verre, who has overseen the research and tests that have confirmed the play's authenticity and William Shakespeare as its sole or primary author. Professor Verre submitted the text to a battery of computerized stylistic and linguistic examinations, solicited the critical opinions of his peers on three continents, and supervised the forensic study of the 1597 document's paper and ink. Academic opinion has steadily grown in volume and certainty over the past year, and there is now no notable voice in Shakespearean studies who questions the authenticity of *The Tragedy of Arthur*.

Our gratitude extends equally to the dozens more professors of English language and literature, theater directors, linguists and critics, historians and Shakespeare experts who formed our ad hoc advisory board, as well as the specialists in ink, paper, and printing led by Dr. Peter Bryce, and a legion of researchers, editorial assistants, and legal experts. The contributions of Professors David Crystal, Tom Clayton, and Ward Elliott (whose Claremont Shakespeare Clinic conducted the stylometry tests) demand particular recognition.

This first edition comes with a unique appreciation by a Random House author, Arthur Phillips. As his family played a central role in bringing the play to light and corroborating its authenticity, he was invited to write a brief introduction to this monumental work, even though he certainly does not claim to be a Shakespeare expert. He also edited and annotated the text of the play. Professor Verre has kindly amended some of Mr. Phillips's notes.

Despite Phillips's importance to the work's discovery, we would suggest that general readers plunge directly into the play, allowing Shakespeare to speak for himself, at least at first. Then, if some background is helpful, look to this very personal Introduction or to the many other commentaries sure to be available soon.

THE EDITORS
Random House/Modern Library
January 2011

. The

MOST EXCELLENT AND
TRAGICAL HISTORIE OF

ARTHUR,

King of Britain.

As it hath beene diuers times plaide by the right
Honourable The Lord Chamberlaine His Seruants.

Newly corrected and augmented
By W. SHAKESPERE.

LONDON
Imprinted by W.W. for Cutbert Burby.
1597.

INTRODUCTION

ARTHUR PHILLIPS

INTERNATIONALLY BESTSELLING AUTHOR OF
Prague, The Egyptologist, Angelica, AND *The Song Is You*

If you do not feel the impossibility of this speech having been written
by Shakespeare, all I dare suggest is that you may have ears—for so has
another animal—but an ear you cannot have.
— SAMUEL TAYLOR COLERIDGE, about *Henry VI, Part One*

•

Shakespeare never did this. He never did this.
— THE BLOW MONKEYS, "Don't Give It Up"

•

Believe me, my friends, that men, not very much inferior to
Shakespeare, are this day being born on the banks of the Ohio.
— HERMAN MELVILLE

•

Phillips himself evidently wanted to carry the performance outside the
walls of the playhouse.
— STEPHEN GREENBLATT, *Will in the World*

1

I HAVE NEVER MUCH LIKED SHAKESPEARE. I find the plays more
pleasant to read than to watch, but I could do without him, up to
and including this unstoppable and unfortunate book. I know that is
not a very literary or learned thing to confess, but there it is. I wonder if there isn't a large and shy population of tasteful readers who se-
cretly agree with me. I would add that *The Tragedy of Arthur* is as
good as most of his stuff, or as bad, and I suppose it is plausible (vocabulary, style, etc.) that he wrote it. Full disclosure: I state that as the
party with the most money to be made in this venture.

As a cab driver asked in an ironic tone when I told him I was contractually bound to write something about Shakespeare, "And what hasn't been written about him yet?" Perhaps this: although it is probably not evident to anyone outside my immediate family and friends, my own career as a novelist has been shadowed by my family's relationship to Shakespeare, specifically my father and twin sister's adoration of his work. A certain amount of cheap psychology turns out to be true: because of our family's early dynamics, I have as an adult always tried to impress these two idealized readers with my own language and imagination, and have always hoped someday to hear them say they preferred me and my work to Shakespeare and his.

Even as I write that—as I commit it to print and thereby make it true—I know it is ridiculous. I cannot really feel that I am in competition with this man born four hundred years to the day before me. There is nothing in the clichéd description of him as the greatest writer in the English language that should have anything to do with me, my place in literature, the love of my family, or my own "self-esteem," to use an embarrassing word stinking of redemptive memoirs. I should be glad for the few lines of his that I like and think nothing of the rest, ignore the daffy religion that is the world's mad love of him. (Or, in the case of those troubled folk who don't think he wrote *Hamlet* or *Romeo and Juliet*, equally mad disbelief.)

I am not by nature a memoirist, any more than Shakespeare was. I am a novelist. But if you are to understand this play, its history, and how it came to be here, a certain quantity of my autobiography is unavoidable. Nobody comes off particularly well in the story of how we arrived here, except perhaps my sister, Dana. I certainly am not the hero. But I do have the legal right to occupy this discovery space outside the play for as long as I wish. No one may lay a red pen on me here, so if these turn out to be the last words of mine that Random House ever publishes, they will at least be true, and the record will be set straight, if only for a while, before it rewarps.

I will perform my contractual requirements—history, synopsis, editing, notes—but I have other things to say as well, and a few apologies to issue, before I creep offstage.

2

M Y PARENTS LIVED TOGETHER until Dana and I were six. Memories of that early age are untrustworthy except as a measure of the predominant emotion at the time. When I summon images of the four of us together, I recall happiness: pervasive, aromatic, connected to textures and weather and faces. (I suspect those faces are not real memories, exactly. They are memory-animations of old photos I have, or imagined snapshots of old stories I've heard.)

My father emerges first as a man who conquered night, who never slept. This is not an uncommon idea children have of their parents: kids at five, six, seven have to go to bed when the adults are awake, and they wake to find those adults already in action. If you do not live with them again after this age, parents will survive in memory as creatures magically exempt from slumber. But my father was even more a figure of the night than that. I remember several occasions when he woke me in darkest black (perhaps only nine P.M., but by then a five-year-old is already deep beneath a wash of delta waves), excited to share some great news or show me some once-in-a-lifetime event. "Wake up, Bear! Bear! You have to see this. Wake up!"

I was asleep, my beloved solar-system book fallen on my chest, my fingers still voyaging over its black and starry cover. I was asleep, and then I was in his arms, flying from my bed, awake and asleep and back and forth, and then I was out on the wet lawn, still cradled in his arms, barely able to peel open my crusted eye, to look, at his whispered urging, into his tripodded, heaven-angling telescope's eyepiece. And there I saw Saturn, my favorite: ringed, unworldly, a giant top among specks of dust. And then he turned some dial, fiddled somehow with the telescope's lenses and settings, and he brought the view much closer, and I could see a dozen of Saturn's inhabitants, moving back and forth in their excitement, taking turns looking through their telescope, gesturing at what they saw, up in their own sky, amazed at the sight of me, trying to get my attention.

And then I was brought back to bed, and he kissed me back to sleep.

A little boy wakes from that and—first thing—consults with the most reliable and trusted person in his world for clarification. I asked my twin sister if she had had any dreams, as we often shared them in those suggestible days. "No, because Dad woke me up to see Saturn," Dana replied matter-of-factly. "I love the rings. It's the best planet. Except for Pluto."

"No, Saturn's better. Did you see the people?"

"Yeah, but Pluto's better."

This was as hotly as Dana and I ever disagreed about anything in those days.

Pancakes shaped like Saturn, pancakes shaped like Mickey Mouse, which, my father said, could occur accidentally. He would dramatically cover his eyes while dribbling the batter, and sure enough, every fifth pancake (we were five years old) was unmistakably Mickey. I used to take pleasure, even at that provably selfish age, in donating my Mickeys to Dana, and every time she thanked me with real amazement. I recall, too, a pancake with the uncanny profile of my mother, placed before her with a long kiss from the chef to the top of her head. "You've got butter on your nose," he said, placing a dollop on her pancake's leftmost tip.

(I made pancakes for my own kids in my day. Perhaps it was the Czech flour, but my repertoire consisted solely of ovals and Pollocks. Their Aunt Dana never did any better when she visited.)

Our mother took us to an exhibit of Dad's paintings. She made us dress up. I had a little bow tie. Dana and I were allowed to walk around on our own, soda in paper cups, hand in hand, and we made each other laugh with stories about each painting, Dad's and others in the group show. We sat on a wooden bench and watched our mother put her hand on our father's back, his tumbleweed of black Einstein hair swaying slightly from the rotating floor fan. We blew bubbles in our 7UP, and I made fart sounds for Dana.

"Those last group shows," my mother reported much later. "So depressing."

But not for us. My father's increasingly desperate and pathetic final efforts at being an acknowledged artist had no effect on me and Dana just yet. His anger at the world's indifference was imperceptible to us, and that is to his credit, or due to children's natural indifference. For us, the adult world was soda on wooden benches, paintings and stories, midnight glimpses of Saturnine astronomers, magic pancakes. Our father amazed us and won our love not because he treated us like children, but because we thought he was treating us like adults, and adulthood was just a much better childhood.

3

"I<small>N</small> S<small>HAKESPEARE'S</small> <small>DAY</small>, kids your age could speak Latin. Brains can soak up anything, but if you pour in Nancy Drew and TV shows, that's all you'll learn." Our father started reading Shakespeare to us when we were six, and it worked for one of us: Dana was reading it to herself within a year. Her love and knack for Shakespeare were, to my eye back then, maybe a little forced—at least at the beginning, an obvious effort to please Dad. But dye sets in, and what was once an affectation can become our truest self.

More significantly, this was the first time Dana and I did not agree about something important. I just didn't like the stuff; Dana did. It is extraordinary to note it now, but I don't think that had ever happened before. Still, I saw that it bound her to Dad, so I faked it for a while. That didn't last, and soon I started wandering off when that fat brown book came off the shelf. This was a little—not to overstate it—traumatic for both me and Dana, I think, because, not long after the realization of this disorienting distance between us, Dad "went away" for the first time. Somehow those two events seemed related. They still do.

My father's arrest and conviction that first time was—to a seven-year-old—the bloody birth of awareness that the adult world is dangerous, a place where you could lose badly, and where my father was by no means in control. "Your father has to go away for a while," says the brave and tearful mother hustled over from subconscious central casting when recollection fails.

At that age, one is too selfish to understand it as her loss or even *his* loss or his imprisonment at all, only as *our* loss, and particularly *mine*.

The child is punished with the father's absence, and some arbitrary evil is to blame—not Dad, not yet. Possibly the child committed some crime himself and so has had his father taken from him? I'm told I cried for many nights running, scouring my conscience for the nasty thing I did, and even—God help me—trying to read Shakespeare as penance.

Fortunately, I had a twin. Twins enjoy what the rest of humanity craves: a perfect communion with another person, the absence of all loneliness. We are born with that certainty, two yolks in a single shell. We carry it with us into consciousness. When self-consciousness is born in us, we feel part of something and someone else larger than ourselves. (We pay a terrible price, however. Unlike the rest of you, we know what it feels like and we have to give it up, breaking eggs to join you in this vain search for an omelette to absorb us.)

Dad wasn't gone long, that first time, and then he came back to live with us. But he went away again less than two years later.

When we were eight or nine, after our parents were separated but before our mother remarried, she woke us early one winter Saturday. It was still dark, but that's not saying much in a Minnesota January. She had already sprinted out to the garage to unplug the car's core heater from the wall outlet, start the engine, and leave it to warm up as she sprinted back inside. Forced to eat and dress as if it were a school day, I crept along unwillingly, like a snail, but Dana was quickly ready, refusing food and hurrying into her coat and lunar footwear. We rode through the Minneapolis cold as the sky bleached and streetlights winked. We drove out of the city, through two-story suburbs, then one-story, through dreary flatland, past white and hibernating farms until we reached daylight and the minimum-security facility, where we were led into the Family Room, as that windowless, barred space of gray concrete was whimsically named.

Our mother pointed out the table where we were meant to sit, and then she stepped away. I may be misremembering, or she may have said hello to him when I wasn't looking. Either way, we were to present our belated Hanukkah gifts to him while she stayed far across the room reading the newspaper.

Our father was brought out to us. I recall being disappointed that he wasn't shackled. I don't think I wanted him to suffer (although maybe I did; I don't underestimate children's preference for color over kindness). Rather, I was searching, I think, for some evidence of harsh treatment so that I could imagine rescuing him, or begin to accept that my crimes had led him to a dire and unjust end. Instead, his world just looked boring.

I had spent some allowance on modeling clay and made him a diorama: the four of us together in our house (three shoe boxes cut open and taped together), our hands joined in a circle around the kitchen table, upon which was spread a vast, if not entirely recognizable, clay feast. This work expressed many of my fixations at eight years old: a reunited family, food (I was in the midst of one of my chubby spells, which correlated pretty well with his jail time), and religion (a short-lived fever, but it was climbing fast that year). The sculpture had suffered a bit in the cold, and white cracks had shot through most of the furniture and figures. I felt a round of pre-crying trembles revving up in my face. My father thanked me, complimented the "evident skill and passion involved," pointed out his favorite parts, seemed pleased, I suppose. He promised me some lessons working with clay when he came home. He apologized that he couldn't keep the gift where he was but asked me to protect it for him. That's when my tears broke through the flimsy dam. I think my mother should have warned me that he wouldn't be allowed to keep the diorama. I snuffled my promise to guard it until he was set free.

By then Dana couldn't keep still another minute, and had no patience for me to have some emotional attack before her big moment. "Daddy, I have to give you mine now."

"Can't wait," he said, and I thought he meant he literally could not wait because the guards were coming to haul him away.

"You have to wait, Dad! She worked hard for you," I sputtered, rushing to protect Dana from heartbreak.

"Artie, it's okay: I can't wait, meaning I'm excited. Let's have it, Dana."

Her eyes were wide and she stood up at the table, her hands

clasped in front of her chest. She began Portia's big speech from *The Merchant of Venice*, Act IV, Scene i. She shouted it at first, directly at one of the startled corrections officers standing next to the grated door leading back to the cells. The guard actually put up with it, or was too surprised to stop her, for a few lines, from *The quality of mercy* until *Upon the place beneath* before he barked, "Little girl, sit your ass down and keep it quiet or we are done today."

Dana was never easy to cow; she was always much braver than I. She wasn't scared by this giant with a nightstick, but she didn't want to cause her dad any trouble or have her visit cut short. And so she surrendered her initial plan to recite the twenty-two-line monologue to the entire penitentiary Family Room, transforming it into the law courts of Venice. She had even picked out—she told me later, in the car ride home, weeping much more plentifully than I—which guard she intended to look at on line 197 with a piercing "therefore, *Jew.*" Of course, we were Jewish, but that didn't mean she identified with Shylock or his vindictive interpretation of the law against the gentle Gentile merchant Antonio.

Shut down by the authorities, she composed herself and began again, more quietly. Too eager, too fast at first, she slowed down by the middle, and I watched them, from outside their circle of two, the two of them staring intently at each other in profile, an optical-illusion vase. My father's upper lip hid between his teeth, and he nodded slightly as he tapped—pop POP pop POP—his stained and chewed-up fingernails against the flecked Formica tabletop to keep his girl in tight iambic rhythm through the speech.

She came to the end: "*We do pray for mercy . . . This strict court of Venice / Must needs give sentence 'gainst that merchant there,*" opening her palms to Dad as if he were Antonio, persecuted by some vengeful Shylock. Dana looked at him with a naked desire for praise, but then something happened that I didn't understand for many years, if I understand it even now. My father took the next line (Shylock's). He groaned, rather than shouted, "*My deeds upon my head! I crave the law.*" He was turning the original meaning ("don't waste time with mercy, give me what my enemy owes me") into something else ("punishment is what I deserve"). It seems to me now that it was an apology of sorts to his daughter, and an indulgence of his occasional taste for self-flagellation.

Despite her triumph performing an inconceivable task no eight-year-old could possibly do (reciting, probably flawlessly, twenty-two lines of gibberish), filling me with pride in her ability to thrill Dad, she was convinced she hadn't been good enough. That's what she murmured to me in the back of that old blue Plymouth Valiant, her mittened hand in mine, my orange down jacket stiff from her tears freezing on my shoulder while the car strained to heat up in the twenty-below Minnesota air (forty below with windchill), our faces red and tightly inexpressive from the cold, our fingers burning blue, the hard vinyl seats and useless twisted blue seat belts. Of course she was crying because of having to say goodbye to her father, again, already in his second short prison term of our young lives, and she was crying because our mother had never sat with him, spoken to him, acknowledged him. But Dana told me, years later, that she was also crying because she had just suffered a strange disillusionment, the grisly death of a childish fantasy: Shakespeare didn't crumble the walls, fell the guards, melt the system's heart. Shakespeare didn't fix everything, or anything, just gave a moment of pleasure that would linger on in two people's minds (she didn't think to include me or already knew better), and this was a thorned disappointment for the little girl prodigy, whose love for words and fantasy had far outgrown her ability to understand the real world.

"Enough, Dana, please. Enough," sighed our exasperated mother, tired of all the bawling.

4

DAD WAS OUT AGAIN the next year, 1973, when we were nine. In *The Tragedy of Arthur*, King Arthur is portrayed as a charismatic, charming, egocentric, short-tempered, principled but chronically impulsive bastard. He is a flawed hero, at best, who succeeds then fails as a result of his unique personality. Unable to find a solid self upon which to rely, he ricochets from crisis to crisis, never quite seeing how he has caused the crisis until it is too late, and then flying so far to the opposite extreme in a doomed effort to repair his mistakes that he inevitably makes things still worse. This description also fits my father, Arthur Edward Harold Phillips.

In American literature and movies, the reigning Jew is still the meek scholar or the mild family man, although I've lately noticed a growing cinematic population of tough Jews, surprising hero soldiers, rebels, kickers of Nazi ass, the occasional gangster. But the Anglophilic, artsy, bohemian Jew is a rarer bird, assimilating into the Gentile world not from any desire to blend in but because he is too florid to prune himself to fit available Jewish types. This, somewhat, was my father: not bookish, as Jews in his day were meant to be, but flamboyantly literary. Not self-hating, but self-creating. Not interested in himself as a Jew at all, but by no means interested in anonymity.

His imprisonments before the final one seemed even—sometimes—to amuse him, or at least he was so intent on playing out his created character that he would not let on to any disappointment at being convicted of a crime. He refused, at least in front of me, to take any of it seriously, as if it somehow had nothing to do with him. It was only much later that he ever indulged an urge to blame someone else, to resent or regret his life. A psychiatrist would (and did) perceive in this a diagnosable medical disorder. In older, more romantic days, though, it would have been a heroic attitude or the sign of a profoundly philosophical character. He was able to keep it up until that last sentence, when they snatched most of his life away.

To this day, I do not know the extent of my father's crimes or even most of his employers (clients, in his parlance). I know everything he was convicted of, some of which he admitted to, some of which he stubbornly denied in private even when he had pleaded guilty. He tended to downplay the seriousness of his offenses. "It's really a question of misvaluation, an uneven distribution of knowledge between buyer and seller, just a market inefficiency, and so I'm going to jail," he told me. This was in the case of a collector at auction paying more for a drawing than it might otherwise have been worth because my father had added a signature and a long, very supportive, typed and aged provenance, transubstantiating the small picture, temporarily, from anonymity to Rembrandtivity.

When pompously asked if he had anything to say for himself before sentencing, my father, putting on a good show, reminded the court that he hadn't drawn it, only signed it. "That hardly speaks in your favor," lectured the judge, whom I, at thirteen, instinctively disliked, a puckered school-principal type, later to appear in various guises in my novels. "At least drawing it would mean you'd made something of value."

"No," my father rebuked the judge. "Your Honor, I have to object to that. The drawing was, and now again is, without much value. While it supported belief, thanks to me, its value swelled a thousand-fold, and people loved it a thousand times more. Punish me for doing it badly: all right. For getting caught: fine. For failing the world: guilty. But don't say I didn't make something!" I applauded, expecting others would join me. If it had been a movie, the courtroom would have shaken with cheers that swallowed the limp gavel's tapping, and some new evidence or technicality would have bubbled up to the attention of counsel.

"Without parole," concluded the judge. That was 1977.

Truly criminal people, in my father's view, were men like the Rembrandt Research Project, a squad of Dutch art experts who swept through the world's museums a few years ago, like avenging angels of facts or Santa Clausicidal maniacs, downgrading this or that old master (even *signed* paintings) to the status of "School of . . ." or "In the style of . . ." or the smirky "Attributed to . . ." My father ranted about these guys when I visited him in the late 1990s, as if it were the only thing on his mind. "Who wants to be *that*?" he stormed from across some other Formica. "What kid dreams of growing up to be the tight-ass joykill who travels the globe waving his facts around and denying people pleasure? As if his facts prove anything."

"What difference does it make?" I asked.

"All the difference in the world."

"Why? It's the same painting. It just means you can't be pretentious about it. But if you liked the picture before, you still like it now. It doesn't matter who painted it."

"Aesthetic empiricism," he replied blandly. "I know, but that's rare, Artie. Fact is, most people like the brand name, and the brand name helps them enjoy the product and opens them to trust other products. So being the big Dutch queen who prances around snatching off the brands—even if he's right, which there's no saying he is, although I do know the truth in one case, and he is right—that stops a lot of people from learning what they like. They don't want to say they like it, because they're afraid the Dutch guy's going to call them a fool for liking the wrong thing."

A few years ago I was reading a book of essays I'd been asked to review for *Harper's* called *The Curtain*, by the Czech novelist Milan Kundera. In it he writes, "Let us imagine a contemporary composer writing a sonata that in its form, its harmonies, its melodies resembles Beethoven's. Let's even imagine that this sonata is so masterfully made that, if it had actually been by Beethoven, it would count among his greatest works. And yet no matter how magnificent, signed by a contemporary composer it would be laughable. At best its author would be applauded as a virtuoso of pastiche." I was at home in Prague, lying in bed next to my wife, who was humming in her sleep. I hadn't been to the United States in a few years, hadn't seen my father in years, and I had lately noticed with some relief how rarely I thought of him with anger or pain, *finally*, and then, at Kundera's provocation, I began to cry. I still don't agree with the sentiment—that a name on a work of art matters—but it was my father's view of the world, and that day in court when I'd applauded him alone, he'd won me over, when I was an overweight and otherwise underdeveloped thirteen-year-old, and my father could still, for a little longer, do no wrong, no matter how many times the state said otherwise.

I would have said it was a strict borderline: I loved him without reservation until the age when reservations were required. And yet, my mother told me a story last year that I had forgotten (and still cannot recall), of an event from when I was nine years old and attending a summer day camp in Minneapolis. According to her, one afternoon the bus dropped me off at the corner where my mother always met me, but this day my father was waiting. I stepped to the last stair of the bus and saw him instead of her smiling in the sunlight. I turned back to the drug-addled camp counselor who was vaguely in charge of not losing us or giving us to strangers, and I said, "My mom isn't here yet. I'm not supposed to wait alone."

"It's all right," said Dad, stepping up to the bus. "I'm his father. Come on, Arthur, let's go get an ice cream."

"Great then," said the counselor.

"That's not my dad," I said. "I don't know that man."

The counselor's laughter grew nervous as I retreated back onto the shadowy bus and refused to budge from my brown plastic seat. I suppose a request for my father's identification must have occurred to someone, and he must have been lacking. A call on a pay phone to my home may have been made, but it must have failed to draw out my mother. Apparently, I stuck to my story.

"He was very patient about it, evidently," my mother told me. "He seemed to think it was reasonable. I would have been furious with you, but somehow he just smiled through it all."

"I really did this?"

The counselor spoke quietly to me on the bus seat, trying to winkle some clue out of me, and I can imagine, but not remember, his expression of mingled doubt and concern. If this persistent man, standing laughing to himself on the corner in the August heat, wasn't the kid's father, what sort of criminality was he up to? And if he was the father, what was wrong with this annoying fat kid? And why wasn't the dad shouting, settling this through force of will and parental entitlement?

"You held out all the way to the police coming," my mother laughed. "I think you only gave in then because you were afraid they were coming for you."

The police car arrived, and I glumly descended at last, forty-five minutes into this ordeal, took my father's hand, and walked off with him for ice cream.

What was I thinking? I honestly remember none of this incident, and if it hadn't been my mom—the least imaginative and fanciful member of my family—recounting it, I might have said she was trying her hand at fiction. But she was telling it straight. The most direct interpretation: I didn't want him to be my father. I must have been so angry with him for the divorce, so ashamed of his imprisonments, so jealous of his relationship with my sister that fantasy's appeal outmuscled reality's prerogatives. Or, since I can't remember a traumatic emotion, maybe it was all in fun. Maybe I was trying to play a misguided game with him, something I thought he'd enjoy. Maybe I was trying to impress him with my ability to re-create the world or myself. Maybe I already understood enough of what made him tick that I was imitating him. If so, by the time the police came, I would have known that I, like him, wasn't good enough to do it forever. I may have stepped off the bus preparing for my first arrest, another Arthur Phillips off to serve time for failures in fantasizing.

Perhaps it was aggressive, a challenge to him to keep up. If he was so good at this sort of thing, I may have been dimly thinking, then I would be as good or better, and I deserved his respect as much as Dana did, or Shakespeare (who, by the time I was nine, had become a bullying, noxious presence). And, in this interpretation, his patient and friendly insistence that he was my father, his loving explanation to the mildly amused cops, his purchase of ice cream for me nevertheless, his general portrayal of a "father" (albeit one who didn't discipline me for this irresponsible charade) was his victory: he had portrayed a dad more convincingly than I had portrayed an attempted-kidnapping victim.

5

BUT IF IN FACT that is how I felt one summer day at age nine, it was not permanent. Disappointment and separation were halting and uneven processes, shuffling back and forth like over-Thorazined mental patients. If I was resistant to my father's gravity at age nine, he could, without much evident trouble, draw me back in before I was ten. I am a writer of stories, trained to think in terms of a character's emotional "arc," but my real-life, untidy path resembles not an arc but a failed rocket program, liftoff followed by repeated crashes back onto the launchpad, short orbital flights followed by long groundings, until, far off in the future, escape velocity is finally achieved and deep space collects me.

But not yet.

After the bus incident, he was still able to induce wonder, to preach wonder, and I could still love, listen, and gaze at this star, my sister's hand in mine, my eyes on my father.

When we were ten, we started spending weekends with him in his studio apartment on Lake Street, above the bookbinder where his friend Chuck Glassow had found him a job. He'd been out of jail for more than a year, had stuck to his probation requirements, and seemed to have become a reasonably normal divorced guy. Our mother was more than willing to enjoy weekends alone with her new husband.

We slept on an air mattress and, at bedtime, he would read to us: Alexandre Dumas or Arthur Conan Doyle if things went my way, Shakespeare if they didn't. One June Friday the evening's soporific, to Dana's pleasure, was decided based on the date: *A Midsummer Night's Dream*. It did the trick for me quite quickly (especially as there was no baseball game on the radio that night), since I'm with Samuel Pepys on this one: "The most insipid ridiculous play that ever I saw in my life."

But I must have fought off sleep until at least Act II, Scene i (and that's due to Dad's vocal prowess), because I remember the conversation that followed from my father's reading of the line "*And I serve the fairy queen, / To dew her orbs upon the green.*" Dana asked what that meant, and Dad described "fairy rings"—little dark circles that appear in grass, which in Shakespeare's nature-rich youth in green Warwickshire would have been a source of mystery and wonder mingled with fear. I may have mentioned that it sounded like a dull childhood if some rotting grass was a highlight, but I was nevertheless spun back under his spell, Elizabethan England greening in my imagination.

Now, some future moments flow from this spring: (1) My sister's dreadful college punk band, for which she "played" bass, the Fairy

Rings (better than her other, earlier effort, Discomfort Women); (2) my eventual career as a novelist, possibly, since we were lying down, drowsy, in the drabbest conceivable space, and my father—who did have a way with his vocal effects and vocabulary—was extolling the greatness of anyone who adds to the world's store of wonder and magic, disorder, confusion, possibility, "the wizards." If he had been trying to hypnotize me for life ahead, it wouldn't have been much different. (On the other hand, if I'd ended up a urologist, I would now point elsewhere for the first seeds of my adult splendor, I suppose); and (3) the very odd weeks that followed, the pinnacle of my love for the three of us as a team, culminating, however, in Dad's arrest and plea bargain, fines, and community service down in farmy Nobles County, Minnesota.

He said something along these lines (I am reconstructing thirty-five-year-old conversations to the best of my ability; they are almost certainly inaccurate): "In those days, you walked outside your house, or twenty minutes outside of London, and you were in an endless forest, as magical and terrifying as you can imagine. Wonders were in the grass, mysteries. Something invisible was trying to communicate with you, frighten you, charm you, maybe steal from you, or help you, lead you to riches or just laugh at you. Now, boring, boring, we *know* there aren't grotesque fairies out there. We cut down those forests to prove it. We *know* what causes twenty varieties of discolorations of the turf. We have so many facts, and with them we can cut down anything."

I agreed wholeheartedly: Dad, forests, adventure, wonder, Dana, and I versus prisons, bulldozers, boring people, facts. That seemed precisely to explain the world.

The following two weekends he asked for us again, and our mother continued to be improbably generous in sharing us, considering his performance as a first husband and her full, inarguable custody. But my mother's way of judging people was her own, and she never hesitated to let him be a father when he could. She didn't hold her or our repeated disappointments against him. "That's the way he is. Don't expect anything else," I heard her say more than once, though decades spun by before I could consistently follow that advice.

He took us out to an extremely nice dinner two Saturdays later, at the Normandy Hotel, a Minneapolis fixture back then. The gift certificate he used to pay for the meal (without incident) is tinted in retrospect with a shading of doubtful authenticity. "The gift of a lady friend," he claimed as provenance, a forged girlfriend vouching for a forged voucher. (The "lady friends" of those years when he was out of prison were often referred to but never produced, and, before I understood that they never existed, they may have inspired in me another strange unilateral competitiveness with my father. My subsequent compulsive behavior toward women, I can admit now, may have been an effort to show him and the world that I was not a forger. And there, just there! I wonder, replaying that meal, whether life really works like this: if he had thought of some other explanation for the gift certificate, or said nothing at all, would everything have ended differently today?)

He returned to his theme as I tore into a tenderloin of pork covered in apples and cream: the world's vanishing faith in wonder, in relation to the vanishing natural world, and in inverse proportion to its growing store of dubiously valuable scientific knowledge. Dana was rapt, I recall. I remember watching her watch him, and I began to be aware of how he looked at me slightly less often than at her when he spoke. I suspected I was getting less of his eye, which in turn made me mad, so I looked up less often from my food, which led him to address the only child who was showing any interest in him, so by the end, he didn't look at me at all. I was already able to make others fulfill my own worst fears.

After dessert (a wedge of chocolate cake the size of my head cragging like an Alp through a cloud of sugar-gritty whipped cream), we returned to his apartment, but instead of changing into pajamas and lying down for some blank-verse torture, we were instructed to trade our dress-up clothes for jeans and sweatshirts, and my resentments scurried back down into their hole. He filed us back outside to his elderly station wagon. We drove west, then south through the late-gathering July evening, the mosquitoes pursuing us through the night, the sound of them sharpening their beaks like sirens' songs luring us to slap our own ears.

He drove on through curiosity, then boredom, answering no direct questions. "Fairies have to travel farther to reach us nowadays," he teased, while Dana and I played hot hands in the back seat until one of us smacked the other's knuckles hard enough to produce tears. His face in the rearview said, "All our skill at disproving things is like a wall we build between us and wonder. To jump that wall, you need a long running start."

I woke when our tires crossed from asphalt to dirt. It was totally dark: our headlights were off, and there was no moon. Far from the city, it was night in a way I have never seen since, a darkness that may no longer exist. "From now on," he whispered, "only whisper."

He parked on dirt. I held the flashlight. "Down!" he hissed. "Only point it down." From under a tarp in the back of the station wagon he pulled a machine I'd never seen before, or ever again. Wheeled, with a chimney-chute on the back, it seemed related to a snowblower, but it had huge flywheels and loose, dragging cables of various lengths fixed to its sides and top. He had red gas cans and plastic barrels, shovels, two handcarts, and a long wooden board with ropes attached to both ends.

It is a photogenic memory: he took the flashlight in his mouth and led our stumbling little parade with the machine, wheeled it across a road and down and up a ditch, up to a fence. He cut the fence wire at one post, rolled it back to the next. Dana and I were highly excited by now, even though we were only performing manual labor by flashlight, each with our loaded cart.

He seemed to know where he was going, around a grove of trees, along a path next to a field of corn stalks as high as my ten-year-old waist. "From here, step only where I step. Put your feet in my footprints. We have to start in the middle." This was now positively exalting, the opposite of daily life, our father at his best when we were at the age most receptive to his power. And we did it. It was work but it felt like something else, something higher.

Laying the guide strings, dragging that board on ropes, doing the cutting, spreading the material, brushing over the wheel tracks and footprints, restapling the cut wire fence, sweeping our tire tracks all the way down to the road. All this took probably six or seven hours. The three of us stank of that material. On the ride home, Dana and I slept despite our questions and bewilderment. I don't remember going upstairs to his apartment or how I woke clean in my pajamas, with my cleaned clothes folded next to the air mattress, or when the doughnuts and chocolate milk had arrived. Dana and I both suspected a dream until we saw the other's face (although this didn't definitively settle it, since we did still have identical dreams now and again). It was past noon.

"*It seems to me / That yet we sleep, we dream,*" my father said, and Dana climbed onto his lap to hug him.

"What did we do?" she asked.

"The hard part is still coming," he said. "The hard part of magic is letting it happen and not telling anyone. Anyone."

"You mean Mom," I said, suspicion prickling in me at last.

"I do mean her, but I'm not so worried about that. I mean *anyone.* Your friends. Anyone."

"Because we can get in trouble?" I asked, finally realizing the obvious.

"Well, yes, I suppose so," the convicted criminal gently granted only now, "but I'm not worried about *that* either. That's not why the secret is important."

"Who cares about getting in trouble?" Dana said, braver than I, as usual. "It's not like we committed a *crime,*" she laughed.

"I know," I protested.

"No, here it is." His voice became very serious, and he had our attention. "You can't tell anyone because that sucks the life out of what we did. All the fun, all the magic bleeds out, and it's just an empty, stupid thing. But if we don't tell, then we spent last night brilliantly. That's the only difference. You decide, and you make our night what you want. Brilliant and ours. Stupid and theirs."

My father made no money from this exploit. He spent a fair amount of money (invested it, he would say). The equipment, the time spent in researching the site (easy road access, unelectrified fence, good visibility from the air, long distance from the farmer's house, no dogs), the time spent in building the Machine (adapting a snowblower to cut symmetrical, tiered paths through early July corn), the slime he concocted to slather over those paths, and, of course, the fines he had to pay to that farmer near Worthington, and the community service he had to perform. And what was his payoff? Why bother? To astonish. To add to the world's store of precious possibility. To set the record crooked once and for all, so that someone's life (some stranger's) was not without wonder. It almost seems like a charitable act, if you subtract his ego.

To this day, the record remains a little crooked, thanks to us. If you Google "crop circles" you will find aerial photos of our work, although our circle, in 1974, was very basic, not like the overwrought ones nowadays. You can find our creation breathlessly described, and you can read the testimony of some of the first witnesses, neatly detached from any mention of subsequent arrests or human involvement. You'll find descriptions of the alien sludge (now a common occurrence at crop circles), though its actual recipe (my father's invention) remains unpublished, as far as I know.

He kept the clippings from the *Minneapolis Star*, the evening paper in those long-ago two-paper days, but it was Tuesday before our work appeared on the TV news. By then we were back at our mother's for the week, so Dad didn't have the pleasure of watching the WCCO coverage with us, listening to local anchor Dave Moore and seeing our faces as we slowly figured out what we had done. Instead, we were sitting next to Mom when the farmer told the reporter with absolute certainty, "There is no human machine or tool that could have done this. Stalks are bent all the same but not broken? No such tool. I cut corn for a living, so I know. And it wasn't here last night, when I walked out before bed. To do all this in one night? You'd need fifty or a hundred people to do this, and believe me, I would have seen and heard that. I'm a light sleeper. And there'd be footprints all over the place. I'm telling you: there's nothing. And this goop? This stuff? No, there is no animal product that smells like this. The whole thing—did you see it? It's—I don't know what this is—but it is damn spooky."

They showed the farmer walking the circle's perimeter, kneeling down in the smooth corn trench to draw some thick salivary strands of the muck off the soil. The station's traffic helicopter was tasked to fly over the field for aerial footage. Soon other witnesses appeared, testifying to bright lights in the sky that fateful night, and a dozen volunteer conspirators—lying or believing—enlisted in my father's project. I don't know what lesson I drew from watching them, back when I was ten, but I certainly recognize a pattern now.

My mother watched the news with us, made fun of it without knowing we were involved, and then she walked off to cook dinner while Dana and I sat very, very quietly in the haze of our own wonder. Remember: we were ten. We knew we had done this, but we didn't believe it. We didn't know what we had done, but we were proud of it. "Do you believe in UFOs?" I asked her, belief and understanding all jumbled.

My father didn't want to make people stupider or mock stupidity or celebrate stupidity. When the farmer said, "The shape. The shape is so . . . beautiful, so . . ." and trailed off, my father was right there with him in spirit. I suspect that he wished, of all the participants in this whole enterprise, to be that farmer, to be fooled. My father had given him (and the world) this glimpse of something hidden. He was only dissatisfied to be the giver and not the recipient.

This may be the closest I ever felt to him. Together we had re-shaped the world, changed how some people viewed life, the universe, everything. Adulthood, ever more alluring to a ten-year-old, was where magic happened, thanks to this superman who was my father. We were an elite. He had chosen and trained us. The judges and jailers were *my* enemies, too.

It was two weeks before he stole this feeling from me. "Say, listen, Arthur, I know how hard it is to keep secrets. And when you let one slip, you know, it can feel like it won't go any further, or that it didn't even really happen. You can almost make yourself believe you didn't do it." I immediately struggled to look as innocent as I was, which made me look spectacularly guilty. Despite my father's history, I was not totally aware what it meant that my best friend at school, Doug Constantine, was the son of Ted Constantine, a prosecutor in the Hennepin County attorney's office under Gary Flakne. But my father thought he knew what it meant, and he was convinced that I had boasted to my buddy, who told his father, who then contacted the law in Nobles County, who in turn had politely requested that my father pay a call at the sheriff's office within twenty-four hours. "No one is saying you squealed on us," he said, though my eyes stung that he was saying precisely that. "It's just that it must have been hard not to let your pal know about this great thing."

My denials never moved him, I know. To his credit, even though he thought I had unbagged the cat, he wasn't obviously angry at me. It was not going to be a big deal for him. He didn't mind paying the fines, since he did acknowledge that the farmer ("a working man," he said in one of his expansive friend-of-the-proletariat moments) had lost some money (though not nearly so much as he'd made from tourists paying to roam slack-jawed through our art).

His anger would have been preferable. Being wrongly accused of anything by anyone is bad enough to a boy, and I certainly didn't like feeling myself pushed out of my father's magic circle. But worse was that our wonder-working was wondrously worked into something grubby. All his talk about wizards fell away. He was just a semicompetent conspirator rethinking whom in the gang he could trust, like kids on a playground reshuffling, again, who was in and who was out. My father's confidence in me (which was the early entry ticket to adulthood) and adulthood itself (a place of wonder-working and pranksterism) now both appeared childish, petty. I wasn't very good at articulating this anger, other than to tell Dana over and over that he was a jerk.

"He knows it wasn't you," she reassured me, adjusting the troll dolls in the tabletop theater he had built her, the little black one smothering the little blond one with a tiny red pillow. "He believes you."

"I know," I lied, the troll grinning mischievously in its violence, its orange hair standing erect in murderous ecstasy.

My disappointment didn't last. It wasn't quite corrosive enough to free me permanently, and I look back now *"across time's moat"* and I wish I could shake sense into that kid: "Enough," I'd say. "That guy's not what you want to be." But younger selves refuse to follow older wisdom.

For my twelfth birthday, when I was deep in an espionage fetish, he made me a high-quality Soviet passport, with my stern photo expertly installed behind Cyrillic seals and visa stamps from my travels to North Korea, Vietnam, Hungary, and Czechoslovakia. I knew that the work involved—the research, the hand stitching, the specialized glue and paints—reflected his sincere love for me. I also knew by then that love was only one element of such an extravagant gift: the rest was professional vanity and a quantity of probable felonious rehearsal.

For my thirteenth, he gave me a baseball signed to me by my hero, Rod Carew, the Minnesota Twins' star second baseman and, later, first baseman and a Jewish convert from Panama, easily the coolest Jew within ten thousand miles of my house. It's not that this item was so difficult to obtain. It's just that by the time I was thirteen, I had started to assume that *anything* that passed through his hands was fake. I threw the ball away.

Later he gave Dana a sweet-sixteen present: a "consolation" driver's license after she failed the exam twice. Since Dad was in prison when we turned sixteen, the license was made by Chuck Glassow, Dad's college friend who, officially, owned a grocery store. We had known Chuck for years, and he used to come out for dinner with us occasionally when Dana and I spent weekends with Dad. He was a little like Dad, very well-read, but less flamboyant about it. He was taller even than my six-foot-one father. When I was twelve or so, with all my contradictory feelings about Dad and manhood simmering up to a boil, I still liked Chuck, though I was also ashamed that I thought my father lost in comparison. This diminishment of my father may have been unavoidable anyhow at that time; that's part of being a twelve-year-old boy (as my own sons, now fifteen, continue to teach me).

I liked how Chuck swore. It was, I see now, an affectation, like quoting Latin and Greek (which he also did); his cursing was Runyonesque, calculated, cooked up. "She should consider blowing that attitude all the way out of her ass and lighting it on fire," he said of one of the grumpy, antique waitresses at the Embers restaurant, and I thought he was a figure of high glamour.

He was an especially slender man, long and thin in every direction and every limb. "Artie," he said after he saw me talking to a neighbor, a girl my age but already quite a bit more developed. "She's too big for you. But I'm drawn in that direction, too. My lady of the moment? She and I? A Giacometti putting it to a Botero." I didn't understand the references, but the line made him laugh so hard he shook. I laughed, too, of course—a twelve-year-old having a grown man crack dirty jokes for him.

And then, a few days later, he mailed me a photograph—apparently taken in front of the Greek temple façade of the Minneapolis Institute of Arts—of a grimacing, wire-thin Giacometti statue putting it to a plump Botero statue, beatific at the rear intrusion. The huge composite statue stood to the left of the grand staircase. I had never noticed it there before, remarkably.

So I puffed my Huffy over to the museum, where I found the usual sculpture to the left of the main stairs: an angel with a sword standing on a wolf, or something, even more improbable than Glassow's, all things considered.

From nothing, from a passing joke that occurred to him as he said it, Glassow had made this crazy and pointless photo, implying a sculpture that never was, a collaboration and history between two artists who never met, and a ribald sense of humor in the city's fine arts museum. He remade the world in his own taste for no other reason than that it amused him. And he shared with me the fruit of that imagination because I had laughed back when he first thought of it, though I had only laughed because he said "putting it to."

Glassow was (I noted with a dash of preadolescent bitterness) what my father *wanted* to be but wasn't. (Of course, it was only due to my father's training of me that I could appreciate and admire him.)

I remember him at Embers one weekend evening, taking coffee in the brown plastic mug and giving ten different explanations for the ten times we asked him, "Why are you wearing a tuxedo?"

"I'm going to the casino after, but I wanted to see you kids first."

"There was a mix-up at the dry cleaner," he sighed, shaking his head, breathing out smoke from his Chesterfield, a line of gray that tracked along the top edge of the red booth.

"Ask your dad. His idea of a practical joke, saying dinner with you three was black-tie tonight."

His imagination inspired me and Dana to try out personalities around him. Something as mild as this game led us to put on different voices, attitudes, vocabularies, to see if, in disguise, we could sneak closer to the truth. "Baby," said Dana like a tender mother, "baby, really, why so swank?"

"I'm going to a ceremony, a roast for a friend who's getting a prize for his charitable work. Couldn't *be* prouder."

"Cut the crap, Chuck." I tried a twelve-year-old tough guy. "What's up?"

Chuck accordioned his cigarette butt into the black ashtray permanently stained gray inside its crenellations. "Fact is, compadre, I'm trying to impress a broad. I'm taking her first-nighting at the opera."

"Come on, for real, Uncle Charles, please," cajoled a young, young Dana, avuncularizing Glassow for the first and only time.

And this man, whom neither of us has seen in decades, now owns a quarter of my family's coming fortune.

But I'm ahead of myself.

6

WHEN I WAS FIFTEEN, two gallants at school called Dana a dyke, and so I tried to fight them. When it was over, and my nose was broken into its current alignment, and the two bravos had triumphantly kicked me in the stomach, adding, "Arthur is a fag," Dana, back home, set to work nursing my body and lacerated ego.

She didn't bother with "you were really brave" or "those guys are jerks" or "you were outnumbered" or even "thank you." We knew all that, and we both knew the other one knew it. And she knew how small I felt, how useless, how badly I had fallen short of some idea of myself as courageous and chivalrous, and, most of all, how ashamed I was that I couldn't destroy someone who had hurt her.

I lay on the sofa, replaying the battle in my head, but with better results and snappier repartee. Dana brought ice in a cloth and laid it gently across my purple nose, unbloodied my cheeks with wet paper towels, dropped aspirin into my mouth, and recited, *"Being your slave, what should I do but tend / Upon the hours and times of your desire?"* A puff of laughter started to build in the back of my throat, despite my condition, but it struck the bones and hollows of my face and quickly retreated as my eyes crossed and flooded.

"Listen to this. Listen," she said, as if I had a choice. "The younger son needs to make money, and so he goes to the fair and challenges the wrestler, who is a complete brute, for a prizefight. Everyone says he's insane, begs him to back out, but he won't. Stubborn like you. The princess in the audience, probably really hot, sayzzzzzz . . ." She dragged out the word, and I heard the pages riffling, and I knew exactly what book was on her lap across the room from me, though behind my eyelids, closed under acid ice, all I saw were black fireworks. *"Young gentleman, your spirits are too bold for your years. You have seen cruel proof of this man's strength: if you saw yourself with your eyes or knew yourself with your judgment, the fear of your adventure would counsel you to a more equal enterprise. We pray you for your own sake to embrace your own safety and give over this attempt.* That's good, isn't it? That's what I would have said today. If I'd've known what you were going to do. And been able to speak that well."

"Does he back down?" I mumbled and picked at the dried blood on my cheekbones, then wished I hadn't.

"No."

"Does he get his ass kicked?"

"No," Dana admitted. "He beats the bigger guy and goes off to make his fortune. But that's not the point."

"The point is," I hurried to conclude in self-pity, "I'm not a hero, and if you had stopped me you would have saved yourself this embarrassment."

She was silent for a while. In my darkness, I complimented my stupid self that I had stymied her. After a bit, I heard her sigh, stand up, sit down again, more pages turning. "More? Really? Do I have to?"

"Wait," she said.

Like most fifteen-year-olds (and most people), I was not delighted by Shakespeare, despite or because of my father's indoctrination of us. The little of it I had read under duress in school had only confirmed the damage done by my family and had put me off the man forever. Most of it is a foreign language, excessively wordy, repetitive. It was either too much work to understand the characters or, alternately (since fifteen-year-olds are programmed to produce endless reasons why they don't like anything), too easy: those awful soliloquies where bad guys reveal their plans or good guys swoon because they're so in love.

"Here," she said at last, a little victory in her floating, disembodied voice. "Here. Now listen. You're seventeen years old. You don't know how to fight, but you're brave. And suddenly, you're in charge of real soldiers. They push you out front, tell you that you're king, tell *you* to rouse *them* to war. You don't know anything about anything, about men in a group. You're a kid. You've been raised as everyone's favorite little boy, sheltered, coddled by women, and suddenly men are listening to you. To Arthur. Relying on Arthur. You don't know war. Here's what you know: girls, school, getting in trouble. But you're naturally a hero, even if you're not trained yet. So now listen to yourself."

And she read his battle speech from Act II, Scene ii. Her voice was just deep enough an alto to pass as a teenage boy's, and it worked. For the first time, it worked. The scene came to life for me, in my enforced darkness, and for this one moment, and then a whole afternoon, I thought Shakespeare was okay.

> "Who waits for us within, fell Englishmen?
> This Saxon pride set sail o'er Humber's tide
> And then conjoined to Pictish treachery
> For but to cower, spent and quaking-shy,
> Portcullised fast behind the walls of York,
> As guilty lads will seek their mother's skirts
> When older boys they vex come for revenge.
> But Arthur's at the gate! 'Tis Britain's fist
> That hammers now upon the shiv'ring boards.
> An English blood be thin as watery wine,
> Then sheathe we now our swords and skulk away
> With Saxon language tripping from our lips.
> You'd con th'invader's tongue? *Absit omen.*
> Let's school them then in terms of English arms,
> Decline and conjugate hard words—but hark!   *Chambers*
> She sighs with gentle pleading that we come!
> Now wait no more to save her, nobles, in,
> And pull those Saxon arms off English skin!"

When she finished, she said, "Listen to it again. Arthur starts out with: the enemy is a little boy hiding in York because he pissed off us bigger boys, and we're going to kick his ass. The soldiers don't really go for that, so you reach again and you say, 'If they conquer us, we'll have to learn their language, and that'll be like Latin class, which was a drag, wasn't it? Anybody?' Figure by now the troops are getting a little dubious about you. And then the cannons go off"—*Chambers*—"the battle's going to start, and so you try one more time, last chance, and this time you nail it: York's a babe and she wants us *in* her. And suddenly everyone starts to nod and grip their hilts, if you know what I mean.

"You could do that," Dana said softly. "That's what I saw today. You could figure out how to be a hero when you have to. You were outnumbered, didn't know what you were doing, and you still fought like a hero."

The Tragedy of Arthur was not necessarily her favorite back then, but she gave it to me that afternoon in April, in our living room, read the entire play to me. It took more than four hours, I'd guess. She patiently stopped to answer my vocabulary questions, stopped to replace the softening ice on my hardening face, stopped to make me something in the blender that I could bear to swallow, and April spring floated in and out through the open window, our mother and stepfather both late at work, our father far away in prison (no threat or irritant or better man), just me and Dana and this play, her thank-you to me for fighting for her honor.

She read to me from her little red hardcover of *The Tragedy of Arthur*, a simple but nicely done 1904 edition that has managed to accrue contradictory sentimental value for several members of our family. Its Edwardian frontispiece engraving (in a very nineteenth-century style) was of Act II, Scene iv, in which Arthur (depicted in an anachronistic late medieval suit of plate armor) hands over his shield and regalia to the Duke of Gloucester, the crucial scene in which Arthur orders the duke to swap armor with him and do battle in his colors so that Arthur can chase some Yorkish girl instead of going back to war.

I own that 1904 edition now. I have it in front of me. It is, as they say in the used-book trade, "slightly foxed," with two or three small stains inside the boards. The cover is slightly frayed at the bottom corners, and the spine is faded. But otherwise it's in excellent condition.

If curiosity has nibbled at you while reading this, you may be asking yourself why you can't find your own copy in these easy Internet days. Where is the $285 used edition on your preferred online outlet? Where is the recent reissue by a small press looking for something quirky to win some buzz? Why is Random House bothering to publish the play with such fanfare if there was already a 1904 edition? Patience, please.

After the publisher's information and date, the first blank page bears an inscription in faint pencil and formal early-twentieth-century handwriting: *For Arthur Donald "Don" Phillips, with the compliments of the King's Men Dramatic Society, King's School, Edmonton, Ontario, June 14, 1915.*

Always kept inside the book is the photo of my grandfather Arthur Donald Phillips appearing in that boys school production of the racy, violent *Arthur* play and the folded playbill, on canary-yellow paper, canary feather–soft at its creases, listing his name in the title role. The photograph is, as you can see, insane:

Whatever he is wearing, it has nothing to do with this play. The costume is neither of Arthur's ostensible period (around A.D. 500, if he even existed) nor of the style worn by actors in Shakespeare's time to depict the early Middle Ages (some bits of armor over contemporary sixteenth-century clothes). No, my grandfather seems to be dressed in leftovers from a production of *H.M.S. Pinafore*, or something else eighteenth- or nineteenth-century and decidedly weird. The back of the photo, though, insists in black ink (and female handwriting?) that it depicts *Don, as Arthur in Shakespeare, June '15*.

"Your grandfather, I gotta say, would have been perfect for that part," our father used to claim, shaking his head at this photo and chuckling with hard-earned wisdom and acceptance. "The flawed hero. His personal charm wins him everything and his personal failings lose him everything. That fit your grandfather to a *T*," sighed my dad.

And, sure enough, the second inscription inside the book, in multidimensional ambiguity, in blue ink, under the blue ink line drawn beneath the penciled school inscription, reads: *To a new Prince Arthur, from his ever-loving Papa. 11/1/1942.* My father would have been twelve when he received this gift.

I first learned of this 1904 edition when Dana and I were eleven, I think. I'm reasonably confident about the era: Dad was out of prison but had moved to a different apartment downtown. This one was above the Gay 90s, a progressive nightclub on Hennepin Avenue. I was lying on the sofa bed reading a comic book (Archie? Spider-Man?). Dana and Dad were in the kitchen, talking in low voices until Dana burst out with, "No way, José! And you have it? How long have you had it? Why didn't you ever tell me? Can I please see it? Where is it? How did you get it?" Dana was in one of her states that can go by a lot of different names. The modern ones (manic, polar, over-stimulated, hyperactive) never much appealed to her, for good reason. It was an excitement my father found endearing but that my mother tried to tamp down as soon as she saw signs of it. Later, Dana would take pills, which she hated if they too much dulled these moods, but when she was a child, they were still just part of her "bubbliness."

I came into the tiny kitchen at this point. She could not calm herself down; there was a slight edge of anger to her voice. I could detect it, at least, even if my father was laughing with a sort of condescending pleasure at having triggered her state. She resented the existence of a secret from which she had been excluded, even one to which she was now about to be admitted.

Usually, the more excited Dana became at that age, the more my mood matched hers. She was the emotional leader, quicker to both joy and despair, and I would generally rise or descend after her, never quite as high or low, though always wishing I was up or down there with her. This day, however, the discovery that her buzz was Shakespeare-induced prevented me from joining in with anything other than the most quenchable curiosity, and I wandered back and forth between couch and kitchen.

I tried not to care, but it was impossible not to want to be part of their excitement and to win back, a little, some piece of both of them. "Arthur, good, you'll find this interesting, too," Dad said, but not very convincingly. "Grab a perch."

They were sitting very close to each other, and my father had the book on the table, with his hands pressed on it, holding it closed and holding it close, away from Dana's impatient fingers sliding back and forth on the wooden table's white plastic surface. He began to explain to me again what he had told her, but she interrupted, bouncing in her chair: "No, no, let me tell him, please, let me." She almost swallowed her own lips trying to push the words out to me, childishly taking credit by retelling it, proudly sharing knowledge, but shaking mostly because this stuff made her happier than anything else, especially since it was her primary connection to Dad.

The news bursting from her: Dad owned a very rare copy of a Shakespearean oddity, a play that people argued about, that no one could decide about, and "he thinks we should read it and make up our own mind about it!"

He nodded along to her pleasure. "That's it exactly." He was very interested in her opinion of the play. He wanted her to read it as often as she liked, change her mind as often as she liked, but to report back to him what she made of it. "And you, too, of course, Arthur, if you're interested." I took a quick look at the play, which seemed no different from all the rest, and I retreated to the sofa and my comic book.

Dana had long since read all of Shakespeare, had cried when she'd reached her last play, despondent that there was nothing new to explore, faintly consoling herself with Dad's promise about the joys of rereading. She had already, at that young age, experienced something coming to an end, a love affair's first flush, and now, to discover that there was still (possibly) one left: she was torn between wanting to stay up all night reading it and rationing her last virgin pleasure over weeks or months.

My father only had the one copy and, in those pre-Internet days, didn't know if he'd ever be able to find another, as it was long out of print, long discredited, just a novelty item, and so he attached very strict rules to Dana's borrowing of it. She could read it only in his home. She could never lend it to anyone. She was free to tell people about it, of course, but under no circumstances was she allowed to Xerox it for herself or others. The book's rarity and importance and ambiguous value were impressed upon her. Unsurprisingly, the next inscription on the flyleaf reads, *April 22, 1977 For my Dana on her 13th birthday, with eternal love. Dad.*

The fussy rules, the improbable interest in her eleven-year-old opinion, the clubby and ceremonial sentimentality: all of this bothered me. I was forced to be bored so as not to face my anger at my father's obsession, which took my best friend, Dana, away from me, not only in the close quarters of his sad-sack parolee apartment, but increasingly in the relative space of my mother's small house as well, where Dana read Shakespeare and wrote my father self-assigned book reports.

I am reminded of a childhood fantasy from about this time, which now appears quite explicable, a recurrent daydream, conjured in moments of solitude and boredom. If, for example, I peered through the glass porthole behind which wet clothes leapt and fell in graceful arcs in their hot drum, the hypnotic effect of the abstract patterns numbed and nudged my mind off its tracks, and William Shakespeare sat at my side on the laundromat bench, where he would ask me what the dryer was and how it worked. Shakespeare was stranded in the twentieth century, helpless and desperate to understand everything he'd missed in the intervening years, relying on me.

I was forced (by my father? my sister?) to babysit him and explain everything (clothes dryers, air travel, vending machines, vaccinations), and it was a chore. I loathed having to look after this fifty-year-old man, his frisky mullet warming the back of his neck above the stiff collar. I don't know why, if I was so discontented with the task, I didn't either (a) in my fantasy, demand to be relieved from my duty, or (b) in reality, stop fantasizing about punitive tedium.

Still I went on with my odd assignment, explaining the plot and premise of *Hogan's Heroes* and *Gilligan's Island* to the great man. ("The *conceit* and *argument*," he would correct me.) He quite liked these shows, evidence to me even then of his limited brilliance. I demonstrated how to peel a Band-Aid when I cut my hand (and thus distracted myself just enough to prevent tears). I would send Shakespeare back to his own time with cures for the plague, explanations of electricity, suggestions for telephones. Later, the fantasy improved when I began to fuck with the Bard. "Some genius," I scoffed, after I told him to cross the street only on a red light and he was crushed by a truck.

More pop psychology: the writer writes to create a world he can control and manipulate because he finds himself stymied by what the rest of you so blithely call "reality." Yes, possibly.

The fourth and final inscription on the inside cover of the 1904 edition—*For Arthur, from Dana*—brought the book into my possession, but that was several years later.

7

FOR DANA'S THIRTEENTH BIRTHDAY—the day before my own— our father gave her the 1904 edition (with the same rules still in force) and a framed poster: an old Morris column ad for a 1930s London stage production of *Shakespeare's Tragedy of King Arthur* starring Errol Flynn as Arthur and Nigel Bruce as Gloucester. Dana loved it and claimed never to be able to read the play again without picturing Flynn as the ne'er-do-well king. "Inspired casting," she used to say. The poster hung above her bed. Don't rush to Google that one.

Dana and I were, obviously, not identical twins but, as the family phrase had it, we were "something more than fraternal." Our resemblance was not magical enough, not nearly, to fool anyone, to let us engage in Disneyish trickery against parents or teachers; nor did we even share enough of a vocal similarity before puberty to lure telephone Romeos into embarrassment. Still, thirty-eight or thirty-nine minutes her junior, I found her waiting for me in Abbott Northwestern's delivery room, and if I depict her as waiting impatiently for me to emerge from our mother, as the clock swung past midnight on April 22, I don't think it's really too fanciful. Thirty-eight or thirty-nine minutes was the longest we'd been apart for months, since the moment we two ova had snuggled into place together (one of us cheating the rules, luging down our fallopian chute as the gates slipped shut behind us), and thirty-eight or thirty-nine minutes was the longest we were ever apart for some years to come. Bathed, fed, bedded down together, nursery schools through primary school (every year in the same rooms, at my mother's request), we literally were never away from each other for more than a few minutes until we had our own friends in third or fourth grade. Even then—me playing baseball in some boy's yard, her playing dolls in some girl's rec room—there was a feeling that the separate time was in some way a research project *for* the other. I was experiencing baseball for her. Even if—practicing with a team after school—I wasn't literally thinking of Dana, I was somehow gathering everything in to give to her: the weather, the plays, the feeling of a badly hit ball stinging my arms, the homoerotic towel whippery of the locker room. Even if I didn't end up telling her everything, or anything, I stored it for her, lived it for her, and she knew it was all there if she wanted to ask.

I used to think of us as essentially identical if physically dissimilar. There was something beneath the surface that matched more closely than other people ever felt. Not everyone could see it, but for some (I'm thinking of Margaret Wheeler; I'll come back to her), we were literally interchangeable. I recall, when we were very young, an old woman in a beauty parlor asking us over and over, "And tell me again: which one are you, dear?" and my mother smiling at what she took to be the lady's joke about obviously unidentical twins. But I saw the old woman's sincere confusion. "Dana," I answered, lunging at the rare opportunity, and the lady nodded, peered at me to find some distinguishing mark she could pin to her memory for "Dana." Dana and I searched the beauty parlor's mirrors together, then looked at each other, seeing plainly that whatever it was, you couldn't see it.

She cried when she learned of Shakespeare's own twin children, the brother dying young, the sister living on. "If something happened to you, I'd be alone forever," she told me. A sweet and dreadful idea, but it leads to problems if nobody dies. If you're alive only when you're with the other, what remains for, say, a wife?

Shakespeare's work teems with twins: perfectly identical twins who don't know of each other's existence, fraternal twins identically lovable despite different genders, separated twins in the employ of other separated twins, and it was through twins—*Twelfth Night* and *The Comedy of Errors*—that Dana first fell for Shakespeare. There she is on Dad's lap, the fat collected works open on her own lap, both of them laughing about some Dromio or other, cheek to cheek and assigning each other parts, while I arranged blue plastic knights and archers on the black pentagons and white hexagons of the kitchen floor tiles, a monochromatic Agincourt raging on a flattened soccer ball.

My father looked down at me and recited from memory the famous band-of-brothers battle speech from *Henry V*. I listened until the odd words—*Crispin Crispian?*—reminded me of a breakfast cereal, and, hungry, I wandered across the room, looking for food, while Dad and Dana held off the French assault without me.

I admit that this seems a long way from an Introduction to a newly discovered Shakespeare play; this essay is fast becoming an example of that most dismal genre, the memoir. All I can say is that the truth of the play requires understanding the truth of my life.

That said, with the best of intentions, still I fall prey to the distortions of memoir writing. The memoir business has lately been an uneasy, underregulated one, full of inflated claims and frenzied Internet debunkers, too many exciting drug addictions and Holocaust misadventures, too much delirious abuse. But even when one is *trying* to tell the truth, there is no guarantee to accuracy: I realize I have completely misportrayed my youth already, because retrospective importance (to me) doesn't necessarily jibe with what actually happened (to everyone else). My strongest memories, my sensations of meaning and significance are all attached to the parent I saw less. The mathematical realities of incarceration and divorce dictate that the vast, vast majority of my youth occurred under the eye of my mother and her second husband, but it is my father, Arthur Edward Harold Phillips, who continually shoves his way to the foreground, wherever I turn memory's camera.

In other words, this memoir is, despite my best efforts, already misleading.

8

M Y SISTER PLAINLY PREFERRED our father to our mother, and I preferred my sister to both of them. When he was gone, first to prison, then to his own apartment after the divorce and Mom's marriage to the eternally patient Silvius diLorenzo (Window Sil, our father called him, citing his transparent personality), Dana was all mine. She and I fell into each other naturally, joyfully, once he was gone. Our mother encouraged it or, at least, didn't discourage it by trying to be a child along with us or straining to impress us with wonder or Shakespeare.

My father delighted in us, sincerely if sporadically, but also delighted in being noticed and *witnessed* while being delighted to be a dad. Mom's love was different. She felt she had done right by us by having twins and felt no need to intrude in our special relationship. She provided, disciplined, paid, drove, lightly applauded. She was a marathon parent, not a sprinter, an old-fashioned parent who could exist in her own world without longing to be part of ours.

Her name tells a uniquely American story: Mary Arden Phillips diLorenzo. Mary: the assimilationist gesture of small-town Jews, second-generation Americans ready to use Gentile names to reassure the Lutheran majority. Arden: shortened from Sardensky somewhere between Vilnius and northern Minnesota. Phillips: the misguided first marriage, striving for something exalted and above ethnicity, something untenable in the real world. DiLorenzo: safety and stability restored, fantasies repressed, thanks to another straight-thinking, unromantic, early-generation immigrant group.

My mother was born in 1930 on the old Iron Range of Minnesota, a child of relative privilege in that humble community and depressed economy, so her family's thorough-going and instinctive modesty was even more wisely self-protective. Her father was something of a town elder in tiny Ely, Minnesota, even serving—extraordinarily for a Jew—on the town council. As the town's most successful grocer, Felix Arden was able to survive, if not exactly prosper, through the 1930s. The family didn't suffer as much in the Depression as others, and Felix was known to provide free and discounted food for those in need, for which he was later honored by the town. As a result of his Christian generosity, the entire family shared in his reputation. Mary worked as his delivery girl to the housebound, and so gained a rather saintly aura. Her very un-Minnesota taste for fine clothes and displays of wealth were therefore largely forgiven, where anyone else would have been mocked or shunned in small-town Lutheran style. She was a regular at the Quality Shop over in Virginia, where the finest clothes on the Range could be had without the trek down to Minneapolis. She was a figure of powerful glamour there, looked up to by the shopgirls and even by the owner's own beautiful and brilliant daughter. Silvius told me that the Quality Shop's owner, in his annual trips to New York, would come back with gowns he chose particularly for the Arden girl from Ely. My mother's clothes, hairstyles, and very unladylike motorcycle with sidecar (which I later used in one of my novels) were only admired and smiled on, since she had been the little girl bringing food through the snow not so many years before, never forgotten by the Swedes, Finns, Italians, and Poles of Ely.

It was one of those Italians, Silvius diLorenzo, who set his heart on the grocer's daughter with the long black hair and eyes so gray they were almost silver. Religious and class distinctions were very real, though, in 1950s small-town Minnesota, and Sil would have had to be a stiff-spined rebel to buck everything in his way for her, even if he could have won her. She might possibly have been in a position to make an unconventional marriage, if he was inclined to convert, or if she was inclined to marry at all, but she still had wispy ideas of moving away from Ely to become an actress in New York or Hollywood, or to achieve some other undefinable glory. She had never tried acting; it was just that too many old Swedish ladies had petted her hand as she delivered their food and told her she looked like a movie star.

Sil was the son of Italian immigrants (whereas my mom was the granddaughter of immigrants). His people worked, when there was work, in mining or on the docks over in Duluth. Sil tried his hand at boxing before being "knocked out enough to knock some sense into me." His mother had a make-work servant's job in the Arden household, though the notion of actually using a servant offended Felix and Annie Arden's modest sensibilities, and Annie had to stop herself from doing Violeta diLorenzo's work for her, lest she reveal just how much charity motivated the employment.

And so, for years, Silvius told me, he ached for my mother, the daughter of the house where his own mother folded the laundry. A fair student at Ely and a second-line wing on the school hockey team, he watched as she was squired to dances, as she rode through town with this or that boy in her sidecar, and as she prepared to go down to the University of Minnesota in 1949.

He declared himself to her that summer before she left, in a scene I heard from both of them. In Sil's version, she barely noticed his presence, seemed puzzled by the whole thing. "She was imagining herself performing for the crowned heads of Europe or marrying one," he said. Sil slunk away, embarrassed but lighter for having faced down his fear. "She was cold as a common executioner," he told me, laughing by then, the late-round victor. "Silly, she called me. That was rough. When you're beneath her contempt, when your mother's cleaning her toilet. Now I can take it."

"What, she still calls you Silly?"

"For years."

I had never heard that.

My mother recalled it differently: "I was astonished. And felt so sorry for him. He'd gotten himself into quite a knot, really unnecessarily, and not for anything I did or was. I was hardly the best-looking girl in town. And, there was something else, too. Are you sure you want to hear this?"

"I really do," I said, just last year, after Sil had died, and I was in the midst of my own middle-aged romantic muddle and agony.

"I was terrified," my mother admitted. "I thought, 'Well, this is not a particularly strong offer for my hand, as an alternative to all my fantasies just over the horizon, and yet it's not without some appeal.' That's what so worried me: I was tempted. And, really, by what? I didn't know Sil that well. I didn't know his finer qualities yet. All he was, then, was an offer. My first offer. I wasn't in love with him, but he was a sweet, handsome man, strong, who seemed to love me, I don't know why, and all that almost felt like enough. I could have said yes! And then I panicked: didn't I want all the things I wanted? When you suddenly realize—even after a lifetime's study—that you don't know yourself very well, it's a little terrifying. Sil, too: he couldn't have done it, married a Jew, converted, done that to his family. If I'd said yes back then, we never would have gotten married."

My mother went away to the university down in Minneapolis, and Sil took work as a builder, learning engineering on the job ("like sergeants learn the lieutenants' job while the lieuts are all at West Point"). After a year in the big city, a year of studying English literature during that department's golden age (Allen Tate held a chair, hosting guest lectures—in the sports arena!—by the likes of T. S. Eliot), she came back for her first summer, and, she told me, "I was torn in half, really. I tried acting, once. Dismal. Studying was very hard for me. I lost all my confidence that first year. I didn't think I could accomplish anything or even trust myself to know what I wanted to do, or could do. I thought I was just hopeless. But, still, Ely seemed smaller than ever, and there was Sil outside my door every evening asking me to go with him to shoot rats at the dump."

As near as I could ascertain (a sweet, elderly modesty settling over their recollections now), some kisses were exchanged (in more hygienic surroundings, I hope), and the contractual significance of those kisses was interpreted very differently. According to Sil, my mother returned to the university for her sophomore year confused but determined to try her way in the larger world again, "without tying herself to a wop builder. A kiss doesn't mean anything, Artie. You know that at your age, don't you?" According to my mother, Silvius saw off his unpredictable fiancée, who was not yet tightly enough tethered to the kindly, safe fellow with a job and a modest plan for the future.

And that second year in Minneapolis, she met A.E.H. Phillips, as my father styled himself at the U of M. He was the wider world my mother had suspected was out there somewhere, and he was exploring, like her but less tentatively, the possibility of other selves. He was a painter already and dressed the part—berets, open-neck shirts, even capes. He was also better read than most of her Lit. classmates, with an uncanny memory, she said, "at least for seduction poetry. 'To His Coy Mistress' came pretty fast off his tongue, and Sonnet 119, and the cajoling parts of *The Rape of Lucrece*, if memory serves. And he taught me about my name." Mary Arden, he informed her over wine, had been Shakespeare's mother. She hadn't known. "Probably what attracted him to me," she said, not only out of modesty.

And here, finally, was the love she'd been expecting and fearing. The love that cannot be ignored or reasoned through, negotiated with, tamed, made cute or quaint or optional, a love as avoidable as act-of-God weather or resistant bacteria, the rebel army arriving in darkest night. I have known it only once, and I understood when she told me she felt herself voluntarily enslaving herself to him, "and if he'd said we were moving to Ely and I was going to wash toilets and he was going down the mines, I'd have had to do it. I wouldn't have asked if I was *happy* about it. I just would have gone. That's who he was."

She delayed bringing him home, left Sil's letters of inquiry unanswered, avoided introducing him to her parents when they came down to Minneapolis. When she told Arthur of the existence of a mild rival back north ("I was just trying to keep him in the game," she insisted), my father took note, smiled pleasantly, and set quietly to work. When she finally did take A.E.H. up to Ely to meet her family, Silvius was gone. "Oh, I suppose I noticed," my mother told me. "I may even have asked. I don't remember."

Sil was nowhere to be seen because he'd received his draft notice. It had apparently been delayed in the mail, because he was expected to report to a fort in North Carolina for basic training in ten days' time, prior to deployment to Korea. Sil certainly didn't have the higher-education waiver my father had, but he didn't argue, didn't make the valid claim that he was his mother's and sisters' only real source of support. Having arranged something with Felix and Annie to take care of Violeta (a loan, Sil insisted, which he swore he would repay), he set off on the trains to Minneapolis to Chicago to D.C. to North Carolina. When he arrived, the army had no record of his call-up. The clerk examined his notice. It was absolutely authentic in every way; it simply didn't correlate to any list or file the army could find, while Sil waited at a motel a mile from the base. At last, ten days later, in some effort to square a bureaucratic circle, the U.S. Army issued him an honorable discharge, granting him the rank of private, first class. "So I owe your dad for that," he said.

In the meantime, my father had met my maternal grandparents, presenting them, at the end of the visit, with a hand-painted Sardensky family tree, stretching its roots back into Lithuania two generations further than the family had previously known, and culminating in the line connecting Mary Arden to A.E.H. Phillips, a proposal Mary had agreed to an hour earlier while Violeta overheard, sobbing, through the air vent that led to the laundry room.

Felix and Annie, both charmed by and dubious of the flashy Minneapolis painter, agreed to the match, and a date was set after their graduation, two years into the future. Mary drove Arthur back down to Minneapolis, averaging eighty miles an hour, and Sil returned to Ely two weeks later, his military career complete, his girlfriend engaged to someone else.

He learned the news from his mother and sent Mary a telegram offering her his warm congratulations and friendship. Stop.

"I felt like I'd won a contest, got cast in a film or a fairy tale," my mother said. "Because I was a fool."

"I really wasn't trying to be clever about it," Sil told me of that telegram. "I just wanted to lose gracefully. And I knew, too, even then, that this was the end for me. I wasn't doing any more love."

9

I AM CONTRACTUALLY BOUND to write a synopsis of *The Tragedy of Arthur*. One act at a time, I think; I don't want to lose readers because Shakespeare puts them off. It's for his own good.

So: Act I: In the Dark Ages, Britain is constantly at war. Uter, effectively king of England and Wales but nominally king of all Britain, faces invading Saxons and also the rebellious northern kingdoms of Scotland and Pictland (eastern Scotland). Mad with lust, Uter rapes the wife of the Earl of Cornwall, then kills the earl and marries the wife, installing a new earl. Because of the ceaseless war, he sends his newborn son, Arthur, product of that rape, to live with the Duke of Gloucester in a relatively safe corner of Britain. There, the boy, rarely if at all seen by his parents, grows up spoiled and impulsive, charming and flighty, despite the duke's loving guidance. He is educated to become king, but also always prepared to flee Britain should its enemies conquer the island.

As the play opens, Prince Arthur is seventeen. In the midst of a boar hunt, he becomes distracted by a shepherd girl and abandons his hapless foster father, Gloucester, to pursue her. Gloucester worries what sort of king he is raising for Britain and, coincidentally, Shakespearily, a messenger then arrives with news of King Uter's death; he was poisoned by the Saxons. Unaware of this, Arthur talks with the shepherd girl, attempting to seduce her. Their flirtation is broken up by the calls of courtiers hunting for the new king.

In the meantime, the northern kingdoms of Scotland and Pictland are thrown into turmoil by the news of Uter's death and Arthur's accession. Mordred, the heir to the more powerful Pictish crown, insists that Arthur is illegitimate and the throne of all Britain belongs to his family. He tries to rouse his father, the king, into fighting for the crown, but his dying father refuses.

Back in London, Gloucester, as lord protector, struggles to convince the squabbling English nobility to support their new king. They do agree to accept Arthur, but only in response to northern insolence: they torture the Pictish messenger bearing Mordred's claim to the throne. Act I ends with Arthur in a soliloquy realizing the difficulties he faces, weighing his legitimacy, doubting his suitability to be king, ashamed that he is not the man his father was, yet daring himself to proceed, more out of anger with his rivals than any real desire to rule.

None of this, I suppose, strikes me as any more stilted or formulaic than other Shakespeare first acts.

Dana kept the 1904 edition of *The Tragedy of Arthur* for all those years, and except for the occasion when she read it to me and my newly smashed nose, I never opened it, never looked at it on her shelf, never thought about it. But after our father showed her the book when she was eleven, the two of them discussed it ad nauseam (my nauseam, anyhow). Dad challenged her to prove its authorship to him, and she rose to the task, producing letters and essays and comparisons of vocabulary and style. They also developed a bantering game about the play: they would propose explanations to each other for its exclusion from the collected works, the First Folio, bouncing theories back and forth. "It was a gift to a lover, a private closet drama," Dana proposed at age fifteen, not coincidentally during one of her periodic all-encompassing romantic obsessions, the details of which only I knew. "He wrote it for a secret lover, and when she didn't like it, he extravagantly promised it would never be performed. She made him swear he would burn it, and he agreed. He wouldn't let his company have it. The play fell into oblivion. When it was time for them to publish the folio, none of them even remembered the abandoned play."

Dad picked up the story and ran, all of us well behaved and calm now on these family visits to prison: "That's good, Dana, that's good. Then his widow found the manuscript. Anne tried to sell *Arthur* back to the King's Men to include in the folio, but they didn't offer her

much for it, thought they could get it from her by preening, all prestige, 'We're the King's Men, after all.' She should be pleased just to
have their attention." Dad was in the first months of his third prison
sentence, and his mind was much taken by treacherous and cheap colleagues, convinced as he was that someone had betrayed him in his
latest downfall.

"While she was stewing over their haughty attitude," Dana continued, "a strange man came to her door with flowers, saying he wanted
to meet *her*, admired *her*. He listened to her complaints about dead
Will, never at home, left the good bed to the kids, all his groupie girl-
friends, and this stranger is very sympathetic. At the end, she agrees
to give him the *Arthur* play for a few pounds, maybe a few kisses
thrown in, and off he goes with the manuscript of the forgotten play.
Now, what did he do with it?"

(Did I on this visit shyly, pathetically show him the short story I
had had published in the high school literary magazine? I hope not,
but it seems quite possible. And if I did, would any reaction from him
have been good enough? I hope so, but I suspect that by then he and
I were locked in unbreakable mutual dissatisfaction.)

Dana's fantasies about secret lovers and seducers who trade kisses
and sympathy for knowledge were not entirely unsourceable. Her
crushes at this time—tenth, eleventh, twelfth grade—were painful
for me to watch. She was so eager and yet so worried about being dis-
creet that she made her desires and her true self invisible to the
beloved parties, even as she threw herself into their company, into
friendship, never giving the slightest hint of romantic interest. For
obvious reasons, she didn't dare confide in anyone except me. She
would probably have avoided me, too, if she'd had to screw up
her courage and reveal herself, but we were still—at fifteen, sixteen,
seventeen—transparent to each other (though some smudges were
beginning to appear). She never had to take the plunge and say to me,
"This is who I am." I just knew. She risked no rejection from me, and
she knew that, too.

In high school, when the rest of us dreamt of being original but
strived to be like someone we knew or some archetype, Dana was already, if uneasily, her own true self. She wasn't the "outsider girl" or

the "artsy girl posing to be noticed for her offbeat originality." I mean that she was already something only a few people ever become, even in adulthood. She could see the world as it was, take it as it was, could usually read people and situations (even if they didn't know themselves perfectly) and then make her own decisions about how she would exist in that world. She understood her emotions far earlier than anyone else I knew, lived unpressurized by peers. She did not fake or judge unfairly. All this would be unique enough, even without the superficial talents that also defined her.

She didn't deny to herself that she was gay, and when that part of her grew enough to assert itself, she accepted it without a blink of shame or regret. Until she called it by that name to herself, she was just someone who looked to other girls to feed her desire for love and intimacy, because that felt natural. That *was* natural. I was the exception, but even then I felt that I was no longer enough for her, and would soon be even less.

She wanted love in general, and this or that girl in particular, so badly that she was often vulnerable to terrible suffering. She was quasi-scientific in her planning and her calculations about whether this field hockey girl or that moody sculptress might possibly feel the same, but when the time came she was always just their good pal. Still, rumors spread (thickly and forcefully enough to break my nose).

In those early days, she was a funny blend: for all her skill in reading other people, she was still inept at gauging their desires. This is probably normal for someone as bookish and theatrical as she was. Adolescence produces all sorts of variations of incomplete emotional development; it's the island of Dr. Moreau of human personality. My own lumpy and bizarre self was top-to-bottom, inside-and-out unappealing, while Dana at least looked good and was certainly motivated by good feelings: she loved art and loved life, loved her family and her friends, and was only sad because she wanted to love more and to feel a flood of such love washing over her in the same volume that she was ready to let it wash over another person. This, of course, led to pain.

She was learning a very difficult skill, much more complex than those being learned by the conventional girls and boys, far harder than the skills practiced by the lascivious would-be lotharios, so Dana necessarily loved awkwardly. She was by no means ready to tell the world what she was; she only hoped by some osmosis to sense others like herself. But in 1979, in a Minneapolis private school where we were scholarship kids with a definite cloud of pathos hanging over us, it was not at all clear that there were *any* confirmed lesbians to be found amid the kilts, or even any girls open to experimentation among the smokers, the punks, the potheads, the actresses, or the field hockey squad that captivated me and my sister alike.

I watched as girl after girl became her best bud and phone confidante and lake-biking pal. She didn't hide anything from me. She told me all about it. She wasn't trying to exclude me. She was probably going to great lengths to make me feel included, *hers*. But that only went to prove the truth echoing in the hollows of my hollowed, crannied soul: to be reassured of one's importance is proof positive of one's failure to be preeminently important. (It's funny: as I reread this paragraph, I can recall the sparks of *hope* that I sometimes felt when my father faced another spell of incarceration. "Maybe *now*," some part of me exulted. "Maybe *now* I will be everything to Dana.")

And so Dana migrated from group to group, a social nomad, always working her way into a clique because her still uncalibrated compass led her to pursue confidential friendships with girls who simply were not gay. They might have been literate, even poetic; sporty, even jocky; moody, even depressive; unconventional, even bizarre. But they weren't gay, or were not yet willing to consider it. And they weren't Dana's sun, her bright angel, her dawn. And when she subdued herself to fit in or exalted herself to stand out, and I watched from a knot of toadish boys, I wished I could help her, and I hated that she was desperate for some other bond than ours, and I felt pity for her and rage at the girls who couldn't see her grace and did not love her enough.

Unlike Dana, I was drowning in a primal soup of undifferentiated emotions. Actions born of confusion, motives crashing off one another, contradictory gestures, opposite and mutually exclusive truths told to different people for opposite reasons, resulting in arguments, broken friendships, fights. Dana was clarity; I was chaos. My love life was far more "normal" than hers, more hormonal, less romantic, alternately sullen and grubby, swollen and grabby. And all along I dreamt of being Dana's . . . what? Not her lover—this is not a report of rank incest—but I dreamt of being something indescribably close, perfectly joined, soulmated beyond the possibility of any rupture or misunderstanding.

Dana was a pretty seventeen-year-old who attracted her share of average-minded boys. She was also smart and published her poetry in the school magazine and was in the Drama Club, and so attracted brainy and artsy boys as well. And while the snobbery arrayed against us for our relative poverty and parental criminality closed some doors, by senior year we fit comfortably enough into the world of Lake Minnetonka boating Sundays and Lake of the Isles Saturday-night house parties. Dana was still divided: she wanted to fold herself into these moneyed routines but couldn't completely erase herself, wouldn't flirt with Evan Wallace, wouldn't encourage the boys at all, and so, rejecting all prom invitations, she insisted that I issue none of my own and instead, both years, we rented a stretch limo with a group of friends (straining to pay our share), migrated in a herd, danced in a circle, threw up on a sidewalk, and I watched Dana watch her latest crush kiss a boy.

We ended up in Kenwood Park after senior prom, just the two of us, at two in the morning, her in a gown Mom had sewn from patterns, me in a leased tuxedo foaming at the chest with flamenco ruffles. (Years later, I actually joined a hipster-flamenco group in Hungary, during my years of wandering. We used the hideous photos of that prom night for ironic publicity.)

It is odd, I know, to think of episodes where she was in pain as the ultimate evidence of our closeness, but there it is. There is something unbearably sweet in memories of her coming to me—and me alone—to open her heart.

The park at that late hour in May would have been very dark, and in its stretches of wood one could, briefly, for the space of a few yards, imagine oneself in a forest, far from city lights or the twentieth century. My night's thrills had been surreptitious—stolen kisses with other boys' dates, pecking at the weak-willed girls of the herd, playing and luring with the darker shades of my father's reputation ("I don't want to talk about, I just can't" being, at eighteen, powerful love poetry). And when the night of heightened sensitivity and thin skin and cruel games had passed, it left me happy, holding my sobbing twin's hand, my arm around her shoulders, draped by my borrowed tux jacket, in a tiny forest, leaning against trees and smoking, carving inanities in the bark.

Her sorrow was proof and vindication to my muddled adolescent mind: she was suffering because she could not find a soulmate in anyone else but me, and when she suffered, she wanted to be with no one else but me. I fear to write this down, but now it is too late: the evaporation of jealousy is as pleasurable an emotion as any I know; it is a release as profound and shuddering as any physical sensation. It is the erasure of fear, the removal of worry, the shimmering tingle once danger—for which your body has tensed—is past. It is not the arrival of permanent courage or trust; jealousy is tidal, and it flows and ebbs forever, and acceptance that it will return is part of the pleasure while it recedes. There is no happy ending, but nor is there eternal pain. Something is still going to happen, so the timing of the dropping of a curtain is largely arbitrary, which is why Shakespeare's endings are so often the weakest parts of his plays. (Someone is getting married or everyone is dead; time to go home now and get on with your own lives. *The Tragedy of Arthur* is no different.)

Dana sobbed so hard she fell to her knees on the grass, and I gathered her up in my arms. "She's not worth this," I said.

"Then who *is* worth this? Why not her?" replied love's logic.

"You'll find one. You'll probably find a hundred. It's just—you're just—*they're* just not ready for you yet." All the limp consolations one hopes will prop up the shaking, desperate, miserable. "You are," I reminded her, "kind and loving and funny and talented and beautiful. That's a pretty good deal."

"How many did you kiss tonight?"

"Depends on how we're counting."

"Just tell me not Amy."

"Not Amy. Not my type at all."

"You don't have a type. You're an angry omnivore. Just not Amy."

"I have a type. I just haven't met a girl who fits it yet."

This stretch of 93 percent accurately remembered conversation is embarrassing. If I was ever such a Don Juan as I was claiming (or wished to be, or pretended to be), it was to a certain extent a reaction to my father's fraudulent claims to womanizing prowess. "Do you think he had all those 'lady friends'?" I asked Dana when she came up to visit me one fall weekend, freshman year of college.

"Are you joking?" She had transformed herself in her first six weeks at Brown into a ferocious-looking lesbo-pug.

"I'm missing something, aren't I?"

"No. Probably he just told you different things." According to her, according to him, he had lived a perfectly monastic existence, in his cells and out, a devoted husband after the fact, a courtly lover, perfectly content to be perpetually separated from his soul's most blessed love, the lost Mary.

Neither was true, Dana pointed out to me. He was just exceedingly lonely since the moment he had—in a burst of self-punishment, aware of his complete failure as a husband—sacrificed his sincere and natural hope for a normal marriage and love, setting Mom free to be with solid, dull Sil. That great act accomplished with a straight face, and rewarded with unlimited child visitation, the curtain should have fallen on a redemptive comical tragedy. Instead, my father lived on, not in Act V at all but in an interminable Act III, claiming to me that he was a swinger and to Dana that he was happy to love Mom at a distance. The truth was isolation and a lot of work—some legal, most otherwise—with an increasing preoccupation with making or finding (or stealing) a large amount of money, which, he had decided, would make up for all his previous failings. This desire led him back to prison—a brutally long sentence on his fourth conviction—but didn't abandon him there.

"I have made a series of rather fundamental mistakes," he told me when I visited him during spring break my junior year in college, 1985. "But I'm on to something big now, I think."

"That's nice. How are you, Dad?"

"Gently used. Slightly foxed. Warmly inscribed."

He was that day very sentimental, even mawkish for my collegiate tastes; during that period I fancied myself to be above a long list of emotions. "Sil took you to a lot of Twins games? When you were a kid?" he asked.

"Yeah, quite a few. He's a statistics machine, you know."

"Taught you how to play, too? Had a catch with you in the evenings?"

"I suppose so, yeah."

"What did you talk about?"

"When?"

"When you'd play catch."

"We did that for ten years. I'm going to a game with him this week."

"Yeah. But as an example. Please."

"I don't know. We usually talked about baseball, I guess. That's what Sil and I have in common. And a fondness for Mom."

"I have that, too," said the oldish man in his orange jumpsuit.

"I know."

"But really no feel for baseball."

"I liked that ball you gave me," I lied about the forged Rod Carew baseball I'd thrown away, eager to call the infield fly rule on this sentimental chat.

"I was lucky to get it. I knew he was your hero."

I am trying—and failing, I fear—to restore dialogue from twenty-five years ago, to be honest enough for a memoir and fair to my father (and my younger self) and still make it clear why *this* moment is worth memorializing:

"I wrote a play," I announced. "It's being put on. Not Mainstage, but the black box."

"No kidding? What's it about?"

"Apartheid. The human cost of institutional racism. The urgent need for the university to divest from South African money. Greed."

"Very impressive," he mumbled, but I could tell it wasn't interesting him, that his momentary thrill of learning that I had written a play was already extinguished, that my writing was not of the sort to produce wonder, that my intentions for a socially engaged theater were somehow wrong. "Where's the magic, though? I mean, does it make your hair stand up?"

He managed not to mention Shakespeare. I had learned enough about prison visits by 1985 to know that you always left on a good note or else regret could crush you until the next time, and so I said goodbye politely enough, although I was in a righteous anger. It was not just blind fury but that rarer kind where you have the icy adrenaline pleasure of knowing you're *right*. I drove, alone, back to Mom's house, fuming at his self-centered sentimentality over his maybe having missed some of my childhood *and* his obvious lack of interest in me right now. After he'd spent most of my childhood in jail, now *I* was not magical enough? "Fuck his magic," I shouted in the empty car. "Fuck His Magic" became a song by the Fairy Rings, and I still have a cassette of them playing it at Brown's Spring Fling.

But making the leap from antipathy to apathy is not something you can achieve just by wishing.

I flew back to Harvard and my great triumph as a playwright. Dana took the train up for opening night. Since freshman year, she had transformed herself again and again, leaving behind her bull-dykery for punk rock and had now become a flower child, a retro pose that fit her least well of all her looks so far. She wore a woolen Latin American serape and had semi-dreadlocked hair. She saw my reaction to her hippiedom and, with a shrug, acknowledged it would soon pass.

"I didn't know you could be so passionate about the suffering of others," she said, hugging me backstage at the theater, a black cube with a single black curtain and a set of four chairs—two black, two white—on a chessboard floor. "You are going to score a lot of taffeta being this noble. But can you keep it up? Or does apartheid awareness evaporate with orgasm?"

It was certainly deflating, though she wasn't being cruel; she just saw through my affectations as quickly as I saw through hers. I wished I could have prevented myself from laughing, but her voice was a tickle, and I couldn't, when faced with Dana, hold myself in a pose.

She came with me to the Drama Club party that night, where I pompously accepted pompous toasts and we all congratulated ourselves for striking a blow for freedom in South Africa. Dana drank with us, smiled at me in a way that invalidated all the nonsense, not smug but desmuggifying, and I truly didn't mind. "I *love* that sweater," she enthused to the girl who played Winnie Mandela. Her gaydar had improved exponentially since high school.

"Seriously," I asked despite myself, several hours later, back in my dorm, Dana stretched out on the common room's futon couch. "Did you like any of it?"

"The play?" she sighed, behind closed eyes.

"The play, yes."

"No."

"Don't soften the blow. Just tell me."

"It wasn't like a play. It was like . . . like a tender for bids on your penis. Please don't waste your talent writing things to meet girls." I liked the mention of my "talent" as though it were a fact. That was more than enough. I thought she'd fallen asleep until she added, "You know you don't give a rat's furry pink ass about South Africa. You as much as said so in every line of that play."

None of this angered me in the slightest, while my father's fainter uninterest had brutalized me. Dana was right, and I loved her. I spread a blanket over her, tucked her in, my best and wisest and never-wrong critic.

10

A S A GIRL, Dana was, like Dad, an author lover. It mattered to her to know about the person who had written the stories, books, and plays she loved. Shakespeare, for example—a man about whom a very small number of things are known—was her friend. She felt grateful to him for what he had made for her to enjoy. I have some of the letters she wrote to our father, describing her feelings as she read each play. Here's part of one dated March 29, 1974, so she was not quite ten years old:

> You know what I thought? In *Love's Labour's Lost*, everyone in court is so mean to the bad actors when they put on their

show. It's a very *cruel* scene, don't you think? Well, guess what I discovered? The next play he wrote after *LLL* was *Midsummer*, and in that one he has bad actors again, and the court watches again, and the play is really bad *again*, but this time everyone in the royal audience is really *nice*. Did you ever notice this? I think I might be first and I think have a theory. After *LLL* somebody in the real court probably said to him, "We're a good audience to *you*, Mr. William Shakespeare, so don't make fun of us. Show us being nice to actors." And he did! Don't forget it's Arthur's birthday next month. Hint . . . hint . . . hint . . . give up? Yes, and mine! And Shakespeare, too, but you knew. First me, then Artie and Will—10 and 410, if you're counting. I would get Will something after reading *LLL*. I love that play. Is it one of your favorites, too? It's one of mine now, and he deserved a big reward from the queen. I hope she gave him a diamond or something for that one. I am making something *so* cool for Artie. I know you can make him something, too. How about a license plate? I am joking. I hope that's funny. Silvius is taking him to a Twins game, I know. And Mom is taking me to the Lincoln Del with three girls of my choice. Have you ever heard of *Love's Labour's Won*? They know it existed and it's by him but they can't find it now. I would like to find it and read it and not tell anyone about it, so it's just between me and Will. I'd share it with you, of course. Please continue to be good, so we can see you, okay? Please? Promise? [He did pretty well: it was three years before his next imprisonment.] "Sir! I love you more than word can wield the matter! You have begot me, bred me, loved me. I love as much as child e'er loved." Dana.

My sister's girlishly precise handwriting (better than mine even now), in pink ink, fills four pages of lined notebook paper on this occasion. The pages still cling to one another at the twisted spade ends where each sheet was from its spiral binder ripped, and here and there my father nursed the creases with Scotch tape, now as yellow as watered Scotch. I asked myself, as I read this and other ones not long ago, biting my lips and grinding my exhausted eyes to jelly with the heels of my hands, if it was possible that my father forged this letter. I didn't recall writing any letters to him, though I did find in his bundles two short, businesslike documents assuring him of my warm birthday wishes to him. But this! Here is Dana as a girl: precociously literate, naturally and profoundly loving, *Lear*-quoting, funny, insightful, looking out for me.

I remembered, thanks to reading this, the details of my tenth birthday. Dana built me a model baseball field, cardboard and artificial grass (from an Easter basket), painted, all in scale to some tiny Twins figurines she had bought with her allowance. It must have taken her hours and days to build it, hours in secrecy away from me in Mom and Sil's modest house, and since there was so little such time in those days, she must have been thinking of me and working for me for nearly all of April. In tiny letters on the back of the jersey of the figure up to bat she had painted PHILLIPS and the number 29 (Rod Carew's number).

Silvius was not yet Mom's husband then but her boyfriend, a stocky and balding fellow whose remaining, not-yet-fatted-over muscles impressed me a great deal. He did indeed take me to Met Stadium to see a Twins game for my birthday, though not until April 28, when the Twins beat the Milwaukee Brewers, even though Carew disappointed, going either 1-for-4 or 0-for-4, I believe. I have my ticket stub still, now that I am older than that stocky, balding fellow was and my own hair has thinned to the point where it looks as if I've had a not very convincing plug job on a much balder head. My mother bought me a boxed paperback set of *The Complete Sherlock Holmes*, which has moved with me from home to home, across oceans, for thirty-six years now and is held together by yellowing tape of its own. And my father presented me with a 1974 Topps-brand baseball card, in mint condition, in a protective plastic sleeve, with Hall of Fame–quality career statistics, of the Twins' second baseman: me. My chubby young face sits comfortably on a man's body in full swing, and visible just behind my blurring bat, a sign held up by a front-row fan: GO, ARTIE!

It was the finest birthday of my life, and I hold out no hope of ever topping it in whatever years remain.

From hate to love to apathy and back again. Therapists and I have schemed and attacked the locked box that contains the answer to the question, "Why did I hate my father for so many years?" Armed with intricate lock-picking tools, we passed aggregate months poking at my psyche, jabbing at its impenetrable front (not a lock at all, only a crafty and detailed trompe l'oeil), searching it for a spring, finally whacking it with the hammer of antidepressants, dunking it in the acid of hypnosis. Still, it keeps its sepulchral secret.

I loved my father, of course, but I did finally have to admit that I hated him. His arrests when I was a boy were evidence first of police conspiracy and harassment, unfairness against my daddy; but later they proved his disregard for us, for me, his apparent preference for prison over my company. In parallel, there was my love for him and my admiration for his work and for his theory that, as a doctor makes the world healthier or a lawyer makes it more precise, he made the world more wondrous. This belief must have had—the shrinks and I are in concord about this—some effect on my becoming a novelist. That and my total lack of skill at baseball. (Somehow sensing this, an online reviewer of one of my novels wrote, "Phillips swings for the fences but manages only to wedge his bat up his own ass.")

Protective of my mother, whom he failed, and jealous of his love for Dana and vice versa, I would gladly dress myself in noble garb now and claim (or just memoir-manipulatively imply) that I hated him for what he did to *them*, how miserable Dana was every time he was taken from her. I could make a case.

We were fifteen when he was sentenced to prison yet again. It was a brutal sentence—ten years—for what I must admit now doesn't seem like that dreadful a crime. And yet I would have had him executed for it when I was fifteen. It could not have been more disgusting to me. Even now, when I am almost as old as he was then, I find myself as embarrassed as a teenager to write down the details. *He was a worker of wonders! He expanded the world's possibilities! He was a wizard! He was teaching me to be just the same as him! I wanted to be him!* Well, he got ten years (and served seven) for a grubby little tax dodge. How measly was this wondrous expansion of the universe? His partner in wonders, Chuck Glassow, owned a chain of mid-market gro-

cery stores and had, for many years, been successfully claiming re-
duced revenues for tax purposes by gathering up newspaper coupons
that hadn't actually been used in his store. Unsatisfied by the tax relief he had won with this game, he had my father print fake coupons
with higher discounts and for products that didn't actually have
coupons, further reducing the store's apparent revenue and tax liabil-
ity. That was it. The marvel of it all. Glassow got five and was out in
two, and Dana only ever admitted being angry at him, never at Dad.
But I took it as a betrayal—of us, of the ideals and philosophy he
taught us—and my anger scoured my insides, burned my love for him
out of me, ablated my heart's interior walls.

When I came home from baseball practice Dana was on her bed,
her eyes bruised from crying, her knees drawn up to her chest under
that Errol Flynn poster: *The Tragedy of Arthur! Held Over!* she had
added as a handwritten banner diagonally across the top. I was raving:
"He's a criminal, and that's all he is! All that talk about art and love
and wonder. He's just a low-life!" Dana started to defend him, but I
was in full howl and would not hear a word for him. "You're the one
mourning this!" I shouted. "He's not coming to your show, is he?"
(Adolescent disappointment is so common because the opportunities
for damning parental absence are berries on a bush: if not her sculpture exhibit, my baseball game, her recital, etc.) She didn't say anything, finally, and the pleasure of being angry *and* right was (and still
is) a delicious brain-chemical cocktail, and a moral license unrevok-
able until the mood passes. "He's a bastard for doing this to you," I
nobly concluded. My sister crying harder and harder proved that I
was right and that I was helping.

The next day was the last of the school's short fall baseball season,
and my anger was the star. I took it out on Doug Constantine, my on-
again, off-again best friend since I was six years old and the son of Ted
Constantine, persistent prosecutor of my father. My anger was
equally unjustifiable and natural. The proximate cause was a collision
over a fly ball, me wheeling back from second base, Doug coming in
from right field, both of us knocked to the ground with the ball dribbling behind us, two runs scoring, game over. Later, I told him that
he'd been typically unwilling to back off where he wasn't needed

while he screamed—*screamed*—that I was a pig, that nothing was good enough for me, that I had to be loved for everything and by everybody, had to snatch up everything.

The most remarkable element of this—far more remarkable than two friends shrieking at each other, then pushing each other, then wrestling, then swinging hard at each other's faces in a locker room while other friends and teammates circled around to watch, none of the twenty boys tempted to step in and end the flailing fisticuffs—was the display of the fractured adolescent mind. Here were two promising young men who could do trigonometry, speak French, recall dates of presidential elections, map atoms, analyze Hemingway and Twain, yet neither one of them could have accurately said why he was fighting his best friend. Both would have cited a common display of baseball clumsiness, but they would have been wrong. I was angry that his father had imprisoned mine and that my father probably still thought I was the snitch; he was angry (to carry on the baseball terminology) that I had reached second base with Ellen Harrison, a girl I hadn't known he liked and in whom I'd had very little interest to begin with and, oddly, exactly zero interest after my hands had touched her breasts, all desire vanishing like October snow on a Minneapolis sidewalk. The battle was joined again in the woods behind school, our wet hair picking up leaves and moss as we rolled in the dirt and smacked at each other's faces with pinioned arms, like boxing T. rexes.

This scene of two friends fighting without understanding the cause gives me some respect for *A Midsummer Night's Dream*, and it is a pity we had no fairies to clean up the mess we made of our friendship in that disenchanted forest. The green, hazy enmity from that day floated on and on and never quite dissipated. Later, in a new twisting away from reality, I convinced myself that it was my father's fault that my friendship with Doug ended. If my father had not been a criminal, Doug's honorable, dull father would not have been forced to prosecute him, and I would not have been forced to choose (as I later interpreted the situation, forgetting Ellen Harrison's role entirely) between friendship and family. *I chose family!* I told myself. *Like a fiery Capulet! And in spite of my own self-interest!* I wasn't invited to Doug and Ellen's 1988 wedding.

11

A CT II OPENS WITH one of those ostensibly "funny" scenes, in which characters speak in something more like the normal manner of Shakespeare's time, not iambic pentameter. They are often lower-class characters and are supposed to be both comic and wise, or at least that's how they're treated now. In the case of *The Tragedy of Arthur*, it's the servant in charge of King Arthur's hunting dogs, reminiscing about what a fun kid Arthur used to be. He discusses with his apprentice boy whether Arthur will be a warlike king or will bring peace to Britain. Does it prove anything that they refer to a dog named Socrates and that my father supposedly had a Scottie named Socrates when he was a boy? I don't honestly know that this is definitive. There must be some statistical likelihood we could calculate: What are the chances that my father could have a dog as a child and then grow up to discover the only copy of a play that referred to a dog of the same name? One in a . . . Or he lied about having a dog named Socrates. Or he lied about finding a play by William Shakespeare. I'm trotting ahead of myself.

Arthur then leads his troops in the siege of York, beating the allied Pict-Saxon-Scot army, forcing them to retreat to Lincoln, where they have secret reinforcements lying in wait. Arthur, thinking he has won the war, decides to stay in York for some vague purpose, telling Gloucester to lead the army to Lincoln in his place, disguised as the king. Arthur promises to arrive before any battle. A chorus of common soldiers leads us to Lincoln, with another dreary scene of earthy "humor," boring me enough to convince me that the whole play is authentic. Lincoln turns out to be a large battle. Arthur is late arriving from York, so Gloucester leads the fight dressed as Arthur and wins a tremendous victory, killing Hebrides, the heir to the Scottish throne. Arthur arrives in time to take all the credit and review the prisoners, including the Saxon chief as well as Mordred and his brother. Feeling generous, even proud of his generosity, and trying to be unlike his father, he frees most of the prisoners on promises of good behavior, keeping Mordred's brother as a hostage. Arthur's most militaristic noble, the Earl of Cumbria, is disgusted by the show of mercy.

Arthur's childhood friend Constantine, the Earl of Cornwall, arrives to offer reinforcements and to share Arthur's vision for a unified, peaceful Britain, a world totally unlike the dark years of his father's reign. Before Arthur can achieve that goal, however, the paroled Saxons break the truce and attack yet again. Arthur is enraged by his own leniency and charges off to yet another battle. Mordred's father dies, making him King of Pictland, and he maneuvers to become King of Scotland as well. Mordred also learns that Arthur has killed his brother in anger over the Saxon attack, and Mordred's hatred for the English king continues to grow. He vows revenge.

Yes, Arthur has a childhood friend named Constantine. I noticed that, too. But Holinshed's *Chronicles* (the Renaissance book of history that Shakespeare used for many plays) tells the story of Arthur and Constantine, so it's probably on the up-and-up.

When Dana visited me in college, October of freshman year, Dad was three years into that sentence for the coupon scam. She came to my dorm straight from the train station, and my roommates and I had her stand in front of a red curtain, directly behind the giant hanging cardboard Ohio driver's license we had made, with a space cut out for a face. Bill attached the removable letters with her new name and new birth date, I took the Polaroid, Ivan trimmed, and Ronnie laminated. An hour after she arrived, we went out drinking on our new IDs, and on our second Scorpion Bowl at the Hong Kong, she confessed that she had squealed about the crop circle to Doug Constantine, back when we were ten. She had kept her mistake from everyone for eight years, and I cycled between awe at her discretion, shame at her indiscretion, and anger that she had let Dad think for all those years that I was to blame.

In the play, Arthur's father kills a noble and replaces him with Constantine's father. Then Arthur kisses and ends up marrying Constantine's sister, rejecting a better offer from the French. In real life, Constantine French-kissed Arthur's sister before she rejected him, and then Constantine's father reported Arthur's father to the sheriff of Nobles County. (If my father did not distort our family life to forge this play, I am left with the uncomfortable possibility that we have lived a distorted version of Shakespeare's imagination, which, ridiculously enough, is what one Shakespearologist claims: we are all the Bard's inventions.)

Dana and Doug kissed when they were ten, I learned with the long straw running from my mouth down into the plastic tub of alcohol. "My first try," she slurred. "And I told him—well, I made him guess. I talked about the news on TV about the UFO, and I let on that I knew how it happened, and then we kissed again, and then I think I told him all of it." So was she giving him a secret in order to win a kiss, making her the john and Doug the gigolo? "No, he wanted to kiss me." So did she let the secret slip and then hope to seal his secrecy with a kiss, making her the incompetent sexual manipulator? "No, it wasn't an accident exactly." So Doug snatched a secret by kissing her into indiscretion, making him his father's agent and her the poor trusting sap? "No": Dana was a women's studies major, and so she described the event as her futile attempt at some sort of "idealized, media-transmitted, societally endorsed, heterosexual intimacy, secrets and flesh co-opted simultaneously." This seems the saddest of all interpretations.

"How could you let Dad think it was me?"

"He never thought it was you."

He'd openly blamed me for years, and continued to associate me with any betrayal he suffered for years to come. That association spread so that every time he was arrested, some part of him wondered if I'd blown the whistle on him "again." Dana's blithe wishful thinking—*he never thought it was you*—was impenetrable. She refused to see how I could take this badly, refused to admit she should have told him the truth.

Her resistance to reality on this point, her insistence that Dad somehow just "knew" truth and always acted in our interest, was a blister waiting to burst.

12

ABSENTEE PARENTS DESERVE their kids' anger. Kids have to get mad to get over it, and if they hurt their parent in the process, that is the healing astringent necessary to everyone. As with many things, Dana was better and faster at this than I was.

Back in 1979, a month after my father began serving that ten-year sentence, fifteen-year-old Dana finally staged her only adolescent rebellion, expressing her pain at Dad's incompetent wonder-working and abandonment of her. Her attack may not impress anyone who's given their parents a truly rough ride, but you have to judge her act in context. Considering that her own personality (gay) was already an unwilling blow against parental expectations, she had never felt the need to "act out," all rebellious energies spent on navigating a world that contained a fair amount of hostility to her. But now she aggressively struck at our father, harder than I could have, because she was braver and more honest, because he loved her more, and because what she did was so piercingly fired at him and him alone.

She became an anti-Stratfordian.

She consciously chose to believe, or tried to believe, or at least pretended to believe—and then feigned amazement at Dad's anguish—that the author of the works of "William Shakespeare" could not conceivably have been William Shakespeare, the semieducated part-time actor/part-time real estate speculator son of a provincial glovemaker from Stratford-upon-Avon, that no such person could have composed the greatest works of English literature, embodying the finest of all psychology, storytelling, artistry, linguistic brilliance, and so forth.

She came home from the Minneapolis public library with first one, then stacks of anti-Stratfordian books, each proving that Christopher Marlowe or Francis Bacon or the Earl of Oxford had written Shakespeare's plays and then decided for obscure reasons to pretend they hadn't. She studied the loony ciphers and the theories of angry outcasts, researched grammar school curricula in Elizabethan England, cross-referenced what those kids learned with what the playwright showed he knew in his plays, read dictionaries of falconry. She spent more time on this project than on her schoolwork and soon dropped her efforts at sculpture. She wrote letters to our father that she would revise and annotate and read aloud to me, to double-check their tone before mailing them. "I don't want to sound *angry*," she claimed sweetly as she composed letter after letter explaining to the friendless convict that his lifelong idol was a fraud and a loser (implicitly like him). The correspondence shuttled quickly back and forth, Dana citing her new books, reading as fast as she could to stymie him (with his limited library privileges).

"Dana, before I go into all the factual errors and half-truths behind every single one of these theories, I have to tell you that at the bottom of all of these notions is a mean idea: only the rich, only the university-educated or the noble can have an imagination, can feel empathy. I know *you* do not believe that, but you are reading books by people who do, and I want you to know where their hearts lie in this. Besides the obvious snobbery, does your own experience confirm it? What do you make of the well-educated rich in your world? In your school? In their houses on Lake Minnetonka? Are they more imaginative and empathetic than you, for example? Do they convince you of this theory?"

"Dad. You are missing the point and clouding the issue. I am sure a drunk street person *could* have written *Hamlet*, if he had the right tools. All I'm saying is: your guy didn't have the tools. He didn't leave any books in his will. Kind of weird for the greatest writer in human history."

Dad replies: "Many people did not leave books in their will. Bacon, who some of your people credit for writing the plays, did not leave them either. That does not mean he did not read books or write them. It just means he did not distinguish them in his will any more than he itemized his socks. If I were to die tomorrow, I would not have a private library to distribute."

"Well, exactly. You're a criminal. That's different. Nobody is claiming you should leave behind evidence of being the greatest writer in the world. But your man is supposedly reading Ovid and Holinshed and Seneca and Chaucer and Terence. Not bad if he can't speak Latin very well and dies without any books. *You're* not expected to leave a will to anyone. *You're* not expected to do anything."

Tone slipped away from her a bit on that one. She did her best to keep the indictments disguised as literary criticism, waiting for his literary discussion in response to amount to an apology to her. She saved all the letters. I don't see an apology in any of them, but maybe it's in ciphers. (It's also worth noting that anti-Stratfordian theories in some sense "expand the world's possibilities," but my father certainly couldn't bear them.)

It was around this time that Sil and Mom had to sit Dana down for the talk about sliding grades and notes home from concerned teachers.

I still admire Dana for all of this. She fought Dad on his own terms and hit him where it hurt. She took chances. I was just sullen, and so required much longer to achieve a safe and healthy adult indifference and separation, and I *still* couldn't make it last. She stormed into battle. She threw herself into something, this massive research project: she had charts up on her bedroom walls, like a Mafia investigator, showing the whereabouts of all her suspects in different years ("1599: de Vere is all over London—*why*???"), and she was obviously letting the unimportant stuff sag. I was much too worried about the unimportant stuff—grades, college applications—which is why I outperformed Dana in school, though she was, by any real measure, quite a bit smarter than I. False modesty, O coy memoirist? Not at all. Let's call in the real greatest writer in English literature: "My dear Watson, I cannot agree with those who rank modesty among the virtues. To the logician all things should be seen exactly as they are, and to underestimate one's self is as much a departure from truth as to exaggerate one's own powers."

Dana wasn't a fool. She soon saw how feeble all the anti-Stratfordian arguments are, but she wouldn't give up. Like all anti-Strats, she was driven by something other than logic. Unlike them, she had a first-class mind and enough creativity to develop her ideas along unexpected paths. Since none of the existing theories worked, she devised her own. Forced to deal with school, she channeled her anger at Dad (and his playwright friend) into her academic work and produced a series of papers and extra-credit assignments that pulled her out of the ditch she'd dug herself into over the previous months. A clever revision of those papers carried her through her college application essays, and she still recycled and refined her work even through some freshman courses at Brown. (The part about the banking system over centuries became a freestanding paper in her Economics 1 class, and mine as well, with my thanks.)

Whenever a teacher pointed out particularly weak scholarship or blatant wishful thinking ("Really, Miss Phillips, what possible source do you have for the bet?" or "Dana, I think you've gotten ahead of yourself here" or "Why would Shakespeare agree to that?" or "If you're right, do you stand to make a fortune in the year 2014?"), she revised and tried to smooth the newest wrinkle.

Her complete project was a strange and beautiful hybrid of historical research, literary interpretation, parody, and outright fiction. She cast her anger into ammunition and—never denying that she loved the plays—she opened a withering barrage of ordnance upon the man credited with writing them and the convict who stood next to him, claiming special friendship.

Starting with a close analysis of the use of *you* versus *ye*, she argued that a preference for one in some plays but not others could not be explained by fashion or formality or topic. They seemed to vary by personal choice. "There is only one conceivable explanation," she asserted with the barking dogma of the frothing scholar. "The plays were written by more than one person."

While many canonical Shakespeare plays were collaborations (*Pericles, Henry VI, Henry VIII, The Two Noble Kinsmen*, etc.), Dana's view was starker: "Two separate men wrote all of these plays, individually, and, for reasons we will explore, allowed an obscure actor to take the credit." This was a unique argument, as far as I know. All the other revisionists handed out Shakespeare's work to *one* of the fanciful alternatives. Dana had a dynamic duo working to write "Shakespeare."

Her theory is, in the end, unprovable, of course, but she insisted (as all anti-Strats do) that it is no more unprovable than the absurd patsy we call "Shakespeare." Her version goes like this:

In 1589, or a little earlier if necessary, a nobleman—Edward de

Vere, the 17th Earl of Oxford will do just fine—and a Jewish money-lender found they had something in common besides the string of debts that bound one to the other. The earl and his moneylender's son were both poets, and neither was able to participate fully in the booming theatrical world of Elizabeth's London. It was beneath the earl to throw himself into rehearsals and company business (though he did write a few things under his own name for court), and the Jew-ish boy, at age twenty-three or twenty-four, desperate to be a part of it all, was, of course, unacceptable in that milieu.

The earl was a Cambridge man, and the banker's boy was a tireless autodidact, spending his devoted and kindly father's ducats on a beau-tiful library, where he loved Ovid best of all but read everything an Elizabethan gentleman ought.

The earl was not going to have an open friendship with his Jewish banker, but was humane (or financially needy) enough that when the moneylender asked him to read a few of his son's verses, the earl con-descended to agree. The father gratefully showed him a poem, the first scene of a play perhaps, and, in his own variety of condescension, granted some leniency on the terms of a bill coming due. The earl read the sample and was immediately aware that he was reading the work of someone with great ability. He summoned the father back and invited him to bring his son.

A strange and rivalrous friendship was born. The earl and the Jew-ish youth read each other's words, peered across the social abyss carved deep between them, and recognized each other with mutual admiration and jealousy. They met again and again, without the fa-ther. Their conversations would have been productive educations for both of them. The earl would have known about the military, the law, court behavior, Latin. The younger man would have provided Old Testament fluency, financial expertise, and, if he had spent time out-side London, an eye for the natural world—the plays' rich language of birds, flowers, country fairs, apples. Each boasted that if he were able to write for the public stage he would be hailed as the greatest poet of the time, outshining Kyd, Marlowe, Lyly. Naturally, one of them suggested a plan.

Next in Dana's fantasy comes a scene that other squinting anti-

Stratfordians imagine as well: a young actor, Will Shakespeare, new to London from the Warwickshire town of Stratford, ambitious but of only middling talent, is invited one night to a private audience with the Earl of Oxford in his London residence and is presented with an irresistible offer. The actor would be given a role to act in his own life, forever. He would play a better version of himself and would win great fame for his performance. He would be slipped works to stage under his own name. He could even take them to a printer and publish them, if he wished. Whatever money he could squeeze out of this was his to keep. The renown would be his as well. The women or boys he charmed with his honeyed verses were his to bed. ("Really, Miss Phillips, is there any evidence of such proclivities in Shakespeare the man?" huffed the twelfth-grade teacher, angry that Dana was saying much more about his hero's unknowability than his sexuality.) Changes made by the acting company in rehearsal were fine; the scripts should be brought back to the earl for reworking, and the earl would have felt the frisson of slumming it, toiling like some common artisan. No mention was made of the Jew at this early meeting where devilish Shakespeare won the souls of two other men and was paid for the victory.

Readily agreeing, the impostor went off with two plays: *The Taming of the Shrew* and *Edward III*. Before he could leave, however, he signed a document, twice, a long empty sheet. At the very top, above a blank expanse of future possibility, he took dictation and wrote: "I, William Shakespeare of Stratford, did not write the play *The Taming of the Shrew*." And, directly below: "I, William Shakespeare of Stratford, did not write the play *The Raigne of King Edward III*."

After the actor departed to try his luck in the world with this unlikely gift, the Jew emerged from behind the arras and shared the earl's wine, and the earl marveled at this dark-haired, dark-eyed, magnificent creature, able to write nearly as well as the earl himself. Though this friendship, this love, was forbidden, still the earl proceeded. (The historical earl also dabbled in bestiality, but Dana let that go.)

"In cases of young artists and older mentors," wrote Dana for a freshman psychology paper, "jealousy and mutual manipulation are hallmarks of the relationship." The younger man surely envied the earl's power and social acceptance; the earl surely feared revelations of his situation and used his threats and superior position to intimidate the youth. Still they produced new material, each in his own world, composing in secrecy before presenting the other with his latest creation.

The actor was summoned again, signed his name twice more by the flickering firelight: ". . . did not write *The Two Gentlemen of Verona* . . . did not write *The First Part of the Contention Betwixt the Two Famous Houses of York and Lancaster*."

Here, Dana went on, it might have ended, and Shakespeare "would have gotten away with it." But people are unpredictable, and people in love—"as we have seen in so many of the wondrous fantasies credited to the dull glover's boy"—are least predictable of all, prey to passions and confusions "overflowing reason's sanded bounds."

With unsurprising success, a name was being made (literally): "Shakespeare" was hailed, paid, even publicly mocked as an upstart by an envious rival. Both of the real artists had accepted their necessary anonymity back at the beginning, but tensions between them were unavoidable: each wanted the other to acknowledge his superiority. The author of *The True Tragedy of Richard Duke of York* faced off against the writer of *The Two Gentlemen of Verona*, and each claimed to be the greater poet. Their debate flared, cooled, was diverted into more plays, into spats and moody reconciliations, vows of love, sonnets, loans and refusals of tokens, yet more plays. "All the while, young Mr. Shakespeare produced new work at twice the rate of any other Elizabethan playwright, and in a dizzying variety of styles, as if he contained multitudes," wrote Dana. "He was credited for being best at comedy *and* tragedy. Most suspicious!"

These two star-crossed lovers met again and again in the hothouse of the earl's estate, between flowers of the New World and Africa. They read each other's latest with envy and pride, competing to outdo each other, stealing phrases from the other's work for later use, leaping ahead to address the other's themes in their next play, collapsing into each other's arms when ribaldry burst through rivalry, and they inevitably wondered how they would be received if they were allowed to be themselves, if they played the roles they had created, if they strolled to the back of the theater to collect the playwright's fees from the box office at the evening's end, earl and Jew, exposed to the world's judgment. They assured each other it could never be.

It did not matter, they insisted to each other—a mutual act of kindness. Their competition was not Marlowe, and their audience was not Shoreditch groundlings or half-brained lordlings. Their peers were Terence, Plautus, Seneca. Their audience was immortal and eternal. Just as men were still reading, these centuries later, the Ancients, anyone of their stature and skill (each included the other but meant only himself) would be read and performed centuries into an unknown future when England's throne would be filled by Elizabeth XXI or Henry LIV. No one would be performing Kyd's absurdities. Monarchy would be admiring the heirs of the two lovers' invention.

"And, come that distant day, which of us will be more admired?" asked the earl in Dana's one-act play of this story. The question was as inevitable as the apple in Eden; they had to ask as they had to breathe. But how could such eternal adoration be measured? Both of them would be known as *Shakespeare*. That would make the answer more difficult to determine, but also more just: neither would have a name temporarily inflated or discarded. Even then it was clear to the loving competitors that reputations could swell undeservedly large and then, like soap bubbles, burst. They would be judged as equals, earl and Jew, though they were in no other way equal. They would wager on some more lasting fame.

Five hundred years before they lay in this fur-strewn bed (Dana later detailed this scene for a theater-design course), Chaucer had not yet been born and English was an entirely different language. Five hundred years into the future it might—the Jew saw far—be a new language again, and the playgoers of the English court in 2095 might speak a tongue with some different words or thoughts differently arranged. "And by such time, the brightness of true genius—like ours—will have outshone all those lesser lights that strut our stage today, that seem as hot as Suns only for being so near." All style and fashion will have changed and changed back a dozen times, and true genius will blaze out, by sheer endurance. The brightest stars will be loved for longevity, not novelty.

How would one of the two men be judged superior? (In a poem for English class—written in modern anarchic randometer—Dana extracted this scene: "pillow talk between lovers / too excited by their visions to fall into sleep.") They trusted posterity in general, but who *specifically* in posterity was qualified to declare a winner? Would sales of copies of the plays measure the difference? Numbers of people who attended all the productions over the coming five centuries? The number of our plays still performed by the King's Men or the Queen's Men in 2095? Use of their invented words in common conversation? suggested the Jew, who had already coined *critic*, *fashionable*, and *eyeball*.

I remember, when we were probably sixteen, that Dana came into my room and asked me, "How would you measure and prove real literary immortality?"

"Royal command performance," said the carl. "That distant king or queen and all betwixt now and then will surely wish to see the best of her players' tales at Christmas revels every year. And from this first Elizabeth to that fiftieth, each monarch will ask for this or that play of ours. How simple to number up all the requests and, at the end, account this the measure of the poet for all time, the scenic master whom all eternity will acknowledge as second only to that uncreated Creator."

Dana elaborated on the wager's mechanism for an economics class, modeling exchange rates and comparisons of currency value over time. If, she hypothesized, two men in 1595 were each to place £200 (say, the equivalent of £45,000 in 1982) into some sort of secure, interest-bearing account, what would be its value in 2014, the 450th anniversary of their invented playwright's birth? A weak math student, Dana calculated the wager's 2014 value at $9 million.

And? And the closest direct descendant of the greater writer—the more royally demanded writer—would collect the money and reveal (with that long list of Shakespeare's signed confessions as proof) that the greater half of the work of the upstart crow was written by either Edward de Vere, 17th Earl of Oxford, or a confused and secretive bisexual Jew named Binyamin Feivel (wrote the sexually secretive religionless Jewish girl from Minneapolis).

"Come now, Ms. Phillips, your fantasy bumps into certain textual realities. The sonnets mention the poet's name as *Will, an actor*. They are plainly autobiographical, plainly revelatory of *himself*. Here is where we glimpse the true man Shakespeare in his world! The sonnets are not some mere literary game! So how do your imagined lovers settle that?" One hundred and fifty-four fourteen-line poems, conceivably autobiographical: how indeed?

With ease, as Dana showed in a staging she directed of *The Sonnets* during the fall of her sophomore year at Brown, 1983: The two men (played at Brown by brown women) write the poems to each other. Soon after their scheme had begun, they were calling each other "Will," both of them, since as Shakespeare's fame grew they both came to identify themselves to each other as him. The autobiography of the Stratford actor that "dimmer readers" thought they perceived in *The Sonnets*, Dana explained, was actually a "photonegative" of reality: these are two lovers writing to each other, not one poet writing to two lovers. First, in Sonnets 1 through 17, the two men take turns encouraging *each other* to marry and have heirs, not some mysterious youth, for how else could their descendants collect on the wager? Subsequent poems reveal varying degrees of submission, love, emotional strife, separation, and reconciliations. One of them accuses the other of stealing a mistress. Then 127 through 152 are all by Oxford: the supposed "Dark Lady" (for whom people speculate Shakespeare seems to have a tormenting, vaguely taboo love) is none other than Feivel himself, dark, as a Sephardic Jew would have appeared by Elizabethan standards. The Dark "Lady" seems to betray the poet. *"Swear to thy blond soul that I was thy Will,"* the black actress recited, dressed as a bisexual English lord writing cross-dressed verse to his Jewish lover.

By the time the two men published *The Sonnets*, their dummy had become a reasonably celebrated figure. *The Sonnets*—the comet dust of their genius—became a bestseller, just like the Jew's *Venus and Ado-*

nis and the earl's *Rape of Lucrece*. The real man, William the actor, found himself embroiled in a bit of a scandal. His colleagues—who admired him, profited from his genius, drank with him—now learned from the published poems that he had had some sort of an affair with . . . a Mooress? A Jewess? An Italian?

By then the actor Shakespeare realized that he *had* sold something back in that first fateful meeting in the spring of his career, and by the time he was filling up that confessional sheet—". . . did not write *The Tragedy of Lear* . . . did not write *The Tragedy of Macbeth*"—he understood that he no longer possessed all the power. He had made his name and liked the name he had made, but by 1604, when the Earl of Oxford died, the potential disgrace of discovery had shifted: it would now be far worse for Shakespeare than for the Jew or the late earl, were the ruse to be revealed. Shakespeare's life, his friends and money, his loves were all products of this lie, and the tangled web in which he had ensnared himself would, if cut, drop him from a dizzying altitude onto a hard surface.

A term paper about confidence men and professional liars that Dana wrote for sophomore psych made no mention of Dad, but hypothesized that a man in Shakespeare's position would have increasing difficulty, at least sporadically, *not* believing that he had written the plays for which he'd been paid and praised ("*made such a sinner of his memory / To credit his own lie*"). And if he were in such a state when forced to admit that he had *not* written them (when he signed the document in exchange for new manuscripts), he might have found the cognitive dissonance so painful that he would have been prone to violence.

A man in such a position—" . . . did not write *Cardenio* . . . did not write *All Is True*"—would have found that document excruciating, would have viewed it as, alternately, a forgery, a coerced lie, or the damning evidence of his teetering life of dishonesty. Its continued existence would have ruined his sleep and his days, drained his every act of reality and meaning. His real estate investments were built on money earned from a lie; his application for a family coat of arms was based on honors won from a lie. With every passing year, the honest proportion of his life was shrinking. The document was unacceptable, but its destruction would mean the end of new plays, which he needed and felt he deserved.

The remainder of Dana's work was openly fiction. Some of it turned up in her creative writing workshop in college, but most of it was viewed as "symptomatic" by her doctor, and even she had to agree.

At some point, the beard decided to shave itself from the face that supported it and walk off a bard. Shakespeare, having decided to retire from the theater, simply stormed into their next secret meeting, grabbed the confessional document, pushed the dainty Jew aside, and thrust the paper into the waiting fire. The evidence was gone. All that remained were stylistic differences within the two men's plays and the money now in the Jew's family's system of interest and accounts, though he himself—Binyamin Feivel—had converted and changed his name to Ben Phillips. (My religionless sister imagined herself as the heir to Shakespeare, and found in Judaism the trick to do it.)

The intervening centuries. Two families, alike in dignity, the Phillipses and the Deveres, carried on a bizarre and secret war, staged in Swiss banks and school boards, critical editions, university tenure committees, by agents witting and unwitting, each family attempting to discredit the opposition's plays so as to discourage performance, having them cited for obscenity or forgery so they would be forgotten, *uncommanded*. Throughout, the families kept one eye on the increasingly peculiar question of what the reigning British monarch requested for entertainment and the other eye on a deposit of cash, moved periodically from one account to another, slowly amassing. Why was it never stolen by a trustee? The trust documents—now and then updated in a new country to adhere to new banking law—were always managed jointly by one member of each family, and only by joint signature of the head of the Deveres and the head of the Phillipses could that swelling amount be moved or altered, despite war, depression, history, greed.

Greed: all it would have required was the simultaneous arrival of a Devere and a Phillips who cared more for half the growing fortune than for a share of the increasingly dubious claim to have descended from the unacknowledged author of half of Shakespeare's plays. And though both families did produce such fathers over the years, ready to trade pride for cash, it never happened at the same time, no matter the financial climate. (Dana, a scholarship kid at Brown while I was a scholarship kid at Harvard, was working two jobs to pay her share of school, and the attack on our financially useless father was evident to me.)

Instead, family pride steadily swells over four centuries, and the moment of revelation from father to eldest child takes on ceremonial significance. A dying Devere explains the situation to his heir. A Phillips boy is usually told of the secret the night before his bar mitzvah (we apparently converted back to Judaism at some point). The bet, the secrecy, the issues, the feuding school boards were all explained to the next head of the family. Papers were signed, introductions made, running tallies of royal command performances updated.

The score was maintained by the same trusteeship, always with the decreasingly science-fictional date of 2014 in mind, when the winner would cash in. But here complexities arose, especially as command performances became rarer and the monarch no longer kept an official company of actors. It's easy to say that between 1603 and 1616, Shakespeare's troupe, the King's Men, performed 187 times for James I, but should they count a 1712 performance of *Coriolanus* where Queen Anne fell ill in the first act? What of walkouts? In 1888, the future Edward VII commanded a performance of *Troilus and Cressida* but was nowhere to be seen at the curtain call, as he was off leading *his* secret life as Jack the Ripper.

And what of films? Elizabeth II went to cinema premieres to see Olivier's *Henry V* and Branagh's *Henry V*, but what about her DVD rentals? Pay-per-view? Dana wrote to the public relations office of Buckingham Palace, but didn't feel the answers were definitive. She was left with her best guess from all her research. By 1985, with twenty-nine years until payday, the score stood nearly tied at 1,401 performances for plays by the Earl of Oxford and 1,384 for those by Ben Phillips, our ancestor, author of the unrecognized and never-commanded *Tragedy of Arthur* and—Dana could prove textually—all of her other favorite Shakespeare plays as well.

13

DANA WAS NO LONGER ADDING to the story by the second half of college, but it still unrolled in her psyche. Her anger at Dad—paroled in March of our senior years—had not completely vanished, and as long as she was still angry, she would cling to a little anti-Stratfordism, her "screw thee" to Dad. And if she was going to cling to rebellious looniness, she was going to cling at least to her own version, the one where she would inherit $9 million in 2014.

Ironically, the (anti-)intellectual position she had taken ("Shakespeare didn't write the plays, *Dad*") led her to this fable in which that same Dad would eventually take Dana aside and tell her the good news about her inheritance: "Here is our family secret, and you are the one to see it to its end!" (It always struck me, though, that 2014, the 450th birthday, was far too convenient for us. The 500th—far likelier a target—would mean it would be my kids' victory, with elderly, whiskered Aunt Dana drooling in the corner.)

In all her research, she never came upon a reference to *The Tragedy of Arthur*. Textually, she put it in its place, dated its composition, traced its thematic and linguistic characteristics to the Feivel plays around it (*King John*, *Richard III*, the *Henry VI* trilogy), but she never found a single word about *Arthur*. "Didn't you think that was odd?" I asked her just last year.

"Nope."

I believe that this smaller self-delusion was part of the larger one gestating in her at the same time, and that the authenticity of *Arthur* was tightly bound in Dana's subconscious to the authenticity of her father's love for her. She could not afford to believe that he could have lied to her about Shakespeare. This linkage was so strong that—as with any anti-Stratfordian delusion or pre–Iraq War WMDs—the absence of proof could not be tolerated as proof of absence.

I don't know what I thought at the time about all this. I really didn't much care or take much note. These ideas were just a continuation of the Shakespeare "thing" I had never taken part in, so I didn't see her trouble coming. But now I think that she fantasized, even believed on some level, that eventually Dad would really tell her the good news. She had thatched together this tale with the sticks and mud of her life and dreams, my father's life, literary history, stovepiped historical research. When I asked, "But you don't actually *believe* this, do you?" she replied, "But that's just it. If it's true, you wouldn't know it yet."

She had begun in rebellion, rejoicing when she irritated him with her letters. But she ended, when he came to her Brown graduation in May 1986, depending on him even more than when she was an idolizing and constantly disappointed little girl, her fantasy life overflowing its allotted space.

I don't want to overstate her breakdown around the time of our graduations. A lot of people feel the stress of that period of life and suffer a temporary loss of bearings. It wasn't the worst crisis ever.

On the other hand, a lot of people suffer the same stresses that Dana suffered without any ill effects. The crisis did knock her out for a few weeks, and did lead the rest of us to treat her a little gingerly in the coming years. I suppose, despite my own flirtations with the psychiatric industry, that this was the first time I really thought of Dana and myself as essentially different.

That is an odd admission, I see. We were twenty-two years old, of different sexes, different experiences, different opinions. I had been angry at her, jealous of her, cruel to her, hurt by her cruelties to me. But this was the first time I ever really saw us as fundamentally different people: I would not have a breakdown. I would not become so involved in an illusion that I would lose track of reality. I would not collapse at the shock of my fantasy's evaporation in the cold air of truth. I was, in fact, comfortable with reality, and, even as I pitied my sister—felt real pain in her pain—I took a certain pride in my healthy coldness. I was made of stronger stuff, and I liked it. (All these beliefs were false, unfortunately.)

Anyhow, Dad arrived unannounced for Brown's commencement in a burst of paternal instinct and insouciant parole violation. (He was arrested upon his return to Minnesota for casually disregarding the terms of his release, thus missing *my* college graduation, making a choice for her and delaying my own healthy arrival at indifference to him.) Dana was so amazed that he had come (to *Providence*) the week she was scheduled to enter real life and adulthood, that she believed he had arrived *to tell her*. She took him to her room, laid out all her later work for him, waiting to be praised by her daddy for having figured it all out. She faced his incomprehension at the end and saw at once that he had no congratulations or legacy to present, no key to a hidden world of elite secrets. She knew all that, of course. She understood that. She had been under other pressure as well, had, I assume, suffered other emotional setbacks. It wasn't the worst breakdown in the world. She just couldn't stop crying. And she started to talk about wanting to "stop feeling this way." She probably didn't mean that the way some interpreted it, but Dad took her to Health Services himself, passing through Brown's campus gardens bursting with spring's crow flowers, nettles, and daisies.

It wasn't the worst crisis in history, not even the worst in the history of Shakespeare-loving, hyperbolic actresses, would-be Ophelias drowning in imagination, obsessive Frannys. But it kept her occupied that summer. When she came to live with me in September, she was very much herself, just with a certain overenthusiasm shaved away. She sometimes talked about having received a "cognitive diss."

She forgave our father for not giving her $9 million, and, more to the point of reality, she forgave him for what she called "his unconvincing performance as a father." I don't know if they formalized it or if there was ever a specific moment when she knew the rebellion was over, but it was over. Unlike other anti-Stratfordians, once her initial psychological splinter was tweezed out, she let the whole stupid thing go. She came out of it where she began and gave Shakespeare back his life's work (and gave her father back a loving, wiser daughter). She still loved the plays. She loved a lot of plays: Ibsen, Chekhov, Stoppard, Strindberg, Beckett, Ionesco, Dürrenmatt, Jonson. She could still quote almost all of Shakespeare, and recited passages from time to time, but she no longer spoke of an ancestor or a paternal genius. She was converted by the fire of her experience into a lover of *works*, not *authors*. I saw her once in rehearsal, when another actress said, "He *must* have lived this. The words are *so* heartfelt." Dana just sighed and said, "Dunno." She no longer cared, really, who wrote

King John; she wasn't grateful to Shakespeare for it—she merely loved it and was grateful to *it*. This is not a minor distinction, and I'll come back to it later.

Fall of 1986, we moved in together in New York City. After those four years of unpleasant separation, I was relieved to be with her, to be able to look after her, to bathe again in the feeling I could find with no other person on earth, of being in company, known and loved, understood, often without even talking.

We could not quite afford a second bedroom in Manhattan. I had been hired as a junior copywriter in an ad agency—one of those jobs deemed so glamorous that they pay you very little. I affected a fedora in my business attire, but photos now reveal that the effect was less Bogart than Hasid. Dana, for her part, lived on waitressing tips. She was still fine-tuning her medications and was sometimes frighteningly manic, as far as diners were concerned: "Please, really, have a great, *great* day today, okay? Okay? Please?" she told some customers with dreadful urgency, or so she claimed. She was determined to succeed as a stage actress and so was waiting tables, modeling a little, and, later, working as an "exotic dancer." She came home her first night from that with five times the tips she'd ever made as a waitress. She didn't mind the work, she told me, but threatened to quit if I ever set foot in the place. She began to call herself a "sex worker" because she liked the exploited proletarian sound of it, although she only ever danced and stripped. Always a Brown graduate in women's studies, she referred to the club's owners as sex industrialists or captains of sexual commerce.

We alternated the bedroom and the living room futon couch, a week at a turn. Of course, if either one of us brought someone home, then the bedroom was the prize. When she wasn't working late or preparing for an audition, we used to go out together, sometimes with friends, but sometimes the two of us would simply feel the same urge at the same time. "Mmmm, you know what I really want to do tonight?" she might ask at the very moment when I was noticing the growling crescendo of my own identical appetite.

I drank more than she did. I say this not as a memoirist's excuse, but only to report accurately the way we lived in those happy years, in many ways the happiest of our lives. We were far from the parents, back in each other's daily influence. We were in love with the idea of ourselves. We were sure something great was coming or, at least, that what we had and what we were would roll forever on. Shot free of the rhythms of college schedules, we were suddenly in an eternal now, with no worries that it would ever end, or that it should.

Dana probably felt otherwise, obviously. I casually threw around those "we"s in the last paragraph. My recurrent obtuseness about those nearest to me has never really been cured (even in those days when I was trying to write fiction late at night, examining the feelings of imaginary people). When I look more carefully at those New York years, I have to admit that what I saw as a paradise of good feeling and absence of anxiety was possibly something else for her, and so her later relationships likely meant more to her than I may have realized. ("May have." How easily the memoirist can make himself seem a little innocent, a little lovable, endlessly extenuating his own guilt, nibble by nibble.)

But I cannot help it: my own memory seems strong and accurate enough; the recollection of my feelings in those days overwhelms all quibbling. I was happy, and, I will insist, she was happy. Retrospective thoughtfulness can make the past too bleak, as if one is gazing backward through welder's glasses.

So I say that it *was* good. We used to go out together, would dare the other to talk to this or that woman in a bar. We shared an appreciation for the female form. "Well, there is a divinity that shaped *her* end, that's for damn sure," I recall Dana exulting over one possible love. By then her eye for likely targets was nearly infallible, far better than mine.

Which was good, because I could absorb rejection after rejection like a fat man taking body shots. Dana, however, had not been toughened up by her summer of sorrow. She was still Dana—impassioned, engaging, lovely, willing to be open and vulnerable—and she took rejections hard.

That said, she was also much more of a man in these matters than I was. She seemed a perfect gentleman in how she treated the women who would pass me on the couch—once in the darkest night, the toilet belching in gratitude for their visit, and once again in the morning, fiddling with the locks and apologizing as I groaned and peeled a resistant eye. In those years, Dana was the sort of man I wished I could be: effortless, honest without hurting anyone, open to others' feelings and needs without bearing responsibility for their assumptions. My one-night stands ended with pained awkwardness; hers left satisfied.

When I think of how I became a writer, I do recall the countless occasions when my father told me something like "There is no higher calling for a man than to create things, and to create worlds out of words is the highest form of creation." This seems a likely psychological seed, obviously. It also equates writing with a sort of con job (building illusions with a reader's own imagination, then being far away when the pigeon realizes there's nothing real at all in the experience).

But Dana's influence was different. She would, on occasion, talk to women in bars and, having decided they weren't gay (or "gay enough"), bring them to me, after talking me up to them. She would introduce me as "a writer." She described my labors sitting on our fire escape going over my words again and again, stumbling in at dawn, exhausted and happy because I'd managed in those long hours to write a few lines that reached to the heart of what it felt like "to be a woman today," she said to the unbelievable hottie with the rack that just would not quit. "He sees that more clearly than any man I've ever known." Not true, obviously, not for a single instant, not in a single detail. I had written almost literally nothing, and certainly nothing of any value, just some feeble efforts at mildly erotic science fiction. I never went out on our fire escape—the window was painted shut.

But I liked me in her version, and I aspired to it. I could not remember the last time I'd wanted my mother to be proud of me, probably not since Little League. Sil's approval had mattered, but only in more prosaic questions of masculinity: "That's no way for a man to act" was very harsh when spoken softly by Sil. I madly pursued my father's approval for many years, with no result. But Dana's praise I wanted *and* I could win. That's the person who will shape you permanently.

I did my hours at my job, hoping to make her (and Dad) smile with my work when I could. Our agency was famous for its print campaign for Absolut Vodka, with the distinctively shaped bottle laid into various disguises. I discovered and passed up through the art department *The Tempest*, I.ii.126: "Absolute Milan!" The *e* was dropped, the island was shaped like the Absolut bottle, and the tiny ship was smashed into its neck.

In a copywriter's dream, I was also able to convince an account director and then the small client to use some of Sonnet 6 as the body copy for an ad. In the posters that went up in bus shelters and nightclub men's rooms, a handsome man at the far end of "young" looks through a rainy window. His finger noticeably lacks a wedding ring, and the only photos on his desk are of him with his aged parents. His face, spotted by the shadows of raindrops, reflects the first melancholy realization of passing time's acceleration. Below him are the lines

> Then let not winter's ragged hand deface
> In thee thy summer, ere thou be distilled:
> Make sweet some vial . . .

and the name and phone number of the sperm bank, as well as the going price for premium-quality, résumé-supported donations.

The references were lost on most vodka drinkers and lonely seed distributors; both ads quickly vanished. Perhaps *that* is why I became a novelist: I stunk at everything else. But no, there it is: the self-deprecating memoirist, mythmaking.

In Shakespeare's case, the mythmaking began seven years after his death, on the dedication pages of his collected works, the First Folio, where my birthday buddy is lauded by his companions, competitors, admirers—"He is for all time!"—as if we are meant to forget that they all stand to make money by this idolizing ad copy. "Read him," urge the collection's editors, his old business partners, blurbing like maniacs. "Again, and again, and if then you do not like him, surely you are in some manifest danger not to understand him." The first stage of turning a writer into a god requires some intellectual bully-ing: if you don't like him, *you might be slow.*

14

BREAKING PAROLE to come to Dana's graduation led to another six months' imprisonment for my father. I sometimes wonder if he knew this would happen and decided her college graduation jus-tified the sacrifice. It's pretty to think so, but then that means he chose to skip my graduation later that month in favor of returning to jail.

At any rate, when he came out in December of '86 from his supple-mentary time, the tireless Ted Constantine had him arrested immedi-ately. My father had cashed in an ex-cellmate's secrets to win that parole in the first place, and the aggrieved man had in turn offered Constantine details of an old unnoticed performance of my father's, news to the prosecutor. The county attorney had taken advantage of the six extra months to build his case on this new offense and was ready to go as soon as Dad set foot on the outside.

I flew to Minneapolis for his arraignment. Dana had won the role of the Wicked Witch of the West in an off-Broadway children's the-ater production of *The Wizard of Oz* and didn't dare give her under-study an opportunity to bump her off. My mother had not paid attention to Dad's legal events for decades, since the last time she had believed in his innocence. My father had spoken of a younger brother from time to time, but the sibling's shifting status—sick, abroad, alco-holic, sick, cruel, abroad, dead, sick—prevented any contact. So I was alone, playing the part of a grown-up coming to advise my father in his legal troubles.

He was broke and so had a public defender, a blond-ponytailed girl of about eight, whom he seemed to enjoy baffling. I joined them in their intense and highly professional planning session.

"Well, okay, so we've come to the plea phase? And it's like they're saying, 'So what do you say for yourself, mister?' I know, I mean, ob-viously, I know that you know all this, but just to square our *T*'s. Now,

I don't want you to say anything to me yet. Let's just lay out what they're all lining up against you? Their side of the story? And then we can see what sort of answer is the best one for us? To make?"

"*I never knew so young a body with so old a head,*" recited my father.

"Dad."

"Is your father up for this?" she asked me and turned, with me, to him. "Mr. Phillips, are you up for this? I know this can feel kind of crazy pressurized? But still, Mr. Phillips? We have to do this pretty much now, because they really do load up my client list. A keep-it-moving sort of feeling is what we need."

I had never seen him like this before, though I had never been present at this stage of any of his jurisprudential adventures. He was no fun, to say the least. He was nearly sixty and was angry, depressed, all the predictable responses at last. He had no interest in defending himself, but he'd lost that old humor about it, the feeling that he was above it all.

Okay, here's the memoirist's self-accusation: if only I had . . .

Told him I loved him? Told him I forgave him? Asked him to come live with me and Dana? Told him I thought he was a great artist? Asked him to go over the evidence slowly with me and the lawyer, to see just how strong the prosecution's case was? I did try the last one.

He wasn't answering her questions, except to mock her in a way he thought she didn't notice. She noticed.

"Ms. Stark, can I get a minute alone with my father?" I had some notion—likely absorbed from movies—that I would talk sense into him.

In truth, I didn't know him anymore. His life was now beyond my comprehension and much of my sympathy—even if I had been a devoted visitor, a loving son, a concerned participant in his life. I was none of those. I found him embarrassing, an obligation with strands of sticky guilt floating off him, trying to wrap themselves around my ankles and throat. Even so, if he'd shown any sign of interest in my being there, if he hadn't resisted my efforts to help, I would have . . . He was only withholding, to use that memoir term of complaint. We spoke such different languages that I wouldn't have recognized a plea for help, a call for attention, a whimper for love, if he ever made such a sound. But let the record show I tried.

"You can't just quote Shakespeare to her. She doesn't even know you're doing it. She just thinks you're odd."

"I used to get lawyers who could quote it back to me. I can't even afford Bert anymore."

"Listen, Dad. Why aren't—"

"Skip it. These jackals want me on this? On this, this offal? Fine. It's five years old. I never finished my piece of it, but your pal's dad has it all, so, I'm—"

"He's not my pal. It was Dana! Dana snitched on that! Why do you harp on that, like you think—"

"I'm not going to waste my time arguing with these people. Hell, I can confess to stuff they don't even know about."

"What? What is that supposed to mean? What are you— Isn't a jail sentence *more* of a waste of your time than defending yourself?"

"Doesn't matter. I can still outlive him."

"Outlive Ted Constantine? What's the point of that?"

He just looked at me, then made aggressive small talk. "What are you doing with your life?"

"Are you insane? You have to focus, Dad. Don't do this to Dana, at least," I tried, playing my double-guilt card, implying that he was hurting her *and* that I was able to acknowledge his lifelong preference.

He was very bitter. Just that day? At that period of his life? It confirms some negligence as a son that I don't know. There was no puckish joy. He was not extolling the creators and damning the gray men who raked the wonder out of life. He was broke, friendless, and humiliated, beaten, unable to pull off his odd crimes because of improvements in forensic detection. Prison and prosecutors had whipped out of him his charming and challenging arrogance. In another, more gullible era he would have presented the king with a taxidermied marvel from the New World, a beast with the head of a lion and the body of a trout, and he would have been loved for it. In our world, he forged, in this case, scratch-off tickets for the New York Lottery, which Chuck Glassow then sold to New York bodega owners for less than they paid the state for real tickets. Unwitting gamblers scratched off my dad's metal paint and lost, just like with real lottery tickets, never knowing they had paid someone other than the state of New York for the pleasure. "Victimless," my father said again, as he said of all his crimes, but this time that wasn't quite accurate. It was simply that he had stolen the state's victims for himself. They didn't know their victimization had been transferred, and if you look at New York's lost revenue—ostensibly used for schools—the claim of innocent wonder-working seemed even further from the old ideals than usual. "Dad, you have to stop and you have to stay out of jail. So, please—"

He cursed Ted Constantine, old Sil, and then me. "What the hell are you doing writing ads?"

"I did one for you with *The Tempest*. Did you see it? I sent it to you."

"I saw. You used him to sell liquor."

"Don't. Please. Please don't talk to me like—"

"Like you're selling out, playing along with this repellent system? Like you're a huckster, pulling the wool over suckers' eyes for nothing more than a paycheck, and you earn your money by convincing fools that one brand of vodka will get you laid? When any pygmy from the African bush knows that all vodka is exactly the same? Why aren't you *making* anything? I confess! Guilty! I wasn't the finest father, but I did teach you that, didn't I? You could help Sil move AC units, couldn't you?"

"Fake lottery tickets? Are you—"

"Go back to New York. Just go."

I hadn't prepared myself for this. He had never been aggressive like this before. Also, I was twenty-three. Those are my justifications, as far as I will go in claiming memoirist's last-word privileges to minimize what I did next: I left.

I left, probably left him (after a few minutes of thinking) in a mood of self-loathing and with an urge to punish himself. I probably knew he would feel like that. I can't say I knew what he would do next, what tool was readily at hand with which he could punish himself; that self-conviction is just beyond memory's reasonable doubt.

I left and stepped into the hall and told Mindy Stark that my father was in his right mind and ready to talk to her now. And I flew back to New York and got very, very drunk with Dana after I picked her up at the stage door.

He insisted on pleading nolo contendere and would not say another word on the matter to anyone. His public defender, with scant knowledge of my father's criminal record and in plain malpractice, had not warned him, or had not even known, that mandatory sentencing, which had recently been introduced in Minnesota, would gravely affect Recidivist Dad unless he pleaded guilty and made a deal. He would do neither, nor trouble himself to plead not guilty and take his chances. According to the draconian tables of the law, the judge had no leeway. It was 1987. My father came out of prison for the last time in 2009.

But that sentence was still *days* in the future. Now I could get drunk with my best friend, and we could go try to score and forget about the whole business.

I was unwilling to talk much about what had happened. I wanted to be free of him entirely, just be a happy young man with money and a buzz and an erection. I also suspected I had done something wrong and, like a child, didn't want to talk about it, because talking about it might make it real.

Dana, however, was eager to talk about it, out of guilt for putting *The Wizard of Oz* ahead of her father, out of dread that she had trusted me to represent sage advice. "He said that? That his goal was to outlive Constantine? What were his exact words?"

I couldn't remember and didn't care to try. I was straining hard for jollity, and Dana was being a sweet, needling drag, extracting detail after detail from me. We had to shout to make ourselves heard over the music. "Look: he wants to stay in prison. I think he's more comfortable there now. He can't get into any more trouble, and he doesn't know how to live on the outside anymore. You see," I added knowingly, having seen a movie or TV show once, "you develop an inferiority complex in there. They do it on purpose. They inculcate in prisoners the idea that they can't make it outside."

She nodded at my great expertise, and we drank. To be more accurate, I drank and told her to drink. "Look: he's done with us," I insisted, mixing up subject and object. "He's washed his hands of us. I'm sorry, but there it is."

We were in some sort of lounge, and I was feeling nervous about how Dana was looking at me. "Drinks are on me, you know," I said again.

"Thanks."

"Okay, no, I guess he said, 'I can outlive him,' and I said 'Constantine?' and he didn't say anything else, just started to insult me. A *lot*."

"Oh." She nodded, looked around the room. "Look at her."

"Oh my. Whose team?"

"I can't tell." She sipped her drink and turned back to me. "Do you think he might have meant that he could outlive Sil? For Mom?"

"That hadn't occurred to me. It's a sweet idea. But, ah—" Of course she was right. It was instantly clear, and I suddenly felt ill, for missing this, for fear that I had done something wrong by not noticing, and in amazement at how little of my father's interior life I could map. "I don't know," I said.

Dana wasn't drinking enough, so I started bullying her into keeping up. A mean drunk, in short, mad at my father, suspecting my sister of having already figured out the depth of my crime while I still had only the dim sense of having done something wrong. She put up with my dumb jokes, my pushiness, and she didn't call me on it.

Later, I saw her looking at that girl shouldered up in a clump of other women on a red curved sofa. She was a striking Asian beauty, I think, long straight black hair and a white T-shirt. Any more detail than that would make a mockery of my efforts to be honest here. But I watched Dana measure her up, and so I insisted in my mood and my cups, "Straight. Boys only. Plain as day. She yearns for a rising son."

"I don't think so." Dana smiled, like a boy mathematician challenging his elders for the first time, and I should have known better. But she reeled me in. "Of course, you're a very handsome man." I should have stopped her right there and punched her, but this was that night, and the moron bowed to his twin sister and said, "Why, thank you, my dear."

"You really don't think I have a chance?" she sighed.

I don't know who suggested the bet. It's not impossible that it was my idea, but I think it more likely hers, more likely still that she slid the idea into my drunk head and waited for me to suggest it back to her as my notion.

A magic lantern turns, and sepia transparencies circle the room, glide over walls, color the picture frames and bookshelves and doorknobs: Dana, serene on a bar stool; me next to the Asian girl, no face on her at all, as if I could hardly focus by then and so could not transcribe any image into memory; my sister and the faceless Asian girl looking down at me from an impossibly high vantage, their faces together, almost blacked out, except for their Cheshire-feline amusement, by some bright light behind them; the neon word, vertically hung, TATTOOS, glowing against total darkness; Dana going over sheets of designs with a shockingly wrinkled lady with shaking hands while I with shaking eyelids watch the light flicker and fade; the wrinkly lady waking me up, taking me by the hand, walking me to a dentist chair set at an odd angle, proposing I do something very strange to her wrist.

I awoke in a great deal of pain. The hangover *ordinaire* was bad enough, but I could have slept through that. I was roused by the flames rising from my crotch, and I am not using that general term euphemistically. The pain was significant enough that its actual source was hidden like the sun behind sunny haze. I certainly yelled aloud. I heard laughter from the bedroom, and Dana called out, "Shut up. We're sleeping." I hobbled, crying, to the bathroom, where I threw up and then attempted to defuse the bomb that was my fly.

Apparently, the bet's parameters agreed upon, I had said, "Do your worst" or something to that effect. The more the Asian girl looked at me from her red couch, the more I'd gloated. (She had actually been looking at Dana; I was having some trouble focusing. On those occasions when she *was* looking at me, it was only to discern my relationship to the beautiful girl she'd spotted as soon as we walked in.) "Are you sure you're up for this?" I taunted Dana. "She's totally into me. You sure you won't chicken out or claim it's not fair? No mercy for little girls. Or former mental patients."

"I'll try to be brave. Besides, I need some ink for lez cred."

"It won't hurt your auditions?" I asked.

"Not there it won't."

The next morning in the bathroom I found in my jeans pocket two neatly folded cocktail napkins. The first had a sketch of a female torso, T-shirt just high enough and jeans waist just low enough, and in the sub-navel space remaining, the ornate words NO ENTRANCE with an arrow pointing toward Dana's groin.

This is obviously not funny, nor did it seem funny ever again after I had (I suppose) found it wonderfully witty at the bar. I don't see any point to it at all, really. It's not amusing, affectionate, profound. It was just a lame joke that I was ready to make permanent in my sister's skin because I was drunk and angry at my father's latest betrayal of my notions of what he owed me. I was owed, and my sister would pay me in flesh after the Asian girl paid me in flesh.

If I had not found the two napkins in my pocket as I was examining my wounds, I would have been entirely at a loss, because the fresh tattoo work on me, especially on that variable surface, was not yet legible.

"Well, in the unlikely event of my victory . . ." Dana had mused.

"In your dreams. Do your worst."

"I think a tribute to the three most important men in my life would be nice."

The brutal Act I, Scene iv of *The Tragedy of Arthur* depicts the English nobles viciously abusing a naïve messenger from the Pictish court. Holinshed's *Chronicles*, the play's source, refers only to an ambassador being mistreated. In the play, the messenger boy, trained to be provocative in order to incite a war at Mordred's instruction, has insulted Prince Arthur and demanded English obedience to the northern king. Gloucester, the lord protector, fails to restrain his touchy English lords. They hold the messenger down and carve with a dagger their reply to the Picts directly into the unlucky boy's forehead: ARTHUR REX—Arthur is the king.

The elderly tattoo artist used a nice black-letter Gothic calligraphy, but the surface of the skin was probably difficult to work on as it was (is) thin, elastic, and has a tendency to bunch, even if I had remained very still, which I doubt I did. Eventually, though, I healed, and the result became clear (though only under certain conditions). Then it produces the effect of a sort of stylized medieval scepter (admittedly for a tiny king) inscribed with a regal motto of sovereignty— 𝔄𝔯𝔱𝔥𝔲𝔯 ℜ𝔢𝔵—although a jester's belled baton has been occasionally cited by select viewers.

Dana's design was certainly more elegant, and it does indeed make a sort of living tribute to her three men. That first week, though, it was an eloquent and burning statement of her anger at me, as there was no position I could assume that was not literally punishing.

Bits of the previous night came back under the clarifying force of the icy damp cloth laid across my lap. "I told Dad I was going to lead my life, and he could do whatever dumb thing he wanted and martyr his golden years to the god of stubborness if that's what he was into," I'd recounted to Dana at the bar. "It didn't matter to me or to you."

"To me?" Dana repeated. "You said it didn't matter to me? How he pleaded?"

"No, actually, as I say that, I don't think I did. No, actually, I tried to make him feel guilty about leaving you behind, or something."

"Well, which? Which was it?"

"Dana, you weren't there. It didn't work. He was so poisonous, I can't even tell you. He was aggressive and manipulative, and he doesn't care. I honestly don't know what else I could have said or done."

"Did you get the impression he wanted you to talk him out of it?"

". . ."

"Arthur?"

"Do you see her? Looking over here?"

"Arthur. Did you get the impression he wanted you to talk him out of it?"

"No," I lied, or thought I was lying. If there's a difference there. "I didn't get the impression he cared at all what I said or did. He just kept— *You* weren't there," I repeated, with accusation.

"Oh. So you think if I'd been there, I would have been able to talk him into defending himself?"

"Yeah. No. I don't know. Buy another round, please."

The wager, I believe, was made shortly after this.

15

A<small>T THE END OF THE RUN</small> of *The Wizard of Oz*, Dana flew out to Minnesota to visit Dad, staying with Mom and Sil. She called a day later to report that Sil had been diagnosed with prostate cancer weeks before. He wouldn't have told us about it at all—not wanting to bother us with such boring stuff—if Dana hadn't turned up in the middle of it. "I don't think he would have told Mom, if he could have figured out how to keep it to himself," Dana reported over the phone.

I was in New York, feeling very alone and slowly beginning to understand my (losing) part in the battle of prideful wills I had waged with my father, the responsibility I bore for what had happened to him. I could feel purer concern for Sil, without second thoughts or selfishness of any sort. That unimpeded response to Sil contrasted, like iodine dye in a scan of the prostate, bright against the murk of my reaction to my father. And with that, as was my lifelong tendency, I took off on a flight from anger to reaction to remorse to reparation. I flew high and fast, soared well past the complicated truth to my next bright clear destination: I was *solely* responsible for my father's sentence. If I weren't such a rotten son, if only I wasn't stuck on what I needed to hear him say, instead of saying myself what he needed to hear, and so on. His original real *felonies* with *victims*, his stubbornness and King Leary behavior: I forgot all of that in the enchantment of self-blame, an act as self-centered as my original behavior (and his), and no more helpful to anyone involved.

I flew back to Minnesota to pay my double homages, visiting Sil at Abbott Northwestern Hospital and my father in his new digs at Faribault, attempting to cook for Mom, staying on the couch while Dana bunked with her.

My arrival annoyed Sil. "You visit for this? Jesus. Come for a birthday, but not this. I got the TV to work, but I can't find the game. This is going to be the year. Puckett? My God. Hrbek? I have to beat this cancer until October."

I helped him pull up the Twins game on his porthole TV, and we spoke of nothing but baseball. I tried to ease my conscience: "Sil, I've been very, you know, in New York, far from here, and, even before that—"

"If you're about to say you've become a Yankees fan, you should just leave. Right now."

"No, God, no, not that. Jesus Christ, that's not even funny. No, I just wanted to apologize, and say thank you, I guess, or sorry, if I've ever—"

"Please, please, stop. Artie, stop. I can't hear the game."

I was not to be thwarted in my quest to make everything right and everyone aware of all my lapses, to be forgiven, not for anything in particular but for my personality. I studied Sil's unshaven face, the translucent gray whiskers like fish bones. Sil was going to die, and my future—my hope to go on with a normal life—depended on not leaving things unsaid, not letting people go without a communion of our feelings.

But Sil was having none of it, deftly blocked all my advances. My relentless pursuit of absolution continued to be of no interest to him. I slapped myself against the stones of Sil, for whom no topic (other than the Twins) justified any sort of emotional outburst or self-examination.

I told him that I loved him. He laughed for a while and nodded. And lived for another twenty-two years.

"Dad," I tried at the prison. "I've been looking hard at myself and . . . I think you're in here because of me, and I'm sorry." Imagine how important I would be if this were true! Having spent some time being a terrible father myself now, this is what I think I was saying: "Tell me I'm important to you. Tell me you're sorry you missed my youth. Tell me we could have been something else." My father, no doubt trying to be kind and rid me of any guilt in the matter, told the truth and said, "That's ridiculous. I put myself in here. Nothing you could have done or said could have stopped that. You're very funny." He also said, "I'm in the right place. I've got something huge to work on, to keep me busy in here. I sometimes think I couldn't be happier."

"Mom," I tried once more. "I'm thinking of moving back to Minneapolis."

"Are you in trouble at work?"

"Of course not. I was just thinking, Sil's sick, maybe you'd like to have—"

"You hang around making me feel old? That's very sweet. You could bring me meals on wheels or change my colostomy bag. First I have to get one, but just knowing you're there for me, I can hardly wait. I'll call my doctor in the morning. Listen, how does Dana seem to you? Has she got herself together okay? I can't tell when she's putting on a brave face to calm me down. Do you think New York is okay for her? You want to be useful, you could make sure she's not letting herself get too stressed again."

And so I flew back to New York with Dana, decided—in my next swing—that I was irrelevant to them all, and that was okay, if I could just be a man about it. I tried to write short stories about all this good stuff, changing everyone's name but little else, and the stories always sucked. I pseudonymously submitted them anyhow to some literary magazines and shuffled a deck of rejections.

Act III: King Arthur, pressured into marrying to secure Britain's peace, rejects a valuable French offer and instead marries for love: his friend Constantine's sister, Guenhera, who has loved Arthur since he was a boy. (It's pronounced GWEN-er-UH, I think.) That dog trainer reappears, discussing the marriage (and Guenhera's pregnancy) in relation to all the illegitimate children Arthur has strewn across Britain. The queen miscarries, and Arthur—as loving of his wife as he once was mad for shepherd girls—demobilizes his army to cultivate his kingdom of peace and art, nostalgic for his own childhood peace. He spends most of his time indulging his wife, failing to be military enough. The Earl of Cumbria voices his disgust at the feminized, debauched court and considers assassinating Arthur.

Act III causes me the most trouble. After Arthur marries, one of his many abandoned loves finds comfort with a kindly shepherd named Silvius, willing to marry Arthur's sloppy seconds. This is more than the most lenient statistician can bear.

16

Dana was cast as Ophelia in a *Hamlet* out in New Jersey. I went out there one night to pick her up after rehearsal. I arrived early, sat in the dark theater, and listened to her castmates up onstage discussing their approach to a tricky scene.

Shakespeare's plays, unlike most modern scripts, rarely include stage direction and never any of those adverbs that force us to read or perform a certain way. No "(angrily)" or "He crosses on her last word and delicately strokes the sword." Instead, each reader and actor is given the chance to make sense of the puzzle himself, to peer into the wavering mirror and report back. This is, I believe, one of the reasons Shakespeare continues to be popular: he offers directors a share of credit, lets them add their two cents. It also makes actors and directors responsible for justifying weaknesses in the plays. To wit:

The older actress playing Gertrude was making a point, reading from her open script: ". . . *fantastic garlands did she make / Of crow-flowers, nettles, daisies, and long purples / That liberal shepherds give a grosser name, / But our cold maids*—see, wait a sec. Why does she do that? I'm telling you your sister killed herself, and that's very sad, but I stop to point out that some flowers look like penises?"

There was much theatrical tittering onstage. The blond boy playing Laertes offered: "She's nervous. You know, people giving bad news sort of go off-point, blurt the first thing comes to mind. You could play it like that."

"That's not bad," agreed the director. "Anyone else?"

"Bollocks," said the bearded Scottish giant playing Claudius. "Big fat hairy bollocks. She's not hemming. Not a bit of it. She can't help it. She's a filthy bird, our Gertrude. She knows Claudius is watching her, laughing at Laertes behind his back, and so, even breaking young Laertes' heart, Gert winks at her man and makes a cock joke, because you and I are All. About. That." And with that he grabbed his stage queen's rump and she swatted at him with her rolled-up script.

My sister laughed but interrupted: "No, because here she's already regretting marrying you. Hamlet's convinced her you're a murderer."

"Codswallop! He didn't convince her of anything, girlie," said the actor, whom I now disliked intensely and strongly suspected of not being Scottish. "When she's rolling about with him in the boudoir and Polonius's blood is splashed all over the place, she's just playing along. She's coddling her pantywaist son. Boy didn't tell her anything she didn't know. She doesn't *care*. She knew all about me from day one. She's a Mafia wife, she is. She lives for a bit of rough, long purple." And he reached again for the ass of the nice middle-aged part-time actress and mother from Montclair.

It was all very precious, and I complained about their manner to Dana afterward, over rum and Cokes. And, boring old me, I couldn't help pointing out my theory: "That was perfect. Shakespeare was the greatest creator of Rorschach tests in history. That's why we keep going back to him for the ten billionth production of this lame play. Look, look: you have a weak spot where Will's not thinking very clearly, and the character rambles on, and Will sticks in a joke that he likes about flowers that look like wieners. It plainly doesn't belong there. Any editor would cut it. It breaks the rhythm and the logic of the scene. And your sweet old Gertrude noticed it and rightly points out the weak spot. Anybody else, we'd say, 'Whoops. Not buying it, Will.' If *I* wrote it, they'd send me home to rework it. Instead, what do you all do? You all talk it out until you make it make sense for him. He wrote it, so it must be right. You six very intelligent people form a committee to offer him your help, and when you've done the best you can, consulting old books of other would-be helpers, when you actually come up with some very clever solutions, you marvel at *him* for composing such a subtle moment."

Dana replied, "When you talk crap like that, riding your hobby-horse all over the room, do you even know it's about Dad? Do you even know you're mad at him, that you won't forgive him because you have a small heart? You've so conflated him with his favorite writer that you want to punish one by taking shots at the other. Do you know that?"

"I do know *you* did that, and you think I'm not original enough to have my own ideas. But that doesn't mean I have to roll over and agree with you. I could even be mad at your father—"

"*My* father?"

"—and still be right about this. You're part of a vast, unconscious conspiracy of enablers, all of whom operate without central control but to the same end: to make a man who died four centuries ago into a god. I honestly don't know what you get out of it, but there it is."

"How is that *not* about Dad?"

Samuel Pepys, the noted seventeenth-century diarist (rather like being noted for writing a lot of shopping lists), judged *Romeo and Juliet* "the worst [play] that ever I heard in my life." He was not alone in that view, but claim such a thing today and you'll be dismissed as a philistine. As Herman Melville already noted back in 1850, before the Shakespeare-industrial complex had crushed our spirit, "This absolute and unconditional adoration of Shakespeare has grown to be part of our Anglo-Saxon superstitions . . . Intolerance has come to exist in this matter. You must believe in Shakespeare's unapproachability, or quit the country. But what sort of a belief is this for an American?" I liked *Moby-Dick* until I read that quote. Now I love *Moby-Dick*.

If it didn't have his name on it, half his work would be booed off the stage, dismissed by critics as stumbling, run out of print. Instead we say it's Shakespeare; he must be doing something profound that we don't appreciate. Compare: a blogger on *The Egyptologist*: "Phillips, clumsy as a newborn calf, totters through the opening scenes, farting exposition as the urge touches him."

Shakespeare and I, admittedly, have a necessarily strained relationship by now, and as I (and others) judge my own writing harshly, I can't help but point out that he is let off easy all the time. You really can't say that this or that bit of dialogue is overdone or undercooked, forced exposition here, unnecessary repetition there, implausibility, inconsistency, haste or languor: no, any apparent crime is excused by some fork-tongued Shakespearologist, another volunteer public defender who leaps up to paper over the fault with some new reading or explanation, for the master can do no wrong, by definition. Any faults we perceive are in us, his faulty readers. (He saw that one coming, too: *The fault, dear Brutus, is not in our stars, / But in ourselves, that we are underlings.*) Everything was intentional, perfect, deep, multilayered, or you can "quit the country." Or "That's really you talking about Dad." And all of us become his fools.

17

B UT DANA WAS RIGHT. I look at my "spontaneous" and "original" actions from this distance and they course with motivation and years of previous history. Here, in this letter of April 23, 1992, written at the end of an agency trip to London, we see the abandoned child running further and further from his resentments and wounds:

> D,
>
> We had a day off after we landed and the hotel wouldn't let us check in early, so I joined a side trip to wander in your woods, yours and Dad's. I visited lovely Stratford-upon-Avon. I've seen your man's house now (a museum with a plastic ham on a replica dining table). I've walked in his magic forest (the sliver of it that remains between two expressways). I've watched actors in drag prance and spittle his words. I've gone looking for his ghost in the streets that remain, the furrowed fields that remain, the churchyard he walked, the tomb he fills.
>
> Back in London this week, I even went to a psychic, one very drunken evening, and investigated my future and yours, and received satisfactory answers, and then I thought to ask if Shakespeare was watching us from the other side. Good news, Dana: "He's writing there. Right now!"
>
> Last night—in honor of our birthdays, or because of his egomaniacal paranormal interference—your Bard hogged the conversation with two Germans I met in a pub near our hotel. Heidi and Günter had come on holiday from Meisen to see the RSC in Stratford and were now taking two days in twentieth-century London before returning home. Over drinks, I explained the earl and Binyamin Feivel as best I could remember, and I asked if they'd suspected that half the plays they'd seen this week were written by a Jewish banker's son.

They laughed politely, not sure if they were the butt of some joke about Germans.

Heidi and Günter were "not engaging to marry," according to Günter, standing at the bar, before we'd even had a first pint together. "We do not see the reason for it. We are together and that is all." One of those premature explanations or unprovoked self-descriptions that fling and gyrate awkwardly in the middle of conversation, implying recent tiffs and incomplete makeups. Heidi's answering silence set my suspicions up on their hind legs.

By the time we'd had a few rounds, Günter had been telling me for an hour how Shakespeare was the most brilliant man ever to write or even think, "more human even than Goethe," whatever the fuck *that's* supposed to mean. He did not stop for an instant to ask what sort of work had brought me to London, but roared on and on, about the plays they'd seen up at Stratford, the "global humanness" he'd witnessed and understood even more deeply this time, how in every culture everyone loved him without fail, how grateful Günter was to great Shakespeare for "making us" and "opening our eyes." Heidi nodded now and then and watched me nod politely. I could see it: when I allowed just the tiniest, most deniable flicker of mockery to sparkle on my face, to cast the tiniest shadow across Günter's earnest, happy performance, she smiled and drank and Günter thought she was smiling for him, and he put his arm around her shoulder and pulled her close so her head cricked away from him, and she looked up at me, drew a swizzle stick between her lips and across the cradling tip of her tongue, draining a drop of Malibu and Coke from it as it passed, and Günter seemed further and further away, and his Shakespeare love was more and more laughable. Less than laughable: irrelevant to this planet. *Inhuman.* The opposite of universal. An annoying hobby. Stamps.

One drink led to another, and we walked out arm in arm in arm, Heidi in the middle, into the London night, until our mouths were sticky with salty mist and hours-old liquor and

German cigarettes. We stumbled along, and then there were bells. "You know, it is today!" Günter yelled, as the clock above Dixon's Gloves showed it was past midnight. "Today is probably his birthday. Four hundred twenty-eight! Do you know this? Happy birthday, Willy!" he shouted, quite pleased with himself, and from dark corners and behind shuttered windows voices called back, "Happy birthday!" Günter supported himself with one hand against an apartment building while with his other he fished out his *lederhosenschnitzel* (much ado about nothing, if I may) and urinated a shadow onto the wall and a black mirror onto the sidewalk, first a drizzle, then a tempest.

I delicately stepped out of view around the corner and was considering whether I'd had enough of my Krauts when Heidi joined me. From our shadow, we heard the bobby arrive: "Oi! You there!" and heard Günter stammer his excuses to the constable, though the sound of his flow continued on and on and embarrassingly on. The cop said, "You a German then?" in a tone implying it would be best if Günter claimed to be Swiss. "Yes, sir, and I am very sorry, Mr. Policeman, for the urining, but you know it is the birthday of your William Shakespeare." The cop put on a ludicrous German accent and hissed, Gestapo-style, "Papers, please." "What do you mean? My papers? Yes, okay, my fiancée has our passports. You need the passport?"

Ah, Dana, now he claimed a respectable fiancée. She would have none of it. Heidi's eyes were so beautifully wide and blue. She shrank farther into shadow, took my hand, and placed her index finger's silken nicotine whorls against my opening lips.

Günter had taken on quite a load back at the pub and was discharging still. He could neither accelerate nor stop, and it seemed the bobby was going to wait him out and hold each passed milliliter against him, each drop an affront to English law. "This is acceptable behavior and hygiene in Germany, is it?" he sneered, though he had likely urinated on his share of British buildings (and German ones, blearily following some football club to Munich, looking for a brawl).

When Günter's untimely release came to its hesitant, dribbled conclusion, he called out, "Heidi? Our-toor? Where are you?" The cop said, "Oi, that's making a noisome disturbance, Fritzy, on top of the indecency. Come on, then. Off we go."

"Please, police, wait. Heidi!"

No indecision pinched Heidi's face as we heard Günter arrested and walked away. She showed so little hesitation, I wondered if she hadn't sent for the policeman in the first place.

"You sure you don't want to . . ." I began.

"No woman shall succeed in Salic land," she quoted *Henry V* in a whisper and took my hands. You'd have liked her, Dana. *"Which Salic is at this day called Meisen.* This is the only line I like. He knows me in this." We heard *"Heidi!"* echo along the stones and streets as we walked in the opposite direction.

"He called you his fiancée," I said, only to know if she felt any remorse at all about Günter's approaching night, or if she meant *ever* to save him.

"Yes, but *fiancée* is a French word," she purred. "There is no word for it in German." And that was the end of Günter.

Heidi was wonderfully distracting. She did not like Shakespeare *at all*, carried a grudge about him, in fact. Obviously, we bonded over this. "Is it okay to say I do not like him?" she asked very quietly, not unreasonably fearing the town's scorn and violence. Her long holiday of plays in Günter's company had driven her to an endearing madness: "Here is what I hate," she said as she pinned me to a tree on the Thames embankment and sniffed at my neck like a werewolf thinking it over. "Macbeth meets these witches. They say, 'You will be king. Just sit still. Wait a little.' And so immediately he kills everyone."

"Human nature?" I suggested as her lips found the pulsing part of my neck. "Maybe he's saying that once we have seen what we want, impatience—"

"Stop excusing him, because this is *scheisse*." She kissed me *angrily*—that's really the only word for it, D. "'Look!' says the watcher man, 'Old King Hamlet's ghost just walked by! Also, wait, don't get yourself excited about this, though, because let's talk about the Norwegian army for an hour first.'"

"Some clumsy exposition," I murmured, feeling oddly defensive of Shakespeare on our shared birthday, as I was reaping the benefits of another man's misguided, expressive love for the Bard.

"Oh, *nein*! 'No, nothing is clumsy, Heidi! He is perfect! If you don't like this, it is *you* who has the problem.'" She was raving a bit now, at Günter, at her holiday, at the playwright. "*Every* play is like this, you know. Every one. You like the *Lear*? It's all about the nice girl making the speech about honesty, and *she would not do this*. But if she do not, then no play for us. *Othello*? Iago knows *everything*. He is a machine devil. General Othello is, lucky for Iago, gullible, needy, easy to make a fool. Like every general, I am sure."

"Complexity of character?"

"Don't be a stupid man, too. You are not like Günter in this, I hope. *The Merchant of Venice*? You are the Jew, right?"

"Well, *a* Jew."

"Okay, so all your Shylock has to tell to that little bitch is 'Hey, it is Antonio's debt to pay me, so he can cut his own flesh without me and give me my pound, and if he spill his own blood or cuts out too much, that is *his* problem. Now *pay* me, Christian bastards!' Am I not right?"

I actually hadn't thought of that solution, had you? (Or of Shylock as "mine.") I told her about your "Antonios" discovery, and she thought that was pretty smart. "*Mein Gott!* This is true. Every one of his Antonios is a sissy boy. Three of them? Four? I wish I told this to Günter." At any rate, she became, Dana, if I may speak frankly to your virginal sensibilities, more and more aroused with each new flawed plot, character inconsistency, technical error, longueur. Any fault she could find was a slap in the face of her pedantic, imprisoned lover, whose crimes, she claimed, held no interest for her when, once more, I tried to ask about him, about her past. But she was done with her past. Very admirable.

I'll write again soon. I'm in an odd bit of travel as I write you. On a plane, actually . . .

Love and all that,

A.

18

THAT LETTER DISSOLVES RAPIDLY into total vagueness there. I censored myself because I was ashamed, I suppose, or at least nervous about what I was doing and what Dana might think of me. And because I was trying, again, to cut off the past and make a clean start. Now the memoirist in me *has* to look bad. The worse I appear, the more vicariously luxurious the reading experience, and the more impressive my inevitable late-chapter redemption, paying for any inadvertent titillation early on.

"I want to go out of London," Heidi said in my hotel room much later that morning. "I don't like England." I had not come to the end of my desire for her, whether due to her innate qualities or my innate needs or her careful dosing and doling out of her charms, I cannot say. But I was, by a long distance, not sated. I was also expected in fifteen minutes down in the breakfast room, to join my colleagues and our British partners before the next client meeting. I would be working for the next twelve hours, presenting and analyzing and lying, a wide enough window through which to lose a new love who did not like England.

"I want to go to . . ." She stretched beneath the sheet and rolled her eyes, considering her choices, putting herself in each place, gauging her satisfaction around the globe, purring in Günterless freedom, only a sheet between her and her next destination. And her next guy. I was not sated.

"What do you want?"

"I want to go to Venezia."

"I'd follow you to Venice."

"Then good. We go. I shower."

She meant *then*. I mouthed the usual words about my job, meetings, hotels, but I didn't mean any of them. It was as if I were reciting
lines, but I kept rushing them, only wanting to hear her lines, hear
her argue me around to what I wanted to do anyhow. I wanted to believe she wanted me to come along. She wouldn't do it: "You need to
be here? So be here. Don't listen to me. We had a nice time. I hope
you write wonderful commercials. Become very successful and make
a lot of money. I am just crazy."

I was already packing my bag.

She enjoyed her aura of risk taking, but it was me taking the risk. I
was paying to keep up with what she did for free. I was abandoning
my job; she was just leaving some sort of fiancé behind, possibly in
jail. Still, with the heightened thrill of transgression and betrayal, we
flung ourselves out of our worlds.

"Don't bring that," she said as I began packing my work papers,
sketch pads, account folders. "I don't want you to be that." So I would
not be that. Her decision cast me instead as . . . not that. "I" would be
her decision, and that was fine with me. She was unlikely to make me
my father's son.

She knew that I was quitting my job, even while I was still kidding
myself that it would all sort itself out later with an apology or something. That command to leave my work behind was Heidi testing her
power over me. She was seeing if she really had me, and so I left my
work behind for her. It made no real difference, but her idea of what
we were doing required a clean break. I broke. And when I came to, I
was different, and I owe that to Heidi.

She was also saying, "Don't bring any fuel for future regret," and I
immediately, instinctively knew she was right. I considered leaving
behind *everything* of mine except wallet and passport but, as always,
was terribly concerned with what others would think of me (in this
case, that I'd been kidnapped).

We were suddenly in a frenzy, dashing madly to dress and escape,
up against some clock we could not have identified. I wasn't running
out on a hotel bill (it was on TBWA, my agency); still, I began behav-
ing at once like a criminal, desperate to be gone. What was I stealing?

That day, twenty-eight years old, I would have self-righteously said, "Happiness," snatched from corporate dullardry. Not true, of course (I quite liked my job and colleagues). Later, thirty-seven years old, I would, self-glorifying, have said I was stealing my "better self" away, becoming a novelist, chasing destiny in the form of this hot Saxon girl. That was certainly the gist of my letters home at the other end of this adventure, how I told the story for years to friends, to Dana, to myself, to my wife. Now, forty-six, I would, slightly more self-aware, say that I was just chasing a girl because I hadn't had enough girls yet, and I was stealing away from adult responsibility because it hadn't yet proven to me its superiority over youthful irresponsibility, and I was trying to achieve *indifference* to my father and my past. Over the years, I have pulled out all these meanings as needed to garb my naked actions. Philosophy is inclination dressed in a toga.

I cut my last line to adulthood: I had Heidi lay my files and folders outside my colleague's door, atop the newspapers, while I lurked, lip-nibbling, behind a corner. She and I then bounced and bounded down the stairs as if pursued or dropped, stopping at the door to the lobby, which we stared at as if on its other side we would face gunfire or fierce barking.

The odds were I could just walk through the lobby. My "team" was supposed to be breakfasting with our London partners in the hotel restaurant, behind frosted and puckered glass. I would be a frosty puckered blur if they even looked up. Head down, I followed the German girl across a vast carpet of turrets and vined ruins in twisted woods. We made it to the front door, where we had to stop to let in two men in their thirties.

"Arthur Phillips," declared the first in an English accent, and I was caught, immobile, the flight impulse only strong enough to make my toes clench inside my shoes.

"Is the copywriter," replied the second man as they passed me without looking, putting a retrospective question mark to the first man's use of my name. "The account manager is Peter Sampson." The back of my scalp burned with unneeded adrenaline. They headed for that wavy glass, and the elevators chimed for attention, certain to hold everyone I had ever known.

"We go?" Heidi suggested.

"*Ja, ja*, we go."

We couldn't stop laughing, and the cabby was excessively chatty. "You been visiting London? First time? I'm Lawrence." Heidi and I suffered some odd hysteria, pawing each other and guffawing unreasonably, my heart's rhythms insisting that this was the great and formative instant of my life, the start of adulthood, curtain up, and that holy annunciation repeated itself every few minutes as some new sensation hit me: the plumed horse guards in front of a palace, the smell of the cab, the smell of Heidi's hair, the smell of a green and misty damp spring park where we idled behind a moving truck whose back panel read—I'm not making this up—DESTINY MOVERS. "Look at *that*," I said to Heidi with urgency. "Look at *that*!"

"What? Movers?" she said, the gaudy omen fluttering its wings, but not for ears deaf to English intimations, and (by kissing her) I put the thought out of my mind that she and I were already off on disparate desperate adventures with diverging lessons and retroactive importance, only sex and scenery in common.

"Flying off to where today?" asked Lawrence, his eyes framed in the black rubber oval of his rearview mirror, a Celtic crucifix dangling from the reflected bridge of his nose.

"Paris," I lied at precisely the moment Heidi lied, "Mantua," both of us covering our tracks for no pursuers.

"Oh, so a sad farewell at the airport, then, eh?" Lawrence clucked sympathetically. "Well, I'll get you there, no worries. We'll make short work of this mess. You know, you probably escaped by a hair. Ten minutes later, this would be two hours' traffic."

We were lucky! We had escaped with moments to spare! We were clumsily lying and our contradictory lies were massaged into sense by this loquacious Cockney. The narcotics of hysterically imagined danger and actual spontaneity carried us to Heathrow, to a counter where I treated, and into the last two (widely separated) seats on a flight to Venice, for which we had to sprint through the airport and onto the plane, our breathless and enforced parting in the cabin yet another stimulant. I sat far in the back, tumescent and aching for Heidi, writing that letter to Dana, trapped between two enraged and tormented babies and the useless adults who sighed beneath them. Heidi—the back of her head calling out to me when I stood to go to the toilet—glowed far away between the ridged and glistening back panels of two Italian fashion-magazine cover boys, back from a show, off to a shoot, back from a shoot, off to a show, Milano, Firenze, Roma, Verona.

My thoughts were an unbridled horse, dragging me through the mud and brambles: what we would be in Venice, hot jealousy of the Italian heroes (out of all proportion to their threat or my claim), remorse at my abandonment of my employers and my girlfriend in New York, fear at my unsalaried future, fear and exhilaration at my unidentifiable self: Who would recognize me where we were going? And if there was no one who could, if I had no job, if I was not in the company of my twin or friends, what would make me me? Surely a new and better me was waiting at the hyper-aptly named Marco Polo Airport. The jealousy I felt for Heidi on that flight was the strongest I have ever known; I nearly wept with anger at the Italian men. I think now this was quite logical, for during this bridge time, Heidi was the only definition of me: I was only "the man who was with Heidi" (whose last name I did not know), and if I'd lost her, already, to either or both of the incomprehensibly handsome man-gods flanking her, then I was in danger of vanishing entirely, shattering between squalling babies.

And so I steamed between my howling colleagues and saw the twin *Vogue uomos* take her between them, bending and forcing, stroking and guiding, grasping and greasing, wetting and chafing, until I was both excruciatingly aroused and shaking with violent impulse: I crushed their heads in car trunks, then squealed the tires on the flesh of their backs until the smoking rubber raked skin from red fibrous muscles snapped off slick and fraying bone.

Restored to her and myself at the airport, I clung to Heidi until the boat came to shuttle us into town, clung to her through the spray until the gulls became pigeons and we stepped onto puddled stone, some inches above the sea, onto a mirage city straining to reach high enough to stay dry for one more minute.

I had both our suitcases, rolling one and shouldering the other, plus her carry-on. I was also trying when possible to hold her hand, nibble her nape, grab her ass in narrow alleys no wider than a man and his roller bag. She must have sensed my urgency, running ahead to a corner while I sweated and tugged her belongings onto towering curbs, around metal posts, across doll bridges, up uneven stairs. She would dose me with her touch with the stingy precision of a medic rationing morphine as too many men in his unit cried out with wounds. She would kiss me at the base of a bridge, her hands in my hip pockets, then begin to retreat until only her lips remained. Then they, too, were gone, and she was waving from a corner, behind which she disappeared. When I reached that corner, I turned it and found a multi-balconied square out of which a dozen bridges sprang into their own alleys, terraced staircases, options. And no Heidi.

There were two hotels in the square. Neither contained her. There were restaurants, cafés, gelato palazzos, but she was not. I didn't dare cross one of the bridges. The smart thing was to wait, on view, in the open.

A richly symbolic young man's moment: across one of these bridges I would find my German stimulant. Across the others, perhaps some other life entirely. But to sit here immobile cannot go on much longer! Cross! Cross! Cross a bridge! If now it seems an author's invention, an overdetermined moment of thematic import, at the time I just felt panic, no consciousness at all of beauty (Venetian or symbolic, literary or life changing), no sense of a Moment at all, only frustration that made my eyes sting and my fingers fist and unfist spasmodically, an anger at Heidi for her alternating carelessness, cruelty, idiocy, sluttishness, prudishness, guile, incompetence.

When the rain came with the darkness, I and the bags waited under lit awnings until restaurateurs and hotel night managers asked me to "move along, *signore, per favore*, to go on."

I checked into one of the two hotels, took a room on a high floor opening onto the square, ready to witness her return, lost or grieving or teasing, and then for us to gaze at each other in wrestling doubt and lust. Morning came, mocking gray. I left notes at both hotels, tried to reconstruct our path from the vaporetto, but I was soon lost in identical streets. I found a staircase jetty that may have been the site of our first steps in Venice, posted a note for her in the tourist office, struggled through the shifting city's float-away alleys and mirror tricks, soaked my feet when the sea would strike up through the paving stones to test for weakness and claim dominion.

She'd taken me for the free airline ticket and was now laughing with her two *Vogue*men. She was lost and seeking me. She was in trouble and counting on me. These were the choices. I was certain of each. I tried to report her as missing. I went to the police station and tried to explain. You did not know her last name? You had known her less than twenty-four hours when she vanished? At the time, you were lovers, *signore*? You met when she left her previous lover in a London prison, because he had irritated her by taking her to too many Shakespeare plays? All of your conversation in that twenty-four hours—perhaps two hours total—was built on a mutual distaste for Shakespeare? The playwright, *signore*?

I had opened her suitcases, of course, before calling on the smirking carabinieri. No documents, no money. Just clothes, toiletries, a novel in German with a photomontage on the cover of a bullfighter and a cadaver on a morgue table. She would never leave all this behind, I argued, though I had left far more behind in London for her, traded it all for a new chapter of life.

I knew then that's what she'd done. Once I was over the pain of not being able to have sex with her again, I didn't blame her, wasn't even that hurt by her rejection of me on such limited acquaintance. She had neatly and pleasantly moved on. And had been kind enough to convince me to do the same, before it was too late for me. Sadly, I realized she had had more effect on me than any woman in my life in New York except Dana. And the significance of that grew as I spent days alone. I was pathologically grateful to Heidi, and if she should read the German edition of this book, then I send her my sincerest regards. But don't read the play, Heidi! You won't like it!

And then, only then, did I arrive in Venice. I had been too busy looking at the Teutonic beauty with the wind-burned cheeks on the vaporetto ride, at her shadowed hips on our last walk, and I had been too busy squinting for a crowd-screened girl in the days after. Now, having accepted that I was not worth her time, that I had been brought here by her but not for her, that I had been chosen by her to be released from my old life, I set off into Venice at last.

I still occasionally saw a flash of blond two bridges away that I allowed to blur into Heidi for a hot, frozen minute, but I was no longer looking for her. I was floating free of everything in this place, as she had obviously meant for me to do, as I needed to do, waiting for something to happen, shedding past selves in the April and May breezes, melting myself down in the June and July heat in the hostel where my budget had necessarily moved me.

I fell in love. I loved Venice first for its surface beauty, just like all the other suckers. But soon enough I loved its ability to hide from prying, to withdraw its essence behind those thousands of cleverly identical façades and squares, to vanish despite a billion grazing eyes, as though the tourists were all walleyed or willfully blind. At first it seemed that no one lived there to man these shops, cafés, and churches. I tried to follow them—merchants, barmaids, prelates— into the spirals of the city. They led me down the alleys, past the street signs that urchins moved or removed from one day to the next, the bridges that shifted their colors from one hour to the next, the buildings whose flags and banners were so easily swapped, the congenially conspiratorial Adriatic, which would as needed bubble up to distract or divert, the throppity-thropping cyclones of pigeons that would, as a last resort, block my view, until, upon this shifting swamp town, the naïve newcomer and the moneyed tourist alike were repeatedly funneled back, tricked back, drained back into the same small area of commerce and snapshots, the impulses Venice allowed you to indulge.

But if you waited and followed, patiently, day after day, finally you saw real stories, real lives. I spent my days now reading secondhand books in dusty yards, eyed up by squat old women in loose housecoats and their feline familiars, guarded and malevolent. I was twenty-eight. I was writing stories about the people I saw, the tourists and priests, about the conversations I overheard. When I wasn't writing, I imagined Dana and my father reading my stories in print. I told myself I was doing something Shakespeare never did. I was the plein air Impressionist rebel and he the stuffy Salon. I told myself that everything about me and my bizarre leap into Venice would produce something entirely new, free of all that came before, free of my life, free of old musty fiction. Something new would pour out of these sun-dried courtyards and pigeon-splattered squares.

Heidi was my muse, I came to understand in a flash of self-love. I have since wondered if I didn't imagine her. I don't remember when I lost my last souvenir of our twenty-four hours—her novel—but with its disappearance and the intervening decades I can almost believe I created her, so perfectly did she make my new life, shove me on to the next thing. It was about then, having cast her as muse, that I realized I would never return to the States but would wander the world wherever adventure and literature led me, learning and loving and writing about the lives of those around me . . . there may have been a Nobel Prize at the other end of this plan.

I don't have access to any more of my letters to Dana, but I can guess their tone, and my manic-Romantic idea of myself based on her replies:

> Darling Runaway,
> Well, well. Venice, is it? O.K. I can see the appeal.
> Things have settled down here at court since your flight, but it is only thanks to me. And now you have had your epiphany, and we are all very excited for you. Though I saw it coming, if I may say so. You had to go somewhere and start over.
> Miss Margaret Wheeler. I can't say you handled that with gentlemanly finesse. She started sniffing around here for you after ten days or so. She had already hunted you at your office, where she learned of your resignation *before your own sister*, resigned to be the last to know anything of importance about you.
> She is sweet, though, your ex-Margaret, and I have attempted to bring her a measure of comfort. [Note: I recall thinking this was a lie, because Margaret had always spoken like a committed homophobe. "Your sister's a dyke? Seriously?" Older and wiser than when I was in high school, I didn't hit her. Because she was pretty. So instead I slept with

her, and was always ashamed of that willingness to trade away one of my few principles for sex.] Her ideas of you were very limited. It seems you presented to her a very controlled and managed version of yourself: competent, ambitious, and businesslike, rather dull. Is this what you think of yourself? Well, she and I have spent many happy evenings now in a sort of Arthur reeducation course, in which I tell her stories of how you really are and always have been. I am giving her a more detailed picture of your life abroad than you have given me. I improve upon what little you have written. She is taken with this, but also, I think, sees the twin before her as the painter of the portrait and perhaps the portrait itself. I think this also comforts her.

The stories of our childhood have tickled her, and she is very ticklish. One's past, you know, is relevant and cannot be so easily erased as you would seem to think right now, judging by your shrieking Venetian rebirth. Dad's son.

The good part is your decision to take writing seriously. Finally. I am really glad about this. I think you're right: your flight from your job and New York and all of us back here was necessary so you could begin something over there. That's great. Don't let the rest of what I have to say take anything away from that. You are a writer. Write. Come home when you know you can.

But. Really. You are kidding yourself if you think you will blossom out of the damp Venetian soil as some new flower, never before seen, with nothing in you of us, of Minnesota, of Dad and Mom and Sil, and those Family Rooms and Lake Minnetonka and all the rest. You will somehow rise from the ashes without influence or history, entirely original in every way? It is a myth and drives its worshippers to madness or bad writing or both.

Seriously. Your new life is (A) already tainted by the past, and (B) already unoriginal. It comes at the cost of that German fool spending at least a night, if not more, in a London jail,

where you left him so you could have his woman. Like King
David. Or Uter Pendragon. *Unoriginal.* And the woman? I
agree you have no choice but to cast her as your muse, the free
spirit who had no life of her own but only existed to pull you
out of your dreary corporate drudgery (which I always thought
you liked and were good at), and launched you with a welcoming
lay into your spectacular new career before flying off immediately
to leave you to your glory and not drear it down with her own
needs, family, aging, stomach flu. But that's because you can't
afford to imagine her as I do: raped, murdered, and sunk
tongueless into a canal when she was wandering, lost, looking
for the sweet American who'd gone with her on an adventure.
Your story is built on many other stories, some of which you
know, most of which you will blithely ignore, understandably.
It is not built on the imagined lives of old women in Venetian
courtyards, though I'm sure those will be good to read. You
can't make "you" without us. And what if *we* are unoriginal?

Because, really, we *are.* It's all been done before, and you
claim that you are free of influences? Anxious brother, he
shares your birthday. Why do you have to deny him for that?
You will somehow reduce him, beat him, ignore him, prove he
doesn't own you? Even if those weren't contradictory, you miss
that he has invented you already. The boy intent on being free
of his family? The dreamy artist who roams Italy for
inspiration? The Jew in Venice? You learned all this from him,
or from people who learned it from him then mushed it into
sitcoms and weepy movies for you. We are all his ideas. To be
fair, he learned it from someone else, too, but he at least didn't
kid himself, claiming to be unique. He was worried that he was
unoriginal, too, you know, just like you:

> If there be nothing new, but that which is
> Hath been before, how are our brains beguiled,
> Which, labouring for invention, bear amiss
> The second burden of a former child.

But he got over it. He hung around with other ones: Marlowe, Peele, Greene, Lodge, Nashe, Watson. And he plundered like a madman from everyone. As a result, he was pretty original. Like a multiple winner of the Oscar for best-adapted screenplay. That makes him sound less threatening, doesn't it?

So go, yes, go, write. I don't say you shouldn't. You will, I hope, put all of the pieces together in some new pattern. Maybe you'll pull off the trick of singularity. Maybe. It's a heroic struggle. But it's not the point. And you definitely won't succeed if you start by denying everything you've ever been until this very moment in Italy. You know what you are now? Dad's son, but in Italy.

I must have snarled at Dana, because her next letter reads:

Your anger at me is totally misplaced. I didn't and don't mean to discourage you. Far from it. I am just trying to spare you some time-wasting delusions. As for Margaret, I don't think you are in any position to criticize or to get a vote. She should have killed herself for you? Please. Besides, I like her private mole, cinque-spotted, like the crimson drops in the bottom of a cowslip.

I took my sister to mean that my goals were futile and that I was already beaten. She didn't have faith in me, I read, and so the confidence seeped out of me. I was just a pretentious idiot who'd quit his job and was trying to be someone I wasn't. And so, when I ran into a little trouble—not liking one of my stories once I came down from a manic, first-draft high, or stumped for what to write about in perfect Venice, where everything was supposed to come easily—I gave up. I surrendered: an exertion of free will, free of Will. It was obviously childish, cowardly, petulant, self-fulfilling: if I could quit, then I was destined to fail anyhow.

So, to prove to myself that it wasn't cowardly, I prodded myself into a few years of ostentatious bravery: boxing badly, running with

Spanish bulls, doing construction work in Eastern Europe, drinking and fighting with Oktoberfesters, dancing mock flamenco in Budapest bars, trying to sleep with rich married women and usually just getting in trouble with their husbands. And to prove to myself it wasn't childish, I composed a dozen semischolarly (not-at-all-about-Dad) essays attacking Shakespeare, each of which I submitted to little literary magazines back in the States. I fled from my father, my mother, my twin, my work, an entire life, which I at twenty-eight dismissed as unoriginal and a failure. Just like my father, I did not come home for years.

19

MEMOIRISTS ARE SELF-SELECTED: they want to tell their stories, nice or nasty. I am something else. A gun to my head—as you will see—I spill my forced confession, revealing me as an indifferent person, a poor friend, a variable brother and son, jealous, hurtful, able to delude myself. I say this not from any pride. It's going to get worse.

Still, I acknowledge that I am growing addicted to the pleasures of self-revelation I once scorned. A memoir requires a courage that we can fairly assert Shakespeare lacked. ("What?" squeals the wild-eyed Bard lover. "Did he never use material from his own life? Did he not reveal himself in his works?" A million words over twenty-five years: yes, it's very likely that he did secrete dollops of oily autobiography into his crisp fictions. But the existence of such revelations does not mean—especially four hundred years later—that you can sift them from the fantasies, fears, and imagined selves, not to mention his masked revelations about other people you don't know: his friends, family, and enemies.)

But now I must explain some more years in order to explain the play. So, enter Chorus: Imagine, then, within this paper V we've crammed the spires and shadows of Prague, the Czech Republic. I settled there and married a Czech girl, because I honestly thought I was in love, and she was beautiful (a model, I was glad to let my friends discover without having to tell them), and she was as far from my old life and self as she could be, since, under the superficial beauty, she was a country girl from a land of which I knew nothing. She'd lived through various political turmoils I had to learn about from books. She was entwined in centuries of cultural, religious, and social networks that proved, when she loved me back, that I must be free of my own past. Heidi separated me from the United States, and now a desire not to be separate, to rediscover with a wife the feeling of my youth with Dana, carried me through compromises and misjudgments. Some part of me thought I had to roam to a land as foreign as possible and find the most unlikely mate to solve this problem. You can wish to be indifferent. Oh, Christ, the unconscious, the psychologizing, the myth, the instinct: I can write and theorize and still not fully explain: I loved Jana. I did.

How long does the geographic solution work? How long can you strive for difference and indifference? Eleven years. Time whips us through each accelerating year, January, Janua, Jan, J, as through a centrifuge, shooting out particles of regret, shreds of memory, a distillate of recalled loss, squandered potential, wasted opportunities, scrambled priorities. Those eleven years—the onset of adulthood at last—brought some of the happiest times of my life: wedding, birth of children, professional success.

"Bohemia!" my father wrote me back in '94, congratulating me on my wedding, sending his well-justified regrets for the ceremony, where Dana served as my best woman and Sil and Mom were graciously entertained by Jana's mother, an unwilling tour guide guiding unwilling tourists. "A magical place with a wild sea," Dad rhapsodized. He preferred, no shock, the imaginary oceanic country of *The Winter's Tale* to the landlocked but no less beautiful reality of Kafka, Havel, Kundera, Skvorecky, Stoppard, me. That was okay by then. I could laugh at my father by then. "And Arthur, his wandering and resistance complete, has taken a wife and accepted his crown! It reminds me of a story, and this time it may end well."

In 1995, genetics, uninspired in its patterns, coughed up twins again, two boys who developed, to my obtuse surprise, into little Czechs who for a while thought their foreign father was okay, but then grew increasingly embarrassed by his accent and general air of

not belonging and his stupid answers to their czildhood predica-
ments. This period has mostly passed, and we understand one another better now. I harbor hopes for their twenties.

I intend to keep my kids out of this except to make three relevant
points:

1) As twins, they were fascinating to watch. They were indepen-
dent of me and Jana in a way monos would not have been. They had
that same sense of completion and confidence—visible almost as soon
as consciousness flickered on behind their oversized brown Slavic
irises, my own blue eyes receding back into the gene pool. Their version of twindom involved more fisticuffs and flaring conflict than
Dana's and mine, but Jana and I learned early that our well-meaning
intrusions in their intra-twin broils only made them go on longer and
with more fragile conclusions, whereas left to their own violent de-
vices, they would pummel each other only so far and so long as was
necessary to institute some closer, still more conspiratorial partner-
ship.

2) They loved their Aunt Dana instantly and with a laughing, un-
Czech joviality that began when they were about three. She visited, as
she did twice a year for seven years, until her conflicts with Jana made
visiting untenable, and the twins would keep her to themselves—in
their room, in the garden, in the woods, later in the streets of Prague.

3) They are fifteen now, and though as tightly bound to each other
as ever, they will face struggles ahead that I would like to prepare
them for, and perhaps a candid explanation of why I no longer live
with them will help more than it embarrasses. And so I have written
such an explanation for them, but elsewhere. This is not the place.

Except to say that I did not find my lost half in Bohemia after all,
try as I did to fit myself against the unique edges of a lovely, kind
woman, wounding her in the process with my own incompatible,
jagged shards.

But I did write in Prague, and with some success, publishing four
novels from 2002 to 2009. Each time I wound myself into ridiculous
states of affectation and superstition, convinced that I could not fin-
ish a novel without sacrificing something: attendance at the twins'
birthday party, kindness to my wife, a visit to a sickly parent, honesty

to one of my rare Czech friends. I returned to the States on book tours and for family visits, though the tours became shorter and rarer as the book business shrank and publishers looked to more and more eye-popping product to halt the collapse. (Which, I have to admit, would include a new Shakespeare play, so we may save each other yet.)

I did not achieve true indifference to my father, and Jana would testify to that, having spent so long trying to nurse me through my anger and recurrent fears and sorrows, scolding me only when I would declare myself "over him," since she knew she would bear the brunt of my renewed grief and furies the next time he let me down. She, in her Central European wisdom, knew that the goal itself was inane, and she would mock Dana's forgiveness of Dad as American sentimentality, weak and self-deluding. You don't get over things, Jana taught me. *You suffer infinitely.* It's hard not to love the Czechs.

And how right she was. I sent him a personalized copy of my first novel, named after my new hometown, waited vainly for a response, then visited him about a month later. *To my father, who taught me so much about creativity. With all my love . . .* I sat across from him at yet another of those Formica-topped tables in yet another windowless room with carpeting the color of vomited-up oatmeal. In those surroundings, my feelings of having arrived (I was a novelist; I was a father; I was thirty-eight years old) merged with all the emotions of childhood visits to other Family Rooms. They were all present at once, and I realized how much of my life had been about him, and how much I wanted to hear him tell me that I was a great writer, as important to him as he was to me. This moment waited and trembled, and I did not know how to speak.

After ten minutes, at the most, asking after his daily routine and complimenting him on his retained youthfulness (he did look pretty good for seventy-two, not much older than my last visit, three or four years earlier), I couldn't help myself any longer. I very uncoolly asked him if he'd had the time (!) to take a look at my novel yet.

He nodded eagerly, was very kind, effusive, really, in his praise of it, the imagery, the story, everything. It's difficult to describe the relief and love, the pride and love, the happiness and love, the sense of having forgiven and having been forgiven, both at the same instant. I should have been satisfied. I should have kissed him and flown back quickly to the Czech Republic to work on my next book and my indifference and my adulthood and my marriage.

Instead, I blundered on, blubbered forward. "There was something of you in the character of Imre, you know."

"Was there? I—I didn't . . . sense myself in him."

He met my eye, and I knew, and I didn't even call him on it, just felt disappointment as a sudden outrushing of all my air, almost of muscular control. I slumped against the table, trying to catch an in breath.

"I think he traded it for cigarettes," I told Dana back in New York on the way home, futilely garbing pain in a joke for her.

"First edition? Warmly inscribed? Must have gotten a carton at least."

"I would hope." I melted into her couch.

"Well, come on, what did you expect, really? It was already written out centuries ago. The half-made man, self-loathing, comes to his wizardly father for approval, for his freedom to become fully human. Sound familiar, Caliban?"

"No. That sounds forced and irrelevant and annoying."

Dana was reading a book by Harold Bloom, a Yale professor who traveled all the way to the maximalist and insane thesis that Shakespeare invented how people now live, communicate, think. Before Shakespeare, we were different, and since the plays have sunk into us (taught, explained, performed, filmed, turned into other works by later artists), we have all slowly but surely become like his characters. We think as he showed us people could think. Life is true to his art, not vice versa. The logical extreme evolution of our slavish love for this one writer ends in blasphemy: he is literally our creator. Dana, obsessing over the book with an enthusiasm that made me worry she'd stopped taking her medication, had decided that I most resembled the slave barbarian enthralled to the old magician in *The Tempest*. "Tell me you know how stupid that idea is," I begged.

She was still living in our old rent-controlled one-bedroom. It was immediately comfortable to be with her back in New York, to wallow in nostalgia for our younger arrangement, if only for a couple of days of meetings with Random House and my agent, interviews about *Prague*. She seemed at first to be thriving, perfectly suited to her surroundings. (I often used that phrase to describe happiness in others back then, as I realized how ill at ease and increasingly lost I was feeling in Prague.) She had no shortage of friends. People said hello to her all over the neighborhood, and her voicemail and email were clogged with invitations. She was at thirty-eight as physically lovely as ever, maybe even more so. She was single, still went out and met women when the need hit her, but it rarely did. When I arrived in town, I went straight to her rehearsal for an off-Broadway Beckett production, and she was clearly well liked there. Cast members sat next to me during breaks, excited to meet Dana's twin and hear my stories about her past lives and loves, until the director passively aggressed from the stage, "I would hate to clear the house of family and friends, but I will have silence now, please. Thank you."

But for all this, Dana's loneliness emerged, and it was troubling. She took my arm, leaned in close to me, pleased me with her relief at my visit, her need of me, her questions about my next book, about the boys, the gifts she had for them. She didn't want to go out, turned down all invitations from cast and crew.

Instead she holed us up in our old apartment, where we feasted out of white cartons with trusted old pagodas on the sides and watched DVDs of the young actress Anne Hathaway. When Dana was out west with a role in a pilot for a TV show that was never picked up, she had developed a powerful crush on Hathaway, having seen but not met her at a party in Hollywood. She paused each film whenever there was a close-up of the starlet's face, her oversized features, her sparkling eyes. "I get the strangest feeling about her," Dana said, after we'd emptied a village of pagodas and two bottles of wine. "When I look at her, I have the feeling that she is *it*, somehow. She'd be it if we ever met." Dana had even written fan letters to her, an act of subservience she had previously stooped to only for Harold Bloom. She'd invited Hathaway to the opening nights of the off-Broadway and off-off-Broadway plays that made up her own professional life, and, in the most openly affectionate letter, she quoted the sonnet to her namesake: "*'I hate' from hate away she threw / And saved my life, saying 'not you.'*"

"I've never *sent* them," she said to my undisguised worry, but she was lying. "I'm not as far gone as all that." She did, however, suggest, "Maybe you could write a screenplay with a part for her. And then you could introduce us." Dana was a professional actress, but she didn't ask me to write something for her to star in, only something for her fanciful crush. I offered her some of my Czech antidepressants, which she sampled. "Are you still taking something?" I asked. "Forty is coming. Only a fool would go in unarmed."

I don't want to paint her during that week in one color. She was also her amazing self, asking after everything, reporting on Mom and Sil, insightful and funny and loving and generous and intensely interested in my boys. She stayed up all night reading the manuscript pages of my next book before my flight home in the morning. She suggested a different ending, and I rewrote the book to her specifications. ("You're smart to leave out the lesbians this time," she said. "You're not strong at them.") It was my most successful novel, and several reviews quoted a passage Dana wrote in my manuscript's margins.

I returned to my life in Prague, made more alienating by the comparison to home, by the feeling that Dana needed me, by the memory of my father's face when he lied. I tried to settle into my Czech routines, my foreign family. I suffered an odd symptom: I started to lose my language skills. I had increasing difficulty recalling Czech vocabulary and grammar. I grew so frustrated that I went back to language school, even though I had been fluent and at one point had burnished my accent and slang to the point that I occasionally passed as Czech for a few minutes at a time. I ended up talking to a therapist about it.

That old childhood daydream came back: I was saddled with Shakespeare's company again, though he was now fully adapted to modern life, reliant on his cellphone, jaywalking to reach a hot dog stand after a meeting at my publisher's. I still didn't like him: that same haircut, but now in jeans and a Yankees sweatshirt. There was, though, something I was desperate to ask him, the same questions I wanted my father to answer: *Am I good? Will I be okay?* But every time this daydream raged, it had to end with me struggling foolishly to win his distracted attention. "Take those off for a minute," I say.

"What?" Shakespeare shouts, the airplane headphones blocking out everything except the romantic comedy he's watching. I mime and mouth for him to take off the headphones. "There's no pause function on this," he says, half-trying to hide his exasperation at my intrusion. "She's a hotel chambermaid, very earthy. And the guy . . . wait, not him, wait . . . him, that guy, him: he's a millionaire hotel guest, very uptight. They're made for each other, but they don't know it yet."

And I tell him to go back to his movie.

I wrote to my father, still, from Prague, wrote *for* him, still. The definition of insanity, the twelve-steppers have patiently taught me, one day at a time, is to do the same thing over and over again expecting a different result. I wrote for him, still. I have now written four novels, and I devised the idea of an anagram for him to decipher over years. The first letters of the titles of my novels are *S, P, E,* and *A.* I planned to write, with all my remaining years, books initialed *S, H, A, K, E, R,* and *E,* and then, maybe, *A, N, D, M, E.*

Shakespeare's lines are a nursery of titles for other, better writers: *Pale Fire, Exit Ghost, Infinite Jest, Rosencrantz and Guildenstern Are Dead, The Sound and the Fury, Unnatural Acts, The Quick and the Dead, Against the Polack, To Be or Not to Be, Band of Brothers, Casual Slaughters.* At the very least, I have never named one of my books after his stuff.

20

ACT IV: King Arthur has allowed his court to become so feminized and debauched that the queen gets an hour every day to run things, putting knights on trial for charges of rudeness or romantic misbehavior. This ends only when a refreshed Saxon army invades

England yet again, thanks to Arthur's soft and distracted defense policies. This harsh lesson teaches Arthur, finally, that his job, and the nature of life, is to be constantly at war with someone. He has no natural allies to help fight the Saxons because he impulsively married for love, rejecting the French. Since Arthur still doesn't have an heir (Guenhera has miscarried twice), he is forced to name Mordred his heir in exchange for military assistance against the Saxons, barring any natural-born children. Guenhera, pregnant again, waits for news of the battle of Linmouth, and goes into labor. Mordred, having assisted Arthur in defeating the Saxons, finds himself both jealous of and charmed by Arthur and realizes he's been fooled: Arthur will never let him be King of Britain. He vows to force the issue, perhaps even seduce Guenhera himself, proving God's will by producing a child with her. On his way to another war in Ireland, this one a war of choice, Arthur returns to court to see his wife, who has miscarried for the third time. Young Philip of York appears, claiming to be King Arthur's son (perhaps from Arthur's mysterious layover in York back in Act II). Arthur, solving his political problem at great cost to others, impulsively makes Philip his heir and forces the queen to accept him. Later, Philip admits in soliloquy that he is an impostor.

Is it the dialogue headings down the left margin over and over again—"ARTHUR PHILIP ARTHUR PHILIP ARTHUR PHILIP"—that make me leery?

Dana called me in Prague, the night of July 18, 2009, to say that Sil, whose long illness I had come to permanently view as temporary, had taken a critical turn, and that I should fly to Minneapolis immediately if I wanted to say goodbye.

The next morning, on my way out of the apartment to the airport, my wife and I had one of those fights that are entirely unnecessary, in which everyone is simply reciting lines scripted by their worst impulses, a dull sequel to old fights, a dull prologue to later fights, a DVD frozen on the same stupid mid-blink face of a normally good-looking actor.

Jana's mother, once such charming local color, so amusingly foreign and so obviously unrelated to my sexy Czech-model girlfriend, was now a live-in nightmare and plainly the mother of my increasingly foreign and disgruntled wife. Jana's mother and sister had both married men who were relentlessly and regretlessly unfaithful, and so the ladies had seized the opportunity while I was packing for my trip to Sil's deathbed to express their breakfast-table certainty, in front of our twins, that I was having an affair. Jana—very much the child of her mother's dour Czech unhappiness and sullen victimhood—allowed her buttons to be masterfully pushed. Reminders of my authorial unpredictability and American suspiciousness were ringing in the room, and Jana greeted me with tearful accusations in front of the boys and her nodding mother and sister. The script called for her to break something, so she indulged in a single dramatic but economical flying saucer and an alienating stream of Czech obscenities, amusing to Tomáš and Miloš, then almost fifteen and, for the time being, just about done with me anyhow. My steady, then angry (and truthful) denials launched her defensive weapon: she had slept with . . . it doesn't matter whom. I said I didn't believe her, which was a serious tactical blunder because I thought she was unattractive, did I? Broken by giving birth (a rather contemptuous sweep of the arm at my laughing sons) to *them*? I thought she couldn't win another man? *"Arrogant American Jew!"* Oy vey.

And so—on the long flight, the endless day as time zones passed in one direction at the same speed that time passed in the other and noon held on and on for hours beneath me, and, later, disoriented in the JFK holding area where counterterrorism shades into countertourism—if I allowed myself to believe that Jana had cheated on me, then it was a delusion of jet lag and stress and sorrow, but one I could pull from my luggage again, further on in this story, as necessary.

21

I ARRIVED IN MINNEAPOLIS. My stepfather had died while I was nodding off in a pressurized cabin.

It was the end of a love story, great at least for its many possible interpretations. Perhaps it was the comedy of Silvius the devoted lover whose dedication survived my mother's false first choice (Shakespeare taught Jane Austen that trick). Or perhaps it was the tragedy of my mother settling for the dull, second-best offer, because her true love was too unsteady, flew too close to the sun, unable to tame himself to ordinary, human love—the poster on her daughter's wall daily reminding her of *The Tragedy of* her first husband. How to define that second marriage to a first love? Each new scrap of evidence recolors all the rest, just as a good director can decide whether Henry V will be a hero, a brute, or a canny bluffer. The fewer the stage directions, the richer the possibility of each retelling.

"Oh, thank you for coming," said my mother when I walked into the yellow kitchen, too late. She hugged me. She was grateful, as if I owed her nothing at all but was doing her some kindness, and I held her a long time, my carry-on bag trying to wedge its way between us. Dana stood to the side, sympathy personified.

Dana had moved back to Minneapolis six months earlier and been hired as the drama teacher at our old private school. Not long after, she was winning big roles in local theaters, doing much better than she ever had in New York. She had an apartment of her own but had been living with Mom since Sil was hospitalized for the last time. "I love it here," she said when Mom had gone for a nap and we were having coffee in the kitchen, shrunken since our childhood. "I honestly feel"—she lowered her voice to a stage whisper—"that I've never been happier. Obviously, sad about Sil. I am. And I am, I am worried about what happens to Mom next, but I wish so much that you and Jana and the boys would come spend a month here. Everything's different. I could almost say I've lived in a dream until now." Dana took my hands. "It's like I've never been happy before, like I didn't know what the word really even meant. Everything else was just . . . preparing me. I have to tell you about someone I've been seeing. She's moved in, actually."

22

I T IS TIME TO CALL in the memoirist's best friend: the changed
name. I name my family, my poor sister, my German girl, my
wronged wife. I call the villain of this story by my own or my father's
name. Yet one identity must be shrouded. What crime could justify
this protection? Or, more likely, has the memoir come unmoored
from memory's safe harbor and now drifts off into black fantasy, and
the desperate writer must do the legal minimum, lest the whole
freyed tissue unravel?

No, she was real. She still is real, and if she was not as innocent as
some, neither was she as guilty, not by a long distance, and I send her
and her daughter all my worthless love and yet more concentrated
apology.

What disguise can I tailor that will hide her from you while still
showing you what she was? The more one loves, the more each detail
matters. To smudge a line, pixelate the birthmark, drag a censor's
squealing black pen across her eyes, transpose two digits of her Social
Security number—I am destroying her, and making all this more
difficult to explain, because I will claim this one small memoirist's
privilege: if you saw her in every detail, up to her name, which fit
her so snugly, you'd have done just the same as I. If you judge me
harshly, it is only because, in my discretion, I am describing her so
poorly.

No risk in confessing that she was ten years younger than Dana
and I. Can I safely disclose that she was of another race? Of another
religion? (One as irrelevant and inescapably identifying to her as Judaism had become to Dana and me.) Can I say she was a composer
and musician, that she played the theremin, professionally, in films
and in Minneapolis theaters? Or that Dana called her "my tigress of
the Euphrates"? If true, how many people in Minneapolis now know
at once whom I mean? If false, how odd are these colors, how far
from comprehensible I've made her, and thus me and everything
about to happen.

"And thus me." For all I thought otherwise when I began this project, I do want to be understood. I do want to be forgiven. I do want you to believe me and agree with me and approve of me. And if I cannot have your acceptance, then I'm tempted to say, "So be it, I'll play the villain instead." That's what passes for psychological depth in *Richard III*, you know.

May I self-mitigate, allow myself some standard excuses? How about . . . Dana's ties to the girl were weak, as strained as my own to my life back in the wilds of Bohemia? No. I saw no arguments between them, heard no doubts disclosed during twin-to-twin heart-to-hearts. No, Dana was in love, every bit as much as I later became, but she was there first, had made and received promises, had sought so long for just this love and could rightly expect her married and beloved twin brother, her long-ago best friend, to act with a scruple of decency. I knew all this. It was difficult, but not impossible, to will it out of mind.

Can I not blame anyone else, even a little? Perhaps my mother would be willing to bear a tiny share on her old shoulders. Why, yes, I see it now: During the peculiar wake/shivah that Dana had designed, my mother grew annoyed by some of Sil's distant, too close cousins and asked me to take her for some fresh air. She moved quickly out the door and down the street, and I had to pick up the pace to keep up with her. She set off for the path around Lake of the Isles and we silently motored along for nearly half the lake before her energy (or anger) sputtered.

"How are you?" I asked.

"That's a funny question. I just buried a husband." We now walked slowly, arm in arm, me supporting her balsa-wood body, the bikers and roller skaters blurring by on both sides, the cocker spaniels in their Cuban-bandleader pants, the skyline of downtown Minneapolis across the lake, as self-contained as a snow globe.

"He loved you."

"He did," she said as if there were no arguing with that. "And he held up his end of the bargain. Probably better than I did. He loved me all the way to the end. Treated me well. Supported me. 'Not wealth, Mary. I don't think I'll be able to do wealth. But we'll be okay.'"

"You do a pretty good impression of him."

"Suppose. Well, there's not much to master, is the truth." I let that lie, and soon enough she exhaled and her tone changed back. "He gave me everything he promised. Everything he had."

"He did."

"It would be pretty awful to say it wasn't enough."

"I don't know. It depends who you said it to."

"He was steady-state, Sil was. That was how he loved, too. He opened with undying love and, sure enough, it didn't die. Until he did."

"That's beautiful. Love like that. People dream of that."

"Do they? Do you?"

"I don't remember right now, but I'm sure I have. I never heard you complain about him at all."

"No. How could I? Can I? Can you say it was a mistake? It wasn't. Odd: I had two good choices and got to have them both. Can't really complain."

I finally bit: "You seem good and ready to complain."

"*Can* you complain while we're sitting shivah, or whatever that thing is back there?" She pulled over to a bench under a linden tree and let the wheels and paws and running shoes flow past us. A snail, like an ornate, restless 2, crept across the back of the bench. My mother picked it up and carried it to some moss out of harm's way. She sat back down and looked at the canoes on the rack across from us, and she started to talk. "For thirty-five years, almost—this October is thirty-five—thirty-five years he told me in word and deed that I was lovable. And so that's what I thought I was. He was like a mild drug. As long as I was near him, it was enough, and it didn't wear off, and I didn't think I wanted for anything but his humble offerings. But it was *so* humble. I was *so* far above him and he was *so* lucky to have me. Flattery, but sincere. And I loved him. I did. I do. I just—Arthur, can I wonder a little? Your father. I count my blessings I got out when I did and stayed away how I did, and Sil was there to give me something smooth and different and *better* and save me and I was *so* far above him and . . . Honestly. Honestly? God *damn* it." I flinched, then laughed at my overreaction, but I had never in all my life heard the slightest obscenity smirch her lips, no matter how badly Dana and I had ever behaved. "God *damn* it. A little less awe of me and a little more effort to astonish me—to make me think *I* was the lucky one? Would that have killed him? But to sit there and say, 'Gosh, I'm a lucky man to have you put up with my low-grade self.' He never made me feel like I had better watch my step or I'd lose him. God *damn* it." She really liked how that felt now. "I could do *no* wrong in his eyes. What's wrong with someone like that?"

"That he loved you so much?"

"No, that, that, that, that I was just a great idea, and he, he was such a, was so, was such a—" And my mom was crying against me. "And then he up and dies first."

Here's the thing about Shakespeare: at the end of the comedies comes the wedding, the circle of life, the dance, the love that will lead to family and birth and life and then some unknown end. But there isn't *this:* that after the marriage and dance, after the decades together, after the funeral, there is the woman, grown old and thoughtful and angry at herself for being angry at him, after everyone knows that everyone did their best, but who sits under the medlar tree and tries to say, "That was a *bore*" (God *damn* it). "I took the easy way, and I regret it." If Dana and Harold Bloom are right, if we're all just walking figments of Shakespeare's imagination, then where in the canon is my mom, who could not quite say the truth about what she'd lived, that Sil's love was not enough, that kindness and best efforts were not enough?

"Am I an ingrate? A shrew?"

"No."

"I don't really feel like one. I just know that's the word for people who talk like this in this situation. Not even cold in the earth."

"You can talk however you want to me." If I later heard her words as a warning against living too little, risking too little, loving too little, playing it safe, well, one crime I will not cop to is ignoring motherly advice.

I didn't know yet that her words were being banked, in some part of my cunning mind, converted to useful currency. I thought I was just being a good, understanding adult and son. But she spoke of regrets, and I recalled Jana's farewell address to me earlier that week, and I later saw the maternal regret as deeply wise license. She later said exactly the opposite to Dana ("Thank God for Sil. I got what I needed, I owe him everything, and I am so *blessed*"), demonstrating a mental flexibility that is evidence of wisdom or empathy or Alzheimer's. Her conversation with me may just have been steam releasing, only a piece of her.

We walked back home, to the remnants of the remarkable event Dana had organized with help from some theater friends. When Mom and I walked in, the afternoon had progressed to one of Sil's cousins singing Sinatra on the karaoke machine Dana had rented while martinis were being shaken up by a catering bartender in a Twins uniform with MAUER written on the back.

And then I saw her.

Desire was instantaneous, that species of desire that feels like something rarer than mere lust but that no twenty-first-century grown-up can dare call by its proper name: "love at first sight." The body stirs, but above the waist. The mind stirs, and insists something significant is happening, casts you into some pastoral scene, some favorite film, some recurrent dream where everyone used to be faceless, like wooden cutouts waiting for tourists. My urges were celestial, not yet sexual: I wanted to touch her face, to put the tips of my fingers against her cheek, to trace the groove between lip and nose. The beach at sunset, the path of skin that ran from her shoulder up to the tender intersection where jaw, ear, and neck meet and merge: dreary anatomical words, *neck*, *skin*, *ear*, *nose*. They fail.

I didn't know who she was yet. She knew me before I knew her. "You're Dana's twin," the stranger said as I zombie-staggered toward her.

"No one has ever recognized us like that. We don't really look alike."

"You can say that if you want," she answered with a smile, and I began cataloguing all that I would give up for this woman. "But that doesn't make it true. I'm—" She spoke her name, and all was confounded. I have to give her a name now, for textual convenience: something ancient that evokes the Levant, spiced, golden dark. "—Petra."

I had her hand, and I let it drop as if I'd hurt myself. I echoed awhile: "Oh, oh, oh, yeah, yeah, my sister's, my sister's—"

"Your sister's," she confirmed, laughing.

(A pretty good line from a rough critic: "Reading Arthur Phillips' dialogue is like poring over the minutes of a stammerers' convention.")

"I'm so sorry about Sil. I met him a few times. A gentleman, and actually a sweetheart."

"Thank you. He was. How's the dog?"

Dana and Petra had just bought a dog together, a male beagle they'd named Maria, as Dana had dreamt of doing for years, a very specific fantasy of very specific domesticity. Dana had been in high school when she first imagined living with a woman and co-owning a dog. She'd read *Twelfth Night* and heard in Sir Toby's praise of his girlfriend, Maria, all the evidence she needed to know Shakespeare's favorite breed:

> SIR ANDREW   Before me, she's a good wench.
>
> SIR TOBY   She's a beagle, true-bred.

And so Dana decided that someday she would have a beagle, and she and her beloved would name it Maria. She had waited more than thirty years for this woman who, in a second or two, had stormed and colonized my imagination from across a crowded wake.

"How's the dog?" I asked.

"Not just *any* dog: Maria."

"Maria. *Ay, she's a beagle.*"

"True-bred," agreed the woman so foully out of reach, so criminally denied me. "Dana was crazy picky. We had to *interview* breeders. Very much Gay Parent Overcompensation Disorder. Finally, she asks this guy in Wisconsin, 'How are your beagles?' and he says, '*My hounds are bred out of the Spartan kind, and their heads are hung with ears that sweep away the morning dew.*'"

"'*Crook-kneed and dewlapped like Thessalian bulls*'?"

"You know the guy?"

"I know my sister."

23

MY FATHER HAD A LITTLE LESS than two months remaining on his sentence. I suppose I would have flown to Minneapolis for his release if I hadn't already been there to mark the end of Sil's term, but I'm not certain of it. This period was the closest I ever came to my ideal of indifference to him, true-dyed, in the blood, not just feigned with conviction. I was due in Prague, should have been hurrying back to see what remained of my marriage, or what remained of my desire to save my marriage, to see who was still angry, who was offering apologies or planning departures. But I could find no desire to return. I sank into my hotel bed in Minneapolis and felt at home. I spent almost all of every day with my sister. I watched her record a radio ad, which reminded me of Dad's vocal prowess when he used to read to us. I watched her study martial arts under the unblinking eyes of a slate-faced sensei. We cooked and ate long wine-rich dinners at her apartment. I played with her dog in Loring Park. I couldn't help but notice we were almost always in the company of her love.

I visited Dad August 3, two weeks after Sil died, ready to try on the unnatural role of son, wanting to hear his plans for what was certain to be a short and thoroughly depressing last chapter of life, arming myself with as much protective covering as I could strap over my heart.

But I spent the drive down to Faribault recalling details of Petra's face, laughing aloud at how she looked dressed as a man and how her hands felt on my back as she clasped my filled bra for the "Bend It 'til It Breaks" party hosted by Dana's theater friends. "When you cross-dress, you're every bit as alluring as Bugs Bunny," she said. By the time I was passing through the various layers of security in visitor parking, I had a vast store of generosity for Dad bubbling up in me. I decided to see him through to the end as any man deserved, as his best efforts would have merited. One of us would do the right thing for the other. I planned to rent him an apartment, set up an allowance, find him a job teaching art at a senior center. I would expect nothing in return, not a glance, not a chat.

I waited in the newly rechristened Family Hall, which now served food: a bunch of withered, whiskered pre-raisins clung exhausted to their stems. For ten minutes I waited and thought of past visits and imagined Petra sitting next to me and what I would say to her about this room and what she would say to me about the man it had made me. And then they led him in. And I didn't recognize him.

He was, magically, nearly eighty years old. He had been a time-lapse father, but this last leap, especially after Sil's death, was horrific. A rickety man aswim in an orange jumpsuit, a visible skull, mottled lizard's wattle from chin to top button, he teetered a little when I said, "Dad?" in the wrong tone of voice, and he lowered himself by hand into the chair across from me, across that same Formica long since infected as the carrier of loneliness, regret, and shame. All that had grown (or at least not shrunk) were his eyebrows, now as lush and thick as prizewinning mustaches, irresistible to the eye, bricks of silvery turf.

I'd seen him during a book tour only a few years earlier, but he had aged far more than that, and indifference again began to slough off me, molten Kevlar. Worse than the visible changes—the weight loss, the hanging skin, the hair that was sparse where it had been full and vice versa—was his way of talking. "I have an idea, something I've worked on a little, been sitting on, more accurately" were his first words to me in years.

"Hi, Dad."

And *then* he said, "Arthur, thank you for coming. It is good to see you." He nodded awhile, his thoughts unraveling. "I have an idea." He went back to where he'd started. "Something I've worked on a little."

"Sil died," I said.

That seemed to take the wind out of him. He nodded and looked at his speckled hands. "Gentle Silvius. Yes. Your sister wrote about that. He was a good fellow. And he did right. He took good care of her."

"He did."

"Which was my job."

"Yes."

That stopped us both. We waited, both sensing that this conversation wasn't going to be what either of us had planned or even grown accustomed to over Formica tabletops past. But then he began his prepared remarks again, like an inexperienced tour guide trying not to be thrown off by questions: "I've been sitting on it, more accurately. It will be something nice for your mother. And your matched princes of Bohemia, too. It will be good for everyone. This idea. I've been waiting a long time, trying to wait as long as possible, without waiting too long."

This seemed to take a lot of energy to explain. He flagged and I hurried to fill the gap, to pick up what I thought he was saying: "Dad, I know. Me, too. I've waited too long, too. I've left so much for too long."

This disappointed him: "Yes, but." It took no time at all to see that he knew I was heading toward some emotional outpouring and wanted me to stop, and so I stopped myself, but that was okay, even funny. I would not make the mistake of expecting too much of him. I could feel myself re-arming, and he said, "I'm not trying to be rude. I—you're a famous writer."

"Not that famous."

"But you've written all these books," he insisted with a look of despair, almost panic, as if my thoughtless act of reflexive modesty had not only persuaded him but also presented a problem. "You still have a publisher, right?"

"Yeah, I do. I was just saying that I—"

"I'm not trying to be rude. I know how you must feel. I'm old. But that's the point. I made it. And so now you and I—we are going to do something together, okay? I have been waiting. Something great. I need you. You're the only one I can do this with. You're a famous writer. That's a great thing you've done. I am so proud, you know. I don't know who to tell how proud I am. And I haven't told you. You make wonders, Arthur."

It is difficult to overstate the effect of these astonishing words, the flood that washed away all my indifference, that proved how shallowly that dye had ever stained me. My home life was in tatters, my judgment was askew, and now I was hearing this impossible revelation from an ancient, broken man who bore some relation to my so disappointing father and my distorted childhood, suddenly hearing the words I'd been waiting to hear for decades, being told now, of all the days of my life, that I had somehow measured up to the best of him: I was sobbing, coughing, as I never had in any family visit since I was a kid.

"Thank you. Dad, thank you."

"But listen." He was sitting up a little straighter, having absorbed something from me. "So this idea. Now I have to. I want your help. I can't without you. I have to. This is for your mother. Do you have another book in the works? Are you writing? Now?"

I told him that my fourth novel (which featured an idealized affection between the protagonist—an adman—and his father) had been published that April, but that I was since then dry for ideas. I had, unusually for me, no outlines, no notes, no flirtatious offers from coy muses. I probably drooped a little when I admitted this. "I have a lot going on at home," I sighed. "Jana and I—I don't know. And when I get stressed, I can't write. I need to be relaxed, to know I'm . . . *safe*—that's really the word for it. I need the right conditions, and now it's just really not right."

"Are you pulling my leg?" he asked very seriously.

"Yes. No."

"Shakespeare wrote *Venus and Adonis* during an outbreak of the bubonic plague. That must have been stressful." I just nodded. "Well." He regretted that turn of conversation. "You're right, though. Times are different. And you need the right conditions. You're a great artist. I wouldn't know how. But this is for the best. You taking a break. You need a project to sink your teeth into. What are you now, forty-five? And your reputation? You're a figure in the literary world, right? You still have a publisher?" he repeated, troublingly.

"Yes, Dad, I have a publisher."

"Are they a good publisher? Reputable?"

"Yes." I laughed and dried my eyes. "Random House is a reputable publisher."

"I did pretty badly by you and Dana. And your mother. I thank providence for Sil, you know. I really do. I am— I failed in every way."

"No, Dad, no." I took the bait.

And he set the hook: "Don't interrupt or I'll lose my train of thought. It's a problem in here." But he was speaking with more focus and energy than he had been. "You spend a long time with your silent thoughts, and they get set off on the wrong track, from a shout or a clanging door, or an electrical short circuit, what is it called, a switching, neurons . . . synapse . . . so to beat that, you start to talk out loud, to keep track of things, and then you get a reputation—old, muttering man. And then when there is someone to converse with, those are skills that rust over, you know. I'm glad you're here. I'm so glad. There isn't much time." And he stopped talking, seemed aware that he'd roamed afield.

"Dad. We have time."

"Please tell me what I was saying."

"You were saying about being here, the noise—"

"I know, but before, but that's not the point." He shook his head and looked at his hands, then the ceiling, then me, perfectly expressive in his gestures now, maybe a little practiced, in retrospect. "The point is, I could fix, a little, of things that I failed." Even that garbled syntax was a hint: I am unable to grab the man who is playing my part in this scene and warn him of the mistake he's about to make.

"You don't have to fix anything," I said. "You just have to get ready for life outside again. Think about what you want to do. Who do you want to see?"

"Listen to me. Artie. This is what I want to do. I'm not going to take up golf. Hobble over for seniors' coffee at Embers." I couldn't bear to tell him Embers had closed, that Minneapolis was an entirely new city, all its residents altered or dead and replaced. "I'm not going to—whatever you people think an ancient convict is supposed to do. I was a serious person."

"I know."

"And this city, your friend Constantine—they *owe* me. You always told him about me. Helped him lock me up."

"You don't really believe that, Dad."

He looked down and pushed his fingers against his cheek, gnawed at the skin at the corner of his lips, badly shaven, red and chapped. "No, I don't. I'm sorry. You forget which conversations with yourself were settled a long time ago and which ones are still recent. You get mad, you know, and then you forget why, and then you remember why, but that wasn't why, that was an old time you got mad." He laughed a little at this. "That's not important now, and there isn't time, and I lose too much time when I'm mad, I argue all day in my head and the day is gone."

"You'll be out in five weeks. You know that, right?"

"And I'll be out of time not long after that."

"You'll get used to living out there. Dana and I can help with all of it." I was volunteering, and, faster than scheming, an internal projection image flashed: me picking him up, taking him to Dana's for dinner, where I would sit next to Petra, the four of us, our dog.

"There isn't much time. Will you believe me when I say I know?"

"Time may feel different in here. Out there, you'll—"

"I'm not making small talk, Arthur. Listen to me, please. I don't have much time, and I want you to do something. With me."

Was there that gap, that period? Or was it: "I want you to do something with me"? Or was there a hint of another word: "I want you to do something f-with me." I know now that it must have been "I want you to do something for me," but I heard "with." I heard, finally, my father asking for my unique help, not anyone else's, not Dana's. I was forty-five, still barely married with twins of my own, sweeping from my pillow each morning last night's molted hair, but my daddy wanted to do something with me, and I nearly fell over myself.

"You have to call Bert Thorn. Today. Do you remember him? He's still alive. He still has an office. Promise: today. Yes? Tell him I want you to have the key. Right now. And then just keep an open mind and think. I'm going to write you a letter. They let us use the email now, once a week, but they read it all, so be smart."

"I'm right here. Just tell me what you want. But"—and I was ashamed of myself for thinking it—"I'm not going to commit a crime, you know."

"Of course not. That's all over. That's why this can happen. I can't think straight out loud anymore," he stammered, and his lips curled up, and his face crumpled.

"Jesus, Dad."

"I can't. I used to be able to think and talk. Now I have to pick one."

"Shh, Dad, it's okay." His hands started to tremble on the Formica, then bounced, flopped around. I took them and held him steady. The guard drew in a breath to shout us apart (NO. 3: NO TOUCHING), but just shook his head and looked away, and my father wept. "So don't speak, just think," I said, a little stupidly, and my father wept. "Think about being out with us."

After a few minutes, when he'd stopped, he squeezed my hands and opened his mouth, but then just stood and walked off to his escort. He had failed at something, yet again, I thought, looking at his departure, wishing terribly that I could help him.

Like all good pigeons, I took on most of the work of conning me myself.

24

THE ORDER OF EVENTS, which cluster around one another in haze, shimmers and becomes unsteady. And so, I reconstruct based on the recalled emotion: event A must have happened first, because it would have made me angry, and only my anger would have justified my behavior at B. And yet, what if B came first? It shouldn't have, but I can't be sure now. And then, what happens to all my carefully stored up justifications, my story line?

Driving from prison to my father's old attorney's office according to the sultry instructions of my rental car's GPS navigator, I called Jana to say I was going to stay awhile longer in Minneapolis. I reasonably expected resignation, a talk about logistics, half an apology about her send-off, maybe even a softly voiced question along the lines of "Do you want to come home to us?" Instead, she yelled over the speakerphone, "Who is that talking to you? Who is she?"

"What? Nobod—oh, it's the GPS thing."

"She sounds like a *slut*. Of course you pick this voice."

Now I can sympathize with Jana, a woman I loved, in one particular way. My initial intoxicating love never grew into something more adult, more settled, more profound, though she rightly expected that it would. How much shame should I bear for that? I, too, thought we would make it. But either I was the wrong man or she was the wrong woman or we were the wrong pair or it was the wrong time or I was broken from the moment my mother carelessly laid two eggs instead of one or or or. I can sympathize with the woman, who was every bit as frustrated and frightened and angry as I was.

But at the time, her behavior certainly bore an uncanny resemblance to aggression, and I, dressed as passivity for this allegorical masque, gladly let her push me along a path I was eager to pursue anyhow, snapping the last fraying filaments of guilt that would have tugged me back to my odd life as a tourist-husband in the toy-castle town in Bohemia.

Jana told me, over speakerphone as I was driving to my father's old attorney's office, that she was trading me in for a friend of ours, Jiři, whose advances and honest love she had long ago rebuffed. She said he had been waiting for her all these years, willing to be merely a friend, even a friend to me (whose treatment of her he loathed, she reported impartially), but she had had enough of her mistake. She was going. "I hope you'll be very happy," I shouted, the car swerving across lane markers on I-35.

The surface similarities to my parents and Sil were gaudy, and I think, sometimes, of the fairies of Shakespeare's childhood and *Midsummer*, who trick unwary travelers. "*I'll lead you about a round, / Through bog, through bush, through brake, through brier.*" If one of them could do a Czech accent and acquire a cellphone, how easily they could play their fairy games and ruin us all.

How strangely distributed are our scruples. When they are evenly spread across our lives, we are judged good people. Mine, unfortunately, tend to bunch up. I unconsciously provoked Jana until she threatened to run off with some Czech or other, which, in her emotion-strained English, was phrased as a fait accompli, which I gladly took as a statement of our separation and a permit to do whatever I wanted. I don't deny the hypocrisy of my position. I had finagled a license to do as I wished and to feel morally pure as I did it. I was anesthetized to all that came next, heard no better angels murmuring to me, for many months to come—none that I couldn't mock back into silence. (Still, I emailed the boys every night, long letters. Ha! Feeble memoirist: I need to assert that I am a good father.)

"Do I deserve this?" I asked the GPS after Jana hung up.

"Turn left in three hundred yards," she purred. "That's it. Yes. Yes! Just there. Just like that."

25

BERTRAM THORN'S SHABBY OFFICE had likely never been impressive, even back in the days when he had partners and my father could afford their services. The misguided slogan—"Breve, Thorn, Tonos and Ogonek: We put the GATOR in litigator"—with its cartoon illustration hung over his law degree from the University of Florida. The thin dark-wood paneling with its peeling veneer. The dusty files bulging with tedious briefs. The exhausted and sagging venetian blinds with their knotted strings. The hairpiece so obvious, so mountainous, contoured, Mannerist, it could only be his real hair.

"He instructed me about this. The kids would come for it," Bert said with an odd sadness I hadn't expected in this aged lawyer. But a young lawyer defends as best he can a young client, then sees him sentenced again and again, then loses touch as he is locked away from other eyes, then greets that vanished client's son, come to find the odd heirloom left behind those years ago, and the lawyer—I saw it happen—is struck nauseous at the sudden thundering announcement of time's criminal trespass. "You were just little kids," he said to the middle-aged man in his office. "A little boy."

When I was a boy—lonely, chubby, prone to fantasy in solitude—I sometimes imagined that I was Death itself, and that no one could see me, except my next victim. I might be on the city bus—the old candy-red 1B—sitting across from an old man, his hands laced across the crook of a cane swaying between his spread knees. I would imagine saying to him in my kindly little boy's voice, "It's time," and he would nod, rise, walk with me out the bus's rear emergency exit, pass straight though it, leave the moving bus behind and beneath us as I took his arm. He drops his cane, and we walk through air to the destination where only I can deliver him.

I judged them, sometimes, those whose faces revealed (in my imagination) fear or disappointment. One old man, not ready at all, stared at me. "You're just a little kid," he whispered.

"Come on, fella, you had your turn, so toughen up," I chided, a prim reaper.

Bert was like this, a little scared by my arrival, my adulthood, my demand for the family jewels. He covered that fear and sadness with a layer of artifice: he sat down heavily, puffed out his cheeks, and said, "Well, this has been a long time coming. I'm feeling a little old!"

He had the key in his own safe, which he kept behind a painting of an open, empty safe. The key was for a safe-deposit box. There's no way to write that without sounding melodramatic. It didn't feel overdone, though, as this parody of an old family retainer handed over my father's long-guarded secret; it felt pathetic.

The box was downtown, at a local bank whose corporate ownership had switched several times in the recent disorders of high finance but which I always associated with the sponsorship of Minnesota Twins games, delivered to my bedroom on summer nights with the windows open, through a battery-devouring radio and a single white earphone, yellowed from use, pressed in place during the frustrating not-dark of summer bedtimes when I was expected to abide by the clock, not the sky, and so lay in bed clandestinely listening to Tony Oliva and Rod Carew and Harmon Killebrew and Bert Blyleven battle the endless tide of Tigers, Brewers, Royals, Angels. All those warm boyhood nights sponsored by this bank, its name and motto repeated every half inning until I fell asleep, the earphone falling onto the pillow decorated with Twins' logos, the batters retreating into white noise.

Whatever spark of pride I had felt at being chosen over Dana quickly faded, maybe with the sight of Bert's fear or with the thought of my childhood as a time of sleep and warmth, of her. So I called her as I left Bert's. Whatever this gift of our father's was, I would share it with her. "Dad asked me to do some project with him," I said, as if this were the most natural thing in the world, as if he had, no doubt, a dozen other projects in mind for her. Forty-five years old, and I was a little boy boasting, casually cruel, cruelly casual to the woman who'd loved me best since before I was born. But, in the next breath, I self-corrected: "And I want you to come. It's turned odd already, of course. I want to do it with you. We'll have some fun." We agreed I'd pick her up at her place and we'd go to the bank together.

When I arrived to fetch her, though, ready to let her open the box, keep whatever expired stock certificates moldered inside it, she was gone, and Petra was there, bearing excuses. Dana had been called for a last-minute audition and hurried off, urging me to carry on without her. I wondered if it was true, or if Dana was instead giving me my moment and protecting herself against any more of my sharp elbows. And then I asked the bearer of Dana's regrets to join me instead for "a trip to a secret vault."

"Ooh! The family vault! What's it all about?"

"Dark Phillips business. Dana must have told you of our shameful past. You want in?"

"Absolutely," she said, adopting a Scandinavian accent. She finished sending some message on her cellphone, her finger caressing its face. "Okay. The game is afoot!"

We drove my rental Taurus back across the river and spoke of Europe. "So you've got a wife and kids."

"Kids. Not so much wife."

"And you have a key to a secret," she murmured in that Garbo accent, and I had to remind myself that she was talking about an actual key.

"How long have you been with Dana?"

Jana was nothing; Petra was everything. What mechanism can so alter us? How could everything I once thought was undimmable fire now seem shadowed ash? An adolescent could blame it all on (or credit it all to) the new love's dawning glow: she was so much *better*, so much *more*, that all I'd loved before was revealed as dim and dun. Romeo has very little difficulty casting off Rosaline once he sees Juliet, easily downplaying all he had previously felt and suffered as mere fantasy, and we all take his side, and make excuses and say now he's learned *real* love. But when we have middle-aged experience, and when the lover is not a child of fifteen, and when the woman he would forget is not a stranger or a crush but his wife of fifteen years and the mother of his twin boys, then love is not inevitable but shameful, testimony not to the new beloved's heightened perfections but to the man's weakness, disloyalty, cowardice.

All of which I would plead guilty to, except except except that my admission does no justice to *her*, for whom *you* would give up the past, for whom *you* would grow dizzy and drop principles and vows and ties to your old self. Can I say that the woman I wed was a fantasy and this stranger was reality? I don't suppose I can, and yet . . . "Who ever loved that loved not at first sight?" wrote Marlowe, the man Shakespeare feared for many years was the better writer, the man who with those words issued a license to misery to millions of underexperienced teenagers and thousands of overeducated middle-aged jackasses.

Is it surprising that Dana and I would both feel so strongly about her? Not at all: she *should* have fit both of us; it makes a sort of geometric sense, just as Jana and Dana's longstanding mutual dislike should have warned me much earlier that my marriage was doomed.

When Shakespeare was a young writer, in *The Two Gentlemen of Verona*, when the hero's best friend loses his mind and madly pursues the hero's beloved, he says, "*Love bade me swear, and Love bids me forswear . . . / At first I did adore a twinkling star / But now I worship a celestial sun.*" But later, in *The Sonnets*, when such a woman appears, destroying the friendship of the two men, the poet underplays her, says she's not a classic beauty—she's *nothing like the sun*.

So Shakespeare faced the same writerly problem that I now face, and he gave up: to describe that gravitational object of affection— a celestial sun—and justify the effect of her by portraying her charms or to skip the whole thing, admit it's impossible, and say she's nothing like the sun but she had her effect even so. I'm still young enough, naïve enough, competitive enough that I want to capture her in ink and paper, pixel and byte, so she might live longer, unchanged, immortalized by my writing, what every great artist hopes to achieve.

26

P ETRA AND I WERE LED into the bank's safe-deposit basement. "Your box hasn't been opened in"—the dapper boy consulted a blue index card—"twenty-three years."

"If this were played upon a stage now, I could condemn it as an improbable fiction," Petra said. Fair enough: safe-deposit boxes are one of those elements of life most people don't deal with, or see only in crisis. Usually, the vaults exist only in movies, and so entering one makes you feel like you're in a movie, but, really, we're just talking about a chilly basement room of lockers and locked drawers. All the false theatrical majesty that banks employ to make their customers feel safe— Petra and I found it funny. She refused to take off her sunglasses, even in the basement, until the object was unveiled, and even then had trouble shedding that Scandinavian accent she'd played with during all the ID checks and goofy key protocol, ours turning in conjunction with the bank employee's. "Darling," she told the clerk as he left us in a private viewing room. "Do not come in here even if you hear screaming. Am I clear?"

My father's safe-deposit box was a cube, rather than a skinny drawer, about eighteen inches to each side. Inside it sat a small wooden crate, even stenciled on the side in the stern broken capitals of the military or the coffee business: **BANANAS**, as if a tiny cargo ship had recently docked and unloaded gnomish pallets of wee goods. "This is too strange," Petra said. "Your family is, really, just *beyond*." The wooden lid lifted off easily in one piece to reveal canvas coverings. Flap after flap of excess canvas was unpeeled until we were looking at a black metal lockbox, square and only a few inches thick, closed on each side with clasps like those of a musical instrument case. All eight of those released, the black top lifted straight off, sticking at the cracked rubber airtight strips.

Finally, on a foam pad, inside a sealed plastic bag, was a book about the size of a thin paperback.

I straddled the border of laughter and anger. This was not my thing, had nothing to do with me. Was he so cell-shocked that he had forgotten which of his kids liked this stuff? "Dana will be sorry she didn't come," Petra said, her Scandinavian clowning still half audible, and I was even more irritated because I felt suddenly and strongly that I had done something wrong. "I feel like Dana should be here," Petra confirmed my fear. "What is it?"

It was a quarto edition, dated 1597, of the play *The Tragedy of Arthur,* or, to be more accurate to the title page, *The Most Excellent and Tragical Historie of Arthur, King of Britain.* The same play that our family owned in its 1904 edition, given to my grandfather for his contributions to his Canadian high school's drama club. A play Dana read to me when I was a kid, but which otherwise I had never heard of or thought about. A Shakespeare play. His name was there on the title page.

Petra was staring at it, frightened to touch it, her face right next to it. "This is real? He has a real . . . ?" Her excitement now began to affect me in that overly dramatic basement. Her excitement burned through one layer of necessary doubt, because the obvious answer to "This is real? He has a real . . . ?" is "No. Of course not. Of course he doesn't." My father, of all people, a forger, owned and had kept hidden for decades a real 412-year-old document? No. Empirically disproven by everything I knew about him. Yet, that day, it was just me and Petra and an object that reflected her enthusiasm, inspired short-breathed excitement in her, and, as I wanted to inspire that, too, I didn't quite disbelieve. "Can we read it?" she asked.

Belief, credulity, confidence. When one looks back, belief resembles nothing so much as a virus, and only as you recover do you realize how fever-addled you were. My immune system was vulnerable as I stood in that bank vault. What had left me exposed? What had blinded me, left me like a certain talk-show host cooing at the moral power of an improbable memoirist, left me like Dutch art experts certain that Vermeer painted the van Meegerens, left me like all the Shakespeare scholars who daily add their names to the roll of endorsements for *The Tragedy of Arthur?*

I held on to at least a facsimile of healthy skepticism. "This is interesting." We agreed to pack it back up and take it to their apartment, to look it over and wait for my father's promised explanation by email. We were in this together, Petra and I; I felt that more than I felt anything else. We should go find Dana; I felt that second most of all. "Should we wear latex gloves or something when we touch it?" I asked.

"Oh, I have boxes and boxes of them at home," she said, smiling enigmatically, and I let her carry the **BANANAS** out of the bank, to the car.

She wasn't kidding about the gloves, as it turned out, which I found very funny, especially when she pretended to be too embarrassed to explain why she had them (something innocuous to do with cleaning a theremin, she finally confessed). We examined the play and then read it aloud, sitting and standing side by side, our heads together, our hands occasionally touching in their prophylactic latex.

A printed book from the 1500s is not immediately easy to read, even if you are not standing two inches away from a woman you are overwhelmingly attracted to. The type is wobbly and squished in places, faint then blotted. Spellings are strange, and they can vary even from page to page. In *Arthur*, for example, both "moue" and "moove" serve as "move." There are no *j*'s, and *u* and *v* are interchangeable. There are varieties of *s* we don't use anymore that look like *f*'s, and so forth. Acts and scenes are only sometimes numbered, and exits and entrances aren't always clear. Punctuation seems pretty random. There are mistakes and variations of characters' names in the speech headings. On two speeches the Master of the Hounds is inexplicably labeled "Kempe." You get used to it eventually. Petra and I did, together, over a long summer afternoon at her place.

We had to repeat certain sentences several times to grasp their meaning. We often stopped to look up words online. Petra frequently wanted to find a picture as well, to have a visual sense of the play's flowers, towns, rivers, apples.

The play was more or less what I recalled from thirty years before, when I was fifteen and had a broken nose and Dana read the whole thing to me to cheer me up. I could almost feel that odd movement of shifting threads in my fractured sinuses when Petra and I came to the scene where King Arthur rallies his troops for the first time.

"What is this thing?" Petra asked more than once during our reading. She also said, "Oh, I love that line" and "I can't believe we get to read this" and "Do you think Shakespeare ever touched this exact copy?" and "My God, he was so amazing" and "He was the best" and "I have goose bumps—*look!*" and "To read something new!" and I lost a breath as I recalled that we were coming closer and closer to a scene where Arthur kisses his new queen, and my desire and hope galloped far ahead of the main body, and my mouth went dry, and I prayed that Dana would not come home yet.

We had been at this for more than an hour, perhaps two, turning each page with the utmost care, the paper smooth and pale, the thread and glue that held the leaves together still intact but obviously stiff. We stopped to marvel at this wonder. "So is it yours? Did he give it to you?" she asked. "What does he want you to do with it? How does he have it?"

"I have no idea. Let's keep reading." I knew that the kiss was coming and, like a teenager, I imagined it would somehow transform everything if we could read it, like this, side by side, hunched over the booklet, taking turns being princes, kings, soldiers, dog trainers, shepherdesses, messengers. Our hands touched now and then, and if the play—if Shakespeare—told Petra to kiss me, I felt sure she would do it. Act III, Scene i:

> Soft, kiss me, Guen, half-close thy lovely eyne
> And in this wispen dawn of gold-flecked mist
> We catch our breath and hear the lark's first song.
> Soft, kiss me, Guen, and take this flowered crown
> And sit with me in shade and kiss me, Guen.

There were no stage directions. But she reached up and stroked my cheek with the latex-armored back of her hand, and I pressed my cheek against those twice-sheathed bones, certainly justifiable by the script, but my heartbeat betrayed a method actor's seriousness.

"She's waited so long for him," Petra said. "She's put up with all his wandering. It's a strange sort of love, isn't it? She's literally watched him with other women and she's ready to forgive him all of it."

"You don't believe him? He says he'll give it all up for her."

"I do believe him. I don't believe *her*. I think she just wants to be queen and she's taken the measure of him. She's playing him. She knows she has nothing to offer politically. The French ambassador is in the hall ready to offer up a princess with land and wealth. Guenhera has nothing comparable—she plays dumb about it, but that's pretty tongue-in-cheek. But she has something else: she offers up youth, doesn't she?"

"She's not that much younger than Arthur."

"Not her youth, *his* youth. She reminds him of being a boy in the woods, *playing* at being a king. Before the war, before the double crosses, the politics. She offers him a new childhood, and he leaps at it. Look at this: he can't propose fast enough. She plays his impulsiveness like a master. He could be drunk. He's about ready to marry France, and she has him in a few minutes, begging *her* to believe *his* sincerity—not just to sleep with her but to give her the crown. He's *begging*. Shakespeare in fifth gear—man, oh man."

This was the second time I'd had this play explained to me by a woman.

"I don't think so," I said. "He knows what she's up to. He's not a fool. He's just done with the past, or wants to be, and he wants to erase his mistakes, and she needs the same thing. It's not just a power play; she has a past—she only hints at her own errant behavior, but it's there. And any Elizabethan audience would know the versions of the Arthur story where she's an absolute ho-bag. She's made her own mistakes in love. She wants to feel clean and new again, and something happened to them, back when they were kids. Something happened to her that was like imprinting. It was instantaneous. It might not have made any sense, but that doesn't mean she can ever escape it. Look what she did to try to escape: she made herself watch him with other women. She roamed on her own. And she's lived as a spinster, for a time anyhow. But she knows there's only one way for her to go. Let's read that scene again. Back from the start."

But the door opened, and Maria jumped off the couch barking, and Dana came in talking: "Baby, you home? I nailed it, I so *nailed* it!" She came upon the two of us bent over the book, our gloved hands side by side. She had come from her callback audition for a production of *The Two Noble Kinsmen*, a late-career Shakespeare collaboration and, with its intimations of lesbian love, one of her favorites. She crossed to us, hugged me, kissed Petra, and then gasped as she saw the quarto's cover page. "What is— Oh, my God."

"It's Dad's. It's what he told me to pick up. I don't know what it is."

"Oh, my God. Oh, my God! *No*. How?" She was shaking as she took a pair of gloves from Petra, kissed her with an apology for having forgotten to do it earlier, even though she had, and Petra stroked the back of Dana's head. Dana put her face right down to the page and sniffed it deeply, twice, again, again. "It is, isn't it? Oh, my God. How does . . . ?"

She had visited Dad a month earlier, she said, and he hadn't mentioned it. What did I know about it? Nothing, I said; Dad promised an explanation to follow. I peeled off my gloves and collapsed, exhausted, onto their sofa, left her and Petra to surround the little book. I wanted her to deal with it. It was already much too much for me. I played up my ignorance, my incompetence, my Shakespeare indifference, and especially Dad's confusion. I told her to keep it safe and do whatever should be done with it. "Does it need some humidity-controlled chamber or something?"

She looked up, obviously unwillingly, and considered me awhile before she sacrificed herself: "No. No, no. He has some reason. It's not for me." She didn't seem hurt, though I don't know how she couldn't have been. But she insisted that without invitation or instruction from Dad, it was not hers to intrude. "I just want—oh, my God, I just want to read it and touch it. Is it any different than the 1904?"

"I would love to compose the music for a production," Petra said, her arm around Dana's shoulder.

"Oh, you'd make it sing. What does it sound like?"

"There is so much you could play with. There's Renaissance stuff, authentic to his layer, or you go darker, medieval or earlier, authentic to the setting, or you go *out there*, just bang away without a thought to the time . . ." She pulled off her gloves with her teeth and crossed the room to their upright piano, started in with a left hand somewhere between a Gregorian chant and a jazz walking bass line. Dana delicately lifted over the pages, found a favorite passage, and read aloud to the music that shifted tones and tonalities in response to her voice:

> By Mordred's holy seed might not we soon
> Implant a prince ourselves to hold our claim
> And with her womb prove Mordred's right to rule.
> Yes. Then will I obtain from England's lords,
> And vulgar tribune sorts who must be paid,
> Such love, subjection, dread that may be bought.
> Success made sure, I'll turn resistant thought
> To acting as a vengeful brother ought.

I loved them both, loved their love of the play, how quickly and instinctively they both leapt to play with it, to build on it, to breathe life back into it. It was obviously a Shakespeare play because these two women I loved so differently each loved it so much the same. I wanted to be part of it. I didn't know my part or how to play it, but a part was coming, and I imagined it somehow bringing us all together, me with Petra, and Dana satisfied to be our loving sister.

She came out of their bedroom with the red 1904 edition of *The Tragedy of Arthur* and started to compare the two texts. They weren't perfectly matched. They weren't so far apart as to be significant, but here and there a word was changed, a line was changed, even some sequences of four or six lines were in the 1597 quarto but weren't in the 1904 hardcover.

"It has Shakespeare's name on it," Dana kept saying. "I knew it. I did. I always knew it. Pet, Dad used to ask me if I thought it was Shakespeare, and I did, and now this has his name on it! This is so huge. I've never seen anything on this anywhere. Lost *Arthur* plays, you hear about, but this—*so* huge."

"It doesn't settle it," I said. "There were cases of printers using his name to sell books he hadn't written."

"It settles it for me," Dana announced.

She sighed and made me take it with me after dinner, packed it in its bag and case and canvas and crate. "I wish I could keep it," she said.

"So keep it."

"No. I can't. He wants you to do something with it. So. Please take it now and tell me as soon as you hear from him, please."

"Okay." I kissed her cheek.

"Bye, Arthur," Petra called from across the room.

27

THE NEXT DAY WAS EMAIL DAY at the big house, and I read my father's long letter on my laptop at the hotel. The job he had in mind for me was larger than anything I had fantasized, and my predominant emotion was pride—he wanted me and only me to do this for him, with him, because he loved me and my abilities. And we would be partners in something unprecedented, earthshaking.

That pride, in turn, triggered some guilt. He was trusting me, and I still sometimes felt I was partially to blame for his lengthy term, and that old daft desire to make everything right rushed through me. By helping him, I would fix what I could of all that I had broken.

And guilt, in turn, triggered resentment, the nibbling feeling that if I was going to help, then I was also owed, or would be rewarded by some universal system we wishfully call karma or God's bounty or whatever, but is really just the little child in us expecting a prize. And I thought of Petra.

And then came the scheming: this project would require me to stay in Minneapolis for quite a while. I shook that off, scolded myself, sent Dana and Petra my silent blessings.

DATE: Tue, 4 Aug 2009 15:05:02 -0600
You went to Bert? You found it OK.? It was there? You have it somewhere safe? So now you have seen it. Do you need to put your

finger in my wound? FIne. Do what you need to be sure. Be careful
with it Itis old. And it cannot be out of your sight with another
person. They cannot copy it. That is important. This is the most
important, No copies. It iss complicated. Do your worst. Be
skeptical. I am counting on you for that now too because I do not
have any doubts anymore and that is surely not helpful.
Microscope it or x-ray it or bombard it with lasers. I do not know
what they do nowadays. My residence here would imply that I never
really did. Ask experts to read it and judge the words and style. I
could recommend people for some of this, but you would not trust
them if I do, so do your way. When you are done you will know what
I already kno. Which means whatever you are doing now is a delay
for us, so go fast. But do what you need to do to believe. Catch up
with me. That is not fair, because I have a fifty year lead. But catch
up. And when we are together, and you know you are holding a play
written by William Shakespeare, then you and I will be partners,
though you, my son, will be the senior partner (not including
Shakespeare).

"The senior partner (not including Shakespeare)." That line
still affects me strangely. I feel it like one of these twinges in my
lower back that make me compensate immediately. The surge of
pleasure (then the parenthesis with a counteracting dose of resentment). I am his favorite (except for others). I am necessary to him
(though not as much as some). I am his writer (not including that
other guy).

When you are ready, we start. But motives, I suspect. You suspect. I
suspect you suspect my motives. O.K. that's O.K. You should, of
course you do, though I could wish you didnot. Or I could wish you
need not That I had not done all this to make you need no
suspicion of my motives. Or that despite all I had done, you would
recall that I NEVER DID IT TO YOU, never sought your unearned
confidence, or with your confidence filched a dime or a dime's
worth of prestige from anyone. So. Motives. The noise in this place

shatters concentration. I cannt keep a straight line. When I left you, I went and laid down. Someone was banging on his bunk up a few levels shouting "MARRY ME! MARRY ME!" Fine. Motives. Obviously money. I will explain when I see you next. When can you come again? No, I will write. Money obviously. There is a lot of money in this. But not for me. None for me. Arthur. I do not need money, and I wiill not be around to spend. Money for you. Dana. Your mother. Finally. And honorably gained! At last. What else? A gift to you. Fame for you. Your own writing is grand and you are rightly praised for it. And your name is crucial to our task. But this is a different magnitude and success in this gambit accrues to you (and Shakespeare).

(There it is again.)

You will be toasted for this! The proximity of your name next to his! You introduce this for him, and he then introduces you to millions of readers. You do him this favor and he owes you and repays you right away in spades. He lights the way and you can do whatever you want after this. You said publishing was in trouble. He will save it. And you.

I didn't understand what I was supposed to do. I didn't understand what it mattered if this quarto was real or what it proved, considering someone had published the play before—we had the 1904 edition, and my grandfather had acted in it in 1915. I was no expert in any of this and didn't keep up with the latest Shakespearean discoveries, but finding a copy of a play that everyone already knew about seemed pretty minor, though if it was a museum-quality relic, then I assumed it would be worth some thousands, perhaps. I may even have fantasized that it was worth $10,000 or $50,000. Still, why so excited, Dad? Perhaps that sounded like a million to 1987 ears.

I do not claim to be above idealism. Old men have privileges. We all get to say that everything is going to hell in a handbasket, but I

get to do something about it. He deserves this, doesnth'e? The
world will take pleasure in it. Think how many aggregate hours
of joy you will bring the world. Add up everyone who reads this,
who goes to see it. Theaters, classrooms, lecture halls, and
bookclubs. Courtship moments in campus bars, letters to reluctant
girls, boys quoting this play to make time. You will be responsible
for all that. And say what you want, but your books are not good for
that.

A touch, a palpable touch. I might also add now, considering my
own semesters of unhappiness choking on dry bits of Shakespeare,
that this aggregate of joy will not come without terrible cost to generations of schoolkids infinitely into the future.

You said you have no book in you right now. So the timing is swell.
Publish this. Tell the world it is his and it is good. Get it onstage.
Get a movie made in Hollywood. Movies! I could wish Olivier was
alive. Is Branagh? Schools. Write about it. Write footnotes. Explain
it in newspapers. Defend it. Get scholars onboard the ship. They
have computers now that can count his words, prove he wrote it,
what year, collaborators. Do all that. They will prove it is him and
his. And you know it, don't you, Arthur? Ask Dana. She knows. And
when you know it, when you're working hand in hand every day
with me (and him)

(Sigh)

youwill feel it in every line. I envy you! You will
be collaborating with him! Reading every line a hundred times.
Those lost words, puns, allusions. Follow his creative path. Help
everyone see how he worked his wonders. You will feel his
presence. I have felt it. He will be a friend who visits. You will
understand him as a fellow writer, as a peer. Read how he used his
sources. Read Holinshed. It is almost a straight lift of the Arthur
chapters in Holinshed. I envy you so much, my son! You are one of
the real creators! You have made people, worlds, plots. In so many

ways, you are more of a creator than he was. He adapted, expanded
other men's characters, puffing meaning into other men's flat
worlds. But you! You have made things from nothing and none but
your imagination. I am out of time. I will write in a week, but write
m e what you need from me. Always your loving father.

I floated along on the waves of his most excellent flattery for several hours, until I fell asleep, not even curious to open my **BANANAS**,
as I was without Dana and Petra's enthusiasm for them. Instead, I
nodded off thinking my father loved me and judged me more creative
than Shakespeare.

28

THE SWIRLING NONSENSE of his email finally woke me and, still in
bed, I called Dana.

"Is he mad at you about something?"

"Not that I know of."

"Then why is he asking me to prove this play? This is not my
thing. This is your thing."

"True, but he wants . . . I don't know. Read it to me again."

And I read the whole email to her again.

"Well, maybe he just wants you because he knows you're, you
know, far from him. Farther than me. He and I are sort of square. He
can give you this, you know, to say how he feels. It's a handshake."

"Oh."

"And he wants you to publish it," she said. "That's why you, too."

"But it was already published. What's changed?"

And so I went online and started looking for this play. There must
have been other copies, other editions, essays, some history of its
controversial standing. This was the first time in my life I'd ever
thought to look. I called Dana back.

"Why can't I buy another copy of the 1904 edition on eBay?" I
asked her.

"I have no idea."

"Why is there no reference to it on Google?"

"I have no idea."

"There's an apocryphal Merlin play and an Arthur play by Thomas Hughes. But there's no Shakespeare play about King Arthur. Not even a discredited one. Not a word."

"Uh-huh?"

"Why haven't you ever looked for it?"

"Because I already own it," she said. That made a certain sense. Having learned of the existence of this play in 1975, having had it read to me once in 1979, I never gave it another thought. Dana, having loved it since 1975 and owned it since 1977, never doubted its reality, never thought there was anything to do other than to love it. We rarely go looking for proof of the things we own and love; their existence is usually pretty evident. "When I was doing all my research," she said, referring to her years as an anti-Stratfordian, "it was pre-Internet. Mostly I just figured the play was lost, and lost things usually get more lost."

"But listen: we're post-Internet now, and it doesn't exist," I said. "Anywhere. Amazon, Alibris, Google, eBay. There's no such play. It doesn't exist."

"But it does. It exists in that crate in front of you," she said. "And in this book on my lap." I heard Petra chime in, revealing that I'd been on speaker the whole time: "And I read it with you yesterday, Arthur. That existed, didn't it?"

"No, seriously. Listen. This makes no sense, unless we admit the obvious."

"Which is?"

"Are you kidding?"

Here is the billion-dollar question, with boffo money for me and Random House and lawyers and academics and theaters and now a film studio hanging in the balance. How did I travel from August 2009, scenting "the obvious," to October 2009, when I signed a contract in all good faith with Random House in order to edit and publish (for the very first time) a previously unknown, undocumented play by William Shakespeare?

"Arthur, seriously?" said Dana. "He didn't. Look at it. Touch it. Smell it. *Read* it. He couldn't. He *didn't*."

29

I THANKED MY FATHER for his kind words, his trust in me, and I asked a few basic questions. They seem surprisingly polite now.

1) Where did you get this?
2) Since Dana has the red hardcover, why is this a big deal?
3) If it was published already, why can't I find it anywhere on earth except Dana's shelf?

And then I waited six days until he had email access again. He replied very briefly, just asked me to come in person. The next visiting day was three days later, August 14, and I pushed my rental car through the wall of mosquitoes that had descended onto the Minnesota prairie.

"Dad, what's going on? First you can't tell me in person, now you can't tell me on email."

We were back at the Formica of Infinite Gloom, but this time he was focused, intent. He leaned forward and made a visor with his hands, his middle fingertips meeting above his 3-D eyebrows. He whispered: "Answer me one thing first. You saw it. What do you think it is?"

"I have no idea. This really isn't my thing."

"Okay, fine. Okay." He wasn't angry, precisely, just frustrated and trying to hold that in check. "You doubt me. Okay. It's just . . . *time*."

He started talking. "In March of 1958, I traveled to England to do some work for a wealthy client. I went by ship. You can probably find the records, ship manifests or whatnot, prove it to yourself. Please do that. Please. Anyhow, my client, this fellow, he lived in a big country house."

"*What*? Come *on*. Who? What kind of work? What country house? Where was this? No offense, but this sounds total—"

"Stop. Just please. I'll get to all of it. I promise. You'll see. You can check *all* of it. Anybody can."

In March 1958, he traveled to England to do "some work for a wealthy client." This fellow lived in a big country house, even though since the war, he'd had to open it to tourists two days a week, to help pay for upkeep. On this vast estate, in his big manor (sketched once by Constable, Dad mentioned), he had one of those inherited libraries that the family had been adding to for centuries. My father in that library was a fat man at the Jolly Troll smorgasbord. "He had a Third Folio, second issue," among other treasures. "When I wasn't working, I was there. Gardens and grounds and horses were not my cup."

"Working. What work?"

My father had been asked to make a replica, "for insurance purposes, perfectly legal," of a small painting in the house's art collection. "I was doing a lot of that back then. My own stuff didn't sell, I don't know if you know, but. I had a good run at this sort of job for a while."

"What painting was it?"

"Stop. Will you stop? For a minute? I'll get to it."

It was a nice gig. He was resident at the great house for sixteen days. He worked six or seven hours a day, while the light was good. The rest of the time, he was something more than staff and something less than an honored guest. He slept in an extra room and was allowed unlimited access to the library in his non-painting hours. He explored every shelf. "I wasn't going to read the Shakespeare. I had read all of it, memorized half of it. I was looking for things I hadn't seen before. I read a ton there. There were things you couldn't get in those days, unless someone like this guy let you see his."

Alongside that 1664 Third Folio, on the Shakespeare shelf, were a dozen or more homemade anthologies. "This is pretty common," explained my father. Apparently, people used to buy those pamphlet-size quartos, and once they owned six or eight, they would have them stitched together according to whatever system they fancied, like a playlist, and then they'd have the assortment bound in a nice cover, "Morocco leather, maybe stamped *Seventeenth-Century Drama* or *Shakespeare Comedies*, which they then kept in the ancestral library."

They would handwrite a table of contents inside the front cover. "So this man, my client, had a couple long shelves of these homemades. Heaps of things to read."

"Do you need to wear latex gloves with that kind of book?"

"What? Of course not. Why?"

"Nothing. Go on."

So, one evening late in his stay, my father opens another of these books, and the handwritten table of contents on the inside front cover lists *The Taming of the Shrew, Sejanus, Every Man in His Humour, Much Ado About Nothing, Love's Labour's Lost, A Midsummer Night's Dream, Mucedorus.* "It was a very odd grouping, this one," he whispered to me conspiratorially, as if one mustn't let Minnesota corrections officers catch a whiff of such delights. His hands were still over his eyes, his elbows on the table, not so much to protect the privacy of our talk but to screen out distraction, and he told his story without losing track of his thoughts. "Very miscellaneous. Four Shakespeare comedies, two Ben Jonson plays, and an apocryphal thing." He'd never read the apocryphal thing, *Mucedorus*, so he asked his host if it would be a gross liberty to take the volume up to bed.

Permission granted, drowsy by lamplight, he flipped to the last play in the volume, but it wasn't *Mucedorus. Mucedorus* was second to last. It was the seventh play, as promised in the table of contents. But there weren't seven quartos stitched together. There were eight. The original anthologist ("the first Viscount Numbnuts") had neglected to inscribe the eighth title on the front board. The eighth play was a 1597 quarto my father had never heard of, credited to William Shakespeare.

"Shakespeare's name first appears on a title page in 1598," he said, no longer the confused senile prisoner of two weeks before. "This was completely unknown. I'd never heard of it. That was odd, to say the very least. I read it that night.

"So. Breakfast. I ask my client if he reads much Shakespeare. He's a boor. He doesn't read anything in his staggering library, any more than he knows anything about the artworks he's selling off to pay for his house. So I ask him: Does anybody in the family read the books? Is he going to sell them?"

"What was his name, Dad?"

And off my father went to the room given over to his work of "preserving the painting in duplicate." That night he considers the anthology again, locked in his little guest room, considers this *Arthur*. He reads the play again, and he believes the cover without a doubt. And he realizes that if it is real, it is a discovery of monumental proportions. "Anyone who knows Shakespeare would realize it was him, that this was absolutely his." Seeing a short distance into the future, he takes his nail scissors out of his toilet kit and trims the last quarto out of the book, lays it in the bottom of his suitcase, and the next morning makes a show of reshelving the violated volume in front of his much scorned host and employer.

"It came out very easily," he said. "It all came off very easily. And philosophically quite pleasant: its owner never saw it in the book, and it wasn't written in the table of contents, so the play can't really be said to be missing, because it was never really there."

He took it back home to Minneapolis, to Mom and their little prechild apartment in Dinkytown, smelling of oils and turpentine. "You told her?"

"No. I sat on it. It wasn't her passion in the same way it was mine. That's okay, that's how marriages are. And I didn't think of it as an object to *do* anything with. I just loved it. That's why I took it. I loved it and the limey didn't care. I loved it. I love it. And it was mine. I deserved it more than he did. Besides, it's not stealing if the owner—no, not even the right term, the *holder*—doesn't realize he owns it and then doesn't realize he doesn't own it. Nothing has been done to him. He has suffered no loss. There isn't even a word for what happened to him."

"Yes, there is. Stealing. That's stealing. It's a word. In English. Who was he?"

He smiled now, the first time, really smiled at me. "I'm not going to tell you, and I'll tell you why I'm not going to tell you. Because you'd give it back, wouldn't you? Or tell his heirs? You know you would. Besides, I was there helping him commit a crime."

"You just said it was perfectly legal."

"What *I* did was perfectly legal. What *he* then did with my work doesn't require a genius to figure out. But that's not the point. Please. I waited a long time to see if he ever noticed. It's been more than *fifty* years. He didn't notice because he never knew he had it in the first place. If he's alive, he won't be filing a claim if we proceed with this."

"Proceed? Am I supposed to fence your swag? I'm not going to—"

"No. *Please listen.*"

At first, my father just kept *The Tragedy of Arthur* to himself because he loved it, and because he wanted to find out if he was going to get caught. He read it and studied it and looked up all the words he didn't know and liked to touch it. "I was like those Japanese businessmen or gangsters who buy stolen art masterpieces and then keep them in their basement to look at all alone, naked." (A comparison that vaults right to the forefront of the normal mind.) "And that was enough for me. I was the *only* one. I liked that. Shakespeare and I were secret chums. We only met in secret. I like the idea that if there weren't many of these, then maybe he even touched this copy. He might have. At any rate, I was the only one reading it. Like he wrote it for me. I have to admit: his Arthur seemed familiar. I liked that, too."

And then, unclenching a little, suspecting he'd scooted away unnoticed, he started to do some research. He corresponded and spent time in the libraries, in downtown Minneapolis and over at the U of M. And he slowly let himself believe as a fact what had dawned on him as a strong possibility back in England: he had never heard of the play, despite his knowledge of Elizabethan literature, because there was not a single other copy. Nor—and this was somewhat troubling—were there any references to it, as there are to the famously lost plays *Cardenio* and *Love's Labour's Won.* "*Arthur* isn't in Meres, or the Stationers' Register, the repertory listings of the Chamberlain's Men, lists of court performances. What records we have of the theaters. Nobody mentions it. Not that I could ever find, but you might have more luck now. It would be *very* good if you could find a reference."

"There was that Errol Flynn performance. Dana still has the poster."

"What? No, come on. No, no, tell me you know I made that for her." It had never occurred to me. "No, nobody ever mentioned an Arthur play by Shakespeare."

"So it's fake."

"No. All I said was, nobody mentions it. That's true of some plays we know are his: no mention at all until they are collected in the First Folio, after he's dead. *Arthur*'s real, and we can guess *why* it's not mentioned, but that's another story." The story my father was struggling to deliver in a straight line (despite the babies, bells, and doors, despite my twitchy questions and surges of doubt in him, like gastric reflux) was about his realization. "But this one is not in the folios, obviously. When his friends compiled the complete works from their own marked-up scripts in the playhouse, they didn't include this."

"So it's a fake."

"No. Stop saying that. It's real. But for some reason, they didn't include it. Please let me talk."

"Sorry."

Instead he only fell silent and started to shake his head and bite his lips. He pressed the knuckles of his thumbs to his eyes and asked, "Where was I?"

"Not in the folios. Not a fake, but not in the folios."

"Yes. Not a fake, but not in the folios. Only one copy, no contemporary mentions, and not in the folios. Zero copies or four copies or what have you, but for there to be just *one* copy and for the play not to be in the folios: I owned the only *text*—"

"Stole the only text."

"Owned the only text, and the importance of this did not dawn on me for many years." (That was definitely a practiced line, and he sort of Gielguded it.)

He did some research with a lawyer with whom he'd once shared a cell, and with very hypothetical letters to Bert Thorn, back when he could afford his time. By the time my father finally understood the financial significance of owning the only text, he wasn't in a position to do anything about it, as he was in prison. This, as it turned out, was lucky, and why—I now believe—imprisonment was not always too troubling for him. It kept him from acting prematurely.

That day, over Formica, my father had his legal situation firmly in mind. "We have to prove not only that it's authentic, and that there isn't another copy, but that we have the right to own this, that we can treat the text as *ours*."

"But Shakespeare wrote it."

"Yes, but if there is only *one* copy, then whoever has it has the right to do with it as they please."

A few days after this conversation with my dad, I paid out of my own pocket for the opinion of a copyright lawyer in the United Kingdom, since questions of English eminent domain over the work of an English writer demanded an English solicitor. About two weeks later, the lawyer confirmed, with slightly more detail and legal terminology, what my father had discovered all those years before (see the next page).

That day in the Family Hall, my dad called it "a fountain of copyrights." You don't own the copyright on the play, but you are the only party permitted to license anything to be printed or produced *from* that copy. No one can copy those derived licensed works; you copyright *them*. Other people have to go to some other copy if they want to make a free copy. And there isn't any other copy.

"And no one is going to say we don't own this copy." He was now speaking very quietly and very slowly, in the limited-lip-motion monotone of a veteran co-conspirator. "You're going to say Silvius gave it to you, and that's all you know. He told you he found it in an attic in a house he owned. That's where the only copy of the *Titus Andronicus* quarto was: an attic in Sweden! An *attic*. Your stepfather found it in an attic. That's all you know. Doesn't matter, because now you own it because he gave it to you. Nobody else has one. Nobody else has the right to it. Not in England, though, Sil didn't find it in England, because maybe the Crown will claim it, and then we're out of luck. Ely. He owned a little house in Ely once. There are records of that. Your stepfather found this quarto in the attic of his house in Ely, Minnesota. In the 1950s, in a house your stepfather owned outright."

Mr. Arthur Phillips
c/o The Marquette Hotel
700 Marquette Avenue
Minneapolis, Minnesota
55402
United States

Strickland LLP
18 Wood Close
London E2 6ET

T +44 (0)20 7729 3760
F +44 (0)20 7729 3760
E info@strickland-law.co.uk

www.strickland-law.co.uk

29 August 2009.

Dear Mr. Phillips,

This is in reply to your letter of 18 August following on from our telephone conversation of the same day.

As I hope I made clear, such a hypothetical situation requires a somewhat vague reply. I do apologise if that is the case here, but perhaps with more information, we would be able to provide a more precise assessment.

Within the limitations of that caveat, if you come to possess a published document, and if more than 75 years has passed since the death of the document's author, then the document's contents have passed into the public domain. You do not own the copyright on the contents of the document. No one can. However, if, as you say, you were to possess the only existing copy of the document, then certain conditions pertain.

Under such a circumstance, the right to produce new editions of the document would rest solely with you. And, further, any edition which you authorise to publish of the document could be copyrighted by you. In effect, you would control and own all rights to the publication of editions of the document.

Certain limitation must be added. You may not exercise these rights without first undertaking a search to assure that no other parties may have a stronger claim to them. This includes heirs to the author, heirs to the original publisher, heirs to previous owners of the document itself. This is a long and costly process. Our office can be of some assistance in this.

Furthermore, if the original author of the document had been a British national, you face the possibility of the British crown determining that the document is of national interest. Under such circumstances, your ownership could be affected by the UK equivalent of what US law

(MORE)

Strickland LLP is authorised and regulated by the Solicitors Regulation Authority. Registered company no: OC343590. Registered office: 18 Wood Close London E2 6ET.

"And why didn't this alleged stepfather of mine do anything with it for fifty years?"

"You have no idea why. What's it to you? What's it to them? Keep it simple. Stick to the truth. Much easier to remember."

"But this isn't the truth."

"You're missing the point. No one is going to be able to say this isn't Shakespeare, because it is. *That's* the truth. It's got his name on it, the paper is authentic, the ink, all that. I've had it tested enough that I am sure. Fire photons at it, whatever you want—it's real. And I'm confident that there aren't any others in the world. If there are, we're out of luck. A second copy turns up, and then ours is just nifty, not without some value, of course, a museum piece, fascinating, but the only money—the real money—is in having the *only* copy. An oil well. A gusher. A field of gushers. That's what we have. What I'm giving you to manage for your mother and sister. And to make you famous as a writer."

As Mr. Piers Strickland later clarified on the phone when I told him what the document in question was: "Every edition. Every version for theater use. Every school copy. Every audiotape. Every children's illustrated edition with tear-out coloring pages in German or Swahili. Film. Film in Latvian. DVD sales in Malaysia." Strickland was unknowingly echoing my dad, whose eyes became younger as he explained the loot he was leaving his poor misused family: "William Shakespeare just signed over to you one hundred percent of his worldwide profits on his newest play. On a play the world will be endlessly curious to read, see, evaluate, interpret, debate. Even if they *hate* it."

"No, Dad, you're forgetting. I'm sorry to ruin this. It's not the only copy."

"What? Really? Someone . . ." He was as sickened and horrified as I'd ever seen him. His hands fell to the table.

"You gave Dana that 1904 edition."

And then he wheezed a little laughter and started to guffaw. "Jesus Christ, you almost gave me a stroke. No, no, I made that."

"What? Why?"

He brushed off my idiotic question. "Please. I couldn't walk around with a *quarto*. I couldn't read a quarto on the bus. I didn't want to damage it. If it was worth a hundred million dollars, I thought it was worth hiding. Are you . . ." He stopped himself before he asked if I was smart enough for this, I could tell. "I couldn't take it to the library to do research, you understand? To get opinions on it. You—more Dana, really—are the best readers. When Dana reads *Arthur*, she can tell it's the same writer. She knew right away. I wanted her opinion back when her eye was educated but still fresh."

Of all the questions I remembered to ask, I forgot to ask the ones that matter most to me personally, if not financially: Why did he forge the inscription to his own father from the drama club? And then inscribe it to himself from his father? And include that picture of his father, if that *is* a picture of his father, with its fake caption on the back? He gave Dana—with sincere love, I'm sure—a family heirloom going back generations that he'd made himself.

But I did ask this: "Why aren't you going to Dana on this? She loves Shakespeare. She still has that fresh eye, right?"

"You're the writer. And we'll have some fun, won't we? Aren't you having fun?"

"I kind of am, actually." I kind of was. "But why now?"

Because he'd had to wait. He'd had no choice. Patience—enforced by prison—had been necessary. He'd had to wait to see if other copies emerged, wait for shouts of "Thief!" to ring out from that country house. He'd also had to wait until he couldn't expect any personal profit from the venture, or the whole thing would be tainted by his record: "Boy-and-wolf problem. My career is ideally suited to make my word on this useless. 'Read all about it! Convicted forger discovers Shakespeare play!' I would sink him. And that would be an unforgivable tragedy. That would be a sin. Even if nobody makes any money, we have to do this for him."

"Novelist isn't much better than forger," I pointed out.

"It is better." He took a breath and started counting off things to do on his fingers, but he only got to one. "It's going to take time for copyright investigators. You have to do that. The guy I bunked with explained this, and Bert agreed. Prove no one else has any right to the text. Obviously, there's no line of Shakespeares anymore. The only serious claim would be the estates of William White or Cuthbert Burby"—the printer and publisher. "We have to prove they died out. You need a U.K. guy, I think. Then you win. You and your sister. And your mother."

"What about the guy in his country house?"

"I won't tell you who it was. Never. I don't trust you not to go to his house and give his grandkids your mother's oil well."

"Thank you, I think."

"It's not really a compliment, under the circumstances."

"So we're all accessories to your theft."

"Not accessories. There's nothing you could have done about it. Beneficiaries, yes. Accessories, no. And really, it's more like your father was some tycoon who outsmarted some people years ago to build his business, and now you're inheriting stock certificates. What are you going to do, go apologize to his early partners he bought out when the stock was cheap?"

"You didn't buy anyone out. You *stole* it."

"You're picking fly shit from pepper, Artie. And I never tried to score off Shakespeare. I don't want to. But I do want your mother and sister to get rich off him. And I want you to get famous off him. That's why you."

30

For two afternoons and nights, I sat with Dana and Petra and Maria in their apartment and reread the play aloud and tried to poke holes in it. I solemnly made Dana hold her hand to her heart and promise to read the play with a harsh, cynical eye, to play devil's advocate and viciously attack anything that didn't sound perfectly Shakespearean. We scribbled down any doubt we could muster: vocabulary that rang false, characters who seemed too modern, compositor's marks on the bottoms of the pages, the thread that stitched those pages together, anything. I was out of my league; I mostly sounded like a fool or a smartass: "Oh, come on, Shakespeare wouldn't do that, would he?" And then Dana or Petra would smile and cite some canonical play where he had done just that. "P-L-A-I-D-E?" I bleated, pointing at the cover. "Dad's pulling our leg, right?" They went online and found legitimate quarto covers with just that spelling of *played*.

The problem was harder than I'd expected. I had thought that with some effort, the play might crack under pressure, like a frightened suspect. But even our strongest doubts were very abstract. Petra thought time passed strangely in Acts III and IV, that it seemed too much like montage in a film. She couldn't think of any Elizabethan play with the same structure. In I.iv, Arthur is explicitly seventeen. In III.i, he recalls his adolescence as if it were a long time ago. By III.ii, several more months have passed, and at least nine more between III.ii and III.iii. Several more months pass before IV.i, and so on. By IV.iv, Arthur must be at least about twenty-six, since he might have a twelve-year-old son, or at least be able to pretend so for political purposes.

"Yes, but no," Dana argued, reasonably enough after all that wine. Maria slept on her lap, pointed outward toward her knees, and Dana smoothed his ears over her thighs. "He did all kinds of strange things with time. Hardly ever did the same thing twice. He was always trying to break up the unity. Time in *Hamlet*. It's like the theory of relativity: a day or two seems to pass in Elsinore, but ships have gone all the way to England and back. *Henry VI, Part Three* is totally wacky. And in *Part One:* the historical king was actually an infant in those first scenes, but he seems to be at least a teenager. Years pass in *Pericles*. *Winter's Tale* has a sixteen-year jump. He might have been trying something new here, way ahead of its time. Time-lapse or montage before the term. Maybe that's why the play didn't stick; maybe it made the audience feel queasy."

In other words, things that *weren't* like Shakespeare simply expanded the possible range of his innovations. If I was having a paranoid reaction, looking for signs of forgery where there weren't any, Dana was having an opposite response, taking any oddity as proof that it must be authentic. If, for whatever reason, you choose to read the play, I am certain the same thing will happen to you: If you think it's him, it sounds like him. If you think it's not, it doesn't.

"Does Arthur even seem like a Shakespeare character at all?" I asked when I hit that exhaustion common to circular debates. By then I was lying on the carpet in the middle of the room, and Maria had migrated to sleep on my chest, his nose pressed against mine. "Why does he do what he does? Is it how Shakespeare characters think?"

Dana was on the other side of the bar in the kitchen, opening wine. "He's actually a fool," she said as I was looking over Maria's snout at the way Petra's legs pressed against each other, folded under her on the couch. "He goes further than any of Shakespeare's other kings. He questions his *own* legitimacy. He doubts his own fitness to rule. He's really one of the fools, you know? He has that dangerous, licensed skepticism, but he's dropped the cap and bells and carried that doubt all the way up onto the throne. To question kingship while you're wearing the crown? The king himself doesn't even believe in kingship? That's a risky thing to put onstage." Dana was tireless. She refilled our wine and turned the pages carefully back to Arthur's remarkable soliloquy and read aloud:

> "I know I have no right to wear this crown.
> I'll contradict no pope who calls me king,
> But in this privy council kings speak troth:
> No right have I, no higher claim than Loth.
> A bastard, I, from bloody tyrant sire.

"*That* is not the same as the Harry-in-the-night stuff from *Henry V.* That's him saying he's *not* God's chosen, and maybe *no one* is. *That* would make an audience queasy, or the Master of the Revels. And get a writer in some hot water, I would think. And be the end of a play: no more editions, no folio."

She had a point and a semi-explanation for the play's disappearance. From King John to Henry VIII and every king in between, Shakespeare's audiences watched one after another variety of human and incompetent monarch walk in front of them and reveal his inner failings. Shakespeare let people see their kings as men, fallible, far enough from divine right that they should submit to man's law. If

Arthur was Shakespeare's, then they saw this king go so far as to admit he was nothing special. It's amazing the English managed to hold off from executing a real king of their own until 1649. (To this day, theater can still do that, provoke rebellion in subjects or phobia of rebellion in authorities. I was in a comedy revue in college that in one performance was particularly disrespectful to the administration. We were then blamed when some drunk took a dump in a dormitory elevator later that night, just as Shakespeare's company was blamed for a coup attempt after putting on a play about a coup.)

"So?" Petra poked my side with her toe. "What are you going to do?" Dana was in the bathroom.

"What do you think I should do?"

"Me? Well, I think Shakespeare wrote it." She ran her bare feet over Maria's back, one beagle-thickness above my chest.

"Me, too." I put my hands on her feet, held them on the dog.

"So there you go." She smiled and held my eye.

There you go: accepting the play, believing in my father, and her feet and eyes not pulling away. *Arthur*, my father, and Petra: all three of them became credible at the same instant. Can you reset history, go back to where things broke down and "*begin anew upon our proper path*"? So that the decades that followed would change their essence, shed tragedy to become softly sentimental comedy?

31

Date: Tue, 25 Aug 2009 14:23:52 -0600

What news, plaese. Have you had results yet? Are you there yet? I know you lack trust in me. Why would you trust me on any of this? As likely a candidate as ever there was to tiptoe into the Fakespeare bog and claim his finery as my own. Too true, your honor, dead to rights. I could die laughing if after all the abuse I have taken at the hands of others I could put one over on the world like that. To die with them worshipping me as Shakespeare! I will not deny the appeal, Arthur. You would not believe me if I tried to deny it. But I could not make it happen. I could never—infinite typewriters, infinite monkeys, infinite time. I could never write anything as beautiful as this play. I am a faker, in every way. But I never could fake anything of real quality. You said that once to me: a coupon faker is all I am, right?

Methinks this bleak protestation should have given me a lot more pause than it did, but I brushed it off as a guilt-mongering straw man. I had never once thought my father *wrote* the play; I had at most only suspected he'd forged the relic from some other text, forged Shakespeare's participation, found some play by someone lesser, like Thomas Dekker, fiddled with the cover page, at most.

Can you just trust me? Can you just know?

Thus asks the man who forged crop circles with me when I was ten and then blamed his arrest on me.

No, I know you can't.

Thus answers the man in his easy dialogue with my likely thoughts.

But now is the time this is going to happen. Because now is the time that you are a famous writer. Now is the time you and your mother and your sister all need money, and I can give it to you. And now is when I am dying.

Those seven words struck me physically, with far more impact than anything Shakespeare ever wrote (or anything I ever wrote), and in the windless moment before I felt the heat in my neck and face condense into my eyes, I knew I had lost so much of him, wasted so much of him and of everything, and that I would do anything to make it right and to hold tight to every love and opportunity and moment that remained in his life and in mine.

And so now you have to pick up the tempo.

I went directly to Dana's. I had to be with her, be the one to tell her. I went without calling, for fear of breaking the news over the phone. She wasn't home; I had forgotten she was at rehearsal for *The Two Noble Kinsmen*. Forgotten: that's what it seemed at the time. Surely I didn't forget. Is such mechanical self-delusion possible? Well, let us consider that the first person I told of my father's terminal illness, the first person who comforted me in my shock and sorrow and regrets and resolution, was not my mother, wife, or twin but Petra, a semi-stranger with whom I was infatuated, who was there, alone, when I arrived, and if this was not a multitiered betrayal, I do not know what else to call it. Petra learned of Dana's father's doom before Dana did. I meant no betrayal; I followed my feelings, the dictatorial and ever-sacred feelings.

I wept for Petra, with Petra, on Petra's golden hands. I apologized for all of it, and she brushed away my apologies as irrelevant, relics of a different kind of relationship than we now had, and she kissed my brow. "You love him, despite everything," she said, using up words and gestures and caresses that her girlfriend would need from her in a few hours. She would have to forge facsimiles then, as I was stealing the originals. And she seemed original to me in every way, even in her sympathy: "You love him, despite everything." The words are commonplace, but she seemed like an oracle extracting hidden truths from my clotted veins, reading the world to me. "Yes," I agreed, amazed, "that's exactly it. I do," and I laid my head on her lap and she stroked my hair.

I spoke with Jana a few hours later, told her I would be staying longer in Minneapolis for work and because of my father's failing health. She had seen my father's effect on me for years, and she said, "You love your father, don't you? Still. Even with all of your lives and what he has done." It wasn't the same when she said it.

32

M Y CAREER. Yes, after four novels in quick succession, I knew I was doomed to slouch in my study in Prague, if I still had a study there, in an apartment paid for by the novel of the same name, decorated with souvenirs of my publicity and publications. I was going to gaze, glazed, at a blank page until, dispirited, I would stare at a screen rendition of a blank page instead. My father had sensed how starved for inspiration I was. "You're between books," he'd said innocently. And for that reason, too, the *Arthur* project fell like rain onto a dying land.

I have never been strong at getting things done. Decisiveness and action are not my traits. I stumble into situations and then notice I like them well enough not to resist (so I take pleasure in creating characters who are my opposite, men of adventure and certainty). But now I began in earnest, fighting for my father's life. I devolved into a sweaty, sparsely whiskered graduate student, eating strangely. I read the play at least twenty more times, making lists of vocabulary and grammar, noting references to research, labeling files: SOURCES, STYLE, STRUCTURE, DICTION. I read the pertinent bits of Holinshed's *Chronicles* and Malory's *Morte d'Arthur*. I read the RSC *Complete Works*, sitting on a bench in the park with my sister's beagle at my side. I read Shakespeare biographies and analyses (Shapiro, Bate, Tanner, Bryson, Greenblatt, Wood, Garber, Bloom, Vendler), books and articles on Shakespearean language (Crystal) and computer stylometry (Elliott and Valenza), Jacobethan theatrical practice (Joseph and Verre), Shakespearean forgeries (Ireland), and books about those apocryphal plays that haven't made the official roster (Tucker Brooke). It is a measure of my fever—money-hungry, lust-breathing, fame-thirsty, guilt-fueled, daddy-pleasing—that I enjoyed all of it. I let Dana guide my education, spending much of my time at her apartment or in her theater's greenroom, waiting for her to come out of rehearsal, seeing Petra often, but trying to give myself fully to my father's project, to become the world's most devoted and loving son for his dying months, proving that I meant no dishonor with Petra (and that I therefore deserved to have her).

I had my entertainment lawyer draft nondisclosure agreements, and I sent teasing letters to scholars at local universities, often the very men and women whose books and articles I'd been studying, tempting them with "a remarkable, once-in-a-century opportunity in Shakespeare studies."

I finally began clumsily editing the play, transcribing it onto my Mac, counting out ten syllables per line, one slow syllable at a time, modernizing and standardizing the spellings, checking the online *Oxford English Dictionary*, footnoting, numbering the lines and acts, double-checking the entrances and exits, adding stage directions implicit in the text.

I no longer doubted what I was doing, and for a writer of fiction, that is a rare feeling, worth clinging to. I was doing something important to my family, to my father, and to the world. I was—though it appeared I was just pushing words around, as always—taking *action*, taking sides, standing up in the real world, coming out from behind the hiding places of fiction. I paid calls! I interviewed relevant experts and sought out their opinions! I hired people! I Googled until my keyboard keys were scuffed! I wondered what Petra was thinking of me.

"What is this thing?" I scribbled in my journal. "Is *TTOA* like we've discovered a previously unknown pyramid in Egypt? Or is it like we've just noticed the glass pyramid in front of the Louvre? Or is it like a Great Pyramid attached to a Vegas casino, complete with blond pharaonic parking valets who are all like, 'Nice drive, man, sweet'?"

I liked the work. I liked the play. I liked the writers and professors and lawyers. I liked everyone and felt happy when discoveries went our way (Dad's, Will's, and mine) and unexpected corroborations slotted into place, such as the day I visited my first real Shakespearean in person, Tom Clayton, the University of Minnesota's Shakespeare man.

His office was lined with books, like a lawyer's, as if the Internet didn't exist. "Let's look at 1597 then," he said after I explained my case and he had cast a nonchalant eye at my quarto, which I wouldn't yet allow him to open. "King Arthur? Well, here's the first thing we look at." He pulled down two books: *Annals of English Drama*, an index to every contemporary mention of any play in the Elizabethan world, and the reproduced diaries of Philip Henslowe, manager of the Admiral's Men, rivals to Shakespeare's company, the Chamberlain's Men. "So there was an Arthur play by Thomas Hughes, a Gray's Inn play, that's in 1588. Makes sense: Shakespeare probably arrives in London about then. Might very well have seen *The Misfortunes of Arthur*. He tended to absorb things he saw, often for a few years. He might have seen that Hughes play, then written one of his own eight or nine years on. Then there's *The Birth of Merlin*, Rowley in 1622. They used to try to say it was Shakespeare, but that's discredited. And . . ." He turned to Henslowe's diary. "There. Look at that. That's good." He slid it across to me. "Henslowe's group put on a play called *Uther Pendragon* in 1597, and then here, in April of '98, he paid Richard Hathway five pounds for an 'Arthur play, now lost.'" He tapped his finger on the entry for me.

"That's my play?"

Professor Clayton looked at me as at a not very bright child and spoke slowly, in case I had a disorder he hadn't noticed at first. "No. Your play says it's by William Shakespeare and was performed by Shakespeare's troupe, the Chamberlain's Men. This is a different play, by Hathway, to be performed by the Admiral's Men. The year after your play. You see? That's what they would do. They were rivals. Admiral's Men do *Uther* in '97 and buy an *Arthur* in '98, it makes sense that the Chamberlain's Men had an Arthur play right around '97. And that it would be written by one of their playwrights: Shakespeare."

"So it's real?"

"I have no idea. May I read it?"

I loved the notion of Shakespeare as a man, a working writer given a topic and a deadline because the other guys—literally across the street—had a successful Arthur play. As a matter of honesty to the record, I have to include the following email, playing no favorites. It cannot be excluded without distorting this whole story:

"Dad," wrote the boy not even wise enough to be a fool,

I am having an amazing experience, a peak of my life, truly. Thank you. I have to admit to a sort of astonishment. I feel like I am getting to know him as a peer, as a friend, as a guy whose path I cross now and then at the theater or the pub. Watching him work—following his thinking from Holinshed to the play. Sensing what was on his mind as a writer—seeing how *Arthur* leaks over from the other plays at the time, how it seems like a first stab at plays that came later. Do you see seeds of *Hamlet* and *Henry V* in *Arthur*? I think I do sometimes, in the shape of the soliloquies. He's moved way past *Edward III*, but he's not at *Hamlet* yet, but he's figuring out how to write something more introspective than *Richard III*, for example. Dana has been amazing, helping me think all this out. You know I've never really been there with you and her on Shakespeare, but I'm catching up, and I've never felt happier with work than I do now. It's not even my own stuff, but I feel better, closer at times to this than I have even to my own books.

I dined almost every evening at Dana and Petra's, often without Dana as her rehearsals went later into the night in the weeks leading up to her opening. Petra cooked, without recipes but with inherited mastery, every bite an act of love dusted with fennel powder. Maria, groaning for scraps, would drape his head on my feet as I ate, trying to camouflage himself as my napkin or the rug. When she was there, Dana practiced her lines; as rehearsals progressed, she was living more closely to her role as Emilia, an unmarried girl. It was a remarkable testament to Dana's talent and beauty that at age forty-five she'd been cast in such a part. Petra ran lines with her: "*You shall never love any that's called man.*" "*I am sure I shall not,*" Dana answered. "*I / And she I sigh and spoke of were things innocent, / Loved for we did, and like the elements / That know not what nor why, yet do effect / Rare issues by their operance, our souls / Did so to one another. What she liked / Was then of me approved, what not, condemned . . .*" I ate, a gender-bent beagle's snout snuffling for crumbs in my crotch, and my twin sister took her girl-friend's hand and pressed it to her lips, and Petra looked across the table to me with an expression I took as embarrassment, confusion, encouragement, even apology.

In *Twelfth Night*, after all, a woman falls in love first with a female twin dressed as a man and then, when she meets the male twin, she has no trouble at all instantly transferring all that love to the man. I could almost see Dana wooing Petra on my behalf, preparing her for me by being her own open, lovable self, the better version of me that I would then become by the force of Petra's transferred love.

For this imagined Petra (unlike 99 percent of the world), romantic love would somehow be prior to gender. Identity, the lovable essence, would exist separate from gender. She would not be *indifferent* to gen-der (as I hoped she would love my male body), but she would love my gender only because it was subsequently revealed to be attached to my sexless but romantically lovable personality. (Neuroscience has proven this, what Shakespeare described in *Twelfth Night*: the bit of brain that sparkles with lust is near but not identical to the bit that identifies the sex of others. They can, on rare occasions, operate en-tirely independently, lust without gender, love without gender, just souls finding each other.)

When we were sixteen or seventeen, Dana and I were walking along Hennepin. This was a spring evening, warm and light, so May or June. I can't quite place the year, but I have a staticky notion that we were on our way to see a movie at the Uptown. I was complaining about a girl, though I can't specify which, and I clearly remember Dana saying, "She may be out of reach, killer." I know, too, that I had recently read a novel, I think by Graham Greene, though I can't re-member which, but I am sure the book had taken hold of me in the way adult novels can overpower a young reader's own identity and shape him.

We were walking through the darkening air, and the streetlights were buzzing on, one at a time. On the sidewalk in front of us we saw a sparrow. It was injured. It did nothing to escape our approach. One of its legs dangled uselessly. When I knelt down, it tried to hobble

away but I picked it up. I was surprised and a little uneasy at how fragile it seemed. There was blood on one of its wings and on its chest.
There could be no nursing it back to health.

"Oh, we have to help it," Dana sighed.

"I will," I said, feeling her pity for the bird as pressure to prove my
hard fitness for life and adulthood. I had to channel humane feeling
into realistic manly action. "There were things a man had to be able
to do," I thought, likely misquoting the character from the possibly
Graham Greene novel. In the book, the protagonist comes upon a
wounded pigeon while walking in a London park with a woman he
means to impress, and then shyly, almost embarrassed, he rapidly,
manfully, mercifully twists the bird's neck and drops it into the rub-
bish bin so the woman doesn't have to see the creature suffer. He
knew precisely how to protect her and end the animal's pain.

I, on the other hand, was probably not very calm, never having
done this before, as well as being overexcited at this chance to prove
myself. I had never even touched a bird before this fateful moment.
We walked from streetlight to streetlight, Dana repeating, "Oh, oh,
the poor little thing," and me trying to turn my back on her near a
garbage can so she wouldn't witness the simple, necessary act, although I can no longer fathom why I thought Dana would need protecting from it. I petted the bird and jogged ahead to the trash can on
the corner, green and ribbed, with a black liner bag and painted with
the words CITY OF LAKES. "What are you doing?" I heard her call.
"There's a . . ."

I hurried to do it. I twisted the little bird's head, waiting for a quiet
crack and quick, grateful immobility. Instead, it emitted a tiny squeak:
I was only hurting it, perhaps merely annoying it, and in *my* alarm
and panic that Dana would witness this secret ritual of kind men,
worried that I couldn't do what I had to do and what Dana needed me
to do (whether she realized it or not), I then wrenched the bird's head
so hard that I tore its body nearly in half.

I held its head and much of a wing in one red hand. In the other
clenched fist, shivering with adrenaline, was the organ-bunched
breast, the other wing, the bubbling interior, the tendons and straw
bones connecting the bird's still-trussed halves. My hands and shirt

were sprinkled with blood and clots of stuffing, and I looked down and watched the bird finally, but by no means instantly or gratefully, die.

I pushed it all away from me into the trash, wadded some waiting newspaper over the body, smeared my hands on my jeans, and turned to Dana, whose face reflected my severe distress.

"You looked like a serial killer," Dana said when I recounted this story over one of Petra's flaky, honeyed desserts.

"It was not my finest moment."

"Tell her what I was going to say, psycho, before you freaked on that bird."

"Yeah, it gets worse. Dana stood there looking at me. And then she said she'd been trying to tell me that there was a vet still open on Lake Street."

"And then you burst into tears," Dana added, finishing the old story.

"And then I burst into tears, and Dana hugged me."

"And I got sparrow guts all over my Suburbs T-shirt."

"Oh, my God, you two must have been so *cute*," Petra said, pinching both our cheeks.

33

MY AGENT AND I made our brief, understated pitch to a roomful of people at Random House in New York, and more people were called in as we proceeded, each one signing nondisclosure documents as the price of admission. The publisher and the corporate counsel stayed in the meeting throughout.

To say the least, this was not the manner in which my previous contracts had been negotiated. My father was right: Shakespeare was holding doors for me that I could not open myself. The next ten minutes were unique in my agent's experience. We were asked to stay in the room with water and fruit while everyone else left. Jennifer Hershey (my usual editor), the publisher, and the lawyer returned with a preempt offer eight minutes later.

I had presented the quarto along with the tentative reports of those few local Minneapolis professors I had consulted and a list of other professors around the country who were eager to be advisers and authenticators. I would be paid a very small fee pending the authentication process. Assuming that verification proved my claims, then the prepublication advance would be larger by multiples than any in my career, larger in fact than the total of my entire career, more than any sum my agent had ever negotiated in *her* career, and that advance still represents only a fraction of what everyone expects to happen next.

Random House would take over the Hydra-headed chore of authentication, collating reviews from Shakespeare scholars and from forensic tests of the document itself, though one of my terms (as Dad had coached me) was that the play would remain in my constant possession, with all testing done in my presence, in Minneapolis or elsewhere. ("All Arthur's expenses paid first class if he has to travel for any testing," Marly Rusoff, my agent, noted as if that were a mere formality, and everyone nodded as if that were a mere formality.) All examiners of the play would be required to study it in controlled conditions where copying would be impossible and only after being bound by bloodcurdling nondisclosure agreements. Random House legal would offer any assistance they could to my U.K. copyright attorney to accelerate the clearance of my right to assert ownership of the text.

Jennifer Hershey, the editor, cleared her throat and very tactfully, very sweetly said that they certainly wished to spare me any work I didn't "feel like doing." This included the editing, annotation, and Introduction. I didn't have to put my name on any of it, if I wanted to "get back to your next novel, which we're all really looking forward to." We weren't here to talk about *me*, plainly. I was free to go prepare some kind of high-tension financial instrument that could catch and contain the tsunami of royalties rolling my way.

But I refused to yield to my senior partner. I spoke with unpracticed and sincere eloquence. This was my family's project. And I loved it. It mattered to my family and to me that our name be represented in the process and in the publication. It had to be that way.

Everyone happily nodded. Jennifer asked again, just to be sure I understood what kind of workload I'd be taking on, if I was certain I didn't want to hand off the editorial tasks to an acknowledged Shakespeare scholar? I did not. "I would rather not publish with a house that didn't trust me to handle this responsibility." Silence.

"Fantastic then." Someone new chimed in that they liked "the publicity story line," but I could see them regrouping to attack again on this point later.

As the authentication process achieved "agreed-upon benchmarks of physical and textual authenticity," I would be fed larger slices of my advance. In the meantime, Random House would manage all publicity and marketing, including the cover design and any supplementary material in the final edition. I would write an Introduction, which, I insisted (based on their obvious unwillingness to let me do the job at all), could not be abridged or altered without my consent. They inhaled, smiled, agreed. The Introduction would include a synopsis, a presentation of general historical context, and an essay outlining the evidence for the play's authenticity. I would also oversee, with Jennifer, any other necessary work preparing the play for a "general audience." I would give talks and publicity interviews as needed after publication. I also sold them the license to produce at a later date a paperback for theater use and to co-publish with the university of their choice an academic edition, with essays by eminent professors.

The house's publicity machine was ignited. Jynne Martin, my usual publicist—and an award-winning poet in her own right, since, in this century, poets cannot rely on earls for their patronage—was excited on behalf of both her expertises and began mapping out how much to leak and when. In this dark era of a publishing industry out of joint, with omens of our destruction lighting up the night sky all around us, Shakespeare was galloping to the rescue, a man who'd cared almost nothing for the publication of his own works during his life. He would save our belief in ourselves as literate people.

My contract was drawn up faster than any Marly had seen in thirty years in New York publishing, and conciliatory replies to her clausal quibbles were softly sighed by Random House legal in hours, not days.

Simultaneously, she opened similarly fruitful and nondisclosable negotiations with theater producers in London and New York, and with Hollywood studios. The results of those conversations are even now being rehearsed, financed, scheduled, scouted, shot.

I flew home to my sister waiting for me (alone) outside baggage claim. It was Dad's release date, and Dana and I drove together to pluck him from prison.

34

I RENTED MY FATHER A FURNISHED one-bedroom apartment with floor-to-ceiling glass looking out over Lake Calhoun and the channel to Lake of the Isles, a place found for me by the novelist Robert Alexander, with whom I share an agent. These were my father's first moments inside a building other than a prison or a hospital since 1987. Sailboats bobbed semi-inflated on the lake, and the slim wave crests were beginning to turn green and gold under the settling sun. He was sitting on a couch for the first time in twenty-two years. He wasn't saying much, nor was I, other than obsessively offering him things. But he was more interested in the fine details of the world, an ancient infant. He would pick up throw pillows, squeeze them and laugh, then rise and walk to the window, press his hands against its warm glass. He made me recount and re-recount the meetings with the professors, the publishers, the details of our good fortune in the wilds of Manhattan. And I asked him why he thought the play had disappeared from history until he came upon it in that unmentionable country house.

"You didn't tell them that, did you?"

"Of course not. Silvius's attic."

"Good. Good."

"So what happened to *Arthur* all those years?" I asked with the most tenderness I had felt for him in decades, my hand on his dying back as he watched the boats like a little boy.

"It's a natural question, Artie, but it's the wrong question. No one can prove what happened. I can suggest a possibility that hasn't yet been disproven. I know people will want answers, but the question is unreasonable: Where did this come from? What happened four hundred years ago that nobody wrote down?"

No, that reads too polished, coherent. He couldn't talk like that last year. That was the gist of his answer, but it was not so smoothly spoken.

"People are going to want to know," I said, pushing back, because I needed an answer for my Introduction, not because I had any doubt of my own.

But he said: "Stay calm about this." *That*, he definitely said, and I laughed. I had asked as an interested believer, but he answered me as the chief of a criminal enterprise who has to talk down a jittery confederate, just when everything's coming together so perfectly. "We don't have to know everything. We can openly admit what we don't know. What we may never know. It in no way reduces the wonder that is *Arthur* to say we don't know where or how many times it was staged—diverse times, according to the cover. We don't have to know how many copies were printed, or where the rest of them are. The cover says 'corrected and augmented.' That means there was probably an earlier printed version, an unauthorized bad quarto. But we don't know. We don't know and we don't have to know if it was censored or banned or ignored. We know as little about some canonical plays. Remember: most things didn't survive at all. There was probably more Shakespeare lost than we know. Most things don't survive. This is what passing time means, Artie." I remember those very words, and as he mumbled them he turned to watch the lake, and I felt at that moment—as I did several times in flashes over the coming month—a pity so profound that I would have (were he a sparrow) gladly torn him in half to end his scalding regret.

He turned to me and asked permission to look in the fridge.

"It's yours." I smiled with loving condescension. "You don't have to ask. Dana and Petra filled it for you."

He drank a Diet Coke, *extremely* frustrated (and knowing his frustration was ridiculous) that Tab could no longer be had. "I was really looking forward to that. I've missed it." He smiled at me and nodded several times as he drank, and I assumed it was love and relief, excitement for our project, and I'm sure it was all that, although eventually he asked, "What were we talking about?"

"What happened to *Arthur* between 1597 and the country house?"

"You didn't tell them about the country house, did you?" he asked, again for the first time.

"No. Trust me. Attic."

I took notes, the basis for an essay on this topic, an essay I am contractually bound to place in this Introduction, but which I can no longer honestly write. That was a different time. So now, to fulfill my terms, I offer my sincere notes of September 30, 2009, still preserved in the amber of my abbreviations, unedited. Contract fulfilled:

> Try theories that work with little we know. Dad: 1597 makes sense, but maybe not for composition. Written earlier? "Corrected and augmented" implies yes. Also, early WS: iambic pentameter rigorous throughout. Later WS bends it, stops midline, wraps around lines. This is early. Comp stylometry will confirm. Prob/possib perf'd earlier in decade, maybe even before plague closed theaters '93–'94. Then perf'd again, later, does well enough 4 Burby 2 think he can make $$$ publishing → prints in '97.
>
> Other evidence "squishier." Theme: WS often stuck w/idea from 1 play to next, tried diff. angles. Explored fully before moving on. John, Richard 2, and both Henry 4, all between '95 and '98. All look at king's fitness to rule. All variations on theme, four men (inc Prince Hal in H4), each with diff. ability diff. vocation, legit'acy, rel'ship to legit: desperate, arrogant, worried, cynical. Arthur fits perfect: slightly diff. from those 4, but absolutely of family, maybe 1st try at this, right after H6 and R3. New angle on WS's preoccupation: What makes good king? Who should be king? What happens when king unsuited, or wishes didn't have to be king? Arthur = Hal's opposite, at least

when Hal becomes H5. Arthur can't become Henry V. Arthur never becomes hero, try & try. Too flawed, stained by birth. Idea WS can only safely explore 1,100 years in past.

Squishier: people like to look for WS autobiog. in plays. Total squishy, but here: WS's son dies in '96. Maybe it's in TTOA. Dad feels it. "Feels something." TTOA "manifestly about lost fatherhoods & lost childhoods." Written by a father? Definitely. By a father who lost a child? Very poss. So: writ in '96, perf'd that year or next, pub'd in '97? Maybe.

Seems to Dad to fit between H6/R3 on one side and R2/H4 on other.

No record of perf's, but not damning. No record 2 Noble Kinsmen and others ever perf'd in WS's life. Likely just not recorded. Cover probab. tells truth: "played diverse times." Maybe at Court—no records for Eliz's reign, don't know every single 1 of 100s of plays at Curtain, Theater, Inns, Stewington (?), etc.

Arthur is 1st x WS on cover page.'98 Love's Labour's Lost now 2nd x. So WS name popular enuf 2 sell plays by '97. But TTOA never printed again and excl'd from Folios, even 2nd and 3rd Folios. So. Have to try best guess 4 Y. Y?

Dad's speculate 1: play about sterile queen—bad idea w/60+ y.o. QE1.

Dad spec 2: answer is here, timing explains: 1598: George Nickleson (sp?), Queen's agent in Edinburgh sends letter to Lord Burly (sp?), Lord High Treasurer/adviser, complaining how Scotch portrayed on London stage!!! Very serious. Msg really from King James 6 of Scot. Most people know he will be Eng king when Queen Eliz dies. Absolutely poss. because of this letter, plays banned, publications stop, even copies destr. Not just Arthur. Recall: theaters closed, companies shut down, actors/writers imprisoned, even tortured, for doing wrong play wrong time. 1597 printing Arthur. 1598: anything anti-Scot is out. Arthur more than enuf anti-scot. TTOA Scots and Picts: craven, scheming, villainous, rebellious, murd., kidnappers.

Banned in '98, then forgot. 1623: collected works. But Scot

James 6 now James 1 on Eng throne (TTOA's worst case: Scot
king of Britain.) Hemmings + Condell look through playbook,
come 2 Arthur, share laugh, shake heads, leave out. No Folio =
no survival. All quartos event. vanish. Only Folio guarantee
memory of plays.

Until better theory.

King James complaining about anti-Scottish plays is precisely the
argument used to explain the disappearance from Shakespeare's
canon of *Edward III*, which was printed anonymously in 1596 and
1599. But this explanation was not first proposed, as nearly as I can
tell from my amateurish research, until the 1990s. I know that *The
Tragedy of Arthur* existed in 1975 at the latest, when my father showed
us the putative 1904 edition. And I know the quarto was untouched in
a safe-deposit box as of 1986. So if *Arthur* itself is a fake, then it benefits from an amazing piece of luck: it can justify its disappearance
with a historical footnote that came *after* the play's putative forgery.

Dad made a little joke at this point, which I can reconstruct verbatim from my notes on the yellow legal pad: "Of course, there was no
Anti-Defamation League or women's lib in 1623, so *Merchant of
Venice* and *Taming of the Shrew* make the cut, but the Scotch were apparently very delicate souls, feelings easily bruised, and so two good
plays are lost to assuage the tender kilted folk, 'shrinking underneath
the plaid.' Amazed they didn't demand a *Macbeth* rewrite."

In my father's fond and wishful notion of lifelong dedication and
business-partner loyalty, Shakespeare's friends come together in 1623
to make the folio. They oversee compositors of varying competence
and sobriety at Isaac Jaggard's print shop as they set nearly a million
words of type in their late friend's honor. Task complete, they retire
to the pub and lift a glass to their monumental accomplishment, a
second in old Will's memory, and one each for every play they had to
leave out. *Pericles, Cardenio, The Two Noble Kinsmen*: they can't include
acknowledged collaborations if the co-writers won't agree (and far be
it from me to criticize strict copyright protection). They can't find a
copy of *Love's Labour's Won* anywhere, because no one's put it on for

ages, and no one ever liked it anyhow. And they can't include *Edward III* and *The Tragedy of Arthur* because now there's a Scotsman *on the throne*, and he is not going to put up with that old anti-Scot stuff that audiences used to eat up back in the nineties. So they go with the thirty-six plays they can. It'll have to do. They hire some Dutch guy to engrave a cover picture of Will, they liquor Ben Jonson into the right mood to compose a dedication, and he subdues his own ego long enough to write something quite nice (maybe too nice, Ben's ghost would say, since his preface is the seedling of the mighty oaken myth that Will wasn't one of many or even first among peers but a timeless god who left mere mortals below).

My father came out of the bathroom, his bathroom. "I just closed the door to use the toilet," he said, laughing. "How about that?" He walked over to the fridge, hesitated at its handle, then remembered the new arrangement, went ahead. He drank his next Diet Coke lying on the carpeted floor, and he watched the last light of his last September. "I am so pleased you and I are working on this side by side. It makes me so proud, you know. I am so proud of your success as a writer. You don't have to worry about me fouling this up. I will stay far away from the project. I know that it couldn't possibly have happened without you. I love you, Arthur."

The second-to-last line is certainly a lie: this publication could very easily have happened without me. And that, like a canker in a rose, spreads corruption into all the neighboring sentences, too, and no argument of authenticity is ever enough to prove what cannot be proven.

35

I MOVED OUT OF MY HOTEL and into my father's apartment as his roommate and caretaker. He had finally revealed the details of his medical condition to me and then to Dana, the inoperable and growing lump in his brain, for which all treatment seemed to him (and to me) far worse than the eventual death it promised. He wanted no sympathy and no treatment. He couldn't prevent the former, but he could in exchange for it insist on doing his part for "our work."

"Yard sale," he announced, intending to raise money for the project, though we needed none.

His worldly goods consisted of a few boxes of books, some jazz LPs and 45s from the fifties, papers and letters, some art supplies, all of which he'd stored in my mother's basement. "Seriously? She let you do that?"

"I hope so. Will you call her?"

"You should call," Dana said, the ridiculous, last-moments-of-a-romantic-comedy matchmaker tone convecting through her voice. She opened her phone and dialed for him, held it to his ear until he finally used his own hand, held Dana's hand with his other.

"Hello, Mary," he said, then paused for so long that Dana and I looked at each other with brows lifted, stunned that Mom had so much to say right out of the gate. Finally, he went on and our fantasies deflated: "This is Arthur. I'm in Minneapolis. Artie and Dana got me a place. I hope you're keeping well. Say, I have some boxes with you, I hope, still. I need them. Maybe we should speak on the telephone. You must know how to call the kids. Or there's a phone here, I think. So. Goodbye." He handed the open phone back to Dana. "She has an answering machine," he explained helpfully.

At Mom's request, I picked up the boxes without him. ("Good sense," Dad said, surrendering at once, the same man who two decades earlier had intended to outlive Sil and win her back.)

Meanwhile, Dana and Petra took him clothes shopping, though both of them adamantly denied responsibility for the T-shirt he was wearing the next day that read I WOULD DO ME.

He laid his few salable possessions on a blanket on the small patch of grass in front of the apartment building, everything but his private papers, and we sat on the stairs next to them, drinking Diet Coke. "Too sweet," he said. "Lacks that lingering bite that Tab had."

"That was the cyclamate. Turns out to be bad for you."

"Literary executorship is a lot to ask." He seemed worried about me, offering me an out. "It can certainly demand a lot of your time. Worse, probably put your own writing in the shade for a spell."

I savored the concern; it was well made. "Don't worry about that. My work will be there when we're done. Besides, this is more important than my writing. It is, and that's okay. We're doing something world changing. And we're doing it together."

A year later, I am writhing to escape this web spun by two dead men, and literary executorship has become the most self-eradicating punishment Dante could have devised for an egotistical author. There was another writer born on my and Will's birthday, a hero of mine, whose son also signed his life over to promoting and protecting his father's works. I think of them both as these two other laughing corpses fling their bolas around my ankles.

But that day, I was eager to reassure: "You'll be with us for a while longer, Dad. And, even after, you can count on me." We sat under the painted bedsheet he'd strung up between two posts: YARD SALE—I'M DYING.

"You're dying? Seriously?" asked a typical customer, torn between looking for a bargain and paying her last respects to the chipper old man.

"Well, it's serious for me."

"You're really dying? You seem so cheery."

"There are limited options for my mood. You'll see someday."

"Ha, ha, true enough, I suppose. Well, I'm sorry. And that's amazing. You're inspirational. How much for the Stan Kenton?"

A child's memory is poor because extraordinary events—*I went to a party! I tied my shoes!*—occur in a world where Fridays are frequent but irregular, and hours swell and shrink. Older brains fritz because no event is sharp enough to trench into memory's gravel. Eventually, little occurs that hasn't occurred in a thousand identical yesterdays, yesterday and yesterday and yesterday sinking back and out of view behind you, and your neck is daily stiffer, resists turning to look. Life in prison only exaggerates this. He swam in the blue October sky.

"You know, you start, when your eyes are fresh, you look at a painting like *A View of Delft*, and you say, 'My God! Look what that fellow can do! He can paint like that, and it looks just like the sky over Delft!' and you are happy or ambitious or jealous or all of those. And then, all these years hurry by, all the middle part that clouds your eyes and your brain. And then, you look at real clouds like these, and you think, 'Hmph. That looks like that painting by what's-his-name, the Dutch fellow.'"

"I remember the weather the day we did the UFO," I said. "Like this."

"Well, you should exert your memory a little more forcefully," he said with a non-sequiturial whip crack of anger, "because that was July."

We took in about sixty-five dollars that day, deducting the cost of the painted sheet. We threw out what didn't sell, and after that my father owned some clothes, toiletries, and a box of letters. I asked him if he wanted to go to a museum, a library, a bookstore, a movie, a park, the beach, for a boat ride, if he wanted some cash and to be left alone. "I want to help with the play," he said. "And sleep."

There was real help he could now offer (when he wasn't sleeping, which was sometimes fifteen hours a day): the professors were coming, and somebody had to keep a close eye on them.

As we were not going to let our billion-dollar pamphlet leave our sight, scholars either had to invite me and the book to their campus, or they could visit us on Lake Street. They were allowed as much time as they wanted with the quarto; they could take notes. They could not photograph more than four pages; they could not take the play out of the room.

My father or I would sit, reading on the couch or listening to my iPod—which device quite impressed my dad—and though some of the scholars grumbled about the restrictions (and I caught one with a pocket scanner when I came out of the bathroom), most viewed the situation as a common enough challenge of their field, and just being allowed to read the play thrilled most of them almost to giggling. They were a funny bunch, about what you would expect Shakespeare scholars to be. Some of them I quite like, and I am sorry to have dragged them into this; I hereby apologize, not for the last time.

"He's quite dishy, isn't he?" Petra said late one October afternoon of David Crystal, the world's leading expert in Shakespearean linguistics, who flew in from Wales to study *The Tragedy of Arthur* in my living room.

Petra and I were sharing a bottle of wine and then starting a second in the kitchen while my father slept and Dana was at rehearsal. Across the room, by the big windows, Professor Crystal had the play open on the glass table in front of him, his laptop displaying the online *OED*. He would occasionally laugh aloud or grunt or exclaim, "Well, look at that!" while he read, and seemed quite oblivious to Petra and me getting drunk and punchy across the bar in the kitchen, our hands brushing now and again, my imagination piloting us far into the future.

She left to pick up Dana, and I stayed as the sun set early, still a little drunk, watching this engrossed and happy linguist grow happier and more engrossed by the blue glow of his laptop lexicon, while I sank into melancholy, as the wine wore off, and Petra had been away from me and with my sister for minutes, then hours, and I was left with her lipstick on a wine glass, which I masochisto-moronically held on to while replaying and reconsidering the four moments in which the skin of her hand touched or nearly touched my own. "She's very pretty, isn't she?" I couldn't help asking Professor Crystal, twice because he didn't look up the first time.

"Sorry? Who?"

Which sounds better? (A) I am of melancholy temperament, enlivened now and then by bursts of high or hot spirit, never long-lived, or (B) I've been on antidepressants, antianxiety meds, and a Whitman's Sampler of other mood stabilizers on and off since I was twenty-four, with uneven success.

I like the sound of (A) better, too. Oddly, even after diagnosis, medication, and improvement, I still had the sticky reputation within my family of being unnecessarily morose, something of a drama queen. Dana, despite our twinned similarities and her more concentrated formula of the same psychic chemistry, often seemed the sturdier of us two, living off an extra dollop of serotonin served up with that second X chromosome, happiness guacamole on a celery stick. This impression of her may have resulted because her highs were higher than mine. Her lows were lower, too, but they were offset by everyone's lingering memory of the peaks. That said, she was always more nervous about the pharmacology, frequently mourning the medicated murder of her edge, the melting of her mildly manic pole.

I was sitting on the couch, foolishly having diluted my own limited serotonin in shiraz, squeezing my temples to wring out a few more drops, shaking my skull for how close I had stood to Petra, how impossible the situation was I had allowed to develop. And, also, I festered in envy at the easy happiness of this bearded, spectacled genius Welshman across from me. I watched him read by the light of the single lamp, hunched over, reflected in the deepening black of the window, and he never looked up at me in the murk, not until my dreaming father cried out from the bedroom, "No, those are *my* hands!"

Professor Crystal noticed me then. He took off his glasses, since he couldn't see me anyhow in my shadows, and he rubbed his eyes. "Well, it's a lovely piece of creativity. It certainly *pops* like him at many moments. Guenhera and the nurse is lovely. Not '97, though. No later than 1595, if it is him, perhaps much earlier, in fact. Mightn't be him on his own. Probably a collaboration, especially if it is before '93. He rarely flew solo back then."

"But is it him? Will you authenticate it?"

"I need more time with it. All the language is right. But I need more time." He considered me. "You know, if you had to say, what is the king's tragic flaw?"

"He has bipolar disorder," I said.

"Ha! I hadn't thought of it quite like that, but yes. That is precisely it. Remarkable. They would have called him excessively humorous, unregulated, perhaps even unfit to rule because of his unfortunate birth. An Elizabethan audience might have seen him as doomed because of that misconception, and everything he does would be seen as futile, a prideful struggle against God's will. Still, the playwright makes him sympathetic, gives him some strengths. But no, he isn't a hero that you root for, is he? Except for him to settle down a bit, find some wisdom. Gloucester is right, in the speech about the passions of monarchs. Another failed king on the Elizabethan stage. Do you have to be anywhere? I should very much like to read it again. Will your wife be back soon?"

I cherished his misunderstanding, lovingly nurtured its growth into a fully realized fantasy with another drink, and granted my guest as long as he wished. Eventually my father emerged from the black hallway, not yet reaccustomed to turning on lights when it was dark. "Mmph. Who have we here?" I introduced the two men, and Dana called, telling me it was urgent that I come to the theater right away.

"Petra didn't turn up? She left hours ago."

"Please come."

I left the ex-con in charge of the world-famous linguist and my billion dollars, and I drove badly from Uptown to the Warehouse District, where Dana was shivering on the loading-dock stairs under the stage door.

She jumped up and tried to open the passenger door before I'd even stopped. "Thank you. Drive. Thank you for this. I did a bad thing. Please drive."

"Home?"

"No, no, no, no. No. Let me think."

"Okay. What happened?"

"Will you *please* let me fucking think?"

Here are the facts in a straight line, which is not, by a long shot, how I heard this story: under the pressure of the approaching opening night, Dana had decided that her performance was "still not coming together," and she decided that this was because she was muddled and fuzzed by her own Zoloft-Wellbutrin proportions, and that enduring a little anxiety and depression was a small risk if it meant she could access more "honesty" for her performance, a little more "buzz of life," and so she had lately started fiddling with the dosages, a common enough event in her life, my life, the life of every mildly depressed person who relies upon and resents these drugs. And, as always happens, it's a trial-and-error process, this self-examination, self-prescription, and self-monitoring, except that it is only trial and error and more trial and more error and error and spiraling, reactive error.

But this time she felt she had balanced it just right, and her dress rehearsal this evening had been exactly *it*, and she was so excited— "admittedly overexcited"—backstage after the run-through—bubbly to the point of boiling—that she had hugged the actor who plays her lover, Palamon, and then grabbed his face and "planted one on him," and then he, probably having had some feelings of his own swelling over the weeks of rehearsal, kissed her back, which she, "for some reason, just went for. It wasn't about him at all, or about the kiss as like a kiss qua kiss, or, or, or desire, it wasn't that, although it proba-bly looked like that, and I can imagine that he felt something like that, and I have to say sorry to him, too, but more it was just this thing, admittedly the stupidest thing, it was just me sort of keeping it going, not wanting it to be over, I think because of the run-through, and it was more like I was *celebrating*, not me kissing Tom, certainly, or even, or even Emilia kissing Palamon, it was more like actress was kissing theater or something, or muse, or, or, or, and, and, and Petra saw me."

Petra stood and watched an extremely passionate, deeply sexual moment between her girlfriend and a strange man, entirely unjusti-fied by the play, in an otherwise empty fluorescent-lit hallway be-tween dressing rooms. And after the predictable scene that quickly flew out of control, Petra left the theater and drove off and positioned herself strictly straight-to-voicemail.

"Go back to Lyndale," Dana said. "Left. Left! LEFT!" She di-rected me to a florist, and I idled while she ran in and out, then guided me to another florist eight blocks up, and I idled while she ran in and out again, this time with flowers. "You have to *do* something," she said in a tone as if *I* had made a mistake and owed her a display of masterful repair work. "Sorry. I don't mean it like that," she self-corrected at once. "The sound isn't matching my point, if you know what I mean." I did.

I demanded her promise that she would immediately go back to her last doctor-approved dosage. She didn't hesitate, didn't say her performance was at risk, nothing. She just nodded.

I drove her to Dad's, introduced her to Professor Crystal, who was still contentedly taking notes at the table while Dad sat on the couch in the dark, ensuring that the kindly scholar didn't make a break for it with our quarto. "All the rhymes rhyme in original pronunciation," the smiling Welshman said cryptically. "That's good," he added when he saw my confusion.

And then, following Dana's orders to the letter, I drove alone to her apartment, carrying a pot of pansies, with clear and even scripted instructions to explain how meaningless the kiss was, how important Petra was to Dana, how Dana would do anything to make it right. I was drilled to recite from *Arthur*. "Tell her: *And I would pass my hours of peace with her, / Empillowed on her breast before my ship.*" But I was never any good at memorization, so I let that go as soon as I was back in the car.

"You," Petra said when she opened the door. "All right."

"These are supposed to help," I gasped, suddenly voiceless, my body unevenly hydrated, my throat driest of all, and I handed her the pansies. She closed her eyes and pressed the odorless flowers against her face until they bent. Some even broke, and she let them rub against her eyelids and nose and cheeks. She opened her eyes and looked at me.

"They might."

I joined her on the couch, and Maria immediately parked on my lap. Petra poured me some of the wine she'd already begun. Something jazzy and modal and Middle Eastern was on the stereo.

"She's sorry," I started. "It didn't mean anything and really, truly wasn't what it looked like. You're everything to her. She'll do anything to—"

"I know," Petra said without expression. Masked, flushed with drink but not flustered, she asked, "What else you got?"

"I'm not sure. A line from Shakespeare."

And she kissed me. There was nothing I could do: I was pinned down by a beagle.

She spoke of death and small joys as she kissed me and stroked my face with those same fingers I had once longingly watched stroke the face of her iPhone, turning and unpinching webpages with soft sweeps. "You have to seize what you can of happiness and pleasure," she said. (You did say all this, you know.) "You have to pay later either way. It's all-you-can-eat, and you have to pay the same whether you stuff yourself or go without. Obviously, you pay when you die. And you pay when your parents die. But when the neighbor's kid gets hit by a car and you watch her parents shuffle around heartbroken until you finally move to a new house? That's paying, too. You have no fun, you still pay, it's just that you let death cut your purse. He conned you. You die and you didn't live. You're death's gull. We'll both pay, eventually, whether you kiss me back or not. But it would be better if you kissed me back."

"What about—"

"Don't."

"You're just angry about—"

"Don't. Don't. Do I look angry? Do I feel angry?"

There. That's that.

In Shakespeare's day, they believed in magic. Now we only have its weak residue: magical thinking. If I could count precisely to sixty between two passing orange minutes on her digital clock, starting at 5:23 A.M. and ending exactly as it melted into 5:24, then when she woke she would love me and not say this had been a terrible mistake. If I could close my eyes and guess, give or take five, how many bricks were in the top row of the bedroom wall, then Dana would even bless this relabeling of our triangle's points. If I could do it within three bricks, she would forgive me. If I could guess the bricks within two, then Dana would even be happy, for herself and us, and she would say she had wanted exactly this to happen, and she would believe that she must have subconsciously known that when she'd kissed her co-star in the hall she could speed us all along to this great ending.

I opened my eyes. "You ass," Petra groaned. "Why didn't you leave in the dark?"

"Good morning."

"Good morning."

"Do you want to talk about . . . ?" I glided a single plucked pansy across her eyes.

"Sometime. Not now."

"Fair enough. One of us should say something to Dana?"

"I don't know. No. Later."

"Fair enough."

My muted phone was heavy with eight voicemails and fourteen texts waiting for me, though they all said about the same thing.

36

I WILL NOT PAINT a stirring word-portrait of my troubled conscience or simmering shame to win any sympathy. Nor will I belabor the lies I wove of where I'd spent the night, the tempered and deniable hope I offered my twin sister that morning. I know. I know. "Thanks for all the updates," she said when I walked in. "Not like I was waiting for any news." I know.

She had slept on our couch and was sipping coffee two-handed, beshawled by a blanket. Professor Crystal was back at it in the living room, offering a cheery good morning and stepping far from the quarto to drink his own coffee. My father was still asleep. On the kitchen bar, already arrived in white, red, and blue livery from Random House, was the contract in triplicate awaiting my thrice-inked countersignature. I needed a notary public. Grateful for the excuse, I fled, and Dana was required to sit guard for another hour, my semicomforting lies draped over her ears.

When I returned from the FedEx on Hennepin, irreparably tethered to my publisher and Shakespeare, Dana hadn't moved, though the coffee cup had been replaced by her phone, which she clutched and watched in its stubborn, haughty silence. My father was still asleep. "I need you to go get some stuff until she calls back and says I can go home."

"It's your apartment."

"I'm not going there until she says I can."

"I'm sure she just needs a little time to think."

"I'm such a stupid bitch."

"Stop, please."

I collected her things for her; Petra was not there. For fifteen days in October Dana slept at Dad's, Mom's, or on the couch in her dressing room at the theater. Professors came and went from my living room, and my father snored away more of each day, living on Diet Coke, which he said was growing on him, even when I called a Coke bottling plant and was given the name of a supermarket in Arden Hills that still carried Tab. Petra refused to talk to Dana, and I, semi-honorably, tried to stay away from the woman I loved until they settled their relationship, although honesty demands I admit it was really just good sportsmanship on my part, that I was merely waiting for new arrangements to be put in place to match my hopes, and twice I slipped away from the family squat. Once, Petra accepted me and my pansies; once, she told me to go home.

The Two Noble Kinsmen opened on October 22, and I sat between my mother and Petra and for a few minutes was allowed to hold Petra's hand in the dark. Petra came with us when Mom and I went to meet Dana at the stage door, and they said their awkward hellos. I took my mother home, left them to talk.

I came back to my own apartment, where my father was exhaustedly overseeing a tireless Brooklyn-born Ivy League Bardman, and when I walked in, Dad croaked, "Finally." I thanked him for standing guard and promised him a ticket to Dana's show the next night, told him to get some rest. "At your service," he muttered. "Gentlemen, good night." He stood unsteadily and shuffled down the dark hall to bed.

Dana called a little after two in the morning. "I don't know what's going to happen," she said, again and again. "I don't know how to apologize so she believes me. Something's broken, and I don't know how to fix it." I listened and consoled, worried for her, sympathetic, honestly loving and sorry. Truly. I did also hear in this the first difficult but necessary steps to a new and better arrangement. Better for everyone, it seemed apparent to me. I began planning to find a new apartment for me and Petra, as I didn't feel I'd be able to live in their old place. Maria would go with Dana, obviously, whom I loved and pitied, I promise, and for whom I felt burning guilt. There. Okay, yes:

and I also felt a little annoyance that she wouldn't face up to what was obviously best for everyone and let us all just get on with it. There. "What do you think I should do?" she asked.

"All you can do is tell her you love her and you want to start over, if that's what you want. You deserve to be happy with the person who's right for you."

"You're so smart."

The next morning, October 23, I clutched the quarto in its case all the way to a chemistry lab at the University of Minnesota, where I was met by my editor and a Random House lawyer in from New York, as well as two experts in dating and validating antique documents: a Russian ink specialist up from Chicago and the paper consultant, flown in all the way from London. Both men had been commissioned by Professor Verre, who, though absent, had himself been appointed by Random House to oversee and collate all the investigations into authenticity. The nondisclosure agreements were signed and rebrief-cased.

The Englishman, Peter Bryce, had a white beard, a white ponytail, seemed in every way a retired 1970s rock bassist, the one Jethro Tull fired just before they made it big. He had an attitude of someone having wonderful good fun. "You sure you want to watch today?" he teased. "These tests can get a bit ugly for the owners." Before a single instrument appeared or the quarto was revealed, all was explained to me: the truth would out; twenty-first-century science simply could not be fooled, and the atmospheric assumption in the lab was that I was trying to fool them. "The hardest fact any forger has to overcome is a simple truth: every object contains the history of its own making. That history can be read. All papers age. Gelatin size degrades. Fibers weaken. These things cannot be hurried along to suit a forger's timetable."

"Okay. Let's do it." I began to open the case.

Bryce wasn't done talking, however. I suspected that his best party trick was to win with a lecture, without using a single tool, to crack a forger's brittle confidence with a well-aimed smack from his hammer of knowledge. ("D'ye recall that case where Bryce flew to Minneapo-lis and terrified the bloke into confessing before he'd even looked at it!") He was plainly waiting for me to gulp when he reached the trick I hadn't thought of, to scramble to pack up my quarto and run for it. "Fake paper? The raw materials are not the same as they were. Linen rags are not the same. Flax grows differently now and is processed differently. No pesticides in the 1590s. Did you know that about flax?"

"I did not. How little I know about flax would startle you."

"Well, even if someone found a stock of blank period French or Genoese laid paper, the paper would not take ink properly because of how it had aged. Not to mention that the ink would now be *over* any foxing rather than the foxing over the ink. Only four people on earth can fabricate a replica of sixteenth-century paper, and I know them all. They won't do it. So, if you bleached old writing off printed stock, to print on it again, or found old linen to make new replica paper, modern detergents contain optical brightening agents. The paper would bear traces of the OBAs, which fluoresce a very particular light bluish-purple under UV. Did you know that? All I need for that test is this." And he withdrew a UV light from his bag, watching me for reaction, then firing it up like a reluctant martial artist forced, despite his profound pacifism, into crushing my windpipe.

He asked me to open the case and lay the quarto on the table. I'm a little color-blind, so I wouldn't have known if the resulting glow fluoresced correctly or not, but he waved it over every page and finally said, "Well. Hmm." He was utterly likable and obviously very happy to taste a challenge. "Next we're going to study every detail of the binding. Stitching styles, threads, glues. Then we shall wallow in the text block, the paper, the orientation of the sheets, the wire profiles, the form of the signatures. We have the polarizing light microscope and the FTIR after that, should we still require. Then our friend Viktor here, from Chicago, will bathe in the ink. It doesn't matter how many details appear right. If one or two are wrong, then the beast is mythical."

"Carry on, carry on."

"Okay. Let's have fun." Some answers would be instantaneous; others would require a week or two for a final report.

For six hours, microscopes, lasers, and various doodads of our

century were wheeled in and out. Magnified slides of individual letters were projected next to control samples from other quartos
printed by William White. Surfaces were tweezed, photos taken,
flakes of ink peeled and dissolved in vials, tips of threads were
snipped off the edges of pages and mounted behind glass. Individual
sheets ("Look away, Mr. Phillips, this might hurt a bit") were sliced
open from the side, butterflied.

"It's very smooth. Hardly a stain. It's been pressed all this time,
hasn't it? Bound? No exposure to light. Stored vertically is my guess,
which means there should be a divergence in thicknesses between the
top and bottom." There was.

Hands were shaken, results were promised, and I put my treasure
back in its case. A frustrating but gleeful send-off from the Englishman: "Mr. Phillips, one curiosity of my work is that it is much harder to
prove something is genuine than to prove something is a fake." I went
home.

My father, Arthur Edward Harold Phillips, lay still in his bed. He
had probably been dead for several hours, since before I'd left that
morning, or even when I'd been on the phone giving my sister romantic advice.

37

"I WILL NOT TRY TO EXCUSE my father's acts. His acts were his own.
His mistakes, crimes, defeats: these were his own. As Shakespeare
wrote, *I would not have it any other wise*, and that is surely how my father felt. But I will say this of his life: he believed that the world could
be transformed completely, if only occasionally, if only for one person
at a time, but that was something, and that was worth it. There are
times when I consider some of his greatest creations, his most selfless
creations, and I feel cowardly in comparison when I think of what he
hoped to achieve in his work.

"A novelist tries to capture a person in a phrase (a walk-on character), or a paragraph (a minor character), or a page (a major character),

or a whole book (for the protagonist), but how to describe an entire life of a real person? Not in snatches of action or frame-frozen descriptions, but over a whole life? My father eludes my abilities. I can write a paragraph about him for you, but it seems to miss everything, even though it's all true:

"Arthur Edward Harold Phillips was a dandy and a great artist and a great mind who could quote poetry in three languages to charm you. A self-made character, he was an original. He lived for art and wonder. He loved a woman, and he lost her, gave her up in self-sacrifice. He loved his two children and wanted to give them, more than anything, a love of literature and art and the world's limitless capability to delight, and he succeeded. But he was also a man whose best principles eroded far too early, who was made bitter by the world's indifference to his creativity, who needed money more than he ever would have guessed, who discovered his greatest genius was in his ability to bring back to life the spirit of long-ago geniuses, but who then wasted himself in the least exalted, least wondrous escapades one could imagine, far less wonderful than if he had simply done what he always claimed to fear the most and become an office hack or an advertising illustrator, and come home every day at five o'clock to a loving wife and admiring children in the suburbs. This, too, is a sort of wonder-working, after all.

"As far as an accurate portrait of my father, I don't know if that paragraph is him or not. This writerly method fictionalizes him, cuts off so much of him—so many contradictions, extenuations, annexes, chapters—that what remains is only a shadow of him, a shadow of his hopes, and a shadow of his griefs. It seems impossible to descend through all the layers of him at even a single moment or at a single decision. I consider even one of his pedestrian crimes, and I ask myself, What motivated him? His worst moments can be explained by: his wonder-lust philosophy, bitterness, pride in his craftsmanship, mere habit, inevitability, simple greed and thoughtlessness, genetic selfishness bordering on criminality, love. I can hardly pull the burrs away to find the man underneath . . ."

I include this extract of egocentric eulogy (I went on for quite a while, in love with the sound of my words—*frame-frozen*!) because of certain contractual requirements I am coming to, and because it is the best testimony I have to illustrate precisely my state of mind before the events of the next week.

"And yet, for all of that, there is my father reading to me and my sister, the voices and the lessons, the laughter and the wisdom, so that his twins couldn't wait to spend a weekend with him in his world of wonders. For all of that, there remains his generosity, his willingness to sacrifice for his children, to sacrifice for the only woman he ever loved, giving her an extraordinary gift because he knew he could not give her an ordinary one."

I put my arm around my mother's shoulder, and she patted my hand. She was hardly shattered with grief; she had long ago decided to deny my father any access to her heart, and she had done just fine. Petra stood with Dana, held her gloved hand. The four of us embraced and drove together, silently, out to the Temple Israel cemetery on Forty-second Street.

I was—from synagogue to graveyard—at my most piously devoted to my three articles of faith: (1) My father—despite it all—had loved me, wished things could have been different between us; (2) Petra—despite it all—loved me and would accept my love, and somehow Dana would be spared any real pain, and my boys would love her and me, and we would all rearrange somehow for the best and happiest ending to these early dramas; and (3) *The Tragedy of Arthur* was by William Shakespeare. These three apparently separate trees were one and the same, connected under the soil, sharing invisible groundwater and spliced, inseparable roots.

"I want you to take over this project," I told Dana. "Or do it jointly with me. I want you to keep the play, write some of the essays. We have to share this. I don't think I can back out completely and give it all to you—I would if I could, I swear to God, but I'm too late with the publisher on that. I should have done that in the first place, and I'm very sorry, really, truly sorry. But come in with me now. Please."

A superstitious gesture, whistling in a graveyard, but heartfelt. I suppose I thought it might make Dana feel better, when she learned about me and Petra. I suppose it can be viewed as a somewhat crass offer, as if

I were buying Petra off Dana in exchange for a share of a lottery ticket. I didn't mean it like that, but I was afraid that's how Dana took it, as if she knew how thickly delusion had caked over my brain.

"No," she said. "Thank you, but he wanted you to do this. And you're doing it for all of us anyhow. So don't feel like you're taking something from me, okay?"

38

IT HAD BEEN MORE THAN A WEEK since I had found him and sat on the bed next to his body for an hour. It was easy enough now to throw away the few clothes and toiletries. All sentimental value lurked in the box of letters.

I read through the whole lot sitting at the table in the living room, where all those Shakespeare pros had read of another ambiguous Arthur. I read letters from his kids, his wife then ex-wife, his lawyers, the prison records like report cards. I found souvenirs of his art career, but I had hoped for a comprehensive catalogue of his forgeries, the basis perhaps—I felt the seductive whisper in the back of my mind—for my next novel. He'd kept nothing so rich, unfortunately, no roster of clients, no onymous mention of a country house in England. But there was this index card:

It is in faded pencil. It is undated but obviously old, softened by the caress of years. There is a number 14 in the upper left. The card has a vaguely Australiaform stain on it, which, when I found it, was also crusty and still adhesive enough to have stuck the card to the back of a mimeographed catalogue of a 1967 group show in an art gallery in Dinkytown, which included two pictures by AEH Philips (*sic*): *Girl with Lily* and *Tired Mother*. The back of that booklet's last page has a twin (although inverted) stain to the one on the card.

There are four lines of writing. Under a doodled comet or approaching cannonball, two stylized arrows mark ideas or a to-do list. The first line reads, "explain Arthur in York." The second arrow points to "Cumbria <u>backs away</u>." Below these is a line of verse, lightly seasoned with scansion marks: "When Ríghteous mén would stánd alóof."

The line is *almost* the last line of Act III—*When righteous men in conscience stand apart*—from a soliloquy in which the Earl of Cumbria *backs away* from his plan to assassinate Arthur (who never *explains what he was doing in York*).

My father was working out Cumbria's words. This index card represents an early draft of the play, the only survivor of a deck of at least fourteen, still here only because something spilled on it, and it stowed away to the twenty-first century on the back of something he thought he could safely keep, a catalogue of his failure as an artist working under his own name (appropriately misspelled).

The shock when a con reveals itself is physically sickening, and I felt a shudder of pity for all those from whom my father had stolen over the years. He had escaped in the nick of time, dead and buried, praised by me despite years of better judgment.

Revelation, in my case, felt like a draining, like—to be a little unpleasant—a storm warning of intestinal panic, as if something were being flushed out of me, sluiced away from heart and brain, a voiding that was hotter, more acidic, more thorough and more scouring than the worst movement in my system's muscular memory.

It ages you, this instantaneous purging of belief. Your skin hangs lower off the bones under the eyes, some fat and sinew are lost in the evacuation, and shadows start to fall across the face.

They don't ever stop, those shadows. After they darken the half-moons under the eyes, they darken the room, the world, and then they set off to darken the past. All those warm moments at his end and at our start: the nervous request for help, the emails, the Tab, the apartment, and back, back, further and further back, shadows blackening all the way back. The death of *Arthur* meant the death of Arthur's love all the way back, the nights on his floor, the crop circle, the little people of Saturn as I dozed in his arms, all flushing out with the other filth, all withering as the light went out and the cold wind picked up.

Too much? Too melodramatic? (*By my assent he fashioneth complotment!*) Maybe. But such aesthetic quibbling does not apply at the moment of revelation.

The only payoff in exchange for this loss is the sudden and permanent clarity of vision, the X-ray eyesight, and the charitable evangelist's belief that this clarity can be taught to others before they have to feel the pain themselves. Sometimes this is true: clarity can be suddenly contagious when a group labors together under a forgery's illusions.

What makes something rapidly and obviously a forgery after it was, sometimes for decades, so obviously genuine? Go Google the van Meegeren Vermeers. A child could tell you that those Navajos and Down's syndrome maids aren't by the same man who painted *Girl with a Pearl Earring*. Read James Frey's memoir now: an elderly Amish lady could find a hundred impossibilities. Sometimes better science opens our eyes, but often it feels more as if a spell has worn off. We blink and look around, rubbing the fairy dust from our eyes, wonder whether we might have dreamt it all. Once you know it isn't Shakespeare, none of it sounds like Shakespeare. How could it? If I didn't write *this*, it wouldn't sound like something *I* wrote.

First things first: I was not going to allow the publication, obviously. I would end this farce. Equally obviously, you are reading this, and I have failed. All I can hope now is that the critics do the job for me. The wise ones will quote me right now and say, as they should, or if only out of fear of appearing like suckers, "It's a parody, a pastiche, obviously false, an act of inexcusable chutzpah, temerity, pretension."

Or will we hear instead, out of their fear of appearing like philistines, that it's "a remarkable find, a treasure, certain to keep scholars and playgoers and Bardologists busy for years to come, a ripping yarn, quite possibly from the genius who gave us *Macbeth*"?

One day, someone will find something within the play to match what I found without: the wrong *something*. Maybe not even that, maybe there will be no flash of anachronism, no smoking verb fifty years out of place. Instead, someone trustworthy, far from our family dramas, will feel, as Coleridge felt of *Henry VI, Part One*, "the impossibility of this speech having been written by Shakespeare," and everyone will wake up, and no one will even need to prove it, and this book will creep quietly out of print, and the 2011 edition will join the 1904 edition of this curiouser and curiouser family heirloom.

"He did it to me again," I whined.

"To *you*?" My mother laughed. "Please. This was why I couldn't have a life with him. Couldn't put up with it. What sort of life is it, if the person is going to turn out not to be who you thought he was an hour before? You can't live like that. Life isn't about trying to make surprise and wonder. Life is hard enough when you're trying to cobble together a biding sense of reality from one minute to the next. Life is impossible and unsteady enough. Look what it thinks up! Car crashes and cancer. Pregnancy and heartache. Then on top of that? To be married to someone who might be one person one day and another the next? Who shouts, 'Surprise! All of life so far was just a wonder I worked up in the basement'?"

"But you said you'd made a mistake not staying with him. You said Sil was a bore. You said—"

"Oh, no. Dear, please. Arthur. Really. You seriously think I can give you words to live by? Oh, Lord, you do. Well, I'd best start watching what I say. Is that what you want? Simple thoughts, consistent? How dull we'll be. Tell me again how you think he did it."

If my father forged everything, this whole story is much simpler. Sometime in the 1950s or 1960s, when he is showing *Girl with Lily* in Minneapolis art galleries to no acclaim and starting to win his first commissions "duplicating" paintings for insurance purposes, he thinks it through: What would be the single most profitable forgery he could produce and how long would it take to pay out? What might be possible if he had infinite patience, if he was willing to wait even fifty years for the payoff? He realizes that the biggest prize—a fountain of copyrights—requires an entirely new Shakespeare play, no chance of a second copy ever appearing. That rules out the plays we *know* are lost—*Cardenio, Love's Labour's Won*, the ur-*Hamlet*—because they might still turn up. He writes the text. Somehow. Really? He sits around, stressed for unstressed syllables, in private, in *prison*? Having written the play, he fakes the 1904 edition, tests it, uses it to trick out expert criticism, weed out mistakes in vocabulary. Then, when he's certain of the text, he forges the 1597 quarto. Selecting a real printer of the period, knowing which one would have no heirs, no estate, no possible line of textual ownership to this day (which has taken a full U.K. law office several months to prove), he produces a 1597 document with ink and paper that can pass modern forensic tests and academic readers. Tests that didn't exist when he set to work in prison or before 1986, when he locked it in a safe-deposit box. Writing a play the disappearance of which can be well explained by Shakespearean studies that were developed only in the 1990s.

My mother interrupted me at this point. "Hmm. Arthur, you know the old line? Sometimes liars tell the truth. Listen to yourself. There were barely libraries in those prisons. Somehow he's concocting sixteenth-century ink?"

"Maybe he had a partner. Why not Glassow?"

"Because Chuck Glassow's a grocer and a thief, not a genius. And he's been out of the country for twenty years. But, really, by now, who cares? Why are you getting so exercised about this? You have other things to worry about."

"He's willing to wait fifty years to see a profit, so he can leave it to his family and feel sentimental and like he made it all up to us. Nauseating."

And more. He gets to know he's pulled it off, his last thought as he dies, a smile on his face, alone in a furnished rental, paid for by his pigeon son. It's the pathetic part of forgery, the snickering little mischief-maker. Still and always the wonder-worker, which role, no matter what he said, always contains an element of laughing at the suckers, the farmers, the fake-Rembrandt buyers. And the ego! He adds to the world's pleasure and mystery. Just a big fairy ring. It's pitiful. He gets to feel like he's Shakespeare. As good as Shakespeare. Not as good as 1600 Shakespeare, not as good as *Hamlet*, but as good as 1593 Shakespeare. As good as the first batch of history plays. He fooled everyone: academics, scientists, readers, critics. Us. Me. "He didn't ask Dana to manage this," I said, "because he knew she wouldn't have done it. He couldn't sucker her like he suckered me. She's smarter than I am. And she's not greedy enough."

"Of course she is," said Mom. "She's an actress. You think she wouldn't like more press time? 'Actress Finds Shakespeare Play'? Please. But, Arthur, I don't think . . . are you sure that index card says what you think it says? This is a lot of money."

I have total sympathy for that position: it is a lot of money, and one should think very hard about one's purported principles before throwing away a lot of money, especially money your long-suffering mother and romantically betrayed artist sister could use. I promised Mom I would think it over before I acted, and I wasn't just being nice. I also wanted to drive to Petra's to see who was where, reciting my one remaining article of faith as I motored over.

I tried. I waited and mulled over that index card, but I could (and still can) see only one interpretation.

39

B ERT THORN CALLED TO REVEAL that there was a will. In the same call, he requested my "word as a gentleman" that his time consulting on the probate, as well as a lingering balance from my father's old accounts, would be "taken care of appropriately out of proceeds."

Besides that unfortunate reminder of my father's legacy, the will itself cattle-prodded my most predatory suspicions. He had drafted it two months before his release from prison, *before* the visit where he haltingly, so sincerely, lured me into this folly. Nevertheless, he wrote it as if my participation were a certainty. First:

"I direct that my son, Arthur M. Phillips, serve as my literary executor, and I direct that he see to the publication, protection, and promotion of the play *The Most Excellent and Tragical Historie of Arthur, King of Britain* by William Shakespeare, so as to maximize the financial return from the play to its beneficiaries. I hereby give and bequeath ownership of my copy of the 1597 edition of that play, and all monies which may be derived therefrom, in the following percentage shares: 28 percent to my said son, Arthur M. Phillips; 24 percent to my daughter, Dana S. Phillips; 24 percent to my former wife, Mary Arden Phillips diLorenzo; and 24 percent to my friend, Charles R. Glassow, if he survives me. If he does not, I direct that his share be divided equally among the three other beneficiaries just named."

Upon hearing that last name over the phone, my mother interrupted my reading with salty Iron Range profanity, circa 1945, in original pronunciation. I had been a little puzzled by the division of revenue when I first read it, but at the time I had only felt a bitter, head-shaking amusement at my father's manipulations of me. I wasn't moved to my own full-throated obscenity until his next stipulation:

"*The Most Excellent and Tragical Historie of Arthur, King of Britain* was written by William Shakespeare. Should my son and literary executor, Arthur M. Phillips, at any time in the future attempt to publish, or cause the performance of, or in any other way disseminate the play under his own name, or in any way publicly imply that it is his own work, or the work of any writer other than William Shakespeare, then I hereby revoke the said gift and bequest to him, and his said 28 percent share thereof shall belong in equal shares to the other three beneficiaries named above, or their survivors, provided they take all available legal steps to enforce my direction."

In other words, he could conceive only of a son as thieving as the father. Before he'd even asked if I would do it, he was defending against the possibilities that I would steal his play for my own fraudulent literary ambition (*Look at me! I wrote a Shakespeare play!*) or I would sink his plans out of spite (as I was the snitch who had squealed to Doug Constantine), and in either case, I would lose my inheritance. And he would sic his wife, daughter, and criminal chum on me to make sure I did the kingpin's bidding.

I don't think that in my entire life of wavering anger issues I have ever been more furious than I was at that moment in Bert's crappy office, blinking up at his drop-tile popcorn ceiling, my jaw muscles straining, almost sprained, from the contortions and tensions of my face. Dana had come over after her matinee to join me for this meeting, and she laughed as I raged, broke a pencil, spluttered at the dead man's lies, insults, hypocrisies. She patted her loony twin's shoulder as I vowed to torpedo the whole smeared business. "His pathetic little performance, his sad-ass delusion, although that's generous, the idea that he was insane, not just a liar." That said, it seemed possible that by the end he thought he *was* Shakespeare, writing Will's will. "I'm shocked he didn't leave Mom his second-best bed."

"Well, I do hate that guy," Dana said as we left Bert's office.

"I know. He's dead and he's still playing us."

"No, no," she laughed, down on Nicollet Mall now. "*Chuck Glassow*. I hate Chuck Glassow."

"Really? You think about him at all?"

"You don't? How can you forgive him? How many times did Dad go to jail while Chuck got off?"

Charles R. Glassow, owner of a quarter of our projected millions, did two years for the grocery store coupons tax scam and came out with fair prospects from other friends; my father was paroled after seven, mentally worse for the wear, and soon to go back in for the long one.

Before that, there was the wine. I honestly can't remember how that one ended, and I don't care enough about the unquestionable accuracy of this to look it up, but Chuck and my father had the idea of printing up exquisitely crafted labels for a French vineyard that didn't exist, the promotional materials for the château and grounds, the history of the denobled family, even a pedigree of the vines, including scientific analyses of the soil and grafts. This was pre-Internet, so the arrival of an elite French red, priced above $150 a bottle, available only in small batches, preordered for the very best customers, was an unexamined boon for Minneapolitan oenophiles. The wine was a cheap American blend, chosen by Glassow and my father for its price, anonymous flavor, and unmarked corks and cork foil.

I don't see any other explanation: Glassow's presence in the will only confirmed what the index card had already revealed.

"Where are you going from here?" I asked Dana, a vague question, as I was desperate now to be told I was forgiven and free to move in with Petra, that Dana was happy. "What's the latest?"

"We're talking. I don't know. I didn't know there was so much wrong before all this. We have so much to sort out. Depths of mis-understandings—I can't see to the bottom. Can't see how it can end right. I don't know. I think . . . I think she's already seeing someone."

"Really?"

"I wonder what Shakespeare would have made of psychopharm," she sighed when I couldn't find the air to form the questions I wanted to ask. "You know? We've taken all this crap for so many years. We're more like everyone else when we're on the junk, everything seems clearer and easier and less fraught, but a little less real, too. Hard to believe that would have seemed like a good idea to him. 'Here, take this: you'll be happy to be a glover like your dad. Here, take this: you'll be happy to be a Protestant. Here, take this: you'll be happy enough married to that old hag and living in Stratford.' I don't think so."

"What if it was for his daughter, though?" I said. "For someone he loves. Judith has been distracted with melancholy ever since her twin brother died, she's hanging out down by the river, making bouquets of symbolic flowers. You think Shakespeare wouldn't run down to the apothecary for some Zoloft?"

"And some Mucedorus for his cold."

She had a double that day—matinee and evening shows—so I dropped her at the theater, hugged her, and flew to Petra.

I came in talking, a little buzzy. "Are you going to tell her, or should I? I think she knows already, on some level. I think she senses a shift is coming. I think she's okay with it. I think she's going to be happy in a way. We're all going have to work on this, obviously, but—"

"This isn't where you should be," Petra said. "There's nothing more here. We're done."

It's a storytelling puzzle, really. What breakup has ever occurred that is dramatic to anyone other than the participants? In *A Midsum-*

mer Night's Dream, it makes for a passably entertaining show because the lovers are driven literally insane by fairies, and their breakup talk is unhinged and vicious. In my case, I just went into a state where I didn't hear her, and hoped if I didn't acknowledge it, she'd stop saying it.

"Are you going to tell Dana?" I asked again.

"Of course not. Why would I want to hurt her?"

"Because you— She thinks you're seeing someone else. Are you going to stay with her?"

"I don't know. No. I don't know. Please go."

"You're going to change your mind."

"I won't."

"This is just nerves. Jitters. This is just before the ending. We decide the ending."

"It's not nerves."

"This will pass. We just have to get to—we have to decide, or it won't—the ending is ours to decide."

"No."

"I love you. Petra, I love you."

"That will pass."

"No. It won't. It won't pass."

"But it will. Of course it will. It always does. And then something else can be the ending instead."

"I'm going to prove to you that we work. Just wait. Just promise me you'll wait."

40

THE NEWS OF THE FIRST scholarly authentication came by voicemail. My editor called, jubilant. She whooped, "It's happening! It's really happening! You *knew* it and they're proving it! Congratulations!" and some other people cheered in the background, an office full of pigeons celebrating because they'd stumbled onto a bag of poisoned corn. I pitied them for how they would feel when they learned the truth. I knew this had to be stopped; I'd put it off long enough.

Although, yes, true, the temptation was to keep my mouth shut. I won't deny it. Especially upon learning that we had at least one professor on our side, which moved me around the board game's path to another payment. "A check will go to Marly's office this week. I'll make sure of it," Jennifer said, signing off. I confess: I wanted the money. I like money. There.

I didn't really expect there would be any more assenting professors after this; I assumed we'd only brought aboard some junior adjunct monkey from Podunk Polytech, probably an anti-Stratfordian anyhow and thus easily deluded, or some tenure-famished conniver ready to authenticate just to make a name. The payment for first authentication wasn't all the money in the world, and I figured there wasn't going to be any more money since we would never achieve the next benchmark. And so I decided to—shall we say—think a bit longer. Guilty.

But other impulses were stronger: pride in my own career, for example. I did not aspire to be famous only by dint of my father's crimes, even if we were never caught. And I was plenty afraid we would get caught, which would be worse for my career and pride: I'd be unmasked and unread. Nobody reads Clifford Irving's novels anymore. (Look him up.) Even if we weren't caught, and my millions typhooned in, I'd be earning criminal revenue, just as my father would have done. This was my shoulder angel's conclusive, pitchfork-bending argument: I refused to resemble my father in any way. Also, let's not forget vindictiveness: I was not going to let him get away with it, even if that cost me $10 million. A display of virtue might also impress Petra, whose faith in me could be restored and who occupied those thoughts of mine that were not wrestling the play.

41

DANA TURNED UP at the apartment, now a dull bachelor pad, an hour after I'd left her a voicemail saying I was going to call off the publication. "Oh, how could you?" she asked at the door, and I feared she was talking about Petra.

"He played me. He played both of us," I moaned, hoping we would land in comfortable old patterns of emotional discharge, hoping she wouldn't say Petra was taking her back. "He thought he could put this past me? He didn't know me." I showed her the index card, which didn't interest her for very long.

"That? Are you kidding? Have you even read the play? He gave it to you. Have you read it? What sort of person— How can you back out now?" She was very angry, which triggered my own anger in response.

"*You* didn't want to do it at all. You told me you wouldn't do it."

"Yeah, but *you* did do it. He counted on you. You promised him. He was making it up with you. I didn't need that. And he wrote the will before you two made your— You can't take the will as an insult. You and he hadn't yet— Besides, you have Glassow to deal with now. If he thinks you're degrading the value of our shared property? He'll sue you. You think he's in this for your reputation? Or literature? You debunk his money at your own risk. Mom could probably use the money, too, you know. If you care. You can keep my share if it soothes your issues."

"I'm not negotiating for more money. Thanks. And I don't have issues."

"Have you read it? Really read it? You didn't notice that it's about you?"

"Oh? So you agree he wrote it."

"You chuckleheaded, whinnying, braying *ass.* It's about you, like a dozen other books I can think of. So either Dad wrote it for you, or he asked you to make it famous because he recognized you in it. So don't come wailing that he didn't know you. He gave you this, this *everything.* What do you still want?"

(That's an illusion, of course, a trick of perspective, the idea that the play is in any way "about" me. It can equally be said to be about a man born in Stratford in 1564—maybe on April 22 or 24, by the way—or about an apocryphal boy king in Dark Ages England or about my father or his idea of me or my grandfather or Dana in armor or or or.)

"Who wrote the play, Dana?"

"You promised Dad."

"But it's a fake. It's a crime."

"What a Puritan prig! What do you care?"

"My reputation?"

"You believe your press kit now? Your reputation? From those novels?"

"Nice."

"Sorry. But come on. Seriously. I don't care who wrote it. It's beautiful. I've loved it since we were ten. Dad gave it to me first anyhow, you know. It's not yours to humiliate. It's beautiful. It's part of my life now. More than *Measure for Measure*. More than *Cymbeline*. More than *Pericles*. *Henry VI*. It's better than *Edward III*, you shit, which everyone is canonizing as fast as they can, and that doesn't even have his name on it. What's wrong with you? Seriously, answer that: what is wrong with you?"

"He gave it to you first? That's grotesque. He gave you a forgery. With his father's forged dedication. An heirloom of bullshit. How can you forgive him for all that?"

"Forgive *him*? I don't think— It's not an issue here."

"And you know that this is all a scam. For money. He's dancing in Shakespeare drag to make money."

"But he didn't sell it when he was alive. He sat on it. If he forged it, he forged it for you. It's his love for you."

"So you admit it's a forgery."

"I don't care. You're going in circles. If Shakespeare wrote it, then you're a dick. You're going to lose Mom a pile of money, and you will go down in literary history as that moron who couldn't tell the real thing when he read it. Or if Shakespeare didn't write it, then you're still a dick, because you're throwing Dad's love for you—and for me, by the way, if you care—back in his dead face. And why? Because your feelings are hurt? You want me to tell you that *Angelica* is as good as *Othello*? Fine: 'Arthur, *Angelica* is as good as *Othello*. Dad thought so, too.' Good enough? No? You have to kill both fathers at once: that's what this is. You're the first person ever to suffer from a double oedipal complex, and one of your dads is four hundred years old. Quick: muster up a grievance against Sil and you could do a triple lutz. Man.

If Dad wrote it, he's got you bound up but *good*. You have to say *Arthur* isn't good enough to be Shakespeare, don't you? And you *hate* Shakespeare! Or are you going to say *Arthur*'s not bad enough to be Shakespeare?"

"It's a fake."

"It's a gift."

"If it's a gift, why didn't he admit he wrote it?"

"You are such an ingrate! He had Shakespeare write a play about his boy! Like when he got that baseball player you idolized to sign a ball for you."

"That was a fake, too, Dana. I threw it out years ago."

"Oh, my God. You are such a bastard. I was there when he signed it. I was *with* him."

"Well, there you go then."

"No. *Him*. Dad saw your guy downtown, in front of the IDS, and he asked him to wait while he went and bought a baseball. The guy— Crew?—"

"Rod Carew."

"—Carew. Carew was in a hurry, and he said, 'No, sorry, mister, let's just do it at the ballpark,' all that, and Dad could see he was going to lose this opportunity *to make you happy*, and so he said, 'Guard my little girl, Mr. Carew!' and then Dad just ran off and left me there with a strange baseball player. First, your hero was a little annoyed, then I got him to see it was funny, and he laughed about it, and then I talked to Rod Carew for fifteen minutes, told him about you, and then Dad came back with a ball, and Rod Carew signed it for you."

"I don't believe you. Why have you never told me that?"

"What's the matter with you?"

"Who wrote the play, Dana?"

"Ask your professors."

"I'm asking you. You can't tell who wrote it? I thought Shakespeare was a god, the giant, head and shoulders better, the greatest writer ever to touch English, *inimitable*!"

"No. The plays are inimitable. *Arthur* included."

"Who wrote it? Come on, who wrote it?" I kept demanding, more and more aggressively, the best words available to express my anger at her for taking Dad's side, for standing between me and the love of my life. "Come on, Dana. Billion-dollar question. Who wrote it? Who? Teach me, smarty. Who?"

She stood up, picked up her coat, and walked out, yelling from the hall, "Shakespeare wrote it! Dick."

She cooled off enough to write me a few hours later:

FROM: dsp
DATE: Sun, 8 Nov 2009 23:41:42 -0600
SUBJECT: you suck you suck you suck

Ok. You make me a straw man. You make me hold all the dumb, weak-ass arguments so you can whip them (me) and prove how smaaaht you are. You are, but not because of this.

I don't care who wrote it—plain enough? I don't want the money, so don't publish it on my account. I don't love the man from Stratford more than I love you. I don't even say I like his plays more than I like your books, ok? Sorry about that before, but isn't this good enough? How'd I do?? That's the real thing you want to know, isn't it? You're as original as he is? As good? Fine. You are. I promise. Now please please cut it out.

Just leave well enough alone. Because you don't know what you don't know? Because you might do more harm by meddling? Because I like it very very much. Each time I read it I like it more.. I am fully prepared to continue loving it if it's his or if it's Dad's. (Has it ever occurred to you, by the way, that maybe mom wrote it? Or me? And dad only helped us with the paper and ink? All three of us toiling away, just to impress you?)) I think it should be read and performed. I might stage it myself if I ca nwrestle the rights from you, Shylock.

What about "A thing of beauty is a joy forever"? He didn't say "an accredited thing". So let it go out into the world and make some people happy. A thing of beauty. A joy.

Let it happen, please. Please. For me. Let people think it's
Shakespeare's, because it is, or it might be, or it might as well be,
and then people will read it. And some of them will like it. And then
if it's actually Dad's? And people like it? Then what a gift *you* are
giving *him*! He wants to impress you and you're letting him show
off to the world FOR YOU (even if you know better).

Your reputation. Ok. Think of a reputation not as a monument, but
as a bank account. Now you spend a little for Dad. People read it
and think it's Shakespeare and if Dad was so pathetic as you think,
then what a kindness you're doing his ghost, the ghost of a
pathetic failed man, unlike you in every way. The single most
generous gift you could ever give him, proving you forgive him
everything else—maybe *that's* what he was asking for, in his clumsy
way: forgiveness. And he was asking YOU because only YOU would
know the real value of such a gift. A writer.

You'd be doing such a mitzvah, baby!

If it IS Shakespeare—just give it one teensy moment of your
wise consideration—IF IT IS and you kick and scream that it's
not? Then either people will believe you and you'l succeed in
tearing down Shakespeare himself, denying him a readership,
proving, I suppose, once and for all that you're his equal, if not
absolutely his daddy. You could do that. So what of a little
unstrained mercy for the lesser writer? As the better man—
which I know you are—couldn't you let him win this last one?
400 years from now no one will be reading him, but they will
be reading you, so you could graciously lend your name to this
project, say something nice. Stand aside and let the fellow have
his day? As a favor to your sister, who still has a soft spot for him,
even though she hereby acknowledges THAT SHE PREFERS
YOUR WRITING AND YOU ARE A BETTER WRITER! Hemingway
admitted he was no Tolstoy. Mailer admitted he was no
Hemingway. I am sure Shakespeare would admit he was no
Phillips, if he could.

Or, on the iron-fisted other hand, hold on one more second! THEY WON"T BELIEVE YOU. You'll scream "fraud!" and they'll laugh. You'll be worse than the anti-Strat clowns. The serious American novelist who can't even recognize Shakespeare when he reads it? Not good, Arthur M. Phillips, author of this, that, and the other thing, not good at all All your work will be dismissed at once: "You read Phillips? That Shakespeare dolt? Nobody reads him anymore."

Think about it, bitch!

ps: Seriously? Seriously? Seriously? Shakespeare wrote it.

42

DATE: Tue, 10 Nov 2009 08:33:56 -0600
TO: Jennifer Hershey
CC: Marly Rusoff
SUBJECT: Bad problem

Jennifer, I am so very sorry to write this, especially considering your excitement last week. I really am at a loss. I am kind of in a state, to be honest. I feel like an ass. But we have to stop. I have changed my mind about this. I think we're dealing with a fake. A really good fake, obviously, but a fake. I'm so sorry. Can you start turning this ship around? Of course, I will return the advance in full. (Please arrange, Marly.) SO SO sorry. Arthur.

FROM: "Hershey, Jennifer"
DATE: Tue, 10 Nov 2009 10:22:42 -0500
SUBJECT: Re: Bad problem

Dear Arthur,

This is probably a normal part of doing something like what we're doing. I have to confess, I had sort of a weird night the other night.

I woke up at one in the morning, and I was sure it was all wrong, somehow someone took us for a ride. Have you had nights like this too? I have never been involved in anything like this. Duh! Who has, really? I think your reaction is pretty normal. Did something happen? Did you learn something you can share with me? I hope, of course, that this is all still good, but, truly, if it's going to go bad, let's find out now, okay? If I don't sound more worried, it's because we got another off the Scholars List this morning. Just before you wrote, I heard from Ball, and he writes that he "can find in the text nothing to disprove the cover's claims." I love that line. Not the most courageous, but still. I really think when Verre gets the final forensics report we'll be on much thicker ice. Even better, the copyright search is going great. White has no line of heirs or assignments, and the legal team is almost done clearing Burby. Piers Strickland has been fabulous. Really, I think it's going to be fine. Are you around today? I'm going to try your cell right now. Otherwise call me after 3 your time?

Jennifer

PS: I can't make out the jpeg. Is it a postcard? Speaking of postcards, I'm attaching some stuff for you to look over. I think the art dept did a great job on these. "pdf2a" is a card that would go out to all the accounts, review pages and bloggers.

The pdf showed the two sides of a postcard. The obverse had the iconic Chandos portrait of Shakespeare (with that appealing but very unlikely gold earring) and the reverse had the words "Do you believe in miracles? April 2011." She also sent cover designs and plans for Twitter blasts and Facebook pages. Marly, meanwhile, sent suggestions from a consultant: tchotchke proposals. T-shirts with: I'M THE DEATHSMAN OF REPOSE. Bobbleheads that, when squeezed, recited, *"Thou turnmelon!"* and *"Flea-bit tench! Jordan-faced Pictish scroyle!"* Greeting cards with black-and-white photos of little children holding hands and inside the words *"One's heart gone forth is hardly whistled home / Not when it leaves behind true-weeping love*." Online contests. Win a trip to Stratford. Win two tickets to the opening night of *The Tragedy of Arthur* in London's West End. I, of all people, had enlisted in the Shakespeare Industry, twittering for him (and, like flatterers with a king, weakening him with every overstatement).

DATE: Tue, 10 Nov 2009 09:30:17 -0600
TO: Hershey, Jennifer
CC: Marly Rusoff
SUBJECT: Re: Bad problem

No, you're not totally getting me, jen. I'm saying it can't happen. The jpeg is of some notes taken by the actual author of the play. It's not 400 years old. We have to stop this. If you don't see it my way—I'm not trying to be a jerk—but you have to see it my way, because I'm pulling out of this. I'm so sorry. I totally feel for you in this, too. But this is the way it has to go. A.

FROM: "Hershey, Jennifer"
CC: Rusoffagency
DATE: Tue, 10 Nov 2009 10:50:44 -0500
SUBJECT: Re: Bad problem

Dear Arthur,

Wow. This is a big deal, I get it. Let's just talk later today, and maybe think about this option, which is that you can take your name off this. As I said, we don't know yet, none of us know for sure. Let's wait for a dozen more reviews from the Scholars List. Let's definitely wait for forensics and stylometry. We're not ready yet, none of us, to say it's a definite. And IF the conclusion is that it's authentic and IF you still aren't comfortable with that conclusion, then you can take your name off it. The Intro should be an academic's problem and responsibility, anyway, to be honest. You've done enough, you don't need that headache. I'm sure we can make it so you still own your share of royalties either way. Let's talk today, okay? We don't need to rush anything yet. One thing I won't let you do is make a rash decision, and I know you won't let us proceed unless we're all 100% convinced.

Jennifer

I considered telling her that I'd written the play myself, just to move things along to the *"swift and sure conclusion of this show of cozenage,"* but I did sense that this might adversely affect my future publishing career. I chickened out.

I didn't answer my cell that afternoon, watched her name drift across it in blue, and then my agent's, over and over, the both of them blinking for my attention. I had a quarto visitor scheduled, though not an official one, and I soon preferred his company to their calls. Dana's castmate Tom, who played Palamon in *The Two Noble Kinsmen*, and whose passion for my sister had set so much in motion, had asked her if he could see the play. He was much younger than he appeared onstage, much younger than we, much younger even than Petra. Also, I had thought his English accent was weak on opening night but, in person, he was English.

I didn't bother with a nondisclosure agreement, but he mugged, "Dana says it's all very cloak and dagger, so my lips are sealed."

"Whatever."

He sat down, looked at the cover, and turned his head this way and that. "Really?" he said. "Is this it?"

About thirty seconds later he laughed outright. "Are you having a . . . Is this it?" His reaction was pure and enormously relieving, as if I had finally been released from wrongful commitment in a particularly whimsical insane asylum. "This is not Shakespeare. I'm sorry. Is this really it? The play Dana was bashing on about? I think someone is having you on." He read a few more pages, then said, "Well, let me read the whole thing."

I and my wine were leaning forward in eagerness by the time he finished. "Well?"

"It's a parody, right? It's not even remotely convincing. It's nothing at all of Shakespeare. The texture is all wrong. It doesn't move the same. This isn't his pacing. It's not his mindset. He was . . . This is not. He wouldn't do that, start a soliloquy like that. How can I put this? The feeling of Shakespeare, which you absolutely cannot counterfeit, it's like a fingerprint. You can't just sound like him. You can't sound like Mozart, either. You just can't. Nobody can. You're a writer, aren't you? You know that. Nobody can sound like *you*, and you're not Shakespeare. No offense. This ain't him."

I normally dislike "ain't" in any accent, especially an English one, where it sounds like a smug, coked-up viscount trying to pass as a prole whilst scoring heroin. In this case, however, I was delighted. And he was glad to go on, preening a bit while I took notes to throw back at Random House. He picked out a dozen phrases and words that had tipped him off as "dead giveaways, I'm afraid. Not raining on a parade of yours, am I?"

"Not at all. Let it come down, Tom. Ain't my parade at all."

FROM: "Hershey, Jennifer"
DATE: Tue, 10 Nov 2009 18:26:35 -0500
SUBJECT: Re: Expert input

Arthur,

Now I think you're messing with my mind. Please call me back. I'm going home now but call me there or on my cell. Seriously.

Did you look up the lines and words that were his "dead giveaways"? Every single one of them (even the one you said he called "not a chance in blue hell") occurs in canonical Shakespeare. Every one. Check out www.shakespeareswords.com or some other concordance. I'm not saying he's a fool, and I appreciate you passing on the opinions of naysayers, too. We definitely want all opinions. But in this case, I think this guy's reaction reflects something other than careful reading of the play without prejudice. I actually think, if we get the authentication and we publish the play (IF IF IF), we're still going to get a lot of responses like your friend's here. People might be more afraid of looking foolish than of missing the boat. I think that's sort of natural. You say to yourself, "This can't be. It's too good to be true." And then you find reasons to disbelieve and get mad, prove you can't be suckered. It's almost a false syllogism. "I do know Shakespeare and I don't know this, so this must not be Shakespeare." Anyhow. Please call.

Tom had gone (dissuaded with difficulty from a long, boozy chat about Dana and her possible feelings for him), and I did go back and check online: *terms of manage, extraught, endamagement, whinyard*, archaic spellings like *unckle*, phrasings like "*In litter sick, did he still lead*." ("No," said Tom. "Just come on. Not him. No chance. No.")

Jennifer was right. Nothing wedged under Tom's skin more irritatingly than words Shakespeare had used but that Tom didn't recall and that then seemed to him to be parodies of Shakespearean writing. His certainty was odd, because nothing else he'd said could be measured or proven. Pacing? Mindset? Texture? Fingerprint? I don't know, but I'm sure that this lovesick actor was, in general, right, even if all his specifics were wrong. Still, Jennifer was right, too: his reaction demonstrated something about how a certain type of Shakespeare lover will feel at first exposure to a newly discovered work (if such a thing ever comes to light).

I also felt sympathy for Jennifer and all of Random House, and for my agent, who had sat in those meetings and put her reputation on the line and whose nurturing voicemails I couldn't bear replying to. Random House has gone to great expense, and they expect a massive return, and everyone in publishing is on the ropes right now, and this would be grand, "game-changing." I get it. But, more than that, Jennifer is a true believer, and she was (still is) about to attach her name and credibility to something that she understandably views as the most important event of her career, and a monumental gift to literature and culture. And there I was muttering, "Get out, get out, get out." I'm sure that was unpleasant. But she's going to feel worse next year, after publication. Sorry, Jen.

FROM: "Hershey, Jennifer"
DATE: Tue, 10 Nov 2009 23:11:08 -0500
SUBJECT: Re: Mounting evidence

I'd rather do this on the phone. But I'll stay up all night emailing if
you want. I feel like I'm talking you off a ledge. But I promise you
can go back on the ledge later, all right? We will figure this out.
Nobody is going to push this if there's real evidence that it's fake.
You do know that, don't you? I don't want to publish a fraud. You
don't really think I would, do you? Do you think I'm that far gone?
Nobody at RH wants that. Nobody. Can you still trust me that far?
We and you have not been partners for eight years now for nothing.
Have we ever pushed you into something you didn't want to do?
We changed the title of one novel. That's it.

OK. Let's get into this. I don't think the index card proves what you
think. It doesn't. I've looked at it a lot and that's not how I read it. It
could be notes of someone writing about the play, studying it,
misremembering the line. Making a list of research questions?
Something to take to the library instead of a 400 year old play?
Don't you think he'd be on a card numbered higher than 14 if he
was already writing Act III? I also wouldn't put it past you to forge
the card! ☺

Can I ask you a personal question? Have you thought about what
you would do if this hits like we all think it could? You're going to
be well-off to say the least. Do you think you'll still write? I've
always been curious about what happens to ambition and
ambitious artists when suddenly money becomes no problem at
all.

Maybe this is cheap psychology on my part, but is some part of you
possibly scared of that event? It would make sense. This is a big
deal for everyone, but maybe we haven't talked enough about the
fact that it's the biggest deal for you, of all of us. This is going to
change your life more than anybody's. If I were you, I think I'd be

wondering if I'd still be a writer the morning I become a millionaire. Even Shakespeare retired when he made his bundle. And Dr. Johnson has a great line: "No man but a blockhead ever wrote, except for money."

But you want my opinion? I know you. You're a writer and I think you'll still be one after all this.

Please call me.

DATE: Tue, 10 Nov 2009 22:51:17 -0600
TO: "Hershey, Jennifer"
CC: Marly Rusoff
SUBJECT: Re: Mounting evidence

Jen, no. This isn't about my psychology or money or fear. It is simple. I am pulling out of this, and I am taking the quarto. We're done. I am really sorry, but it's done.

43

IN HIS TIME, Shakespeare was one of many writers. He was admired, but not out of all sane proportion. Others were rated more highly. Opinions varied, as they should, outside of dictatorships. The poet Michael Drayton composed an ode to all the great authors of his day: Shakespeare was one of more than a dozen, just above Samuel Daniel, right in the middle, praised for comedy and "clear rages," whatever that means. The playwright John Webster listed the men he admired around him: Shakespeare was buried in a long roll, recognized not for being the creator of the universe but for being *prolific*, of all things, like Joyce Carol Oates. William Shakespeare was, in other words, a man, a working writer, one of many. So why is he now forced on us as the single greatest? How did he pull this scam, and who abetted?

It isn't an obvious answer, and for the newcomer to Shakespeare, or to those of you who stopped paying attention as soon as tenth-grade English was blessedly over, the idea of someone being unconvinced or even bothered by Shakespeare's easy, royal afterlife may seem a bit odd.

But we have allowed this man to be inflated, to our disadvantage and his (and certainly to the disadvantage of all those other writers of his time whom we never study or read or perform because they're cast as eternal also-rans). But this is a trick of perspective, a rolling boulder of PR, a general cowardliness in us, a desire for heroes and simple answers. Laziness: it's easier to think one guy had it all.

(A) We judge him the best. (B) He has survived all this time. But, really, what if it's the other way around? Is he who we've got because he's good, or do we judge him good because he's who we've got? We now find it hard to enjoy any of his contemporaries very much, but at the time, the same people who liked his plays liked the other guys', too. We've lost the ability to appreciate those others, because we've been too obsessively appreciating him.

His business partners—for love, money, sincere belief—published that folio, the collected works, and in so doing preserved far more of him than we have of anyone else. A sixth of all Elizabethan plays that survive to this day are his, a huge share because his friends had that canny business idea to publish a collected works and include an over-the-top blurb from Ben Jonson, inventing modern literary publicity, pushing a blockbuster. That disproportion—a sixth of all the stage!—gives us a disproportionate view of his value and importance. Another contemporary ranked Shakespeare as one of *four* who were "the best for tragedy," including Thomas Watson. But *none* of Watson's work survives. What might we teach in schools and print on T-shirts and quote to get girls to sleep with us if Watson's friends had been as devoted and savvy as Shakespeare's? How might we speak English differently, or reimagine human psychology?

Because he survived, Shakespeare set our rules for quality (although at the time he was sniped at for breaking previous rules). And who fulfills his rules the best? If "Shakespearean" means "good," then which Elizabethan writer is the best? The one who is the most Shakespearean. And that isn't Dekker.

Merely by surviving time's withering breath, by being studied and taught, he has shaped the world's tastes. We are trained to appreciate him and his distinct qualities, and we ignore the others. Only he does what he does (yes, Tom, his fingerprint), and that's fine. But then we call him the best because we have been shocked and rewarded and bullied into believing that that one fingerprint is the standard of all truth and beauty.

And now we program computers to count up all the phrases he used and scan other texts, and if one of those texts has enough of "his" phrases, then we say he wrote that, too. Jennifer emailed me the computer stylometry results on the twelfth of November. One hundred and twenty-three pages of report for a seventy-six-page play, covering enclitic and proclitic microphrases, semantic bucketing, feminine ending percentages, modal blocks, and on and on.

But as my father used to say, "There's one thing that stylometry doesn't measure, and that's style." It also can't measure my father, who would dig crop circles for the fun of convincing people that aliens had landed, and who colors *The Tragedy of Arthur* in every line.

One faces these terrible *why*s, frustrating in their nearness yet total impenetrability, like strippers behind glass. Why did he do it? Why did he hide it and then reveal it but still lie about it all the way to death? I can untangle a knot of explanations (plausible, partial, plausibly partial, partially plausible), but they always seem to lead me to some other *why* and leave me feeling foolish, made foolish again by my feelings for an incomprehensible father (or for an unknowable playwright).

Let's say, just for the length of this paragraph (because that's now the maximum length of time that I can fake it), that Claremont College's Shakespeare Clinic's stylometry computers are right and that *Arthur* "scores the closest match to core Shakespeare since the foundation of the Clinic." Then why did my father give it to me and not Dana? It's not as if my literary connections and luminosity are so potent—anyone walking into a publishing house bearing a newly discovered Shakespeare play would be whisked to the top floor. You don't have to say you wrote *The Song Is You* to win their attention.

Dana says it was to show me he loved me, to apologize. But if it's a forgery, then those claims are worthless.

And, no matter the stylometry report, it is a forgery. And since the play isn't authentic, we have to ask instead: why did my father write it? The forgery of a nonexistent item requires a very particular trick of the mind, as an artist friend explained to me over drinks in his studio in Minneapolis after I bemoaned my predicament. "Beyond facility with the brush and being on top of the science of the paint and the canvas and the tests for age, beyond talent, there is a skill that the copied artist didn't have or didn't need. Empathy. That's a forger's real knack. The technical stuff can be second-rate and we won't mind."

It is difficult to think of my father as empathetic in the usual sense of the word. Though, semantically, the prison psych report in his box of papers concurs: "Mr. Phillips is capable of remarkable leaps in empathic reasoning, able to rapidly assess the emotional state and needs of others. However, this capability is significantly narcissistic in its orientation." He could see into other people very well, but only so he could manipulate them.

The revealed forgery demands of us, "What sort of person *bothers*?" Well: "The act is paradoxically arrogant and self-effacing. In extreme cases, it can be read as a form of psychic suicide. It is a plea for attention and an ashamed desire to be invisible (as unimportant compared to the esteemed original). It is simultaneously a desire to fool the whole world and, by fooling it, to be assured of one's own unrecognized greatness. Those who accept the forged work as authentic participate in building a monument to the ego of the criminal." That's the psychiatric casebook speaking, and this classical description generally fits. Take van Meegeren ("That pathetic little man," as my artist friend described him). He forged a whole period of Vermeers. "He couldn't really paint like Vermeer, of course, so he invented the idea of Vermeer's poor early efforts. Clever idea, dismal paintings," my friend remarked.

"Remember, the experts couldn't tell; they swore these for Vermeers until van Meegeren painted one right in front of them.

People couldn't see it because the sense of knowing the subject, of knowing Vermeer, was so strong in van Meegeren that he could feel like Vermeer, even if he couldn't paint like him. He could still make us feel like we were in Vermeer's presence, seeing the world as Vermeer did."

Is that my father, then? But my father didn't forge juvenilia; he aimed for the 1590s, when Shakespeare was beginning to break from the pack. Certainly the monument to his ego sounds right: as the professors write in with their tentative or gushing authentications ("It's not unconvincing," said the one from East Anglia, "not unconvincing at all"), they each polish my father's monument.

How large the monument is! The editorial team at Random House excitedly hung up a giant map, and as each university professor weighed in, assistants pushed in a little labeled pin—red for yes, blue for no. Oxford, England, and Oxford, Mississippi. Two Cambridges. Hampshire and New Hampshire, York and New York, Jersey and New Jersey, Wales and New South Wales, and on and on. The red tide seeped across the map, the swath of a flying epidemic of credulity flu.

Was that my father? A man so gifted with empathy—specifically, empathy for a glover's son born four centuries earlier—that Shakespeare experts read his fake and scratch their heads? If my father wrote *The Tragedy of Arthur*, then we have an unpalatable portrait of the artist with a capability for extraordinary love and understanding who was unable to direct any of it toward me. "Can you see how I would find this embarrassing?" I asked him, age fifteen, when Career Day required an essay by me about a parent's job.

"I don't," he snapped. "It doesn't have anything to do with you. I'm me and you're you."

A biographer asks, "What would my subject likely have done, even if I have no record of it?" The forger asks a slightly trickier question: "What would my subject have done that he definitely *did not do*?" And in turn, the forger makes all of us ask ourselves the potentially terrible question, "What actions or thoughts out there are like mine—are *me*—even though I've never done or thought them?" This leads to that paranoid and extreme Shakespeare-philic/Shakespeare-phobic idea that there is nothing we can do or think that some actor from Warwickshire didn't plan for us between 1589 and 1613.

My mother was a victim of my father's inability to be empathetic to the living. I am another of his victims, and yet I have in turn treated my children and wife and sister no better, and day after day Petra did not come to my door to say I was forgiven and that a new start would be granted me. All my empathy has gone into trying to understand fictional characters, fantasies of my own making.

The Random House Publishing Group

Ballantine Books · Del Rey · Modern Library · One World · Presidio Press · Random House · Random House Trade Paperbacks · Villard

Frances Collins
SVP, GENERAL COUNSEL
RANDOM HOUSE

Mr. Arthur M. Phillips

November 13, 2009

Dear Mr. Phillips,

Re: October 7, 2009 contract for production of "The Tragedy of Arthur"

We are counsel for The Random House Publishing Group.

After a review of your e-mail to Jennifer Hershey on the 10th of this month, and of the terms of your contract with The Random House Publishing Group for this book, it is our opinion and that of our client, The Random House Publishing Group, that your proposed actions would constitute a breach of your contract. Such actions would severely damage our client and your reputation as well.

Please deliver your manuscript of the annotated play, your Synopsis and Introduction, as well as supervised access to the original copy of the play for photographic reproductions by the Delivery Date as required by the contract.

Your failure to make such delivery would constitute a material breach of the contract.

In such event, we are instructed to pursue all available remedies to protect our client's interest.

Yours truly,

Frances Collins
Senior Vice President and General Counsel

1745 Broadway, New York, New York 10019   TEL ███████   FAX ███████   E-MAIL ███████

Of all Shakespeare's pithy quotes, most people recall the one that goes something like "First, we kill all the lawyers." My father cited it often enough, and I hear it from a lot of people who, I am certain, have never read or seen a Shakespeare play but who like his authority for their natural instinct.

The sentiment shouldn't really be credited to Shakespeare (as it was on the T-shirt that Chuck Glassow once gave my father). Shakespeare was in the business of making up characters with fictional views, and should not be held responsible for advocating, for example, mass advocatocide. The character who speaks these words in *Henry VI, Part Two* is a henchman of Jack Cade, a revolutionary, a blood-covered ideologue not interested in fine justice or sparing the theoretically innocent in his passion to scrape away the existing order. Cade is a Lenin, a Pol Pot, and he is often cited as an example of Shakespeare's quasi-prophetic powers: Shakespeare wrote Cade, and then Pol Pot appeared three hundred years later to fulfill the imagination of the creator.

Unless . . . what if Pol Pot, as a student in Paris, read *Henry VI, Part Two*? Saw a French production? What if Lenin read it? Or Hitler? And a man of certain tendencies and politics sighed with pleasure to find a role model, a character with whom he so closely identified that he adopted some of his policies? "First, we kill all the people with glasses . . . First, we kill all the kulaks . . . First, we kill all the mentally ill." I think a case could be made that Shakespeare has twentieth-century blood on his hands.

An absurd position, I know, but if critics insist that he showed us how to live and think and love, then surely he taught us how to run an efficient terror-based revolution and how to commit genocide, too.

A Buddhist critic wrote that Shakespeare helped ruin Western civilization by giving such eloquence to resisting change, to analyzing emotions, to the despair over passing time, to exerting one's will: in short, to enunciating so stirringly the opposite of a Buddhist worldview.

He can't win, I suppose. That's the price of his deification. To be fair, I don't hate Shakespeare, and that's to his credit as a writer, because I can't imagine anyone who's been given more good cause to hate him than I. But I cannot find myself in his works. I identify with none of them, no matter how many fawning critics bleat to me that he captured all of humanity in his eye and pen.

Dana saw me splattered all over the canon, citing Richard II's arrogance, Iago's pointless and free-range resentments, Benvolio's friendship, Mercutio's loyalty, Tybalt's fire, Romeo's idealism, Falstaff's appetites, Arthur's passions. Arthur most of all, and I still have to laugh, because if Shakespeare can be so easily imitated by one of those he cast in his likeness, then he is no god at all.

"Of course he's not," she would have chided me now. "He's just a writer. Like you. He deserves only what you deserve: to be read and treated like a writer. A reader likes something you wrote, but something else not so much. Good. That's what he deserves, too, not to be punished with this religion of his perfection and prophecy. Who wants to read something unquestionably perfect for all of us? That's not good for us or him. He wouldn't have wanted it."

44

I AM NOT A FEARLESS PERSON. I am not proud of it, but I cannot claim much courage when faced with letters like that one from the Random House lawyer. That sort of letter, I know, is designed to cow people. I was cowed. There it is. I sat back, did nothing, wrote nothing, was not openly uncooperative, responded noncommittally to every email from Jennifer and Marly, and waited for someone smarter and more persuasive than I to settle this. *Something* would come along to prove it, even to them, and it would all go away. I would be right, but I would not stand up to be right. Or to be sued.

Jennifer sent me notices every time a professor from the Scholars List rendered his or her official opinion. Some *were* refusals to certify; there were even a few very well argued essays against Shakespeare's authorship of the play, and she honorably sent me those as well. But as November rolled on, such emails and faxes were in the needle-thin and oppressed minority, and late in the month she sent me a digital photo of that big map over at 1745 Broadway, now a view of Mars from the pins of authenticating red. That email's subject line was "Preponderance of scholarly opinion."

It was torturous to watch these views come in wrong. I occasionally rose to the bait and clicked off angry little e-rants to her:

> Seriously, listen to this guy: "Scholarly opinion now holds that he did write some or all of *Edward III*, and similarly *Arthur* is, in my view, largely or entirely written by William Shakespeare." Well, which, Jen? Some or all? And why is scholarly opinion now ready to let him have *Edward III*, more or less, when, for two hundred years that same scholarly opinion was certain Shakespeare had nothing to do with it, a play they dismissed as beneath his talent? This is not a serious field. It's fashion and PR.

Dear Mr. Phillips,

I wished to send you a copy of my report directly because you and your family were so hospitable to me during my stay in lovely Minneapolis. I do hope we might see one other again in the coming exciting months. Please send your father my very warmest regards.

Ours is not an exact science, but a matter of the most precisely described and fulsomely supported guesswork. Some things do strike one as so unlikely as to cross over into the absolutely impossible, it must be said, but other questions are not fully answerable these many centuries later. It seems to me that, from a textual perspective, *Arthur* is in the realm of the entirely possible.

Our taste and cultural point of view are not eliminated by computers. You know, the century before last, some critics simply *knew* that Shakespeare could not have written *Titus Andronicus* because they didn't like it. Today, most of us do not think too much of *Henry VI, Part One*, and, lo and behold, the computers tell us he probably didn't write too much of it. Well, we must be a little more careful than that.

The *Arthur* text is consistent with the Shakespeare whom we know in the early to mid-1590s, contemporaneous, in my opinion, with *3 Henry VI* and *Richard III* or a bit later. The vocabulary is either attested to by sources of the period or, in cases where it seems he was inventing words and compounds (admittedly rather more heavily and rather earlier than we have seen him do elsewhere, if my dating is correct), it is in a manner consistent with his style. None of the hallmarks of forgery are present in the text. It should go without saying that this opinion does not take into consideration anything you have learned from examination of the paper, ink, and binding.

The computer stylometry report I read certainly does not conclusively prove that Shakespeare wrote *Arthur*. Such tests are not perfect, of course. They are just a little supportive of our hunches, one piece of the puzzle, if you will. (There are passages of Shakespeare that fail the tests, you know!) In this case, some of the phrase and frequency tests imply that Marlowe might have had a hand, which I think unlikely. Perhaps Robert Greene. Some elements point to Thomas Kyd, which I do find somewhat more persuasive. Do I sense Dekker? Perhaps. But, yes, certainly, examining the data over the length of the entire play, there is nothing to rule out Shakespeare, specifically the Shakespeare who still finished his sentences at the ends of his lines, who rarely used caesuras or broke his verse. Shakespeare of the early to middle 1590s, no later, in my opinion, than 1594.

If our generation does not like something Shakespeare wrote, we are tempted to say he did not write it. And if someone, imitating Shakespeare carefully enough, writes something we do like, we are tempted to say Shakespeare did write it. In that way, he edits himself, and he has the luxury, every generation, of receiving help in crafting only the best possible collected works. He keeps the best of the day and can rely on us to pooh-pooh his own worst stuff for him. Which brings us to the question of *Arthur*.

I must say, I think it reads quite well, and I like parts of it very much indeed. I think Arthur and Guenhera's courtship scene is especially fine. The play in its entirety is not my favourite, but I feel similarly, for example, about *All's Well That Ends Well*. Thus, when a computer says it isn't *not* Shakespeare, I am tempted to give it to him. It has his name on the cover and a date that makes sense, which—I expect you know— hardly proves it is him, but also does not weigh against him. All told, I enjoyed the play, and, more to the point, I rather *like* the idea of it being his. I like that he might have written that scene of Guenhera's labour pangs. (Not terribly scholarly of me, I confess!) I am glad to offer you this good news. I am happy to add my name to the authentication process. Congratulations, and I sincerely hope you and *Arthur* continue to win over fans.

A nice old lady, certainly. I don't wish to mock her scholarship or her kindness. But, really. A science dedicated to proving that all the bad ones *were by someone else*? This is typical of the industry. "After God, Shakespeare has created most," mooed Alexandre Dumas, another better man kowtowing to the plaster bard. Shakespeare could not conceivably write bad plays; therefore, bad plays with his name on them are fraudulent. Even the bad parts of the things we know he wrote! The worst of *Pericles* is now by Wilkins. The computer says so.

If all this is circumstantial, speculative, well, there is something else. I remember Dana's responses to our "old" "1904" edition, back when she thought she was being shown a play many people debated, like *Edward III* or *A Yorkshire Tragedy*. She read it in a frenzy, failing to ration her pleasure, and she rushed back to our father with *her* stylometric report, which, as an eleven-year-old, she was very proud to deliver, proud that he cared about her opinion. "I think it's him," she declared, every bit as scholarly as that Irish don whose letter I just transcribed.

"Yes! You just *know*, don't you?" he told her. "When you read it, aloud, you know it's him. It's his—don't count the *you* or *ye*, the *'em/them*, forget all that nonsense. Just read it out loud like your performance matters, like you can impress the groundlings and the nobles, maybe the queen, and you *know* it's him. It makes you laugh like him, gives you gooseflesh just the same." He recited from memory a few lines of Arthur's from II.vii:

"Imperfect is the glass of other's eyes
Wherein we seek in hope of handsome glimpse
Yet find dim shapes, reversed and versed again,
Which will not ease our self-love's appetites."

Dana applauded. "It *is* him," she said, a girl with an idol—my father and Shakespeare interblended in her loving gaze. "It *has* to be."

"It does have to be," he agreed. "His attitude, his amused skepticism—of kings, of knowing ourselves, of knowing all our own motives, of love. He loves all of life, but he tells the truth even about the bad parts."

"So why doesn't everyone see it's him?" Dana demanded. "Why don't people put it on?"

"They don't have a *license* to like it. They need precious proof, a piece of paper, an explanation. They don't trust what you and I can hear. They want trivia: Where did the play go? Why this, why that, why isn't it proven? But we don't know. How could we? Anything's possible: maybe it was censored, maybe he meant to work on it a little more. We can't know, but really, who cares? *You* know, don't you. You can hear it. God, Dana, that's wonderful."

At the time, I thought they were just annoying. Now I know what he was doing, because he told me as much: he trusted her opinion, and if she was convinced—*an eleven-year-old girl in 1975*—then he felt his play had passed some test.

Even after stylometry and the Scholars List, the argument isn't really any further along than that: some people (he and Dana, some professors, some software) have loved *The Tragedy of Arthur* as much as they love if not *Hamlet*, not *Lear*, then *King John*, *Richard III*—and with the *same* love. "I love you because you look like your mom," Dad once said to Dana, and she hugged his shoulders from the side at this odd disclosure, which he then quickly amended: "And because you're you, and all that. But you do look like her." I wasn't there for this conversation, reconstructed here for memoiresque purposes from Dana's testimony and my knowledge of my father, as he conflated his loves for his estranged wife and his daughter. "When I haven't seen your mom for a few years, because, you know, and she appears at her door when I come to pick you and Artie up, and she's wearing clothes I've never seen and glasses she didn't need the last time and a new hair color and all, you think I don't recognize her? Don't love her as much as ever? That stuff doesn't hide *her*. Well, it's the same."

That's precisely how the computers feel. And with that, the argument in favor of *The Tragedy of Arthur* comes to its end. Contract fulfilled.

These professors! Once they wager their egos, they never quit. More than a reputation or tenure is at stake. They bet their very souls. By the time you are (to pick one of these indistinguishable biographies at random) "one of the world's leading experts on Shakespeare's history plays," the possibility that you can't recognize a Shakespeare history play when you see one would be enough to make *you* feel like a forgery. That must sicken you, a very hollow thud in the heart, which is why only the most courageous critics are going to come out strongly for or against this play.

"A work of a creative genius," writes an English fence straddler, on the other hand, "though whether it is by the same genius as the one born in Stratford in 1564, I am not yet prepared to say."

It's maddening that it's even close. It should be intolerable to any of you who actually love Shakespeare that *Arthur* has made it this far. It should be obvious, plain in every line that it can't be him. *Arthur* is bad. The play is bad. It is bad. Don't read it.

I love this one: "Shakespeare was drawing on his own experience of lost fatherhood in Gloucester's wrenching soliloquy in Act I. I think it might only have been written by a man with a painful loss in fatherhood. Recall as well, please, that Shakespeare's only son, Hamnet, died in 1596. I would wager any sum that this play is by his hand and dates from '96–'97." Give that man a Pulitzer.

Still, there was one last hurdle that my father absolutely would not be able to clear with his pre-1986 technology and his almost perfect career record of getting caught. When the forensics report came in, we would all just go home and forget this ever happened.

"As of 19 November, we have found nothing out of period in the materials or production of this document. We must stress that this is not a certification of authenticity. Further investigation could still produce evidence of an anomaly." The forty-eight-page report went on to declare the ink as being of appropriate chemistry and the paper as unbleached sixteenth-century Genoese printer's stock. The font used to produce the text showed no evidence of differing from the equipment responsible for the 1598 *Love's Labour's Lost* quarto. The print history examination included comparisons of variable spelling, signature numbering, et cetera. I stopped reading.

FROM: "Hershey, Jennifer"
DATE: Tue, 24 Nov 2009 09:46:09 -0500
SUBJECT: FW: Blinded me with science!

AP!

I love that stuff like this even exists. It's amazing what they know, isn't it? Be sure to read the print historian's sub-section. *LOVE* it! Read page 41. He goes into what they can trace to White's print shop. They can say how many little p blocks he had in his font case in 1598 because when he set a page with a lot of p's, for the last few he had to use inverted d's. And the same thing happens, *after the same number of p's,* on two pages of Arthur. Unbelievable.

Verre says the forensics battery is now an all-clear. I honestly can't believe there's anything to doubt here. Do you still? I think it is impossible that a forger could fool all these tests.

That smug certainty of modern science's all-seeing eye, that conviction that there is no human ingenuity still to come: this gives me some faith in the falseness of the otherwise disorienting forensics report.

I will only assert that there is always a way to fool a test. That the most complex tests are being fooled right now by someone who hasn't been caught yet. The good forgers, recall, will never be known. Peter Bryce said as much to me: "I suppose by definition I only catch bad forgers, don't I?" Tomorrow's tests will catch today's master criminal, just as today's scientist feels safe mocking yesterday's master criminal. There has always been erroneous, arrogant certainty on the part of some technicians that they could never be tricked by artistry. Always has been; always will be. I don't know how my father did it, but he did it. If I'm the only one who can see it, that doesn't make me wrong. He did it.

Arthur, the more I think about it, the more I admire your tenacity in double-checking every possible explanation of your good fortune. I can understand—if I were holding a lottery ticket such as yours—the overpowering sense of disbelief.

45

Petra came to me, shaking and wet from the snow, and she let me wrap a blanket around her and hold her, the first time in weeks. She said nothing, just stood there and let me hold her, and I knew everything was going to be fine.

And then she stepped away from me, said she had just come from her doctor. She was pregnant. She had only meant to punish Dana, she said, maybe more, and Dana never wanted a baby and Petra did, and maybe she had felt something else about me last summer and fall, but it didn't matter now, not at all. She wanted the child, and she wanted to leave Minneapolis and go home to her own family in a different city in a different country, and she had come to say goodbye and tell me this news, but she expected and wanted me to do nothing about it.

"But I love you. That's not nothing. No poetry, Petra. No lies. Just: I love you and I want us to take this gift and be happy. The end."

"That seems possible to you?"

I laughed in my certainty. "Yes. Wait. Don't you see? This fixes everything. It's *authenticating*." God help me, that was the first word that came to mind, and I can picture (I can't stop picturing, unfortunately) Petra's face in response. "My kids, our baby: you'll see. We can put this all together. The pieces all fit. It's a great thing, a great start to a great story. You have to trust me. Stay. Trust me. I'll take care of everything." I tried to hold her again, but she stepped away, shedding the blanket and me.

"You're wrong."

"But you're not—you're not *indifferent* to me?" I asked hopefully, though even as I said it, the expression before me was projected back over the faces, the poses, the images of our nights together, and they changed, recolored by how she was now, passion becoming indifference, wonder becoming regret, love becoming hate, shame smearing a gritty film over all of it. "What are we going to tell Dana?"

"That's not really your problem, is it?" she said, with a look of bottomless disgust.

"I'll tell her," I said. "Tomorrow. After her matinee. I'll pick her up at the theater. You can come if you want, or I'll do it alone."

She left me in the dark apartment, watching the snow come down, my father's ghost still snoring in the back bedroom. I sat alone on the couch. There was no more wine. That feeling of a con being revealed—the nausea and instant aging and fury and shame and humiliation: I tried to imagine learning that your brother has impregnated your girlfriend.

DATE: Tue, 8 Dec 2009 21:51:08 -0600
TO: Jennifer Hershey
SUBJECT: The end.

Dear Jennifer, my editor and friend, I hope,

I have had a rotten couple of weeks. You keep sending me the good news, and I just don't believe it, and I can't bring myself to start writing some Introduction I know is a lie and I don't want to make money on a lie and I keep staring at this very bullying letter from RH's legal office, which I have to say pisses me off.

My "failure" to deliver "The Tragedy of Arthur" by William Shakespeare is predicated (to talk like a lawyer) on the fact that no such item exists. I signed a contract with you in my good-faith belief that it did. I was wrong. It doesn't. Something else exists, which, published over my name and your colophon, will make us both look like fools or worse. I am sorry for any damage this does to you. I really do sympathize. I know you put a lot of career capital into this. As for real capital, I'll pay back the advance, and then you and I will both say goodbye to our mutual dreams of avarice and fame dreamt in other days. Hershey, "I charge thee, fling away ambition: By that sin fell the angels." For my part, I'll burn this atrocity of an old criminal's fevered, feculent ambitions.

I put off telling Dana. Characteristically, I suppose, even predictably, it appears. Friday, I resolved to do it. *Kinsmen* was off that night, and I left her a voicemail asking her to meet me for dinner. And I waited. And practiced what I would say. I think I would have done it. I was ready.

Petra called instead. She was sobbing, just sounds, until a few words emerged, incoherent. "Do you want to come and do this with me?" I asked. She just cried and cried. "Pet?" I told her to calm down or some other pointless inanity. At last she said, "I told her. I'm so sorry. Tonight I told her. You never did. And she told me to leave and I did. Please, I'm so sorry. I'm here. Now. She took something. I don't know. Arthur, she's hurt herself. She's . . . oh, God . . ." My sister was dead.

46

M Y FATHER SPENT HIS LIFE pretending to be other people, the creator of other people's work, creating pretend things, things everyone knew were impossible, whether they realized it right away or only later. He gave himself over to his unoriginality. At the end, he had stripped away everything but the unkillable urge to convince me (and the world) that Shakespeare wrote *Arthur*, when obviously Arthur wrote Shakespeare. As he lay dying alone, all that mattered was an act of self-immolation.

To strive to break loose, to skin oneself down to the unique germ under all the layers of other people's effects, and to try to rebuild on that one unique element, to avoid at all cost any hint of pastiche, imitation, anxiogenic influence, and then to burst out and display colors never before seen in combinations never before imagined: this is the chimera I have been scrambling after in response to what I thought of my father back when I was an ordinary, common disappointed child. But we *all* seem to pray at this cult of our own originality. This accounts for our flood of dull memoirs, which tend to be, ironically, quite similar: everyone feels they are unique and the story of themselves will be unique, too.

But, on a planet of seven billion, it is unlikely that very many of us (if any) are literally unique. That blow to the beloved identity can feel fatal, and so the forger settles for second best: he finds the acknowledged and accredited unique figure (Shakespeare) and says to himself either (A) "Well, if I can be him, then he's not so unique, so I don't have to feel bad for being a bundle of low-grade copies myself," or (B) "Well, if I can be him, then I'm unique, too, just like him, unlike these seven billion walking duplicates."

But Dana. Beautiful Dana. Her job was to pretend to be other people, to speak words written by someone else, while other such people pretended to love or hate her, to make a darkened room full of strangers admire her in her artificial imitations and recitations.

I sat between Petra and my mother on the opening night of *The Two Noble Kinsmen*. Dana made her first entrance.

She was dressed in fanciful Elizabethan costumes in a play set in an imagined ancient Greece, a prequel of sorts to another, better play, and based on a story written by a fourteenth-century Englishman, adapted by two seventeenth-century Englishmen, one of whom was trying to write in the style of the other, including a scene that was patently an homage to a previous, much better play, based in turn on an eleventh-century Danish legend. Dana recited these men's rhymes, took only those steps and made only those gestures predetermined by her director, a Croatian journeyman Antonio who, after finishing work on this play, hurried off to direct an episode of a well-loved and well-worn network hospital drama.

But for all this artifice, there was *Dana*. I wasn't the only one who thought she (Emilia) was a unique and original figure on that stage. Strangers—hundreds of strangers five times a week for seven weeks—looked at her like they'd never seen anything like her, and they hadn't. There is nothing in Shakespeare to predict Dana, except, perhaps, Guenhera in *Arthur*, proving only how much my father loved her.

When we were sixteen, I earned my driver's license on the first try, outscoring Dana by one crucial point. I passed; she failed. The next day, I took the opportunity to visit Dad alone, the first time I'd ever done that. (My own limited empathy fails to provide subtitles to my mother's nodding, expressionless silence when she handed me the keys. Nothing new there, I suppose: a famously vicious and dismissive New York newspaper book reviewer—whom I made the career-bashing mistake of kissing and feeling up at a party at Yale decades earlier and then never calling—faulted my last novel for "a curious absence of empathy.")

I have better luck reading Dana's heart. I didn't tell her I was going to visit Dad because I didn't want her to come with me, and I didn't want to say no if she asked. And so when I returned, obviously both-ered by the visit, I saw her swallow her anger and hurt feelings in order to be ready to listen to me. I lay on her floor, next to the bed, where she'd been reading by lamplight. She switched it off, and we were in the near darkness of a Minnesota April evening. I turned on my side, away from the window, to see the old dolls under her bed, sidelit from the hall, ignored for years now but still carefully glued in position under their sleeping mistress, awaiting her renewed interest, voices, animation, never to return. Their tea poured, forever ignored, hands touched surreptitiously under the table forever, glances forever discreetly exchanged in the crowded tea party, hopes forever sup-pressed behind pursed plastic lips.

"How is he?" she asked in the dark.

"He's him."

"How are you?"

"I'm me, unfortunately," I whined imprecisely.

"I feel for both of you," Dana said, as if she were being ironic, but she actually did feel for both of us, and I appreciated her feeling for me, but then an instant later I denied myself that balm and found it cheap, because if she felt for him (who deserved none of her fine feeling), then her feelings were indiscriminate and therefore worthless. My God, what a curiously contorted bastard.

All I said was "What's with these stupid dolls? Why do you still have them? Are they supposed to be gay?"

"Yeah. Lesbian Barbie," she sighed. I thought that was pretty funny, and I valued her again at once in my storm-front sentimentality. "Why does he piss you off so much?" she asked.

"He's just so awful." I don't disagree with that, but only now can I translate it into adult: *Why doesn't he understand that his behavior affects my happiness and that I am ashamed and angry and embarrassed and confused about what it means to be a man and a father as a result?*

This is not so remarkable. It *is* remarkable that Dana was able to answer me back then as if she already spoke adult. That is empathy. "You're stuck until you forgive him," came her voice through the darkness.

"'There's no forgiveness without an apology first,'" I snipped, stingily quoting some puritanical pamphlet of self-reliance I was reading, besotted as I was back then by Ayn Rand. "'And even then, apology-and-forgiveness is just a compact of shared weakness.'"

"No, it's strengthening, I think. Forgiving him means you don't need him to help you be you anymore," Dana said, or something along those lines, and I remember feeling uncomfortably, almost painfully, hot, down there on the floor, silent on my side, in the dark on her white shag rug, angry again, certain that she, too, was in on whatever conspiracy was afoot of people who knew what I was thinking and wanted to make me admit I didn't understand myself at all. And then, on cue, Dana asked from the dark (though it looked like one of her dolls speaking), "Now you're mad at me, too, aren't you?"

I could say so little, couldn't say why I was crying, why I loved Dana more than anyone I'd ever known, why I only felt truly myself when I was with her. But at least I knew it, and my hand was already up above me, squeezing hers on the bed as I coughed on my tears.

Desperate to be unique and desperate to be joined to someone else; desperate to be free of my father, of influence, of expectations, of limitations, and yet desperate to be contained and defined, known and understood; desperate to be lauded for my distinctiveness and loved for my similarity. I was desperate to be like my sister and loved by my sister, who had somewhere found the secret to originality.

Those mystifying dolls under the bed, lit from the hall like stage actresses, dressed in incongruous outfits—stewardess skirts and pill-boxes, Regency high-waisted drawing-room dresses, military fatigues, cheerleader sweaters and kilts, tiaras and ermine robes—they, all of them, were enacting some scene from inside Dana's head. They, all of them, were aspects of her, all abandoned under the bed the day she no longer needed them to sort out who she was.

So much of Shakespeare is about being at a loss for identity, being lost somewhere without the self-defining security of home and community, lost in a shipwreck, confused with a long-lost twin, stripped of familiar power, taken for a thief, taken for the opposite gender, taken for a pauper, believing oneself an orphan. But Dana had somehow settled all that on her own. I knew she would never be at a loss, no matter what life's drama did to her. Dana was never an article of stupid faith for me. She was my only undeniable fact.

I drove to her apartment to face what I had done.

47

I POUNDED ON THEIR DOOR, out of breath, hoarse. It was unlatched and swung open on my first blow. I ran in, ready to gulp down whatever pills she'd taken, ready to join her, ready to fall on her body, ready, I promise, to die for my mistakes. I swear it: I look back at that moment and I see no hesitation or posing in what I meant to do. I deserved to die and I meant to die.

"Arthur Rex," Dana clucked, as if at a naughty boy.

I slumped down onto the floor at the sight of her and Petra sitting on the couch, sipping hot drinks, Maria on his back between them, a two-woman tummy rub in progress. His head hung backward and upside down over the front of the couch, the tips of his ears almost touching the floor. Our mother was in the kitchen. I shook and hyperventilated and gagged, laughing and crying and shouting. My nose ran uncontrollably, and I asked half questions that everyone ignored, and I ended on my knees, trying to hug Dana's legs. "Don't do that." She kicked me away gently but firmly, like a dog humping her shin. I couldn't stop shivering. "Go warm up in the bathroom. Come back when you can listen."

I stood for several minutes under the warming lamp, looking in the vanity mirror, trying to recognize myself or anything of what was happening. I didn't move until I heard impatient scratching on the door. I opened it and followed Maria back into the living room.

I stood before them and heard it all recited back to me from a different narrator's view. When I winced and turned my eyes to the carpet, Dana said, without any humor at all, "Look at me when I'm speaking to you, please." She had suspected me the night it began, but she knew it all by her own opening night. She knew it all when she called at two in the morning the night Dad died. She knew about us at the cemetery. She knew about us down on Nicollet Mall after we read the will at Bert's office. She knew about us when I told her about the index card, when I told her I was going to stop publication of the play and she stormed out. She knew about us the night Petra came to tell me of the baby.

"I kept waiting for you to figure out a good ending to this story," Dana said. "You're a writer and everything. Famous novelist? Not so good at endings, though, it started to seem. You really couldn't think of one, could you? Lame-ass. You just left me there to find out by myself and then give up? I was supposed to just realize you were right for her, and I should get out of the way, leave you with her and the baby. Because you're such a great husband and father? You can't even think of something consistent with the characters. That was the best you could come up with?"

"I'm sorry."

"Too late for that. We need a good ending," Dana said. "Do you have any suggestions? Last chance."

"I'm sorry." I was still shivering. "I'm really, truly—"

"We need action, not words, I think, at this point." She just stared at me and shook her head. "Did you really think I'd drown myself, Hamlet?"

"I don't know. I don't really understand. I feel—"

"No, no. No more feelings. Just plot now. Come on, buck up. Pull yourself together. This is important. Give me an ending, writer. What do you have? Nothing? Really? Well, then, let's turn to a better man. What's your favorite Shakespeare ending?"

"I don't understand."

Petra said, "Please don't pick *Antony and Cleopatra*, where the Middle Eastern girlfriend has to kill herself. I don't dig snakes."

Dana looked sideways at Petra and laughed. "I hadn't thought of that one. That's good. You are good." They had sorted everything out somehow, I don't know when, but Petra looked grateful.

"I don't understand," I repeated feebly.

"Well, I'll make it easy, killer. Do you think we've got a tragedy or a comedy here? I'll give you a hint: I'm not going to kill myself for you. And neither is she. Or Mom, I don't think."

"Okay. A comedy."

"Atta boy. Now we're moving. So which comedy?"

I tried to play along with whatever this was, even though I was so cold I was biting the insides of my cheeks until I tasted blood. "How about the one where the jerk realizes he shouldn't have tried to steal his best friend's girlfriend, and he apologizes, and everyone forgives him."

"*Two Gentlemen of Verona*?" Dana scoffed. "That wish-fulfillment piece of shit? Total crap. A man's calculated effort to steal, then rape his dearest friend's lover, and everyone just gets over it? I don't think so. Not Shakespeare's finest moment: nobody's that forgiving. Try again. A little more realistic, please."

I was hunched and shaking before them, still wet, my stomach churning and beginning to cramp, naked, but for my clothes, in front of the five encouched female jurors: my mother, silent and miserable, her crossed leg bouncing with caffeine and unhappiness; Petra, kissing up slightly to Dana, positively delighted by whatever reconciliation they had come to without me; Maria, on his back again; Dana, smiling and angry at once, a curtain lowered over her soul, her disappointment in me and her exclusion of me from her sympathies the most brutal punishment I could imagine at the moment. Did I say five females? Yes, from time to time, Dana's hand would leave Maria's belly to rest on Petra's.

I chattered, "Is it *As You Like It*?"

"Is what *As You Like It*? Speak up, boy."

"The one where everyone sort of dances around and gets married and forgives the one guy who ends up without a wife?"

"Spoken like a true Shakespeare scholar."

I just looked it up, by the way, and I was right, although I didn't have all the details at my fingertips that night, obviously. (I also noticed just now that in that play the faithful shepherd-lover is called Silvius, so that name's appearance in *Arthur* isn't that suspicious after all.) At the end of *As You Like It*, Jaques the cynic has, by his own choice and errors, removed himself from the party and the dancing circle. And that, I was hoping, was how we could end, me on the outside, but still not far away, still not utterly banished, their anger at me softening by their love for each other. That would be fair, while everyone else joined hands in celebration of life so far, inhaling together for whatever comes next—births, weddings, deaths. This would be a good time for the curtain to fall: the god Shakespeare descending deus ex machina to bless us one and all, even his faithless priest, me. Dana and Petra back together, eventually my mother forgives me, then cashes the first of many giant checks left to her by her devoted first husband, his shade in peace at last because he's made everything right. Meanwhile, Uncle Arthur lives quietly and alone, visited occasionally by his mother, sister, estranged sons, baby niece. Dana and Petra raise a child that, with only sixteenth-century technology, resembles both of them, a twenty-first-century crowd-pleaser. We pray our little comedy has not offended. Good night.

"No, I don't think so," Dana said. "You're no Jaques. Try again."

"I don't know, Dana. I really am so sorry. This just got all confused—"

"You and I are way past that now. We need something definitive. Action. Proof. Something we can trust is a real change. A new footing for all of us. A baby's on the way now, and everyone needs to know who you are in this."

"So tell me who I am. What do you want me to do?"

My mother finally spoke, though she didn't look at me, only at Dana, who was firmly in charge of this scene. There was no fun in my mother's voice when she spoke, just the starkest disappointment in another Arthur: "Isn't there one where the lech is tied to a tree and pinched and frightened by little children with torches or something until he gets the point?"

"*Merry Wives of Windsor*," Dana sighed. "Yeah, funny but not very conclusive. You get the sense that Falstaff isn't really going to change." She looked me up and down, my incessant shaking, my weak effort at a smile, my increasingly obvious intestinal discomfort. "We could force the villain to marry the girl he's wronged. *Measure for Measure. All's Well That Ends Well.* What do you say, Petra? That's really your call."

"No, no, no, I'll pass," said Petra, waving one hand in front of her nose, her other resting on Dana's hand on her still-flat stomach.

"Hmm. Running out of canon, Artie. How do you feel about the end of *Love's Labour's Lost*?"

"I could never read that one," I admitted.

"Too bad. It's worth the trouble—you should go read it. Because it's the one for us. *To weed this wormwood from your fruitful brain.*"

"I don't even know what that means."

"I suppose you don't. You're the guy who doesn't even know Shakespeare when you read it. Pick up your coat."

"What?"

"Get your coat. I see you had time to take it on your way out the door to view my corpse. Wouldn't want to catch cold doing that."

"It was already—I was already wearing—I had it on me—already on," I stumbled. The truth.

"*A heavy heart bears not a nimble tongue.* Whatever. Fine. Get your coat." I picked up my dripping coat. "Put it on. Zip up. It's cold out there. Now take out your car key. Good. Here's your ending: *This shall you do for me / Your oath I will not trust.* For a twelvemonth, probably more, depending on publishing, you will not see any of us, or call, or email, or anything. Not one word. Right, Mom? Just nod, Mom. Not one word. None of us. And if in that period you can prove something to us, then you will be welcomed back, and we will be right joyful of your reformation. You will publish *The Tragedy of Arthur*. Yes, you will. Don't talk. Listen. And you will divest yourself of your precious reputation and self-love, which has led us to so many unfortunate dead ends these long years. And you will prove to us that we matter more to you. And you will publish our story, but mostly your story. You will tell the truth. You will write a little nonfiction for once in your life, and you will learn its lessons in public, where everyone can see you and judge you, not hidden behind your imagination or ambiguity or characters or your famous scorn of memoirs, but right out front, naked. And you will be judged for what you did. By everybody. Because with a Shakespeare play attached, everyone is going to read it. And if we are impressed by what you write, maybe we can talk about the ending to *As You Like It* again. If not, well, I think we're back to the tragedies at that point. No, don't say anything. Nobody here wants to hear it. None of us. Just take your keys and go. Now. And not a word until we've had a chance to read your book. Not the galleys, either. The hardcover. Go. No, just go."

My mother didn't look up, not even at the very end, and Petra busied herself with Maria, scratching him until his back leg kicked the air. Only my sister was still watching as I closed the door. She didn't look sad.

In a burst of childhood jealousy or childishly innocent amorality, I once (or more) poked around my sister's desk and came upon her diary and my father's half of their correspondence. I read their jokes and messages of love and discussions of books and plays, unlike anything I'd ever written or received. She caught me there, hands in her secrets. "Oh, my," she fake-purred, trying to sound grown-up about it, trying to cast me as a boy years younger than she, just because I'd snooped. She was trying not to appear angry, just suddenly removed from being my twin, a distant, amused big sister. "A thief in our midst!" she laughed, and I hated her so much, this version of her who abandoned our identicality, pretended not to understand what drove me, pretended she wouldn't have done the same thing in my shoes, pretended not to be part of our joint agreement against the world. (Obviously, yes, I had broken that agreement by breaking into her desk, except that her secrets in that desk were actually the first violation of our alliance.) I fled her bedroom, pursued by the stuffed bear she threw after me.

In this case I went home, where, shivering and sweating hard and trying to take my temperature, I dropped the ancient thermometer in my bathtub, and a worm of silver mercury slithered from the glass wreckage.

She sent me the 1904 edition of *Arthur* a few weeks later. No note, just the inscription *For Arthur, from Dana.*

Ballantine Books · Del Rey · Modern Library · One World · Presidio Press · Random House · Random House Trade Paperbacks · Villard

Frances Collins
SVP, GENERAL COUNSEL
RANDOM HOUSE

Mr. Arthur M. Phillips

December 9, 2009

Dear Mr. Phillips,

Re: October 7, 2009 contract for production of "The Tragedy of Arthur"

Jennifer Hershey has forwarded to this office your further email of December 8, 2009, expressing your intention to destroy the original edition of the play "The Tragedy of Arthur" by William Shakespeare. Ms. Hershey has been instructed not to communicate with you further in regard to this matter until you have abided by the terms of your contract.

If you fail to do so, Random House has instructed us to seek all appropriate remedies, which may include injunctive relief and recovery of damages, including lost profits.

Of course your contract allows and indeed requires you to write an "Introduction," the final text of which is your own. You can express your dissenting argument to the play's authenticity in that space. Your views will then be weighed against those of others.

Please respond to this letter, and our letter of November 13, 2009, within two days of the date of this letter, indicating that you will comply with our client's request and with your contractual obligations.

Yours truly,

Frances Collins
Senior Vice President and General Counsel

48

A CT V: Mordred comes to court, knowing Arthur is in Ireland. He means to win Guenhera's support for himself as the official heir, or perhaps even to seduce and impregnate her, to prove his divine right to the crown. He is greeted by actors who mistake him for an actor as well. Enraged by them and insulted by Guenhera, he then meets Philip of York, who insists that *he* is the anointed heir. Mordred kidnaps them both. Arthur turns his Irish invasion around to intercept Mordred alongside the Humber River in Yorkshire. In soliloquy, Arthur judges his life and kingdom as failures, but he cannot see what else he could have done. His army is trapped in the mud. Fatalistic, even self-destructive, he is impatient to get on to an ending, even a bad ending. Pictish ambassadors arrive, offering Guenhera and Philip in exchange for Arthur's abdication. Outnumbered, Arthur is ready to accept when a report arrives of a Pictish attack. Angry at apparently having been lied to, Arthur kills the ambassadors and orders an immediate charge against the enemy. Mordred, surprised by the English movement and apparently not having called for any attack from his side, orders the death of the useless hostages and goes into battle. Guenhera and Philip are murdered. Arthur rallies his troops. Mordred kills Gloucester. Arthur learns of this and then of his wife's death. Heartbroken, he rages, seems even to think that he won the battle of Lincoln, which he skipped, a victim of his own knightly PR. He cannot go on, realizes he has been a poor king, and finally places himself in God's hands. At once he sees Mordred and knows he must save Britain at all costs, even that of his own life; this is his only possible legacy. Arthur kills Mordred but is mortally wounded. In his dying breath, he gives his crown to Constantine, who becomes king of a unified Britain.

If I were a better version of me, I would not react faster than I think, would not be wounded when no harm was intended, would understand before too much time had passed to forgive, would not—in my clumsy efforts to make amends—so often make things worse. I would not have lived and written such an ugly story, and I would not so resemble this vile picture of me that my father drew, before I was even an adult (or, worse, that Shakespeare drew centuries before I was born).

Those who know me personally know to a fine degree how much of all this is true, how much an apology (and how sincere), how much a boast or a con job. To the rest of you, it's a muddle or it's a thing of beauty. And if it pleased you, and you found in its candor and lies and sobbing cross-dressed confessions some hours' entertainment, then well and good.

I will send this off to Random House now, proofread the galleys, give this work all the care Shakespeare could never give his own, then cash my checks and send my winnings from this venture to bank accounts established for my boys, my ex-wife, my mother, and for Petra, Dana, and their little girl, whose birth I was not allowed to attend, whose face I have not yet earned the right to see, whose breath I have not yet smelled, whose cheeks I have not yet touched, whose whole first year I will have squandered, whose name I do not know, and whose gender I learned only from a mutual friend (whose indiscretion was subsequently clarified for him, and whom I can now no longer get to return my calls).

I did consider, in chiming midnights of pounding self-pity, killing myself. My favorite line in Shakespeare: *When the players are all dead, there need none to be blamed.* But I'm not the type, and it's not that kind of story. And my sons are coming for Christmas, or a little after; Jana's very generous to allow it, just as my mother was with another shabby father named Arthur. I've planned a lot for me and the boys to do in frozen Minneapolis. Also, they like detective fiction, and I am starting to think I might write a novel with them as the heroes, twin-brother PIs in Prague. Lots of plot.

For now I will do as Dana (and RH legal) instructs. I will not lie and say the play is real, not even for her. She didn't say I had to. I will not say her version of our life is truer than mine. But I will say again that I'm very sorry, for whatever that's worth.

What sort of story is this, then? Not quite a tragedy, not for anyone else, anyhow. Not quite a comedy, not for me, anyhow. A *problem play*, I suppose we could call it. With time we will fit it into some genre or other. Endings are, after all, artificial, until the last one. It all depends on how you like the book. If you think I mean it, it reads a certain way. If you think I don't, it reads another. Just like the play.

So. The curtain drops, maybe snags a little on its way down, and stagehands scamper around trying to free it, while this actor in his one-man show stands there staring out into the darkness with a stupid smile and darting eyes as he squints from row to row, trying to find one particular face, to see if she liked it.

ARTHUR PHILLIPS
Minneapolis
November 2010

THE TRAGEDY OF ARTHUR

BY WILLIAM SHAKESPEARE

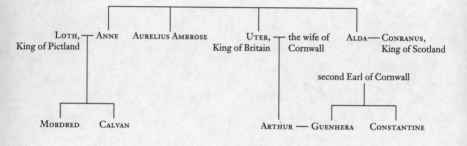

Lines of succession to the British throne in the story of Arthur, from
Holinshed's *Chronicles*, Shakespeare's source material

LIST OF PARTS

THE ENGLISH-WELSH COURT

ARTHUR, *Prince of Wales, later King of Britain*
Duke of GLOUCESTER, *Arthur's guardian, later adviser*
Constantine, Earl of CORNWALL, *later King of Britain*
GUENHERA, *his sister, later Queen of Britain*
Duke of SOMERSET
Duke of NORFOLK
Earl of CUMBRIA
Earl of KENT
Sir Stephen of DERBY
Bishop of CAERLEON
LADY CRIER *and other Ladies of the court*
Guenhera's NURSE

THE PICTISH-SCOTTISH COURT

LOTH, *King of Pictland*
MORDRED, *Loth's son, Duke of Rothesay, later King of Pictland*
CALVAN, *Mordred's brother, Prince of Orkneys*
CONRANUS, *King of Scotland*
ALDA, *Queen of Scotland, sister-in-law to Loth, aunt to Mordred and Arthur*
Duke of HEBRIDES, *son to Conranus*
ALEXANDER, *a messenger*
DOCTOR

COLGERNE, *chief of the Saxons*
SHEPHERDESS
MASTER *of the Hounds*
The Master of the Hounds' BOY

DENTON, *an English soldier*
SUMNER, *an English soldier*
MICHAEL BELL, *a young English soldier*
French AMBASSADOR
PHILIP *of York*
PLAYER KING
PLAYER QUEEN
Messengers, Servants, Huntsmen, Attendants,
Trumpeters, Hautboys, Soldiers, Players

SYNOPSIS

PROFESSOR ROLAND VERRE

ACT I: In sixth-century Britain, King Uter Pendragon rapes a noble's wife. The product of that rape, Arthur, is raised in Gloucestershire, far from his father's constant wars with the Saxons. When Uter is killed, Arthur inherits the throne, but his right is challenged. Mordred, heir to the crown of Pictland (eastern Scotland), asserts his claim to be king of all Britain (England, Wales, Scotland, and Pictland, as well as Ireland). Mordred's father, King Loth, refuses to go to war for this title. Mordred decides to provoke a war. The English nobles torture a Pictish ambassador, offering Mordred an excuse to bring Pictland (and Scotland) into the fight.

ACT II: Arthur leads his men against the Saxons, Picts, and Scots at York, gaining his first victory. Mordred retreats to Lincoln to join hidden Saxon reinforcements. Arthur sends the Duke of Gloucester to lead his army in pursuit, vowing to arrive before any battle. Instead, the Duke of Gloucester, disguised as Arthur, wins a great victory against a surprisingly strong force. Arthur arrives late and allows his enemies to go home on the promise of peace, keeping Mordred's brother for ransom. The Saxons attack again. Arthur, enraged, kills all prisoners, even the hostage brother. Mordred becomes King of Pictland and vows revenge against Arthur.

ACT III: Gloucester arranges a valuable marriage for Arthur with a French princess, guaranteeing wealth, allies, and strength to help him achieve his goal of a unified, peaceful, and prosperous Britain. Instead, Arthur marries Guenhera, the sister of a childhood friend, who has loved him since he was a boy. She miscarries twice. Arthur's nobles complain that he is too solicitous of his wife and has lost interest in military matters, that he has turned the court into a place of effeminate art and recreation. One noble considers assassinating Arthur to save the endangered kingdom.

ACT IV: Arthur is overly submissive to his queen, who is pregnant again. He allows her to put knights on trial for acts of rudeness or chivalric misbehavior. In the midst of this, the Saxons attack yet again. Arthur realizes that he does not have the means to defend his kingdom and that he has, in his rashness, alienated the French and his nominal vassals, the Picts. Forced to negotiate, he secures Pictish aid by naming Mordred his heir. Mordred accordingly assists in the victory over the Saxons at Linmouth, but he suspects that Arthur is going to renege on his promise.

ACT V: While Arthur is fighting a rebellion in Ireland, Mordred travels to London and learns that Guenhera has miscarried again but that Arthur has promised the throne to young Philip of York, one of Arthur's illegitimate children. Humiliated, Mordred kidnaps Guenhera and Philip. Arthur leaves Ireland and makes camp in a muddy field alongside the Humber River to fight Mordred. It is not clear who attacks first, ending the hopes of a diplomatic solution. Mordred then murders Guenhera and kills Gloucester in battle. Arthur, heartbroken and realizing his weakness as a king, sees that his only duty is to kill Mordred, ensuring the end of civil strife in Britain. He does so, dying in the process, and a new king of a unified Britain is crowned.

ACT I, SCENE I

[*Location: A wood in Gloucestershire*]
Enter Arthur and Gloucester [*with spears, hunting boar*]

	GLOUCESTER	Arthur, by noble right your prey now waits.
		Yet stay, my prince. Charge not alone in haste.
		Her rump is pressed against an oak's thick hide.
		And so to left and right command two men
5		To kneel, with sharp-toothed bolts[1] in ready bows.
	ARTHUR	Fair gentle Gloucester, keeper of my state,
		I love thee well for all thy tender care.
		But here alone where war doth not intrude,
		Thou art too careful of this Prince of Wales.
10		Believest thou she'd strike with will to slay?
	GLOUCESTER	With carving razor tusk, she'll pierce your plate[2]
		As if she cut through velvet pilèd thin.
	ARTHUR	Her carving tusk?
	GLOUCESTER	My lord?
15	ARTHUR	We shout beyond
		Each other's ears. While long thou prat'st[3] of boars,
		How is't, dear friend, thy heart did slip the trap
		Laid sly by that reclining shepherdess?
	GLOUCESTER	A shepherdess?
20	ARTHUR	An echo keeps my state!
		The shepherdess who there within a grove
		Doth lie and also lies: she feigns to sleep.
		Speak troth, thou marked her not?
	GLOUCESTER	My prince, I marked

---

1. **bolts** crossbow arrows.
2. **plate** armor. Dogs were commonly armored for boar hunts, men less often, but it did occur. [Roland Verre]
3. **prate** to chatter pointlessly.

25		The boar, your prey.
	ARTHUR	And thee I pray to tempt
		Me not with tales of bacon in the wood,
		When finer cates[4] do savor[5] there below.
	GLOUCESTER	Young liege,[6] I know you will leave off to do
30		These hot pursuits, which ill beseem a prince.
		I'd bid you study of your Christian soul,
		And chaste again you'll join with me at hunt.
	ARTHUR	O, gray old Duke of Gloucester, kindly lord,
		For all thy gifts, sage counsel, and sweet care
35		I mean to clip thee to my kingly breast
		When round my temples flows the stream of gold.[7]
		But be not now nor then a wit-poor prophet,
		Who cloaks his lank advice in piety.
		I would not have my second father's voice
40		Now sing this priestly strain,[8] nay, Duke, not you.
	GLOUCESTER	Do you then call me father, good my prince?
		With love I call you only son, from when
		That night our gate did croak and murder sleep,[9]
		There came a courser,[10] black against the sky,
45		And wondrous dispatch from th'embattled king
		Was read to me, great confidence bestowed.
		Then soldiers pushed th'unwilling nurse to me,
		I marked the fardle[11] in her weak, old arms,
		All swathed[12] were you in clouts[13] of Orient red.[14]
50		And she did sob to you, "Farewell, my boy,"
		And would not ope her fists to give thee o'er.

4. *cates* delicacies.

5. *savor* (passim) One of the ironies of this project is that the first modern edition of Shakespeare's lost play is published with American spellings! [RV]

6. *young liege* a double-stressed (spondee) opening. Gloucester is trying to get the prince to pay attention. It is by such subtle clues of meter that Shakespeare communicated to his actors (and to actors to this day), directing them without overt stage directions. [RV]

7. *stream of gold* the crown.

8. *strain* a melody or song.

9. *murder sleep* cf *Macbeth*, II.ii.43. [RV]

10. *courser* warhorse.

11. *fardle* bundle.

12. *swathed* swaddled.

13. *clouts* swaddling clothes.

14. *Orient red* the color of dawn (which occurs in the east, or Orient).

		Then I and my new bride, yet half abed,
		Before we passed scarce one black night's embrace,
		Did gaze upon a tiny boy's bare head.
55	ARTHUR	A mother more than my own dam was she,
		Your blessèd wife.
	GLOUCESTER	Who lived else issueless,
		And loved you as her son unto her grave. *Cries off*
	ARTHUR	Thy pig attends her shrift[15] and final words,
60		While I do lay in charge my spear at mutton.[16]
	GLOUCESTER	Then have you nothing of a conscience, Prince?
	ARTHUR	I have a conscience of a nothing, Duke.[17]
		And ere I float upon remembered days,
		Or lose a stone[18] to that hog's truffling chaps,[19]
65		I'll take me down the hill to where she droops,[20]
		And dreams soft or of princes or of swains.[21]
		Whiche'er Mab[22] soweth that I'll ear.[23] Now to her![24]
		Exit [Arthur]
	GLOUCESTER	"In Gloucestershire is Arthur safe from war."
		Thus read King Uter's posted words, and
		Gloucester—
70		When time was[25] war-like Gloucester—was
		unmanned.
		Each freshly knighted squire, each new-made earl—
		To hollowed title raised, for lack of pates
		To fill the bloodied casques of warm dead lords—
		Did frown on me, a nurse, far off from war.
75		I nothing chose, but did obey my king:

15. *shrift* the hearing of confession.
16. Sexual double entendre, *spear* as phallus, and *mutton* as slang for vagina. [RV]
17. Again, a sexual pun: *conscience of a nothing* an erection for a vagina. [RV]
18. *stone* testicle.
19. *chaps* jaws. [And, with *truffling*, a double entendre: the boar can find truffles, but truffles were also thought to promote chastity and cool off sexual ardor, which would surely be the result if its tusks or chaps were to cost the prince a stone. —RV]
20. *droops* nods with tiredness.
21. *swain* a shepherd or rustic lover.
22. *Mab* the fairy queen who causes wishful dreams.
23. *ear* reap.
24. *to her!* a hunting cry. Shakespeare makes it clear that Arthur exchanges one prey for another. [RV]
25. *When time was* "Who was in his day known as . . ."

Not only stand protector for the prince,
But warrant him the future of the realm,
Be England's Mentor[26] to the Prince of Wales
And tend a manly heir to wisely reign
80 Then banish war from off our bloodied shores.
I ne'er had other son, nor wife for long.
The day I cut that boy a sword of lath[27]
And leapt for him and made to die when touched[28]
And held him pick-a-back[29] near all the day,
85 Smacks[30] not more distant flown than half a week.
Yet he was never mine, but only lent.
Now bounds away this gallant-springing[31] man,
No more a boy mistaking me for Mars,
But cockered,[32] half-made prince 'pon whose slight arm
90 Anon must trusting lean all Albion.[33]
I am to raise a king or fly with one
As fate decrees, and vicious Saxon[34] arms,
And Scottish breed-bates'[35] whining discontent.
To lead or to be led. For both he's bred.
95 On me will lie the blame an[36] he's not meet.[37]
The censure is on Gloucester's weary duke
Who sacrificed his name to make this prince.
What king forged I? All England will be judge.

Enter messenger

Short-winded, boy?
100 MESSENGER   Aye, save your grace. Am I

---

26. **Mentor** When Odysseus went to the Trojan War, he left Mentor as guardian and teacher of his son.
27. **sword of lath** wooden sword.
28. **made to die when touched** to pretend to die when hit.
29. **pick-a-back** piggy back.
30. **Smacks** tastes.
31. **gallant-springing** growing up beautifully.
32. **cockered** indulged.
33. **Albion** Great Britain.
34. **Saxon** Historically, the Saxons migrated into Britain, either peacefully or as invaders, from about A.D. 400 to 600.
35. **breed-bate** troublemaker.
36. **an** if.
37. **meet** suitable.

	The first to bear you tidings of the day?
GLOUCESTER	There's none of any other, nor of thee.
MESSENGER	Were ten of us when we were sent from York
	To speed to you and Arthur heavy cheer.[38]
105 GLOUCESTER	Is't he or I were meant to hear thee first?
MESSENGER	That wants a learnèd herald to unknot.
	'Tis you, my lord, as you are lord protector,
	'Tis he, my lord, for he is now your king.
GLOUCESTER	My king? How king? What of the king his sire?
110 MESSENGER	It is on this my embassy depends.
	He quaffed of water drawn from venomed well,
	Undone by filthy Saxon perfidy,[39]
	And yet, in litter[40] sick, did he still lead.[41, 42]
	With truncheon slipping from his fingers' grasp
115	He whispered terms of manage[43] few men heard.
	But hoarsely forth he called, to no effect.
	And now on York's high wall the Saxon flag
	Does whip, and Pictish[44] Loth does claim our throne.
GLOUCESTER	Thus one man's death so bolds the bashful north
120	That borderers[45] ally with farland[46] troops
	Conspiring all to reach at Britain's crown.
MESSENGER	Where waits the prince, my lord?
GLOUCESTER	The prince? The king
	Is there, below, at hunt.
125 MESSENGER	Shall I to him?
GLOUCESTER	Anon. Allow him yet one weightless breath.

[Exit messenger]

38. *heavy cheer* serious news.

39. *perfidy* deceitfulness, treachery.

40. *litter* a coach or wagon.

41. See *Henry VI, Part One*, III.ii.95, from which my father stole this line.

42. Or in which Shakespeare quotes the same source material, or in which Shakespeare's likely collaborator on *Henry VI, Part One*—Nashe, Peele, or Greene—quoted Shakespeare's preexisting *Arthur* play. The explanations are both numerous and unconfirmable, but they do not with any likelihood point to the fraud Mr. Phillips endorses in his Introduction. [RV]

43. *terms of manage* military commands.

44. *Pictish* Pictland, which in this play is the dominant northern power, seems to have covered eastern Scotland from Roman times until the tenth century.

45. *borderer* enemies along the border.

46. *farland* foreign.

His office and the times will bide a trice.[47]
The feared-desirèd day has startled us.
Who waits?

[*Enter servant*]

130 SERVANT   My lord?

GLOUCESTER   Go bid the master couple up the hounds
And knot the slips,[48] uncall this day's last pleasures.
Then send to all our friends across the Wye[49]
To speed to London's abbey, thence to York.

135   We grieve a king, anoint his heir, and fight.   *Exeunt*

---

47. **bide a trice** put up with a brief delay.
48. **slips** leashes.
49. **friends across the Wye** troops from Wales. [RV]

ACT I, SCENE II

[*Location: A field in Gloucestershire*]
Enter Arthur for Swain[1] and Shepherdess

SHEPHERDESS   An it like thee, sit and watch my flock with me.
There's grass enough to rest a body on. And trees to
booth[2] thy white face,[3] an it like thee.

ARTHUR   It likes me much, Joan. *Ecce signum*,[4, 5] here's a cowslip[6, 7]
5   for thy hair.

---

1. **for Swain** Arthur is somehow disguised as a peasant or shepherd. [RV]
2. **booth** to shelter.
3. **white face** It is possible she already sees through Arthur's disguise, since his skin is pale, not like
   someone who spends his days outdoors. [RV]
4. **Ecce signum** "Behold the sign." (Latin, and thank God for online translators.)
5. Or professional editors: Shakespeare used the phrase again in *Henry IV, Part One*. [RV]
6. **cowslip** a wildflower. I can only imagine my father straining to find one in a prison book of
   English flora.
7. Again, Mr. Phillips is jumping at shadows. The cowslip—*Primula veris*—appears in three other
   Shakespeare works. [RV]

SHEPHERDESS		Itching,[8] are you? I find my own flowers with none to help, thanks.
ARTHUR		Sweet goose, you speak true. But can you weave 'em to a crown? I was learnèd once in twisting stems in what
10		what form I conceive. Would you a crown, Queen?
SHEPHERDESS		Thou namest me what?
ARTHUR		A queen, a royal lady of all these demesnes about.
SHEPHERDESS		Oh, and wouldst thou be my king then? There's not a Jack sits before me promises less than empires for a
15		kiss. And not a one but delivers me none.
ARTHUR		The wretches! But you stretch 'em no credit,[9] my Joan, or more's the pity. And now I am no common goat-herd. Find me so?
SHEPHERDESS		More pretty, true, but that's a cloud in stag's form,
20		soon enough to turn to other shapes, if only grow its its horns a foot or two.[10]
ARTHUR		She's witty wise enough to be a queen! All's well for me then. Wouldst thou a ring of shoots for thy pretty hand? Shall I shape these flowers into our banns?[11]
25	SHEPHERDESS	Wouldst thou grudge it me?
ARTHUR		No man could, nor highest devoted nor basest knave. For lips as red I'd not begrudge an empire. But talk of kingdoms? Why is this willow not realm enough? Not vast enough for empire the sedge[12] that holds
30		that near bank? And sure this day and night are time enough for friends?
SHEPHERDESS		Sure there's time enough for swains to talk a girl and find yet an hour of sun to run away by.

8. *Itching, are you* Joan hears "ecce" as "itching," or desiring sex. She immediately shifts from the friendly, informal "thou" to the more distant (and chaste) "you." It is in details like this that one senses the work of the master playwright of the sixteenth century, not a convict of the twentieth. [RV]

9. *stretch 'em no credit* you won't let them kiss you on a promise. [RV]

10. *stag . . . horns* Joan is teasing with double meanings. If Arthur is young and pretty, that will change, just like the shape of a cloud, and someday he will become a cuckold; cuckolds were said to grow horns when their wives betrayed them. [RV]

11. *banns* public notice of an engagement.

12. *sedge* grassy plants growing in wet places. [A sexual-anatomical innuendo is not impossible. — RV]

ARTHUR None could be so dull to run, given taste of thy
35   flowered company.

SHEPHERDESS A ring of flowers is nothing to plight a troth[13] for all a
        life.

ARTHUR What girl's tilly-vally[14] prattle! What day are we?
        Come, tell.

40 SHEPHERDESS 'Tis Monday, Jack. 'Tis sure 'twere only yesterday at
        morning the priest talked of such and other.

ARTHUR Monday, then, 'tis Monday. And what knowest thou of
        Thursday still a-foot? Tell, sorceress, that I might
        know the future! Perhaps we'll fly a Saxon army, or
45   this overbold river o'er-wet the fields and town, or a
        pox to carry every third man to his end? So tell me,
        Joan, what knowest thou of Thursday next?

SHEPHERDESS Turnmelon![15, 16] Thinkest thou such serpent tongues
        as thine have ne'er hissed sweet to me? What know I
50   of Thursday! Pah! I know I fear it not. I know it will
        will from this day be different so little as those two
        green grasses are the one the other. I know I'll see it
        from this willow or that one there, where my bell-
        wether[17] likes best the sweet clover. I'll sit here
55   Thursday, my flower-prince, upon this very throne.
        Can I so easy outsee thee by seeing that? Where
        wilt thou be Thursday? Afeard[18] boy, doth Thursday
        next or ten years on danger thee to quaking?

ARTHUR Ha! I do love thee, Joan. Nay, no day at thy side, afloat
60   in this broad main[19] of green can fright me. I tell
        thee, Joan, I know it, I'll ne'er leave thy side. I
        cannot see a day, Thursday or other, when I would
        would not feel as I do now. I am a turtle,[20] have no

---

13. **plight a troth** to make a promise of marriage.
14. **tilly-vally** nonsense. [Used twice more by Shakespeare in his plays.—RV]
15. **turnmelon** See "Step On" by the band Happy Mondays: "You talk so hip, you're twisting my
    melon, man."
16. Meaning obscure. A face so ugly it rots produce? A duplicitous person? Possibly an error of
    typesetting, but no alternatives have yet been suggested by early readers. [RV]
17. **bell-wether** the leading sheep of the flock. It wears a bell around its neck.
18. **Afeard** frightened.
19. **main** open sea.
20. **turtle** a turtledove. A symbol of faithfulness. [RV]

conceit[21] of a time but this, a planted, growing,

65   swelling seed forever.

SHEPHERDESS   Growing, swelling, aye, aye.[22] Just words, no different
if thou speakest or make mute that voice, the sun
moves no fleeter for all thy wild tongue doth whip.

ARTHUR   Queen of wisdom! Chide me roughly, then! Close my

70   vexing mouth, prison my rebel words under soft lock.
Come, make fast my silence.   [*They kiss*]

                   Flourish, trumpets off, cries [*of*] *"Arthur," "Prince"*

SHEPHERDESS   They call some royal name.

ARTHUR   Some hapless duke, bid to weigh some caitiff's[23] claim
of law, or called to lead trembling boys to buffets

75   'gainst Saxon steel.   *Cries off*

SHEPHERDESS   They seek him at an inch now. They will upon us.

ARTHUR   I bleed remorse for such a one as this, his days in
chambers, closets,[24] armor. I had fled by breakfast
were I that cursed prince.

80   SHEPHERDESS   They come, they come, now nigh.[25] Yet none of
princely mien[26] are by. Wherefore should they
disturb our close quiet?

ARTHUR   Ah, ah, ah, unless thou art some lady playing at
pastoral belike,[27] beflowering her skirts! I see now,

85   tricksy, thy flock are courtiers, thy ladies attendant
linger above, enbranched and dressed in leaves and
birds-nest. And there thy most lank-lean chamberlain[28]
will slip loose at thy command to bite my ankles.

                                             Cries off

SHEPHERDESS   But still they come at us.

90   ARTHUR   Then I must needs flee ere your highness has me
sequestered at your pleasure into a dungeon, or

---

21. *conceit* idea, imagination.
22. Joan hears sexual insinuation in his words. [RV]
23. *bid to weigh some caitiff's* asked to judge some wretch's.
24. *closets* private chambers.
25. *nigh* near.
26. *mien* appearance.
27. *belike* probably, perhaps.
28. *chamberlain* Arthur is referring to her dog.

stretched an inch or two for my rude attentions.

SHEPHERDESS   Patch!²⁹ Jackdaw!³⁰ Whither away? Thou runnest, thou runnest.

95   ARTHUR   But from your sergeants at arms. If thou art not some hidden queen, be here for me an hour hence and I'll to thee. Stand'st thou affected³¹ to swear it?

SHEPHERDESS   Wouldst flee? Then flee. Wherefore? But here, a token, and from thee.

                                                        [*They exchange tokens*]

100   ARTHUR   An hour, an hour.

SHEPHERDESS   Lies and lies, but here I'll be an hour on and an hour yet 'til folding,³² and days and days if thou wilt have me.

                                                                    Cries off

ARTHUR   An hour, but a single hour, Joan, I swear it.   *Exeunt*

---

29. **Patch** clown.
30. **Jackdaw** a proverbially stupid bird. [RV]
31. **stand affected** be willing, be moved to do something.
32. **folding** returning the sheep to their fold.

ACT I, SCENE III

[Location: the] Pictish court
Flourish and trumpets. Enter Loth of Pictland in litter, Conranus of Scotland,
Mordred of Rothesay,[1] *[Calvan], Alda,*[2, 3] *and others*

LOTH	Too hot, my son, too hot.[4]
MORDRED	There were a time,
	My lord, such heat did blast[5] from your own bile,
	When all did know King Loth of Pictland's moods.

5   For when but crabbed[6] he havoc-shaked this isle,
                     Provoked to whirling bangstry[7] and dread force,
                     He threw down Grampian[8] mount to vent his gall.[9]
                     Think I forgot what was to be your son?

CONRANUS	Leave off, fierce Duke, your father begs his rest.

10   MORDRED   Nay, Uncle, I'm the deathsman[10] of repose.—

1. Heirs to the throne of Scotland were from 1398 until 1603 known as Dukes of Rothesay, much as the English heirs were the Princes of Wales. In this case, however, Shakespeare was committing both an anachronism (if Holinshed is to be believed, these events occurred in the 500s) and an error of place (wherever this ancient kingdom of Pictland was, it probably covered only what is today eastern Scotland. Rothesay is in the west). [RV]
2. *Alda* This seems to be an error of my father's, as she never speaks.
3. *Alda* Likely not. Queen Alda's silent presence in this scene is specifically requested by Shakespeare and is worth noting. *Arthur* is—as other commentators have noted elsewhere, and will no doubt be discussed in some coming work of scholarship on Shakespeare and feminism— a very feminine play, despite its clash of kings and battle scenes. Guenhera's birth labors and marital sorrows, the abandoned mothers, and Alda's enforced presence here—where her right to speak is openly scorned—reveal a sensitivity to women's issues unsurpassed, in my opinion, anywhere else in Shakespeare's works. One might even add—with only a trace of irony—the boar in I.i, which is described in terms both sexual and violent, and which is compared explicitly ("To her!") to the shepherdess Arthur seduces and abandons. [RV]
4. *too hot* We are in the midst of conversation. Loth is replying to Mordred's heated words. [RV]
5. *blast* blow violently.
6. *crabbed* cross, grouchy.
7. *bangstry* violence. [Perhaps especially a Scottish term, as it appears in Scottish law codes under James VI. —RV]
8. *Grampian mount* one of Scotland's three mountain ranges.
9. *gall* the gall bladder, supposedly the seat of bile and anger.
10. *deathsman* executioner.

[*To Loth*] Your vigor melts away too soon, great king.
Think on your crown! Hold on[11] with sovereign's
    cares,
Not fall away from temporal affairs,
To forward[12] dwell in heaven's seigniory[13]

15   While yet your shape doth fill that earthly seat,
But bridle all events to your control.—
[*To Calvan*] My brother, chafe[14] your father's icy hide
With selfsame news was read to us below.[15]

CALVAN   Prince Arthur flies to London's Roman tower[16]

20   So soon as he doth make a potent head[17]
And therewith at the Abbey butt[18] the crown,
From whence, with benison as Britain's king,
He purposes with fearful sway[19] to York
To venge his father's death upon the Saxon.

25 MORDRED   To make a head! And post with sway! To venge!
Who acts thus, Calvan? Say you? Mouldwarp[20]
    Arthur,
Bescreened in Wales, now dares to ope his eye!
That vain and liberal[21] boy would stain the crown,
Would brave the London air and Saxon blades,

30   While valiant Pict and Scot—with whinyards[22]
    sheathed
And buttoned belts[23] left hanging by the wall—
Do ladylike sit fond and bluntly[24] still.

CONRANUS   What though, if Arthur is of Uter's seed?

---

11. **Hold on** Continue.
12. **forward** prematurely.
13. **seigniory** realm.
14. **chafe** to warm.
15. **below** downstairs.
16. **Roman tower** The Tower of London (in fact begun in 1078) was popularly believed to have been left behind by the Romans. [RV]
17. **make . . . head** to raise an army.
18. **butt** a pun: Arthur will use his "head" to butt the crown. [RV]
19. **sway** force, authority.
20. **Mouldwarp** Mole.
21. **liberal** licentious, promiscuous. [And here pronounced in two syllables. —RV]
22. **whinyards** short swords.
23. **buttoned belts** armored belts. [RV]
24. **bluntly** stupidly.

For legacy he gains but bonny[25] strife.

35   Long may he live as his dead sire did live,

Distract[26] by constant war 'gainst Saxony,

Who'll parallel[27] the English king along

For ev'ry season of the years whilst we,

From Tweed to Tyne to Tees, extend our claim.

40   Let o'ercharged[28] Arthur bleed and hold his crown

As northern tide flows unrelenting south.

MORDRED   You'd move our bound by modest ell[29] or inch

When Britain all, this island whole entire—

All England, Wales, this Pictland, and your Scots—

45   By one crown all is ringed, and that crown mine.

CONRANUS   Your father's.

MORDRED   Aye, my father's, aye, if he

But stretch his gripping hand toward Arthur's scalp.

CONRANUS   This wind of rhetoric racks not the heir.[30]

50 MORDRED   No lawful heir did sprout from Uter's seed.

By lust made frantic, stole that vicious king

Into the absent Earl of Cornwall's bed,

And there did scratch with steel[31] th'resisting itch.[32]

The lady swelled with this false Prince of Wales

55   And Uter then grew bold to slay the earl,

Conspired to kill, like David of the Jews,[33]

In this alone resembling royalty.

That he did condescend to count the countess

Queen doth shade[34] this Arthur no more king

60   Than dressing meat blown[35] full with clouds of flies

---

25. *bonny* beautiful (ironic), and specifically Scottish. [RV]

26. *Distract* driven to distraction.

27. *parallel* remain equal to.

28. *overcharged* overburdened.

29. *ell* about a yard. [45 inches to the English, 37.2 for the Scotch! —RV]

30. *wind . . . racks* a pun. Lit: "All your talk doesn't change things." Fig: "All your wind isn't strong enough to move the air [heir, i.e., Arthur]." [RV]

31. *with steel* with force, or at point of a sword.

32. *scratch . . . th' resisting itch* to satisfy his sexual appetite, which satisfaction was literally resistant, as the earl's wife was raped. [RV]

33. *David of the Jews* In the Second Book of Samuel, King David sent to war (and certain death) Uriah, whose wife, Bathsheba, David had impregnated.

34. *shade* make.

35. *blown* tainted.

Give th'relish to't fit for royal feast.
Thus Uter was o'erthrown by Saxon arms
For God would straight again the fracted[36] line:
He grants each king his line, each line its king.
65 If Arthur reigns, we violate God's law.
Wouldst thou condemn each Scot and Pict to hell?
Dead Uter's sister Anne, your queen, my dam,
Does give to you, O Father, from the grave,
This lawful seat and pleads you make your claim.

70 CONRANUS But soft! Dead Uter was your uncle twice.
My Queen of Scotland mourns a brother's death.
Too cruel to her your threats to snatch his crown
And rain down death upon her brother's boy.

MORDRED What speaks my aunt in this?[37] Whence voice has
she?

75 Or you, enfeoffèd[38] uncle, vassal liege
To Loth my father. Scots are sworn to Picts:
Conranus king is king by king of Pictland,
Though he wait silent by with Pictish grace.—
[*To Loth*] My father, stand and bellow that your voice
80 Ungently shout down London's stolen walls
Until soft Arthur cap his beaten ears,
And yield to God and you his purse-picked crown.

LOTH [*Low mumbles*] An if our call's not heard?

MORDRED   Speak out,
speak out.

85 I hear but coughing.

LOTH   If our call's not heard?

MORDRED Then let them hear the sounds of righteous war
'Til English ears do note your martial voice.

LOTH Too forward[39] is this talk of making war.

90 MORDRED Then if you would forslow 'til lusty strength
Returns again in you, our guile will serve:
Send embassage to England with our cause,

36. *fracted* broken.
37. ***What speaks my aunt in this?*** nothing, as Alda stands silent now. Cf note to stage direction above. [RV]
38. *enfeoffèd* sworn as a subordinate, given land in exchange for obedience.
39. *forward* early, premature.

And privy[40] order to the Saxon camp:
Clandestinely we'll spur them to our use
95 And prompt them to press south without delay,
Then we, false-troubled[41] of the English need,
May have occasion t'offer them our aid
If they but[42] plant the crown where God would have't.
When you, new British king, from London rules,
100 Then we and our new English vassalage[43]
As one expel the Saxon from our shores.

CONRANUS   My brother-king, dare scorn my peace-soft heart,
Or say old men do always fly from toil.
But I did fight beside you at Iona.
105 My smoking[44] blade did cleave Norwegian skulls.
Take heed of word from lover[45] such as this:
Hot war, so fleetingly combusted up,
Doth hardly[46] snuff itself back down again.
And look! Our arms have built for us high walls!
110 Sit circummured[47] behind the winding Tweed,
Our uplands[48] scoff at foemen's bow and ax.
Say, Loth, what matter is that lack-brain prince
Who weens[49] to term himself all Britain's king?

MORDRED   What peace has man e'er joyed but paid in blood?
115 What dream wouldst thou my father dream abed,
Whilst puppy[50] Arthur, king of laystalls,[51] hopes
To trim aside two-thirds my promised birth?

LOTH   No more. I have no appetite to war.
Send embassy and vouch that Arthur's king.

120 MORDRED   But not of Britain.

LOTH   England then, your will.

---

40. *privy* secret.
41. *false-troubled* feigning concern.
42. *If they but* On condition that.
43. *vassalage* humble subjects.
44. *smoking* steaming.
45. *lover* friend.
46. *hardly* with great difficulty.
47. *circummured* walled in securely.
48. *uplands* highlands.
49. *weens* thinks, imagines, has the ambition.
50. *puppy* foolish young man.
51. *laystalls* toilets, outhouses.

MORDRED	I will discharge it to your terms precise.
LOTH	Duke Mordred, heir, be satisfied.
MORDRED	I am.

125   Full correspondence to my lord's desires
Is satisfaction to your loving son.

LOTH	Embrace me then your uncle-king of Scotland.
MORDRED	With fullest heart.
CONRANUS	It glads me.

                                   [They embrace] Loth swoons

130   MORDRED   Physic,[52] wine!

A cup, a drench[53] of wine! *[To Loth]* How do you, sir?—
[To servant] You! See him to his chamber, I'll anon.

                          Exeunt [but Mordred and Calvan]

Dear Calvan, brother, bearer of my trust.
Two embassies will we dispatch. First, you.

135   CALVAN   How frame[54] my tongue?

MORDRED	To words of amity.

Ride to the Saxon force at York. Their chief,
Flame-bearded Colgerne, takes your embassy.
In York he swills and vows and kicks his dogs,
140   And burns up offal to his red-eyed gods—
The carrion fumes offending Christian sense[55]—
And seizes not his vantage. Whet him on.
In Mordred's name give gold that he from York
Drive out to waste all 'round with Saxon blade.
145   But, brother, still our hands must clasp in darkness.
Teach Colgerne that our love blooms best in shade.

CALVAN   Such toadstool[56] love I'll passioning derive.[57]

                                    Exit Calvan

Enter messenger

MORDRED	What messenger is there?
ALEXANDER	My lord.
150 MORDRED	Thy name?

---

52. **Physic** doctor.
53. **drench** a drink.
54. **frame** shape, prepare.
55. **sense** Likely the sense of smell is intended here. [RV]
56. **toadstool** as an adjective, unique to Shakespeare. [RV]
57. **passioning derive** enthusiastically explain.

ALEXANDER	'Tis Alexander, Duke. I come from Wick.
MORDRED	Great Alexander boasts a comely face.
	Thou hast an air of gentle-seeming manners.
ALEXANDER	It please your grace, my mother taught me well.
155 MORDRED	Then come. We must needs teach thee new to speak
	In terms of harsh defiance and contempt. *Exeunt*

[ACT I,] SCENE IV[1]

[Location: The Tower of London]

Enter Gloucester, Bishop of Caerleon, Somerset, Norfolk, Cumbria, Kent, Derby

KENT	How? Are you then protector of the realm?
GLOUCESTER	With patience, lords, but for a single day.
	The morrow when, at your hand, Caerleon,
	Prince Arthur is in London's abbey blest,
5	He will from flexure[2] rise your perfect[3] king,
	And will no more require protector's aid.
	Today I rate[4] the puissance[5] of our arms,
	For after morrow hie we back to war.
	Prince Arthur wants the numbers, man and beast,
10	To make account of all your mighty ranks.
	How stand your noble lance and common pike?
SOMERSET	But soft, Lord Gloucester waits upon our haste,
	Foresees[6] we will obey with no complaint.
	Yet English barons joy long-customed rights
15	And freely choose ere kneel to any king,
	Though he be Uter's son or no.

---

1. Holinshed's *Chronicles*, Shakespeare's source for this play, says only the following: "The Britons disdainfully using the Pictish ambassadors . . ." It is from this seed that Shakespeare created I.iv, a most extraordinary dramatization of that simple idea. [RV]
2. *flexure* bent knee.
3. *perfect* complete, unquestioned.
4. *rate* measure, settle the amount of.
5. *puissance* power.
6. *Foresees* assumes, counts on.

	GLOUCESTER	Or no?
	NORFOLK	To be black Uter's son makes not an heir.
		By such a stamp[7] ten thousand British kings
20		Do dance a-maypole, yoke the ox to coulter,[8]
		Or skink[9] the wine at table for my thirst,
		Though none so like their sire as Arthur be,
		Who with his mawks on beef and ling[10] doth dine,
		Who'd 'change all England for St. George's field.[11]
25	SOMERSET	He's born on George's day, so 'tis like home.[12, 13]
	GLOUCESTER	Ignoble, rude and slanderous babble, lords
		Ill suits the love that's due your sovereign prince.
	NORFOLK	Come morrow, Gloucester, what names you the king?
	GLOUCESTER	The king will have me England's seneschal.
30	SOMERSET	You'll hold the keys to all the postern gates[14]
		Until the midnight king doth steal the guard.
	GLOUCESTER	These hare-brained comments will find quittance, Dukes.
	CUMBRIA	But who makes doubt of Arthur's godly right?
		These arms embraced King Uter as he died,
35		A man twice me, twice thee, twice any lord.
		Beneath the walls of York he cried to me,
		"Prince Arthur now will be your lawful king."
	KENT	O, tender-feeling Cumbria, 'tis well,
		But you have not seen Arthur sith his youth
40		When that boy sprouted no more manly beard

---

7. **stamp** mark, proof.

8. **coulter** plough.

9. **skink** to decant liquor, or wait tables.

10. **mawks, beef, ling** three slang terms for prostitutes or loose women. [RV]

11. **St. George's field** section of London known for prostitutes. [RV]

12. **George's day** April 23 happens to be my birthday as well as King Arthur's. A little greeting from my father and proof of Dana's claim that the play is "about me."

13. **George's day** is also taken to be Shakespeare's unconfirmed birthday. The mention of it as King Arthur's birthday raises the possibility that Shakespeare was perhaps allowing himself some self-revelation here, in Somerset's description of a man who frequents prostitutes. Perhaps Shakespeare, a man who lived for months or years at a time away from his wife, was intimately familiar with St. George's field. More likely still, April 23 is also the foundation day of the Order of the Garter (which had Arthurian overtones), so there are many far more likely explanations for this reference than that the play was forged to honor a twenty-first-century American novelist. [RV]

14. Another joke implying Arthur is sexually insatiable and Gloucester is merely his procurer: *postern gate* was slang for anal sex. [RV]

                Than trims a raspberry[15] in August heat.

SOMERSET   And sith his beard has grown, you'll find no man
                Hath seen the prince's thumbs.[16]

KENT   So long as that?[17]

45   SOMERSET   Renowned like to a serpent or a tailor's.[18]

     GLOUCESTER   What ancient barons' rights are these t'abuse?

     NORFOLK   These ten and seven summers hath the prince
                In Gloucestershire reclined, whence rumor tells
                That Arthur's luxury-amazed,[19] but king

50   Of milking maids, and each new queen he leads
                By kecksie flourish[20] to a clover bed.
                No continence[21] hath he and none dare bar
                The boy from exercising his mad lusts.

     SOMERSET   The father's passions storm within the son!

55   Will abbey words becalm the prince's rage,
                The ire descried[22] by those who should speak love,
                That Arthur soars to fury when but touched,
                Doth strike a man of noble birth for spite,
                And spends his words of love upon a cook?

60   GLOUCESTER   Thus tales lead beasts, and heads too willing follow[23]
                The boy is stern for war. Come tilt with him.
                First pass he'll lay you on your plated back
                Like to a flea within a walnut-shell.
                He'll lift great sword and drop it on your pate[24]

65   With edge or flat or fig-ball pommel: choose.[25]

---

15. *raspberry* Prior to the discovery of this text, the earliest recorded use of "raspberry" in English dates from 1602, some five years after the play's publication. It is such details that further convince me of its authenticity. [RV]

16. "Since he's come of age, the prince has been almost constantly engaged in sexual antics." [RV]

17. *so long as that* a double entendre. The length of the prince's new beard (reaching his thumbs) is confounded with the length of his penis. [RV]

18. *a tailor's* tailors, and fools, were reputedly well-endowed. [RV]

19. *luxury-amazed* lust-maddened.

20. *kecksie flourish* with royal music (flourish) made by blowing on a blade of dried grass (kecksie). [RV]

21. *continence* self-restraint.

22. *descried* revealed, disclosed.

23. *tales lead beasts . . . follow* pun: tales as rumors, wagging the head. [RV]

24. *pate* head.

25. *choose* "He can kill you (with the edge), knock you unconscious (with the fig-shaped pommel), or just tag you for show (with the flat)." [RV]

In York will he course fast as rolling floods,
As swift as you in thought may cross the globe.

KENT   Like to his father then he longs for war?
The father's war did steal the father's life.

70   The father's son would match the father's feat
And on his feet march all of us to death,
So son might set, like father, in the north.[26]
Forever war, forever war, and on.
Yet Saxons find war-stubbled York a prize

75   And would content themselves in its embrace.
This land's o'er-marched, o'er-bled, o'er-wearied
    o'war,
Yet still Prince Arthur comes to wield a sword!

CUMBRIA   What danger cowards so the southern Kent
While Cumbria is gripped from north and east?

80 KENT   I am not wished to hear thy slanders, cur!

CUMBRIA   Nor Saxons wished to peace by Kent's desires!

CAERLEON   Enough vain heat! My lords of England, peace![27]

Enter Alexander

GLOUCESTER What word hast thou, sirrah?[28]

ALEXANDER   No king is here.

85 GLOUCESTER He comes anon. Again: what word? Make haste.

ALEXANDER   My master bids me say: "No king is here."

NORFOLK   What master, fool?

ALEXANDER   Which is the lord protector?

GLOUCESTER Thou clog'st[29] him, stamm'ring chough.[30]

90 ALEXANDER   He greets
    you thus:
"Vice-regent for unrightful, sneaking prince."

GLOUCESTER What master lays such words upon thy tongue?

ALEXANDER   Grant leave, ye English nobles, I my words
May unconstrained display, as charged by Loth,

---

26. Puns: York (in the north), where the father (Uter) died, and where the son unnaturally wishes to die, a desire as unnatural as the sun setting in the north. [RV]

27. See *Dr. Strangelove*, one of my father's favorite movies: "Gentlemen, no fighting in the War Room."

28. **sirrah** a term of address expressing contempt or the speaker's authority.

29. **clog'st** burdens.

30. **chough** a bird [thought to chatter nonsense. —RV]

95		Great Pictish king, and Mordred, Duke of Rothesay.
	GLOUCESTER	Thou tarried long for license, messenger,
		By now is absolution pertinent.[31]
		Yet doubt[32] no moody welcome here. Proceed.
	ALEXANDER	Then thus speaks Loth, the king of Picts.
100	KENT	And
		Mordred.
	ALEXANDER	Yes, too, and Mordred, Duke of Rothesay, too.
		'Tis thus they speak, in fewness and in truth.
	KENT	So plainly warned do I now hope for neither.
		Come, tell, what would thy dwarfish duke[33] proclaim?
105	ALEXANDER	That Arthur was by boist'rous violence[34]
		And out of holy wedded state begot.
		King Uter stole a womb from Cornwall's bed,
		There planted criminal[35] seed, and slew the earl,
		Ennobled false pretender, spawned no heir.
110		By any Christian law, adultery
		Creates a bastard with no right to throne,
		And crime 'gainst God it is to lift a sword
		To pillar[36] so triobular[37] a claim.
		Nor Uter nor his brother left no issue.[38]
115		Their elder sister, Anne, was wife to Loth,
		Who rules all Pictland, Scots, and Irish lands,
		Who's now, by Anne's bond, English king and Welsh.
		King Loth and Mordred bid you, English lords
		And bishops, rouse up London, ope its abbey
120		Wherein pay homage due to Loth, your king,
		According as the Britons' custom is.
	DERBY	'Tis all?
	ALEXANDER	With this complete and with your love,

---

31. *absolution pertinent* "forgiveness is now more to the point."

32. *doubt* fear.

33. *dwarfish duke* the first of several references to Mordred's height.

34. *boisterous violence* violent rape.

35. *criminal* pronounced in two syllables. [RV]

36. *pillar* to support. Apparently a Shakespearean invention as a verb. [RV]

37. *triobular* worthless. [Literally, worth three oboli, small coins. —RV]

38. *left no issue* If this play was performed in the early 1590s, a childless English monarch being replaced with a Scottish one would not yet have been politically sensitive. By 1597, it certainly would have been. [RV]

		He bids the Welsh and English chivalry
125		Unite with all his lands and western isles,
		Together dash the Saxon from his realm.
	DERBY	Art breathless yet?
	GLOUCESTER	He asks no more than this?

                         Our lives, our wealth, vouchsafe his endless line,
130   And vail³⁹ our pride to serve him as his bondmen?⁴⁰
        ALEXANDER   The duke hath taught me more should you dispute
                         The logic of my principal dispatch,
                         Although the latter words I fear to voice.
        DERBY   How feculent⁴¹ thy northern vapors stink!
135   Would Mercury's low wings be fixed above
                         And beating blow away these winds thou pip'st!⁴²
                         Didst thou us beg pre-pardon⁴³ and free tongue
                         To lick our ears with gleeks⁴⁴ so sour and hot?
                         Come, take my true reply to your King Loth.

He strikes [Alexander]

140   ALEXANDER   Unrighteous knight, this violence⁴⁵ done cold
                         'Gainst embassy's anathema to God.
        DERBY   O, messenger, pay heed to these few words.
                         What writing hand hast thou? A secretary's?⁴⁶
                         Wouldst thou then, boy, my words ink out with pen,
145   And dry with grains of fine white callis-sand,⁴⁷
                         Or can thy cistern skull retain good water?⁴⁸
                         Then tell thy king what Stephen Derby sayeth.

He strikes [Alexander]

---

39. **vail** to lower in submission.
40. **bondmen** slaves, serfs.
41. **feculent** containing, or of the nature of, feces.
42. **Mercury . . . pip'st** Mercury—the messenger god—had wings on his heels. Were they attached higher (*fixed above*) on this messenger, they could blow away the flatulent stench of the words. [RV]
43. **pre-pardon** forgiveness before the act. Earliest known usage had previously been 1625. [RV]
44. **gleeks** jokes.
45. **violence** Shakespeare gives the word two or three syllables as his verse requires. Here, pronounced with three syllables. [RV]
46. **writing hand . . . secretary's** "Secretary hand" was one of several different styles of handwriting in the sixteenth and seventeenth centuries, more difficult to forge and therefore more suitable for confidential correspondence. [RV]
47. **callis-sand** sand of Calais, used for blotting. [RV]
48. **cistern . . . water** "can your leaky memory remember my message?"

	ALEXANDER	Most vicious! Evil! Lawless, graceless knight!
	NORFOLK	Do Loth and Mordred lust for England's joys
150		And long t'embrace our rich and southern earth?
		Then tell them, herald purpled,[49] shamed to rose[50]
		By bold Sir Derby's steely words, that Norfolk
		Doth bid them cool their passion, ice their stones[51]
		In candied[52] Clyde, for England hath her king,
155		A king who is beloved and temperate,
		Extraught[53] from ancient stock of heroes' blood,
		Full master of himself and bred to rule,
		To freeze like basilisk[54] the naughty Scot.
		Tell this to Mordred from the Duke of Norfolk.

He strikes [Alexander]

160	ALEXANDER	Doth mickle[55] England want for righteous men
		As desert towns that God did burn to ash?[56]
	GLOUCESTER	Restrain yourselves, nobility, and cease!
	KENT	From Roman tower ride we north to Loth,
		With war as key shall we unlock[57] his land,
165		Upscale[58] his Highland bounds and chastise him.
		Look close this roweled[59] spur of Earl of Kent
		And tell Duke Mordred, jauncing[60] Gall'way nag,[61]
		That he will curb beneath King Arthur's weight
		Or feel this spur to perforate his hide.

He kicks [Alexander] with spur

170	ALEXANDER	But grant me leave to flee, cruel men! Enough!

---

49. Ostensibly "bruised," but I hear my father's fondness for Crockett Johnson's children's classic *Harold and the Purple Crayon*, the story of a lonely boy who creates the world around him with his art.
50. *shamed to rose* embarrassed and blushing, but here bruising from the blows.
51. *ice their stones* cool off their testicles.
52. *candied* frozen.
53. *Extraught* descended.
54. *basilisk* a monster lizard reputed to paralyze anyone it looked upon. [RV]
55. *mickle* great.
56. *Desert . . . to ash* Sodom and Gomorrah [from the Book of Genesis. —RV]
57. *unlock* perhaps a pun on "loch"? [RV]
58. *upscale* climb over.
59. *roweled* spiked.
60. *jauncing* prancing.
61. *Gall'way nag* a particularly small Scottish breed of horse. Mentioned by Shakespeare again in *Henry IV, Part Two*. This also marks the second reference to Mordred as small in stature. [RV]

GLOUCESTER	Retire, good Kent, this rage ill suits your name.
SOMERSET	Nay, Gloucester, 'tis no rage but honest law.
	Attest, good prelate Caerleon, to this:
	Six liberties are granted embassies:
	Speak peace, or war, or amity, or none,
	Set terms of ransom, voice a lord's rebuke.
CAERLEON	'Tis by the square.
GLOUCESTER	But licenses no blows.
SOMERSET	Demands ill-mannered for our slavery,
	Would have us carry coals[62] to King of Picts,
	Heaps scorn upon our manhood and our king,
	Commits felonious lese-majesty,[63]
	Uncounted ways does tickle us to ire?
	Were't not this knave must hear our measured words
	I'd cut away these hanging letters-patent.[64]
	This froward[65] wants a lesson in his speech,
	And begs our gentle-voiced correction, so!

He strikes embassy

CUMBRIA	No English born, your Mordred and his Loth,
	And loath are English born to bear strange rule.
	To English born belongs this British isle,
	To Arthur, noble bear, belongs the throne.
	Now come, my saucy wayward embassy,
	Bear north what words I will inscribe for thee,

[He draws dagger]

	Steel quill, white parchment of your brow, red ink:
	Arthur Rex![66]

[He carves the letters on Alexander's forehead]

ALEXANDER	Stop! God, O God, too cruel, hellish men, let go!
CUMBRIA	Rest still, my lazy drone[67] and from this nest
	Of eagles thou wilt fly true north with words

Line numbers: 175, 180, 185, 190, 195

62. **carry coals** to bear indignities uncomplainingly.
63. **lese-majesty** treason.
64. **hanging letters-patent** literally, a written commission conferring Alexander his special status; in this case, Somerset is also threatening to cut off his ears. [RV]
65. **froward** evil or ungovernable person.
66. **Arthur Rex** "Arthur is the king." The only Latin I know by heart. [Note: the meter comes to a halt on this line, leaving time for the action. —RV]
67. **lazy drone** a parasite. [Interestingly, Shakespeare uses "drone" in four other plays, twice with the epithet "lazy." —RV]

That weasel[68] Pict might at his leisure read.

Exit [*Alexander*]

200   GLOUCESTER   Unruly lords of England, 'morrow's king

May rue today's ill-judged intemp'rature.[69]

Our gear[70] allows no palfrey's[71] walking pace:

We now must lash your rights along the path:

How many liegemen here swear Arthur king?

205   CUMBRIA   We all our faithful love to Arthur swear.

        ALL   We all do swear. To Arthur! Arthur's king!

        GLOUCESTER   Then waits for you a prince to crown, then war,

And, far-afield, most patient-hopeful, peace.

Exeunt [*not Gloucester*]

Improvidently Loth in haste and pride,

210   If not from charity, hath served my king,

And graciously invited jarring[72] lords

To point unitedly at him their swords.   *Exit*

---

68. *weasel* implying ferocity, bloodthirstiness, and deceit.
69. *intemprature* hasty, ill-considered mood. [Also, "intemperance" in other Shakespearean usage. —RV]
70. *gear* matter, affair.
71. *palfrey* a gentle horse.
72. *jarring* discordant, fighting.

[ACT I,] SCENE V

[*Location: The Royal Court, London*]
[*Enter*] *Arthur* [*crowned*] *solus*

    ARTHUR   So on a sudden am I made a king.

There is no boy who'd have it otherwise:

To step from forest games and don true crown.

But London's gamesters[1] mark at ten on one[2]

5   That Arthur balance still this crown on head,

Or head on neck, ere summer's come and blown.

---

1. *gamesters* gamblers.
2. *mark at ten on one* lay the odds at ten to one.

Those numbers tickle me; I'll Gloucester send
To play a thousand marks that I will fall.
E'en now do am'rous Pict and German hie
10   From north and east to visit me at court,
And finger my own hat on this my seat.[3]
There's something in this wooden chair calls out
To men of vaulting ween[4] but little wit.
What? Dare I hold myself above them? Nay.
15   I know I have no right to wear this crown.
I'll contradict no pope who calls me king,
But in this privy council kings speak troth:
No right have I, no higher claim than Loth.
A bastard, I, from bloody tyrant sire.
20   Unkingly, too, am I from th'angry mood
In which I was conceived, some kindnesses
Neglected, mother forced in loveless bed,
And from my part in this bed's play, they tell,
My monstrous getting surely cursed the land,
25   Which God will ceaseless venge with pox and
            drought.
What action might I take to ease this doom?
I stripe my back[5] at butchered Cornwall's tomb?
Still I th'usurper am, by father damned.
O, Arthur, coward boy! Ungrateful churl![6]
30   Say who art thou that acts as solemn judge
Of own creator, shoves him off thy dam,
With pitying heart unbirths thy thankless self?
What king was he to spawn such king as I?
What king he was now lives within my skin.
35   I bear his blood, his wit, his faults, his sin,
Save he did crave a kingdom for his own,
While crown unsought now perches up on me.
This glistering[7] ring was plucked o' my father's
            corpse:

3. *And finger . . . seat* "And try on my crown and sit in my throne."
4. *vaulting ween* high ambition.
5. *stripe my back* flog himself as penance over his father's murder of the Earl of Cornwall.
6. *churl* contemptible fellow.
7. *glistering* glittering.

Have I no will in me to venge his death?

40 He murdered fell whilst I did weave up stems

Into a crown t'anoint a maiden's brow.

That circlet placed, was she in some sort[8] changed?

Nay, nay. Nor can a crown make me a king.

What king am I to be? Not wise, not bold,

45 My kingdom ought to be the wood and bank,

The vast infinity of summer eves.

But, hear: I talk as if I might now choose.

Cheer up thy mewling self; put doubt to th'axe!

[He looks in mirror]

Here, search this glass: what kingly sight is there?

50 By right or no, this cap doth suit us[9] well.

What foes will come, let come, but no man tell

That Arthur yielded ere he fought to death

For that was his, bestowed by father's breath.

Exit Arthur

---

8. *in some sort* somehow.

9. *us* Note that Arthur begins using the royal "we" here, accepting his kingship, reflecting that acceptance even in his diction. [RV]

ACT II, SCENE I

[Location: The Royal Kennels]

Enter the Royal Master of the Hounds and his Boy

MASTER　　　Raised, lifted, up high I am. There's none less than
the pope who said it so, for say if Arthur is the king,
then is his kennel-duke the king's kennel-duke, and
all his hounds the king's hounds now, not prince's.

5　　　The pope in Rome proclaims it, and that's how we
are all trans-substanced[1] now. Tell the beagles,

---

1. *trans-substanced* The Master of the Hounds commits a few malapropisms. Here, he means "transubstantiated," the Catholic dogma of the communion transformation. Considering the religious strife of Protestant England in the 1590s, a level of Catholic mockery here is possible. [RV]

though they'll likely bide thee no more, now they are king's beagles now, not the same, not at all. They make voice the same, but the meaning's altered. And thou! No more a boy to the prince's hound-master. Stand tall, boy, so tall as great hound's withers! Thou servest the master of the king's hounds now. Cuff the other boys so far thou hast a will.

BOY   And they'll not cuff me more?

MASTER   An if they do, thou sayest the pope will excommasticate[2] 'em.

BOY   They say the king will not see the dogs no more, no time for hunts now.

MASTER   When the king had thy years, he passed all hours with me, slipped his watchers, came tripping to the hounds. Knew them all and one, e'en by their name, called 'em to their slips, learnt to flesh[3] 'em. "Highness," says I, "they'll be wanting you in for lessons," I'd say, but no, I knew he'd stay by. "Or tilting," I'd say, "dancing," and the king—were not the king, then—the king, says he to me, "If it please," talk sweet and crisple[4] up their coats with his light fingers, "If it please, not to give out, leave me just to see to Peritas, his leg ails, his gait's not good." Not for long years, but back then, he knew better than thou hast shown, could make 'em bark or hold mum at his word. "Sing," says he, and there they sing. "Mum now," says he, and all there's no sound. "Sing! Mum! Sing! Mum!" He'd weep when a boar or bear did the the worst to one of his.

BOY   He'll see worse things now, sure. All to war. No time now for hounds.

MASTER   Any other prince become any other king, I'd say thee aye. But this boy loved his dogs, loved his games. And then, now, see, he cannot but stop and admire every

---

2. *excommasticate* again, a malapropism; here, for excommunicate. [RV]
3. *flesh* rile up a hunting dog with meat.
4. *crisple* to ripple, ruffle.

maid or lady passes by. Say there's a king who loves it
so, so strong as any pleasure-jack or apple-squire,[5]
who runs 'em to earth, prefers 'em to all war making,
mark it. Wants to miss the wars, sees no joy in the
noble slashing, the crying out, the gobbets of flesh
and man's blood-sprays. Give 'em his choosing, say I,
he'll visit his tib,[6] have his will,[7] then back in his slop,[8]
then he'll be here, next us two, thou'lt see him, and
him calling for old Edgar and Lucius and stroking
Socrates' long ears. And all us others, we'll do what
the king will do, and not have to go to war. If he's the
same boy, and why not? Who tells me he's of another
sort now? For nothing: a drop of oil and a crown
makes not a man another sort.

BOY   I wot not,[9] sir. There's magic talk as well.

MASTER   Makes no puttock of a wren.[10] Same boy I loved, same
boy. He'll make no war when there's peace to joy.
Watch, thou.

BOY   My mother's brothers twain are pikemen in Sir
David's company.

MASTER   A valiant, and Welsh as one might hope, God save him.

BOY   My mother would their hands were hers sooner their
arms lopped or hacked for Sir David.

MASTER   Might she see the kingdom commodated[11] all to her
liking alone. Now wilt thou come, boy? There's meat
to give out. Wouldst thou tarry[12] on and on?

Exeunt

---

5. *pleasure-jack or apple-squire* hedonist or pimp.
6. *tib* a common woman's name or a strumpet.
7. *have his will* double entendre: Have his way or have an erection. [RV]
8. *slop* tunic or trousers.
9. *wot not* don't know.
10. *puttock of a wren* The wren is small and gentle; a puttock is a bird of prey. [RV]
11. *commodated* arranged.
12. *tarry* delay.

ACT II, SCENE II

[Location:] Below the Walls of York
Enter the King and his nobles and army. Alarum

ARTHUR   Now thick-walled York looms gray and cold above
And bristles all along like porpentine[1]
With spear and bolts that scent out English flesh.
My English friends, my English brothers now,
5   You hear my voice's maiden call to arms,
To urge you on who want from me no urging,
And quicken ire of knights to martial wrath
Who were born fighting men ere I was born,
To lead you where you have already bled,
10   But I have not. What king is this who calls?
An York should be the first and last of me,
Let no man say I was not Uter's son,
Nor valued more than he this bubble life.
But of our foemen, this cannot be said.
15   Who waits for us within, fell[2] Englishmen?
This Saxon pride set sail o'er Humber's tide[3]
And then conjoined[4] to Pictish treachery
For but to cower, spent and quaking-shy,
Portcullised[5] fast behind the walls of York,
20   As guilty lads will seek their mother's skirts
When older boys they vex come for revenge.
But Arthur's at the gate! 'Tis Britain's fist

---

1. **porpentine** porcupine.
2. **fell** fierce, deadly.
3. **Humber's tide** The Saxons have invaded England along the Humber River, disembarked, and invaded York by land.
4. **conjoined** met up, joined forces.
5. **portcullised** fortified behind a portcullis, a castle gate.

That hammers now upon the shiv'ring[6] boards.
An English blood be thin as watery wine,
25   Then sheathe we now our swords and skulk away
With Saxon language tripping from our lips.
You'd con[7] th'invader's tongue? *Absit omen.*[8]
Let's school them then in terms of English arms,
Decline and conjugate[9] hard[10] words—but hark!

                                               Chambers[11]

30   She sighs with gentle pleading that we come!
Now wait no more to save her, nobles, in,
And pull those Saxon arms off English skin!

                       Alarum and chambers. Exeunt

---

6. *shiv'ring* splintering.
7. *con* learn, memorize.
8. **Absit omen** "May the omen be absent" (Latin). ["May this not come to pass" or "Heaven forbid." —RV]
9. *Decline and conjugate* in Latin, reciting or listing the various endings to nouns and verbs, respectively.
10. *hard* probably cruel, harsh, rather than "difficult," although the double meaning of difficult conjugation and declension may be present. [RV]
11. *Chambers* sound of cannons.

[ACT II, SCENE III]

[Location: The road from York to Lincoln]
Enter Mordred, Calvan, and armies

MORDRED   Had cruel Diomedes on Deinos leapt[1, 2]
               To melt our arms and singe our prideful cheeks,
               Still less endamagement[3] had this day wreaked

---

1. *Diomedes* Diomedes was a hero in the Trojan War.
2. *Diomedes on Deinos leapt* While that's true, the reference here is actually to the giant Diomedes, who kept four horses, mad from consuming human flesh. One of the horses was called Deinos ("the terrible"). Hercules' labors included stealing the horses. [RV]
3. *endamagement* harm, injury.

As Arthur did these hours in battled York.

5 No Christian, holy king is Arthur, nay:
He cruelly used our gentle embassy
As I did doubt he might,[4] though 'twas enough
To spur our father back to war-like mien[5]
And dispatch force to force his will in York
10 Yet still doth shame now cloud our northern brows!
Five hard assaults I put to the usurping
Upspring[6] prince of English bastardy.
I rained upon him blows of sword and axe,
And through his beaver's vents[7] I heard the sound
15 Of laughing boy or demon's goblin mirth.

CALVAN The southern gallants drew from him their heart.
"For Arthur, George, and Britain!" they all cried,
Not England's name alone, but Britain's rung.
And on his quartered shield he paints his hopes:
20 The red Welsh dragon flanks gold English lions,
And harps of Western Isles do play light airs
O'er fields of northern thistle.[8]

MORDRED   Bannerets[9]
And horses' coats all colored with that boast!
25 Self-loving Arthur now doth rest a-bed,
While we escape the day by postern gate.[10]
Yet all those buffets paid in York today
Are but an obolus of bloody debt
We'll farm[11] in Lincoln town. You, sirrah, here.

---

4. *As I did doubt he might* A little disingenuous, since Mordred sent Alexander expressly to provoke a war. [RV]

5. *mien* manner, mood.

6. *upspring* upstart.

7. *beaver's vents* the slits or airholes of his visored helmet.

8. *quartered shield . . . ween* The four sections (*quarters*) of Arthur's coat of arms reveal his ambition (*ween*) to be king of all the British Isles: Wales (dragon), England (lions), Scotland/Pictland (thistle), and Ireland (harp). [These symbols are, of course, anachronistic to the period of Arthur. —RV]

9. *Bannerets* pennons, military flags.

10. *escape . . . by postern gate* Mordred unintentionally attaches a fecal image to the northerners, likely amusing to the London audience, and likely sufficient to offend James VI, triggering the Nicolson Letter of 1598. [RV]

11. *obolus . . . debt . . . farm* "He will repay our injuries in greater quantity later." From collecting ("farming") tax or debt. An obolus was a coin of the lowest value. [RV]

30	FIRST MSG.	My lord, your will?
	MORDRED	Go now to Lincoln's walls,

Where Colgerne keeps his tenfold larger strength.
We will entice the foe by seeming weak
To follow thither and therein surprise.

35 Advise him us we hie[12] with Arthur's force
Pursuing, thus he must lay gins[13] with guile.

                                        [*Exit messenger*]

There death will knock from haughty Arthur's pate
The diadem my father's brow to deck.[14]
Another man, another man!

[*Enter messenger*]

40	SECOND MSG.	Your grace?
	MORDRED	To kings of Scots and Picts make speedy haste,

Invite them to descend from highland nest,
And on spread wing to Lincoln fly like fate
T'assay[15] the crown I offer with all love.

45 Go, go!   *Exit messenger*

                    Now, Calvan, brother, Orkney's prince,
To all the captains tell: 'twixt here and there
We leave no crumb, no watery drop but tears
Of those who'd us deny benevolence.

50 May Arthur find upon this road no bran,
No vivers[16] of the basest sort to chew,
Until he come to Lincoln, there to wash
His blazon's quartered fancies[17] in red blood.   *Exeunt*

---

12. *hie* hurry.
13. *gins* snares.
14. *deck* decorate.
15. *assay* to test, sample, try on.
16. *vivers* food. [True enough, but especially in Scottish dialect. In fact, the term was exclusively Scottish until the nineteenth century, demonstrating again Shakespeare's gift for listening to the voices around him in London and imitating the dialects. —RV]
17. *blazon's quartered fancies* the whimsical, wishful ambitions of Arthur's coat of arms (*blazon*) drawn in four parts (*quartered*).

[ACT II, SCENE IV]

[*Location: The town hall of York*]
[*Enter*] *Arthur, Gloucester*

ARTHUR   I did not know what joy awaited me
When dawn did break this morn, when I alone
Had never tasted of the feast of war.
Whilst other men did seem to shy and fright,
5   Full general in my greetings,[1] I did leap
To gratulate[2] each happy Saxon, Scot,
Or Pict I had good fortune there to meet.
I find no better way to sport than this.
The day is mine!

10   GLOUCESTER   And all our thanks to God.
But for the morrow, I'll no wagers take.

ARTHUR   Refuse to rest your pounds upon my arm?[3]

GLOUCESTER   Were all of England York and all its sons
Were Arthur, Pluto's wealth[4] to any odds
15   I'd play and off to slumber vict'ry-ripe.[5]
But 'twixt pacific York and Pictish throne
Awaits no mead[6] but cragged, ungentle path.
And proud the Saxons are to want a fleet,

---

1. **general in my greetings** (ironic) attacking everyone he saw with equal generosity.
2. **gratulate** to greet.
3. **pounds upon my arm** a pun: pounds as weight to rest and as money to wager on Arthur's arm. [RV]
4. **Pluto's wealth** Pluto was god of the underworld and its extensive riches. [Hence, "plutocrat." —RV]
5. **vict'ry-ripe** on the verge of victory.
6. **mead** meadow.

So each and every foe will ask our care.[7]

20   ARTHUR   And so we shall design.

Enter Somerset, Norfolk, Cumbria, Kent, Derby

                              Good morrow, brothers!

     SOMERSET   Great King, O rampant lion emperor!

     CUMBRIA   My stomach wants for yet more bloody broil.[8]

Let fly! I'll draw the culv'rin[9] with my teeth.

25   NORFOLK   But majesty, 'twas you that 'mazed us all!

As evening dyed each Yorkish stone, I flagged:

My foot did slide through pools of Scottish gore

And on my back I lit. Two Saxon blades

Down toward me came, and I prepared my end.

30   But by my halidom[10] St. George careered[11]

With Pictish blood across his bristled cheek,

His limbs still freshly sprung as bent green yew,[12]

He slashed through danger, holp[13] me to my feet,

Then circled round and fought at every side.

35   My lord, bend I this ancient knee with love.

     CUMBRIA   Now foes do run, King, whither turn our might?

     ARTHUR   My nephew, King of Brittany in France,

I writ, and Constantine,[14, 15] young Cornish earl,

His father placed in Cornwall's seat by mine.

40   I bid them come take part at Lincoln's feast

And there to warm themselves and troops withal

By th'embers[16] of this factious[17] mutiny

---

7. Legend had it that the invaders burned their boats upon arriving in England, leaving themselves no tempting option of returning home, so each foe will have to be killed. [RV]

8. *broil* fighting.

9. *culv'rin* type of cannon. [Anachronistic. —RV]

10. *halidom* an oath, "by all that's holy" or "by what I hold to be holy."

11. *career* to charge, gallop.

12. *freshly . . . yew* as flexible and springy as wood from a yew tree (used to make bows). [RV]

13. *holp* helped.

14. Named for my father's perpetual tormentor, Ted Constantine, Hennepin County attorney and father of my best friend, Doug.

15. The name is in Holinshed, Malory, and several other Arthur stories. Shakespeare did not select it to comment on a twentieth-century Minnesota prosecutor. [RV]

16. *embers* inspired, I suspect, by my father's habit of visiting the Embers restaurant in Minneapolis, where I can imagine him writing this play.

17. *factious* seditious, secessionist.

And on its remnants dance a stamp royal.[18]

Enter messenger

What word there, boy?

45   MESSENGER   God save your majesty.

ARTHUR   He seems inclined t'affect thy will a time.

MESSENGER   The foe, affrayed, unranked, beset with pox,
Goes south and drops its numbers as it flies.
Your people worry[19] them, bemock their heart.

50   A child did toss some several stones at them,
Which quaking Picts did in agastment[20] flee,
As though shot out by ranked artillery.

ARTHUR   We'll not await Petit Bretagne's[21] force,
But haste to Lincoln, where we'll cut this tale.

55   Though half and half again the Yorkish brawl
We'll see in Lincoln's fields, an we not speed,
E'en that we grant to boys with slings and rocks.[22]
My lords, two hours to bid adieu to York.

Exeunt nobility [except Gloucester]

My duke, yet stately matters here in town

60   Demand of me considerance a time.[23]

GLOUCESTER   You would delay our march, my king?

ARTHUR   Nay, nay.
Our arms must haste, though even to a pin.

GLOUCESTER   I'll set good men to follow at your hest.[24]

65   ARTHUR   'Tis of no need, though lovingly designed.

---

18. *stamp royal* a kind of dance.

19. *worry* harass.

20. *agastment* fright, alarm.

21. *Petit Bretagne* Brittany, as opposed to Grand Bretagne, or Great Britain.

22. A bit convoluted: "Though Lincoln will only be 25 percent as large a battle as the one we have just fought, even that opportunity to fight will be lost if we don't hurry, since kids with stones will scatter the remaining enemy." [RV]

23. Arthur's mysterious business in York is never entirely clarified in the text. I can see four alternative explanations for this: (1) The 1597 text is corrupt. (2) We are meant to see the arrival of Philip in Act IV as the denouement to a sexual adventure here in Act II. (3) There was some stage business in the original production which is now unclear to us (and modern directors will no doubt find their own interpretations). (4) Shakespeare allowed a mystery to sit at the heart of his character's behavior, as he later did in *Othello*, for example. [RV]

24. *hest* command.

GLOUCESTER   My lord, my wit is blunted by the day.
                     Your mind it is to stay in York alone?

ARTHUR   It is.

GLOUCESTER   Shall I attend?

70 ARTHUR   There is no call.

GLOUCESTER   If I do waver at your word, it is—
                     But I should say, your new-dyed[25] royalty—
                     I would so soon expose—but, stay, my king—
                     I beg indulgence if my love o'erflows

75   The bounds of mannered courtier's smoothing
                                  tongue,
                    But this can no way be—the boy thou wert
                    With holy unction[26] is reborn a king.

ARTHUR   I thank with all my love thy wise advice.

GLOUCESTER   My joy it is my wit can serve your need.

80 ARTHUR   'Tis well, 'tis well. It is my need that you
                    Command and lead our hunt to Lincoln now.

GLOUCESTER   My words have then consumed but their own tails?

ARTHUR   Go, lead our furious arms for us. Take care
                    That you advance no swifter than the rear.

85   The hindmost rank[27] is every army's heel.[28]

GLOUCESTER   The body, lacking head, will range[29] about
                    If king they saw in battle now's dislodged.
                    It is too hard upon your first assay.[30]
                    Your nobles still mistrust and countermand

90   Each other's words, bend not to my impose.[31]
                    Thick-sinew'd[32] Cumbria and saucy[33] Norfolk
                    Will bow to king but never seneschal.
                    Arthur, you are no single man, but king.
                    You must in every act revolve upon[34]

---

25. *new-dyed* brand-new.
26. *unction* anointment with oil.
27. *hindmost rank* rearguard unit.
28. *heel* Achilles' heel.
29. *range* roam, wander.
30. *too hard upon your first assay* too soon after your first battle.
31. *bend not to my impose* refuse to obey my orders.
32. *thick-sinew'd* muscle-bound.
33. *saucy* impertinent, insolent.
34. *revolve upon* consider, meditate over.

95   The country's cares and gracious God's intent

For this the flock of which you wield the crook.

ARTHUR   You show that I am truant[35] in command.

Your warming sun-bright words have dried a path

Which I perceive at last through muddy cares.

100   GLOUCESTER   My lord, I am in all humility

Made glad and do admire this sovereign lord

Pursuing wiser course when 'tis revealed.

ARTHUR   To quell the noble plaints and cheer the men,

The colors of the king will ride on you,

105   My armor and close helm, my flag and shield.

You will not speak, but gesture royally,

Short-tongued[36] for military stratagems

Outrav'ling[37] in your bloodied silent mind.

And I will gallop up anon,[38] to ride

110   With you afore the Humber's far behind.

GLOUCESTER   What gear so notable[39] can stay[40] a king?

This pulls dishonor down on both our heads.

ARTHUR   Smooth not thy tongue, but smooth thy brow its
                              cares.

Though kingdom's needs concern my every thought,

115   A king is licensed still to be a man.

GLOUCESTER   Of this, I fear, my lord, you are mistook.

ARTHUR   'Tis of no moment, none by cock and pie.[41]

You'll make a country ride on sun-gold day,

To glad these moody lords who want but some

120   Brief show of royal confidence, which you

From me reflect on steel and painted skin.[42]

And when, at Lincoln's gate, the arrows sing,

To me they'll sing, in my own proper coat.

---

35. *truant* negligent.
36. *Short-tongued* taciturn.
37. *Outrav'ling* untangling, clarifying.
38. *gallop up anon* catch up soon.
39. *notable* significant.
40. *stay* detain, delay.
41. *cock and pie* a mild oath.
42. *you . . . skin* "My armor and coat of arms (*painted skin*) will reflect my royalty, even if they are on you." [RV]

	GLOUCESTER	Yet list me still, my boy, my wayward boy.
125	ARTHUR	No longer, Duke of Gloucester, but thy king.
		If chartered are thy words to gainsay kings,[43]
		Still king it is that grants these liberties.
		Or, soft, thy boy, but king as well, good Duke.
		Now come and do as I command of thee. *Exeunt*

43. **chartered . . . gainsay** "Though you are permitted to question kings . . ."

[ACT II, SCENE V]

[*Location: The road to Lincoln*]
Enter Denton, Sumner, and Bell

	DENTON	High words ride on high wind,[1] I say. When they would have your guts to stuff their pudding-bags,[2] they start at singing of Troy for us to love our labors more.
5	BELL	I grant York was but first I ever knew of war. Never had I chance until now, I was not able, but what I saw in York's turned[3] roads calls shame on talk like that.
	SUMNER	A new warrior, la! And all the glories fall in for him. And thou'rt equal to the king! Had his first taste at
10		York. Didst thou and he stand with shoulders touching?
	BELL	Why bend thy brows?[4] Do I go boasting? Nay. I walked in tremble-knee'd, sure. But did I skirr?[5]

1. "Noble speeches require a lot of gas."
2. **pudding-bags** a mold or bag for making pudding.
3. **turned** twisting.
4. **bend thy brows** scowl.
5. **skirr** to flee.

		When the dragon[6] belched fire and the ordnance[7]
15		thundered, I stood firm. Knocked two Germans
		down, I did. Lifted one his beaver back when I put
		him on the turf. Put my blade through. I did, thus,
		just pushed it through. Like when I would kill
		coneys[8] with my brother, like that, some, tough, yet
20		not so tough, in truth. It goes in soft. I never cared to
		look the coney in his eye neither, when time came.
		Nor cared to look at this big yellow[9] one. Said
		something in Saxonish, I suppose it was.
	DENTON	Like as not only giving thee "rest you merry."[10]
25	BELL	Think you so?
	SUMNER	Or "fair fall you, valiant soldier."
	BELL	He may, he may have.
	SUMNER	What block art thou? Needest thou be set to school in
		Saxon talk to know he begged thee mercy or swore
30		out upon thy soul or cried for his new orphan or his
		own Saxon mother in Saxonland, which is far from
		York, I tell thee, too far to be wandering in hope of
		friendly greetings. Hast thou hope he did forgive
		thee? Honors thee thy valor? What tales to sing
35		thyself to bed withal!
	BELL	No stories, but what I have seen I'll sing: men do with
		valor face death and all the doom beyond when for
		their king they fight.
	DENTON	Bend, boy, bend thy head, thy battle-mate's on hoof.

Gloucester for Arthur passes

40	SUMNER	His visor down, all silence.
	DENTON	A ghost, like. I first knew battle for his father. Thou
		mightst have eaten butter had I stepped in cream.[11]

---

6. **dragon** presumably a cannon carved into the shape of a dragon. [Anachronism. —RV]
7. **ordnance** artillery. [Anachronism. —RV]
8. **coneys** rabbits.
9. **yellow** blond.
10. **giving thee "rest you merry"** "Sending you on your way with best wishes." [RV]
11. **butter . . . cream** He was shaking so much from fear that he would have churned cream into butter.

	SUMNER	But this one fights the same as his sire, no fear at all in him.
45	DENTON	Is he not flesh? Is he of other stuff and feels not a blade peel off skin? His eyes are agates? They do not jelly if an arrow pinch 'em? His bones so hard as will not splinter out the skin as I saw Nick Safe's arm do?
50	BELL	What serves this talk? To fright a man before a battle's fought is no victory, nor like to win us one. Every fool can say the price to flesh, but marching in withal, as our king there does march, that's a lesson, not to gabble subtle meant to void an army's guts afore the fight. What more corruption could a canker[12] spread in corn or rose than that? Thou mightst be a Saxon tongue to make us weak in heart.
55		
	DENTON	A fig[13] for all thy corn and flowers, boy.
60	BELL	Thy breath stinks enough. A flower might cover o'er thy toothless mouth and worse.
	SUMNER	That stink he borrowed of certain French companions, all now burning night and day, and off to powder tubs.[14]
	DENTON	I'll learn you both some Saxon words, you knaves.
65	BELL	I need no more words of thee, coward, nor can my nose take none. *Trumpets*
	SUMNER	Quiet now, the both. That's Lincoln there and the trumpets sound.
70	BELL	After York, it will be nothing. I had some chance to be at York at all. They'll stand me a spigot at the Pard's Head,[15] if I tell my tale.
75	DENTON	Again a fool, before and after a fool, a fool from claw to beak. You sit mum, not you who tells it, you, the man by you tells it and you sit mute as marble and first you say it was not this, it was nothing, then you

---

12. *canker* an insect larva that attacks plants.
13. *a fig* an obscene, contemptuous gesture.
14. *powder tubs* thought to be a cure for venereal diseases, such as syphilis, the so-called French sickness. [RV]
15. *Pard's Head* the Leopard's Head, presumably an inn or pub.

say you want no talk, and then, when the noise for a
tale is up, then, then you say, "So. I'll tell you how it
was at York, but it's no tale I can tell swift, and—" and
you wait a time, you cough, and say, "Throat's dry."
80 Then old Francis opens wide the taps for a man who
was at York. *Trumpets*

BELL That's the trumpet of our company. To the walls and
later learn me more of this soldier science. *Exeunt*

[ACT II, SCENE VI]

[*Location: Lincoln*]
Alarums and excursions, including Gloucester in Arthur's armor
Enter Mordred, Calvan, Colgerne, Scottish and Pictish nobles, Saxon soldiers

MORDRED What dev'lish hag was mother to this fiend?
Yet Arthur holds the field, untouched by blades!
No man is he but war itself come down
To earth to look upon the death of souls.
5 We melt before his charge, our heart is broke!

COLGERNE No Uter, he: more war-like is the son.
He stalks full silent as with windpipe slit.

CALVAN We are enow still armed and holding ranks
That with a voice to stir us to our task
10 We yet can thrash back south these enemies
And hoist our father's arms on Lincoln's walls.
But ope your throat and lust'ly call the fight!

MORDRED Great Calvan's words do fill my lungs with air:
On northmen, on! To arms, to arms, to th'fight!
15 In Arthur's blood I'll bathe my limbs tonight,
And Britain stride undoubted in my right!

Alarums and exeunt

[ACT II, SCENE VII]

[*Location: Lincoln*]
Alarums, excursions. Enter Gloucester for Arthur and Hebrides. They fight.
Hebrides is slain. Enter English nobles

NORFOLK	The shamèd enemy displays his haunch![1]	
DERBY	'Tis Lincoln now, not York, that English tongues	
	Will speak when they would conjure victory.	
	Four-fold the threat we doubted lurked in stealth,[2]	
5	The city was well-manned and fortified,	
	But Arthur's greyhound-sight did note a gap	
	And lusty-blooded split it with his arm.	
CUMBRIA	While Gloucester passed the battle's day at rest.	
	By this proud flesh[3] upon my arms and face,	
10	All striped these many years in England's wars,	
	That seneschal is recreant[4] and base.	
SOMERSET	But softly, Cumbria, hold tongue. The king	
	Doth wave us off to solitary pray.	*Exeunt*

[*Gloucester unhelms and kneels*]

GLOUCESTER	Deception 'pon deception preys and fats	
15	Itself, the stronger to deceive anew.	
	'Twas ever thus, but now is Gloucester's name	
	All shard bestrewn,[5] so Arthur's fledgèd[6] name	
	Might tower[7] up to all the world's esteem.	
	Because I winked at his small boyish deeds,	
20	Now habit binds me tighter, cuts my flesh,	

1. ***displays his haunch*** turns tail.
2. ***Four-fold . . . stealth*** "We found hidden here four times the force we were expecting."
3. ***proud flesh*** scar tissue, raised as if proud.
4. ***recreant*** cowardly.
5. ***shard bestrewn*** dung-covered.
6. ***fledgèd*** fully plumed, feathered.
7. ***tower*** in falconry (continuing the imagery of "fledgèd"), the action of flying to a high point before swooping down to kill. [RV]

And I omit behaviors grosser still.
What kingdom have we won this day at war?
What rule deserve from such unhonest[8] toil?

Enter Arthur as friar[9]

ARTHUR   [*Aside*] Why here's a glass that shows one's better face.

25   Were I of suppler knee, as there I seem,
I'd bow to earth my joints and plant my thanks.
Would this one here could reign instead of me,
A wise old king, resolved yet never rash.
I would I saw such pious king as this

30   When I do peer into my subjects' eyes.
But no.
Imperfect is the glass of others' eyes
Wherein we seek in hope of handsome glimpse
Yet find dim shapes, reversed and versed again,

35   Which will not ease our self-love's appetites.
But let us make more pleasant now our thoughts:
I'll hood myself and from my bloodied twin

[*Hooding himself*]

Glean news of Lincoln's fate and mine.— [*To Gloucester*] O, King!
Might errant[10] friar ease your soul's distress?

40   In earth and blood you are o'er-crusted, still
The soul may be clean searched[11] and truly healed.

GLOUCESTER   Thou startled, priest, and near did feel my blade.

ARTHUR   Confess and I will shrive you back to war
New-cleansed and shent.[12]

45   GLOUCESTER   But I must hoard my act.
The blackest sins I bear are sins I share,
So my conspirator must kneel with me.[13]

---

8. **unhonest** dishonorable, immoral.
9. **as friar** King Arthur is disguised for safe travel alone from York to Lincoln. As his words below indicate, he is also—in modern parlance—on a "walk of shame," and his changeable mood in this scene is typical of those early-morning retreats from regrettable adventures.
10. **errant** wandering.
11. **clean searched** cleaned, as a wound.
12. **shent** exempt, pure.
13. A modern director has some interpretive choice as to when, precisely, Gloucester realizes that the "friar" is Arthur. [RV]

		And kings, what's more, may whisper[14] but to popes,
		Or to your lord, my Bishop Caerleon.
50	ARTHUR	A friend, i'truth, and his stiff bishopric
		I visit oft, where he and I partake
		Of meals of fish and pear, 'til full to burst.[15]
	GLOUCESTER	What priest can talk such filth upon his lord?
		My blade will teach thee mannerly discourse!

[He draws his sword]

55	ARTHUR	But Gloucester, nay! Slice not this royal meat,
		Or wait until we change again our coats
		So by my carbonado[16] you might whet
		An appetite for vengeance in my men.
	GLOUCESTER	Is't Arthur safely back to us from York,
60		And first of all his business is to sport?
	ARTHUR	But soft, let's dress each one in rightful cloak,

[They exchange armor]

		To each our own apparel and our mien.
	GLOUCESTER	Your time in York, O King, did serve its need,
		Did rightly beg your absence from the field?
65	ARTHUR	Good Duke, take pains not to omit my helm
		Else company might think we swapped our heads.
	GLOUCESTER	You take me for a joint-stool,[17] King, then sit.
		You welcome not my counsel, Majesty.
	ARTHUR	I clip it to my breast at dawn and dusk.
70		There's none save you enthroned within my heart.
	GLOUCESTER	Then hear my words. Today was battle won—
	ARTHUR	Such joyous tidings, Duke, do glad me well.
	GLOUCESTER	By gross deception came this victory.
		Your men believe you led them into war.
75	ARTHUR	An if they so believe, then so I did.[18]
		But now, our royal transformation done,

[*Enter nobles with prisoners including Mordred, Calvan, and Colgerne*]

We greet our men with fettered prisoners—

---

14. **whisper** confess.
15. **bishopric, fish, pear, burst** a rapid-fire series of double entendres: Arthur claims to visit the Bishop of Caerleon and engage with him in orgies. [RV]
16. **carbonado** sliced and grilled meat.
17. **take me for a joint-stool** take me for granted.
18. That's my dad at the quill there, no question.

What guests have you, my English chivalry?

CUMBRIA These bales[19] are but a tithing[20] of our crop.

80 They wait their fate upon this lower world[21]

And we our fortunes as you judge our worth.—

Hail, Gloucester, hail! At battle's end you come

To fright the prisoners with your martial air.

ARTHUR Great lords of Britain, by your arms is peace,

85 So long extirped,[22] replanted on our isle.

ALL Hail Arthur! Hail Britain! To our king!

ARTHUR For two score years these knaves cast pestilence

From north and sea 'pon our abusèd land,

And crushed beneath their tread our wealth, our crop,

90 Our churches, beasts, and golden English corn.

I sweep my eye across these hanging[23] looks,

These villain Saxons, Picts, and shamèd Scots.

With but a breath could our worse nature burst

And wash again this new-dried ground with blood.

95 O, Englishmen! Is there yet one of us

Who would not venge on Scotchman's neck the cries

Most pitiful of murdered English babes?

What joys have they not thieved from out our homes?

My youthful days, my kingdom, and my sire:

100 All this I lost and this far past enough

T'excuse a slaughter of this murrained[24] herd.

Anointed king, still I am but a man,

And men do long for blood to balm their wounds.

ALL Then kill them all! For Arthur! Kill them all!

105 ARTHUR But do these cringing mice contain enough

Of blood to slake and chill our burning thirst?

Or will their cries not satisfy our hate,

But feed and thereby swell our hate's desire,

While their own mothers, orphans, widows shrike[25]

---

19. ***bales*** bundles, as in agriculture or commerce, implying, too, that the prisoners are bound.
20. ***tithing*** a tenth, as in the amount of tax owed to the church.
21. ***lower world*** earth. [RV]
22. ***extirped*** uprooted.
23. ***hanging*** morose.
24. ***murrained*** infected.
25. ***shrike*** shriek.

110		In twisted tongues and curse us to their gods,
		Demand our blood to wash their tear-stained cheeks?
		There's none so swift to carve this tendered flesh
		As I, who look on them and grows hate-drunk.
		But this eternal hatred is a pox,
115		Which e'en struck down and slew my father-king.

In twisted tongues and curse us to their gods,
Demand our blood to wash their tear-stained cheeks?
There's none so swift to carve this tendered flesh
As I, who look on them and grows hate-drunk.
But this eternal hatred is a pox,
Which e'en struck down and slew my father-king.
As royal touch can heal a man's disease,[26]
It can as quick transform man's hate to love,
And in a trice sweep winter from the land,
To reap the fruit of peace.

CUMBRIA   [*Aside*] What talk is this?

ARTHUR Let Colgerne, vassal now to Britain's king,
To German lands with all his men repair
Without delay, but know that they will die
If e'er they do return.

CUMBRIA   [*Aside*] Have I my wits?

ARTHUR Familiarity did breed contempt;[27]
Disloignèd[28] far, love 'twixt us may increase,
And by exampled English mercy shown
May Saxons now embrace our Lord. Cast off
By Lincoln Wash, and from our realm begone.

GLOUCESTER You will I know hold some as surety,
And not deny your iron men[29] their prize.

ARTHUR I do intend precisely that, my duke.—
Here Mordred, thou didst wager dad's own crown,
But frozen luck, thou lost it to thy betters.
To Pictland now and fetch thy father here
T'impress the wax of his remembrance, boy,
That he doth rule his Picts at Arthur's pleasure.
In earnest of this love I bear for him,
We hold for now young Calvan to our breast
And in great London's tower feast our guest.

                    Exeunt, manet[30] *Cumbria*

CUMBRIA Did e'er his father win such victory?

26. *disease* scrofula, a lymphic disorder, was thought curable by being touched by the sovereign.
27. From Aesop's fables. [RV]
28. *disloignèd* removed to a distance.
29. *iron men* men at arms.
30. *manet* indicates that a character remains when others exit.

Did e'er his father cast away the like?
To clutch in mailèd fist his enemies,
145   Then careless drop them back into the fight?
This cock-a-prance![31] This beadsman,[32] preached of
    love,
Yet loved us not enow to preach of ransom.
Bright-armored[33] Gloucester called his mind to it;
War counsel comes from one who shunned the brawl!
150   What man would wink at that one's cowardice
Then heed the stratagems he would propose?
No oath adheres to such a paltry king,
But for the love I bore his poisoned sire. *Exit*

---

31. *cock-a-prance* swaggering fop. [RV]
32. *beadsman* someone paid to pray for others.
33. *Bright-armored* clean-armored, as he supposedly had not fought. [RV]

[ACT II, SCENE VIII]

[*Location: Arthur's camp at Lincoln*]
Enter Arthur, Gloucester, servants, messengers

ARTHUR   Our late inspect[1] of Britain's sorrowing breadth
Shows us a land all brought to waste by war,
From hunger lamed, abandoned of the law.
Now plague and famine stalk our market towns,
5   And gripes[2] make claim of sovereignty for death
Where Arthur would establish gentler court.
Here is a worthy challenge for a king.
No Pendragon forepast[3] hath seen as I
The glory of a king is weighed on scale
10   By what prosperity his kingdom joys.

---

1. *inspect* inspection.
2. *gripes* vultures.
3. *forepast* in the past.

Watch Arthur now drive sickness, dearth, and war
From out his realm as I did whip the Scot.
Send men to learn what towns have stores of corn.
Set reeves to fix my law in every shire.[4]

15 Strong fort each town on coast and northern line.

Enter Constantine [Cornwall]

My dear, good Cornwall! Rise and let me kiss you!

CORNWALL   My king, I bring all love and of more boot[5]
Five thousand Cornish blades as you require.

ARTHUR   Again, again, embrace me, Constantine, brave
20   Cornwall![6] Now help me to remember, friend: when
were we last together?

CORNWALL   'Twas Gloucestershire. Our fathers lived and we
did pass each day at swim and running. You ever
were the best.

25 ARTHUR   And thou, to make a match of heaven,[7] wert always
second.

CORNWALL   Too sadly true.

ARTHUR   And when thou wert king of the woods and I was king
of the waters, or I king of the woods and thou of
30   waters, our pastance[8] was to act great deeds for the
the princess of the flowers. How fares thy gentle
sister? Still pleasant in her humors, the girl we
strived[9] to please?

CORNWALL   No more a girl, but still doth ask in humility to be
35   remembered.

ARTHUR   I remember no store of humility in her.

---

4. *reeves . . . shire* a supervising official with royal jurisdiction. [*Shire-reeve* is the etymology of "sheriff." —RV]

5. *boot* use.

6. It is interesting to note the brief shift to prose here: old friends, once intimates, now talk as intimates, before returning to affairs of state in line 41, where Arthur also returns them to the more formal "you." A similar case of shifting to prose between two characters of the same class can be found at the end of *Henry IV, Part One*, III.i, between Hotspur and his wife. [RV]

7. *to make a match of heaven* to make a perfect match.

8. *pastance* recreation, pastime.

9. *strived* As an example of stylometry, the computer report of *Arthur* noted that Shakespeare tended to use "strived" early in his career and "strove" later. [RV]

CORNWALL   Your wit[10] is most royally acute. But you will observe
            her alterations, for she rides to join with us anon. It
            was her will, and her will is beyond my certain
40   manage.

ARTHUR   You were my joy of younger days, good earl,
            And now I swear upon this fruitful plain,
            That you and I will be inseparate.

CORNWALL   You deem this blasted,[11] war-ripped turf so rich?

45 ARTHUR   Ay, Cornwall! All our enemies are flown,
            And we will in this loam plant seeds of peace.

Enter messenger

            A frantic look in this one's eye.—What is't?

MESSENGER   My king, as you did by their bond require,
            The Saxons lifted sail from Lincoln Wash.
50   But soon a change of wind did hale[12] them back.
            Their priests addeemed[13] this blessed by pagan gods.
            They spilled from ship anew upon our isle,
            Contemptibly stepped back onto our sands.
            They throw their eyes on gold and church and field,
55   They kill our countrymen and burn our land.

ARTHUR   O, God! What scorn I do deserve from thee!
            What villainy is this? What have I wrought?
            What arrogant and idle prince am I!
            And where were men to chide my fond, mad youth?
60   I should be scorned for my vain clemency.
            I am not mocked enough! O sugar-prince,
            A headstrong jade[14] that should be roughly spurred!
            Let those who judge me weak be made at once
            My chosen privy councillors.—Which way?

65 MESSENGER Towards Bath, my king.

ARTHUR   We'll cote[15] them ere they
        wash.
            This crime has touched me; I am powder-hot.

---

10. *wit* mind, awareness. No implication of comic acuity. [RV]
11. *blasted* damaged, ruined, stricken.
12. *hale* haul.
13. *addeemed* adjudged.
14. *jade* contemptuous term for low-quality horse.
15. *cote* overtake. [A term from hunting with dogs. —RV]

To rear now post my word: our mercy's pact
Refused, each prisoner's throat is to be cut.

70 GLOUCESTER The tidings speak but Saxon perfidy,
Not Scot nor Pict. A moment's calm, I beg.

ARTHUR I'll not be tender pitying more, good duke.—

Exit messenger

My men, imperfect[16] is our bloody task
So follow me, unsheathe your late-hacked blade

75 And dispatch hell-born foes to hellish shade. *Exeunt*

16. **imperfect** incomplete.

[ACT II, SCENE IX]

[Location: The Pictish Court]
Enter Doctor and Conranus

DOCTOR I have to all my texts submitted Loth,
To all my wit, invention, fancy, hopes,
To strong balsamo,[1] leeches, pastes, and cuts.
Yet still he falters and outstreams his life.

5 It flows from ev'ry outlet, king. He fails.

Enter Mordred, with train.

CONRANUS The prince with retinue is back from war,
And surely wants the king his father's ear.
Go learn if audience may yet be had.— *Exit Doctor*
Good Mordred, Duke, we missed you here at court.

10 MORDRED I bear hard news of noble death, war's tithe.
The thanes[2] of Bute and Moray, Linlithgow,
And Douglas ride birlinns[3] to Colmekill's shores.[4]

CONRANUS Such heavy loss, so light an argument.

1. **balsamo** balsam.
2. **thanes** Scottish nobility.
3. **birlinns** the large rowboats of western Scotland's chieftains.
4. **Colmekill** the traditional burial site of Scottish kings, on the northwestern Scottish island of Iona; cf *Macbeth*, II.iv.33. [RV]

MORDRED   How light, my uncle? Tell. A crown? A throne?
15   A kingdom stole from thee stirs not thy gall?
                A tyrant who doth threat thy land and clan?[5]
                Who torments lawful embassy, hates peace
                And would lock Pict and Scot in steely yoke?

CONRANUS   A petty prince thou told'st this court was weak,
20   Who wanted nought of us 'til thou like dog
                Didst bite at him as would a bear and now
                Dost whine what thou hast learnt of his sharp claws.
                Speak troth, thou wert impatient of God's will.
                An God did wish thee sat on London's throne,
25   He would not send thee home with thanesmen's
                      dooms.

MORDRED   At Lincoln, King, I fought beside your son.

CONRANUS   Speak thou no more a word. He follows not?
                Waits not upon thee nor presents to me?

MORDRED   Brave Hebrides gave battle like to none.
30   On horse and foot—

CONRANUS   No more. I want no more.

MORDRED   But Scotland! King! We must record his deeds!
                You weep that yet must gaze upon his valor!

CONRANUS   Show mercy on my soul and heed my plea.
35 MORDRED   Art thou a man? But ope thy frighted ear
                That I may teach thy tongue some noble words.
                For God, who makes us labor for our cause,
                Doth bid us praise each death as sacrifice,
                Necessity, the proving of our right.
40   He wants not that we mourn His project's cost,
                But celebrate all blood that lifts us on.

[*Enter Loth, carried, with attendants and Doctor*]

                Make red thy lily heart; my father's come—
                [*To Loth*] My king, you must prepare yourself at once.
                But briefly: Calvan would that we should come
45   To London's tower, thence to bring him home
                In change for some few scarcely valued words

---

5. **clan** Again, as with *birlinn*, Shakespeare's use of Scottish dialect is noteworthy. [RV]

		That Arthur would have spoke at him.[6]
		The hour of our strength will spring again,
		We'll seize anew the vantage in the strife.
50	DOCTOR	Your father's apoplexy, Prince, forbids
		His travel e'en from here to castle gate.
		[Loth makes a sound or gesture]
	MORDRED	What? Would he speak? Explain these signs to me.
		Or would he have me nearer to his ear?
	DOCTOR	His speech is off and on confused, and I
55		Cannot, I fear, know always his intent.

Enter first messenger

	CONRANUS	Make haste.
	FIRST MSG.	The Saxons did forswear their bail,
		Set down again and now lay siege to Bath.
	MORDRED	At Colgerne's word?
60	FIRST MSG.	It was.
	MORDRED	On him the stain.
		Yet should he bloody the usurper's nose,
		It does become the voice of God's reply
		To Arthur's unconfinèd blasphemy.
65		Yet still we'll pay for Calvan with our words.

Enter messenger with bag

		The tidings like the tide do press and press
		Against our bonny shore. What jocund word?
		The bastard's killed? Or Saxons fled to sea?
		This battle cannot end but well for me,
70		With one or other of my foes defeat.
		Thou, sirrah, canst not fail but please, so speak.
	SECOND MSG.	I bear no happy words and beg your grace.
		I dare not speak.
	MORDRED	You choose to speak or die.
75	SECOND MSG.	I speak and die, or do in silence die.
	MORDRED	'Tis thus we all do live, my boy. Now speak.
	SECOND MSG.	The Saxon treachery told to the king—
	MORDRED	What king?

---

6. The line is short by two syllables, implying a pause, perhaps indicating that Mordred waits for Loth to reply. [RV]

	SECOND MSG.	King Arthur, lord.
80	MORDRED	Say not "the king"
		As he is none, or is but for a day.
		Say rather "bastard" or "usurping swine."
	SECOND MSG.	The Saxon treachery told to the swine,
		He put to death all ransom-waiting men.
85	MORDRED	Say rather "ransom-waiting Saxon men"
		As Saxony forswore itself, not we.
	SECOND MSG.	But this in truth I cannot say, my lord.
		He gave command for every ransomed man
		And in unholy anger he did slay
90		One man himself.
	MORDRED	'Twere better thou held tongue.
	CONRANUS	Nay, nay, speak on, go on.
	SECOND MSG.	To honor rank
		He offered Calvan sword and liberty
95		If he could singly⁷ vanquish him.
	MORDRED	No more.
	SECOND MSG.	Enragèd passion seized King Arthur's limbs.
	MORDRED	No more, I say! No more, no more, no more!
	SECOND MSG.	He smote your brother down and raught⁸ his locks
100		And by those hairs he drew his head hard back.
		On Arthur's face there shone a demon's hate.
		He sends to you the head and broken sword
		Within this bag and bids me tell—
	MORDRED	No more!

[Mordred] kills messenger

105	SECOND MSG.	I curse thee, villain prince, and all thy seed!⁹
	CONRANUS	How, nephew? Now thy site's¹⁰ thine own, no word?
		Thy heart that spoke bravado now is cold.
		So whither appetite for chronicle?

---

7. *singly* in single combat.

8. *raught* reached for, grasped.

9. It is not clear whether the messenger is still delivering Arthur's words or is expressing his own (understandable) feelings. [RV]

10. *site* grief. [Only in Scottish use in the sixteenth century. One is tempted to imagine Shakespeare quizzing Scottish friends for dialect words.—RV]

MORDRED	Thou wouldst come o'er me with my right rebuke.[11]
110	Then hear what manly speech I have for thee
	And bastard pup who wet his casual thirst
	With purest blood.[12] *He opens bag*
	O Calvan, brother, prince! O murdered boy!
DOCTOR	But soft. These words do close your father's throat.
115	This rattle sure is death's unjointed[13] talk.
MORDRED	Nay, sire! Can Arthur, malt-horse,[14] paper king
	Still reign while breath itself rebels your will?
	But softly, King, my father's only son
	Doth beg you not to yield t'imperious death.
120	I cannot lose my father now.[15]
	You would yet speak? I bend to you my ear.

> [*He leans close to Loth*]

	Again, again. I swear it, father, aye.
	All shall be done to your precise command.—
	[*To servants*] You, bear him to his chapel, there to shrive
125	His soul and read the verses due to him.

> [*Exeunt except Mordred and Conranus*]

CONRANUS	Such chatt'ring! How the dying king did buzz!
MORDRED	But sure the company imbibed each word?
CONRANUS	We heard from him no sound: thy table's[16] clean.
MORDRED	He urged me on to lose no days in tears,
130	But clad in gimmaled[17] mail and glimm'ring crown,
	Receive thy oath of fealty now and more:
	Assigned me Scotland's heir and with thy death
	Unite two kingdoms as God's certain will.
	And when our strength's restored, fill Arthur's tomb.

---

11. "You would hold my own correct criticism against me." [RV]
12. Note short line for stage business: removal of head, reaction. [RV]
13. *unjointed* incoherent.
14. *malt-horse* brewer's horse, an idiot.
15. Again, a short line. Mordred hears Loth say something? Or pretends to hear something? Or realizes his opportunity? Here, again, a director will have a chance to make the play his or her own. [RV]
16. *table* writing tablet. "The slate is clean."
17. *gimmaled* hinged or ringed, as in armor. [Used by Shakespeare twice more, in *Edward III* and *Henry V.*—RV]

135   CONRANUS   All this the wheezing king did set in charge?

       MORDRED   All this and more, perchance.

       CONRANUS   Loquacity[18]

                   In dying men is rare, though not unknown.

                   And of my death spoke he as urgently?

140   MORDRED   A natural death, years hence. But his is nigh,

                   So let us lend a comfort at his side.   *Exeunt*

---

18. **loquacity** earliest recorded use. The *OED* shows subsequent usage in 1603. [RV]

ACT III, SCENE I

[Location: The court in London]

Enter Gloucester and French Ambassador, attendants

       FRENCH AMB.   Mon duc de Gloosestayre,[1] my king à vous

                   Envoys his royal love and hail Arthur.[2]

       GLOUCESTER   We thank you and your great King Childebert

                   Who hath to France brought peace and gentle ways.

5   FRENCH AMB.   But your Arthur has in small years defeat

                   The Saxons cross the German Ocean's[3] waves.

                   Rebels[4] who fought do now cry up to God,

                   "We are subdued! Who take our side? Hélas!"

                   Arthur will now make for his kingdom laws

10   And art and prosperous virtues, you say.

---

1. **Mon duc de Gloosestayre** The French ambassador presumably has a thick accent. His efforts to pronounce "Gloucester" are transliterated in a three-syllable mock-French concoction: Glue-suh-stair. Shakespeare did, on occasion, mock the French and did try to transcribe the sound of foreign accents in his plays. However, in this case, I am unable to shake the memory of my father's fondness for the Warner Brothers cartoon skunk Pepé Le Pew.

2. **Arthur** In the ambassador's accent, "Arthur," a troublesome trochee (AR-thur) becomes a convenient iamb (ar-TOOR). [RV]

3. **German Ocean** the North Sea.

4. **Rebels** again, spoken with a French accent, presumably this is iambic: re-BELS. [RV]

But still revolters[5] come as always do,
And also more of savages who no
Do love Lord Jesu but false cloven gods.
I am much sad in heart to make these words
15   But King Arthur has not alone the means,
The arms and treasure, he require for all
He wish. He must have loving friends beside.

GLOUCESTER   My lord, we are quite perfectly agreed.

FRENCH AMB.   And France can be to such this loving friend!
20   My king would now make friendship's girdle[6] fast
About the waist of him and of Arthur,
Together joined will both be more of men.
Also, the king has maked a daughter-child
To give and place her on your king as queen,
25   So make Arthur the heir to Childebert!
I bring this portrait covered[7] of the lady,
Arthur may look on it and fall in love.
And here, she writing letters to your king,

He gives letters

In which she make expressures most sincere.

30   GLOUCESTER   Which he will read with all attentive speed.
Good sir, I will return to you anon,
But beg you sit awhile in the hall.

FRENCH AMB.   Merci, bon duc. I think we make good match.

GLOUCESTER   Were't ours alone to make, I know we would.

Exit Ambassador

35   Were all good counsel heeded by our lords
All kingdoms of the world would prosper well.—

Enter Arthur

Your Majesty, I beg, again, a word.

ARTHUR   O, Gloucester! Now doth Cupid lurk in shade?
No more of Florentine grand duchesses,

---

5. *revolter* a rebel. [Perhaps a faux-French neologism, but it appears in English as of 1602, though nowhere else in Shakespeare.—RV]

6. *girdle* not a ladies' undergarment, just a belt, though still the image is quite odd! [RV]

7. *portrait covered* The stage business with the foreign princess's portrait may give another clue to *Arthur*'s disappearance. Elizabeth's father, Henry VIII, agreed to wed his fourth wife, Anne of Cleves, based on a portrait of her. He sued for an annulment after meeting her. This episode of Arthur and Matilde may have been viewed as too close to home. [RV]

40		Venetian doge's[8] girls and Spain's infanta.
		My lord, I would have no more cavilling,[9]
		But ask a respite from this marriage chat,
		A week, a day, to feast our victories,
		And then thou mayst molest me with this prate.[10]
45	GLOUCESTER	You were thrice blest at Lincoln, York, and Bath.
		My king, a marriage now will fasten peace.
		Your hopes for Britain's weal[11] demand great sums.
		The king of France would have you be his heir!
	ARTHUR	How seemeth she to thee, the French *princesse*?
50	GLOUCESTER	There's but the envoy's word and painted cloth,
		Still covered o'er 'til you consent to look.
		But sure she is not loathsome.
	ARTHUR	Mend my soul![12]
		With praise as this, one need not fear of scorn.
55	GLOUCESTER	Her disposition she reveals in this. *Gives letter*
	ARTHUR	I want it not. You know I speak no French.
	GLOUCESTER	Nor Spanish nor Italian, King. I know.
		With exercise your tongue can learn the trick.
		You need but muster out the words "I wed."
60	ARTHUR	If they do love me so, they could learn English.
		Are there no foreign princesses who can?
	GLOUCESTER	My king, I beg of you, a list'ning mood.
		A happy kingdom wants a steady hand
		To steer through white-topped billows, storms, and
		fear,
65		When curdled sea with oily fingers threats
		To fist the groaning crew from greasy deck.
	ARTHUR	Less peroration,[13] Gloucester. Hit the mark.
	GLOUCESTER	The royal sceptre must be straightly held
		And not with ev'ry wind rock left and right.

---

8. *doge* the supreme ruler of Venice.

9. *cavilling* petty argument.

10. *prate* idle talk.

11. *weal* well-being, prosperity.

12. *Mend my soul* a very mild oath, probably used ironically here, as in "Heavens to Betsy!" [RV]

13. *peroration* rhetoric.

70	ARTHUR	Too much synecdoche for this crowned head.[14]
	GLOUCESTER	Too hot, my king, your fancies and vexations.
		For those who sway the rule must needs be led
		By cooler humors, not by passions' pricks.
		In marriage men are spared from wilder lusts:
75		Their anger melts away, they find them calm.
	ARTHUR	You paint a dreaded scene, you god of love.
		An if the lady find me not her taste?
	GLOUCESTER	'Tis not unknown.
	ARTHUR	Come, Duke, thou art too cruel.
80	GLOUCESTER	'Tis not unknown affects[15] do wax with time.

All's one, as in your autumn, you are not
The same young lovers who were wed in spring.
In time new common cause is found, and wife
And husband are as allies in a war

85 They cannot win, yet still are they content
To fight it side by side.

ARTHUR Most nobly read.
Duke, grant me but a moment to revolve,
As you do teach me now, if league with France,

90 Made strong by unseen, sure not loathy dame,
Is best of fate for Britain and her king.

GLOUCESTER Most gladly, lord. I'll sit without.

ARTHUR Our thanks.

Exit Gloucester

Cold fear now grips me closer than in war.

95 Dare I examine her behind her veil?
Whatsoe'er it shows, I must not credit true
For royal painters earn when they omit.

Uncovers painting

"Bonjour, princesse." There's all my Frankish talk.
Can this sustain our weary hours throughout

100 A life of matrimonial content?
"Bonjour, princesse. My kingdom wants a queen.
What say you? Find me well enough for now?

---

14. **synecdoche** Arthur plays dim, claiming not to understand Gloucester's point, but his request for less synecdoche is surely ironic, since "this crowned head" is an example of synecdoche. [RV]

15. **affects** feelings.

Then we must hence spend every day and night
In one another's speechless company
105 Until the one of us should mercy show
And dying leave the other in sweet peace."
Perchance I ought to praise her qualities.
"Within your bluest eye I see reflect
The fleets of France at my behest and beck.
110 The sun is no more golden than your hair,
Which calls to mind your treasury and wealth.
How I do long to press beneath my hands
Your soft and yielding countrymen for tax."
Let's taste of her smooth embassy instead: *He reads*
115 "Great Arthur's famous and heroic acts."
She does write well. "Your loving friend, Matilde."
'Tis all set here as circumstance demands.
Matilde. Matilde. 'Tis as should be.[16]
This then must be, 'tis right, as Gloucester says.
120 I'll call him back and set it to be done.
O traitor voice, why silent now, thou knave?
But call him, coward! Now. Call now.[17]

Enter Constantine and Guenhera

O, brother, what relief to see thine eye!
Just now I want thy wit and company
125 To free my spirits from these chains of state.
CORNWALL   So long as you would have me here I'll stay.
ARTHUR   What lady waits upon thee with such care?
GUENHERA   A lady once you termed a warty toad,
A spaniel, and your most unwelcome shadow.
130 ARTHUR   A warty toad? I unbelieve this lie,
Nor credit you are Guenhera who cast
Enchantments o'er us all in Gloucestershire.
GUENHERA   Enchantments? Ha! O, King, are you not shamed?
For long years have I feared an apple's fall,
135 Which does remember me at once the pain
Of being struck by them upon my head
When you would throw them at me in your mirth.

16. Note the short line: a pause of hesitation. [RV]
17. Again, a shortened line. [RV]

	ARTHUR	I am ashamed if ere that cockerel[18]
		I was did aught that lacked in courtesy.
140	GUENHERA	'Tis possible that I did bear myself
		Without most ceaseless perfect comeliness.
		I'truth, I fear th'most perfect gentle knight
		As soon had hurled a pippin[19] at my head.
	ARTHUR	I am astound that this is truly you
145		In form made real from out my mem'ry's mist,
		And you are changed and unchanged both at once.
		The workings and the crafts of wizard time!
		You are become most perfect dame while still—
		Within you, as behind a mask you wear—
150		I see today that girl, and yet more odd,
		Do feel myself become again a boy
		Now stood beside you feigning I am king.
	GUENHERA	I'll flee an you become again that boy
		Ere crabs and costards[20] take again to wing.
155	CORNWALL	But still art thou a barnacle, my Guen:
		The king hath matters pressing for his time.
	GUENHERA	I hear no plaint from him and sure I would
		For that boy said my ears were long as hounds'.
	ARTHUR	Indictment without end! Where's mercy flown?
160		You'll mark each scruple[21] of my youthful crimes?
	GUENHERA	The bill of charge[22] is 'graved upon my heart.
	ARTHUR	Then care of state must stand aside whilst I
		Prepare defense or plead for clemency.
	GUENHERA	'Tis bootless, still may hope eternal spring.[23]
165	CORNWALL	An if my sister irks you not, my king,
		Excuse me now to counsel with your stabler:
		I fear my horse has taken bots.[24]

---

18. *cockerel* young rooster.
19. *pippin* a variety of apple.
20. *crabs and costards* types of apples.
21. *scruple* iota, jot.
22. *bill of charge* official accusation.
23. An intriguing puzzle. Alexander Pope writes "Hope springs eternal" in 1733. Might he have read *The Tragedy of Arthur* in that same country house from which the senior Mr. Phillips stole the play? [RV]
24. *bots* intestinal worms that beset horses. This looks suspiciously to me like "I need to see a man about a horse."

	ARTHUR	Your leave
		I freely grant to nurse your steed, on term
170		You swear, good earl, to feast with me this night.
	CORNWALL	I take it 'pon my death, your majesty. *Exit Cornwall*
	GUENHERA	You find me altered much from what I was?
	ARTHUR	I cannot stick in speech my brawling thoughts.
	GUENHERA	Then you are not so changed from woodland boy
175		That I unchangingly did love.
	ARTHUR	Not changed?
		But now I wear the costume of a king.
	GUENHERA	So did you in those best of all my days.
	ARTHUR	'Tis true, I clad myself as ancient kings,
180		As Caesar, Solon, Hebrew David, Saul.
		Do I seem no more suited to this garb?
	GUENHERA	No more, no less. I thought you perfect king
		In Gloucester's oaks, when reigning from a branch
		You daily sent me to my death.
185	ARTHUR	Say no.
	GUENHERA	But yes.
	ARTHUR	A tyrant and a fool was I.
		I would have piping now, not drums and fife.[25]
		But soft, did you not say you loved that boy?
190	GUENHERA	I did.
	ARTHUR	But love no more? What love is this
		That sang to you when I was crowned with twigs
		But chokes now when my crown's all wrapped in
		gold?
	GUENHERA	That sylvan king did not requite my love,
195		Remember this, but banished me from him,
		Bid leave him with my brother, much preferred,
		As Constantine was precious to that court.
	ARTHUR	A dreary[26] king he was, that despot child.
		I would that I could reach across time's moat
200		To lay my hand upon this purblind[27] boy
		And tell him love that wondrous nymph he sees.

---

25. *piping . . . fife* music of love rather than of war. [RV]
26. *dreary* cruel, horrid, perhaps melancholy, but not current meaning of boring or gloomy.
27. *purblind* myopic.

Nay, I'll not ever say that he was me,
For were it I who sat a day with you,
And love the issue of our argument,
205 'Tis sure that I would answer you in kind[28]
And offer tenderest affections, Guen.
If, as you say, this forest boy did not,
Then how dare he lay claim to being me?
And yet, if he was never me, how can
210 I hope that you will offer still your heart?

GUENHERA What, what? Will you mock love to me now, King?
Make light of common hearts, kings' privilege?

ARTHUR No mockery but of my wordless self:
No poet, Guen, no orator at all,
215 I am untongued when most I want new words
To lock your beauty in my longest thoughts.
I spent too soon the language I did know,
Like to an actor hoarse from preparation,
Or a traveller of the Afric coast,
220 Who lights with wonder on an unknown bank,
But finds he's burnt his words on duller lands.
What can I say that was not elsewhere false?
And more above, I'd verse upon these sights,
But sure you are the matter's wisest scholar,
225 Thrice-schooled in science of your beauty's paths.
At glass you have learnt all the fields and hills:
I cannot win you with geography
Of your own kingdom's sparkling coasts and leas.

GUENHERA So I am Vanity in your conceit?[29]

230 ARTHUR No saint there is who could resist that sin
Were every glass so richly laid with like
Temptation to't. Say that you love me still.

GUENHERA O! Kings speak love when love is politic!
Was't Gloucester or my brother Constantine

---

28. *in kind* ironically, a little grist for the mill of the Bacon-wrote-Shakespeare school. "In kind" in this sense is used nowhere else in Shakespeare, but is used in 1622 by Francis Bacon in his *Henry VII*. Of course, this may only prove that Bacon imitated Shakespeare or that they were both innovative in writing the spoken language of their period. [RV]

29. *conceit* fanciful notion, poetic figure.

235   Impressed[30] your words to move sad Guenhera,
                               Revive her young days' camomilèd[31] hopes?
                               A king must wed where stratagem decides,
                               Where blind boy's[32] arrows, shot with policy,
                               Do prick the heart but slightly if at all.

240   What promised they I'd furnish Britain's king?
                               Do I bear land or gold or men at arms?

ARTHUR   Though caution urge me hide the case, here 'tis:
                               I was but now set down to study love
                               And think how kings, though men, must sacrifice

245   Their own desires to commonweal's demands.
                               Much wind was blown today to ope mine eyes
                               That Britain's new-made master must ally
                               More closely now to—

GUENHERA   Cornwall?

250 ARTHUR   France, Guen,
                   France.
                               Already are we Cornwall's sovereign lord.
                               There is no policy in Guenhera
                               Being Arthur's empress, yet I stand in gyves.[33]
                               I of a sudden am again a boy

255   But granted better wisdom of my years.
                               My younger sight now sharper with new wit
                               I mark in you far more than Cornwall's cliffs.

GUENHERA   Thy father, too, did love a Cornish girl.

ARTHUR   But not so gently. Sure I am not he.

260 GUENHERA   Were't not for Uter's special[34] appetite
                               My brother would not hold his watery earldom,
                               And I would not appear to royal eyes.

ARTHUR   We entertain conjecture such as this
                               And I do end the worse: unborn, unkinged.

---

30. **impress** forced into service.
31. **camomilèd hopes** Camomile was reputed to grow stronger for being trampled upon. The adjective is Shakespeare's invention. [RV]
32. **blind boy** Cupid.
33. **in gyves** tied, as if with the straps that hold a hunting falcon to a wrist or perch.
34. **special** particular.

265   I'd not be here and hammering the flint[35]
                         To kindle your extinced love for me.

GUENHERA   Extinced? Said I this? I do not know.

ARTHUR   That's tying hope an inch above the reach.
                         To taunt a king with sour-sweet painful words

270   Is sure a crime that stains thy crystal name.

GUENHERA   How swift from love thou sayest I am stained!
                         As none dare foil thee in thy every bliss,
                         See thou art unaccustomed to be thwarted.
                         Like other Pendragons, thou'lt seize perforce[36]

275   What all thy words have failed to win with ease.

ARTHUR   Dear Guen, I say again I am not him.
                         The proof is in my mild and soft reply.
                         Though thou mayst roughly chain me to a stake,
                         And fill the yard, and arr[37] and tear at me,

280   While cries for blood from every groundling[38] rise,
                         I will but roll upon my back and sigh.

GUENHERA   But, noble bear,[39] when I, a lovesick girl,
                         Did love that Arthur, all the world knew him
                         Bound in[40] with dowsabels[41] and ev'ry Joan.

285   No fury then, 'tis true: his smile sufficed
                         To win him what he would.

ARTHUR   While silent Guen
                         Did sadly mind his dog-star[42] scrabbling[43] days.

GUENHERA   One's heart gone forth is hardly whistled home,

290   Not when it leaves behind true-weeping love.

ARTHUR   I would a kiss could drive away that pain.

---

35. **hammering the flint** trying to solve a difficult problem, from trying to light a fire or fire a pistol with a flint. [RV]
36. **perforce** by force.
37. **arr** snarl like a dog (onomatopoeia). The imagery in these four lines comes from bearbaiting. Arthur casts himself in the role of the bear (as his name would suggest) which Guenhera picks up on in her next line. [RV]
38. **groundling** audience members standing in the courtyard of a theater, bullring, or bear pit.
39. **noble bear** As my father tirelessly reminded me as a boy, "Arthur" means "noble bear" in some Celtic tongue or other.
40. **bound in** surrounded.
41. **dowsabels** sweethearts [especially pastoral. —RV]
42. **dog-star** Sirius, but by implication the hottest days of the year, the dog days of summer.
43. **scrabbling** scratching frantically, like a dog.

	GUENHERA	Thy lips, O King, are like Achilles' spear,[44]
		Such weapons that do wound and also heal?
	ARTHUR	Might I not heal myself while healing thee?
295	GUENHERA	O fie! What pain ails thee, luxurious[45] king?
	ARTHUR	Regret[46] can scratch a man so rough as thorns.
	GUENHERA	Invention pains as well. Reports of love
		That touched my ears stung worse than what I spied.
		Oh, yes, I spied from in the tickling gorse.[47]
300		I spied you woo them, win them, weave their crowns
		Of yellow buds that opened for the sun.
	ARTHUR	'Twas nothing but some twisted celandine.[48]
		My nurse did use to grind it when in need
		And made from it a certain private paste.[49]
305		So nothing that thou spied should bring thee grief.
	GUENHERA	I spied them weep, my eyes salt-ripe[50] as theirs.
		I do suspect that now, regretful king,
		'Tis more convenient you should give each girl
		Full half your face engraved upon a coin,
310		Thus binding up rememberance and pay.
	ARTHUR	For all the sorrow that boy moved in thee,
		I strong rebuke him and on his account
		Requit with crown that I have by my hand,
		No crown of weeds that will not live a day
315		But that becomes thy beauty and thy state,
		And may yet cure the harm to thee and me.
	GUENHERA	O smooth, smooth king, what sayest thou to me
		Thou hast not sworn an hundred times before?

---

44. **Achilles' spear** The spear that wounded Telephus, in Greek myth, could also heal him. [RV]

45. **luxurious** lascivious, lustful.

46. **Regret** Somewhat surprisingly, here and below in line 307 are the only two instances of this word in Shakespeare's works, although it was used in books, which evidence suggests Shakespeare read, such as Spenser's *Faerie Queene*. [RV]

47. **gorse** prickly furze. [*Ulex europaeus.* —RV]

48. **celandine** a wildflower.

49. **yellow buds . . . celandine . . . private paste** One hears Shakespeare's Warwickshire childhood in these lines, one of those lovely moments that one is tempted to label autobiographical. *Ranunculus ficaria*, or lesser celandine, is a wildflower of the English Midlands, does indeed open and close for the sun (albeit not after being picked and woven), and was indeed used for a curative "private" ointment, as reflected in another nickname, "pilewort." [RV]

50. **salt-ripe** on the verge of crying.

	ARTHUR	Unjust, fair Guenhera, and here's the proof:
320		For half the month has Gloucester filled my ears
		With policy, alliances, and leagues,
		And all my flaws from when I was a babe.
		One hour ago, by his sharp reasoning,
		I thought to yield the day and bow my head,
325		To play a kingly lover, winning us
		Some foreign fields and rights to levy tax.
		But now I am as mute as any boy
		Who never yet has touched a lover's lips.
		I'm dry. Wouldst have a king before thee kneel?
330		I kneel. Wouldst have a king forsake demesnes?
		Adieu to France attending in the hall.
	GUENHERA	An if it were reversed, not thou but I
		Who left behind to weep discarded loves,
		Wouldst thy new faith in my new bond be strong?
335		Couldst thou forgive and take me as thy queen?
	ARTHUR	Return with me to woods in Gloucestershire,
		Begin anew upon our proper path.
		Thy hand. Thy hand, and in the oakshot[51] sun
		Come walk thy ways with me, o'er roots and earth.
340		Soft, kiss me, Guen, half-close thy lovely eyne[52]
		And in this wispen[53] dawn of gold-flecked mist
		We catch our breath and hear the lark's first song.
		Soft, kiss me, Guen, and take this flowered crown

[He crowns her]

And sit with me in shade and kiss me, Guen.

[He kisses her]

345	GUENHERA	Need call we now the courtiers?
	ARTHUR	Anon. *Exeunt*

---

51. **oakshot** presumably, streamed through the branches of an oak. An invention of Shakespeare's.
   [RV]
52. **eyne** eyes.
53. **wispen** wispy, made of wisps.

[ACT III, SCENE II]

[Location: The Royal Kennels]
Enter the Houndmaster and his Boy

MASTER   He fought his bit of war, yes, but that's all done now.
                And see if it were not what I augured.[1] He sends his
                his army home, the most of 'em, to fields and
                traffics.[2] Those uncles of thine, home again, both
5   arms about 'em. The earth gives up its foison,[3] the
                markets are loud with cries, roads all teem with
                wheels. The queen is round with young.[4] The court's
                a court of music all the day. The king's that boy again
                I loved. He came again last night, d'ye know, and
10   called me friend, and stood at this gate here and
                stepped up to the bar to reach within, and he did
                watch the hounds an hour yet. Asked all their names
                and stepped right in, dropped to his knees and had
                them in his arms, suffered them to wet his royal face
15   and stroked the velvet of their ears. Said he thought
                Hamish was of Edgar's line, noble shoulder, noble
                brow and muzzle, he said, the color minded him of
                Edgar. He has the eye for blood. And now the queen
                ripe to bring a prince, that prince will come to us,
20   mark it, see, and learn the dogs as well. Both be
                here.

BOY   If she whelps[5] a prince, what's that make for Tom, the

---

1. *augured* predicted.
2. *traffics* commerce, trading.
3. *foison* plentiful harvest.
4. *round with young* pregnant.
5. *whelps* gives birth, especially for animals.

boy of Joan? And Phoebe's boy? Not princes are
they, sure?

25 MASTER   With beagles, 'tis no matter, sith, by law, the sire's
good qualities hold strong into the pups. A bad dam
makes no harm upon the litter. Good sire means good
pups: good head, hard tooth, strong croup,[6] there's
thy father, there's thy pup. People: 'tis not so. Take
30   Tom, thou sayest, and mark: his dam found that
Silvius[7, 8] to wed her, so Tom's no prince, or is no
more, if he were. And, mark his face and colors, he's
more to his dam or even Silvius than he do
resemble—thou know'st the word.[9] Though Silvius is
35   fat and gross enough in breadth to stick a cross-
passage[10] while that Tom be slender as—[11] 'tis not for
us. Now Phoebe's got no husband, so the church says
her boy's an orphan.

BOY   She calls him her own prince, says he'll have a
40   kingdom in the sky.

MASTER   She'd be kinder yet to handle him as a good dog and
not talk such. Mark Agnes there. Does she spend her
days in thinking on what heaven holds for her? Does
she think on yesterday's meat or tomorrow's rain? And
45   d'ye know one so content to sleep and bark? Peace,
boy. The king has made us peace, we leave him his in
turn.

BOY   The sun is almost lifted up.

---

6. *croup* rump, from base of tail to mid-back.

7. This is the line that, presented to my mother, prompted her dismissal of the entire play as
"grotesque," not to mention "unreadable." "Better he should have spent his prison years lifting
weights," she sighed.

8. *Silvius* a common name in pastorals, English folklore, etc., and, as Mr. Phillips noted elsewhere,
used for a shepherd in *As You Like It*. [RV]

9. The Master stops himself from saying "Arthur."

10. *cross-passage* another remarkable piece of linguistic evidence for the play's authorship. A cross-
passage was a corridor in a medieval house connecting two opposite doors, one giving onto the
street and one onto the building's yard. There is a cross-passage in the house where Shakespeare
was born and raised. It passes in front of his father's glove workshop and was used to allow a
horse drawing a cart of skins to enter the building, continue through to the yard to make a
delivery, and exit the same way. For Silvius to be so fat as to block the cross-passage is, of course,
a grotesque exaggeration on the Master's part. [RV]

11. The Master was going to say "Arthur" again.

MASTER   Come then, couple 'em, show me thou knowest which
50   hound suits each huntsman's will. Not Argos,
                though. Give him yet another day to lick that leg.

                                                          Exeunt

[ACT III, SCENE III]

[*Location: A hall of the court, London*]
Enter Cumbria and Norfolk

CUMBRIA   These months in court have emptied me of heart.
                We are now imbecile[1] and womanish.
                I counsel thee, O Norfolk, fear what comes,
                How haughty proud is Arthur of his court.
5   Immortal glories he proclaims and scorns
                His father's attributes as barbarous.
                'Tis fools who hope their world will never end,
                That only ancient kingdoms durst[2] expire.
                But search dull tomes of crumbled nations past,
10   And learn that soon before each empire's death
                Was manly virtue banished from within.
                Now Arthur sets us all to scholarship
                Of kingdoms and their ruin: England's next.
NORFOLK   Great Cumbria lends voice to all my fears.
15 CUMBRIA   Each folly doth insist it is first-born
                And nothing owes to madness gone before:
                Our court's decay[3] is nothing like to Rome's,
                'Tis true, yet still will lead us to our end.
NORFOLK   I doubted[4] Arthur's realm would slave to lust,
20   But not to see this meacock[5] court of wives.

---

1. *imbecile* puny, weakened. No implication of mental deficiency.
2. *durst* dared.
3. *decay* downfall, ruin.
4. *doubted* feared.
5. *meacock* effeminate, cowardly.

His youthful passions are reversed left-right,
So lust remains, yet only for the queen.
The queen is all. Her crotchets[6] are his toil.

CUMBRIA He shapes each man of us into his like.
25 We are no men but play at manliness.
From inside we are hollowed empty armor.
The court abounds of players and of tales.
Once mighty battle ranks reform to dance.
Now fablers win his love; all deeds are thought.
30 This dandled[7] king was ne'er a martial lord,
His brows do frown on those who counsel arms.
He longs for heaven's peace brought down to earth,
And does beguile himself to credit too
That England's enemies should find delight
35 To sit and mazèd[8] wonder at his arts,
Whilst all our forces till and sell and sleep,
And will in battle's heat abrook[9] no pains.

NORFOLK The queen had but a single holy task:
She tarried long at it, then bore no heir.
40 King Arthur yet forgives her useless womb.
Whilst each[10] her bloody mischance cheers our foes
He claps her words, proclaims each one conceitful.[11]
Were I King Mordred, great, at least, in hate,[12]
Or Childebert, whose daughter we did scorn,
45 I would rain plague and war upon this land.

CUMBRIA Doth Gloucester not advise the king our foes
Admire[13] at us, wide-lipped[14] as rav'ning[15] dogs?
There will be death upon our kingdom's gates.

---

6. *crotchet* whimsical fancy.
7. *dandled* pampered.
8. *mazed* bewildered, perplexed.
9. *abrook* tolerate.
10. *each* We learn in IV.i that the queen has already miscarried twice. [RV]
11. *conceitful* imaginative, witty. In this context, it echoes also the question of her lack of conception, as in fertility. [RV]
12. Mordred's Short Man Disease is now confirmed. My father once said to Ted Constantine, while being led out of yet another courtroom, "Status can never make up for stature, Ted. You'll be U.S. attorney general and you'll still feel my balls resting on your hairpiece."
13. *Admire* wonder, marvel.
14. *wide-lipped* openmouthed.
15. *rav'ning* bloodthirsty, voracious.

		This minstrels' court will run with English blood.
50	NORFOLK	O, Arthur's queen and Gloucester is his maid:
		He wants but clout[16] and tire[17] to serve this hive.
	CUMBRIA	Unjust to bees who know of war.[18]
		What duty can we owe to folly's prince?
	NORFOLK	But soft, my earl. Be chary of such thought.
55		Our fealty's[19] not chosen, nor can be
		Withdrawn when grievance burns our gorge with bile.
		This king is king by God's own will, not ours.
	CUMBRIA	Let contemplation wander on a path
		Where action need not follow wingèd thought.
60		I speak not of King Arthur's case today,
		But of the gen'ral, philosophical.
		If any king doth die, by loving hand,
		And kingdom thence be saved ere sands run out,
		Then violence diverts no will of God
65		But acts it forth, as if one were His hand.
	NORFOLK	But, Cumbria, this is no end of it.
		That next king, stern and measured to your taste,
		Must every moment fear another blade
		From one erroneously reading signs
70		And thus misprising[20] all of God's desires.
		There is no end to contemplation's path.
		Assassins breed assassins swift as hares.
		We must bear under folly and dispose
		The ends of kings t'the king of all our ends.
75		I pray you, Earl, to let such thinkings go.
	CUMBRIA	Your learning suits a university.
	NORFOLK	Our virtue will prevail by fearless words
		And force of great example. Now, farewell.
	CUMBRIA	Farewell, my friend. I will take heed of this.

Exit Norfolk.

80	To see the conflagration in the spark,

---

16. *clout* rag [especially with menstrual connotation. —RV]
17. *tire* woman's headdress.
18. Note short line. A pause as Cumbria prepares to speak the treasonous next line. [RV]
19. *fealty* The word tended to take three syllables early in Shakespeare's career and two syllables later. Here it takes three. [RV]
20. *misprising* misunderstanding.

But, from some conscience-words of little heft,
Not dare prevent the scorching of our realm,
Would tear my heart from me as with a hook.
I want nor crown nor vulgar admiration,
85   And could in innocence play regicide
As shallow Arthur has too long played king.
Come, hand, couldst thou perform this hellish act?
But think upon't. In mind's eye perceive
The moment when: the start of fear, the cry,
90   The stream of blood, the man betrayed who looks
Into your eye in want of answers there,
The sacrifice of your eternal soul
Which you do willing give to devil's clutch
No matter all your right and high intent.
95   But no, I turn and dare not follow this.
What affect's this? I scarcely know this frost:
Is't cowardice I feel ice o'er my heart?
It is. I see our end, but cannot start.
And so do kingdoms fall by vice's art,
100   When righteous men in conscience stand apart.   *Exit*

ACT IV [, SCENE I]

[*Location: The Royal Court, London*]
Enter King, Queen [*pregnant*], *Cornwall and nobles, ladies bearing scales and lady-whifflers*[1] *with soft maces. Hautboys, harps*

ARTHUR   My lords, give way. All men must bend the knee.
For now the ladies reign their hour in court,
And I dispose of all our sovereignty
Into these paler hands to bear law's scales.—
5   My queen, in whom I have re-breathed[2] my heir,[3]

---

1. *lady-whifflers* female ushers.
2. *re-breathed* apparently Shakespeare's coinage. Next attested use is in 1606. [RV]
3. *re-breathed my heir* "in whom I have again conceived a child."

Abdico meum regnum.[4]

GUENHERA   Loving friend,
God thank thy faith in gentler sex's wisdom,
Which we now sharp[5] upon the wheel of law.
10   Speak, Crier, read the charges to the court!
But where's the Earl of Cumbria, who's charged?
Go, send for him at once to stand before.

Enter Cumbria with lady-whifflers

ARTHUR   Tut,[6] Cumbria! Be not a puling[7] boy.

GUENHERA   My lord, if I do reign, then let me reign.

15   ARTHUR   O, gentle tyrant, mercy on my head.

GUENHERA   Once only do I wink,[8] or else seem weak.
Now, Crier, speak!

LADY CRIER   O, Earl of Cumbria!
As token of accused, uncertain state,
20   Bear willow branch as sign of love forsworn
And fennel leaf that honors lovers true.

                                    She gives two branches

At trial's end, shall one remain on you.   [*Reading*]
Imprimis:[9] The Earl of Cumbria did, upon St. Lambert's
Day,[10] speak love to Rosamunde, a lady of this court,
25   and did move her with his words. *Item*: He having
purchased with words this melting heart, the same
earl did lead the lady to a bosky covert.[11]
Item: This same earl did, at mellay[12] two days later,
wear no token of the lady in his helm or on his
30   person and, when he did smite Sir Stephen to the
ground, asked not the lady's favor. Thus reads the
charge of most uncourteous love.

GUENHERA   The lady stands withal. Her case is plain.

---

4. "I abdicate my reign [to you]." (Latin)
5. *sharp* sharpen.
6. *tut* an exclamation of impatience.
7. *puling* whining.
8. *wink* turn a blind eye.
9. **Imprimis** "In the first place." [A common legalism to introduce a list, the following points beginning with "*Item*."—RV]
10. *St. Lambert's Day* September 17.
11. *bosky covert* bushy grove.
12. *mellay* melée, the open combat portion of a jousting tournament.

And black th'unmitigated[13] crime we hear.

35 If guilt is found then we pronounce the doom:
To Rosamunde forsworn you'll pay a sonnet.
Its two and dozen branches[14] will support
Perfumèd buds of love that you affect,
As every lady here can see in you.

40 Good Cumbria, what answer do you make?

CUMBRIA Will you not ban[15] this childish tick-tack,[16] King?
Discharge your servant from this vanity,
This swarm of tomboy-geese,[17] and swift restore
This wayward court to manly empery.[18]

45 ARTHUR Kneel, slave, to thy dread queen and tame thy tongue,
Which were more sharp, thy neck had felt its edge.[19]
Compose thy fourteen lines to this poor maid,
Or suffer my compulsatory[20] wrath.

GUENHERA Such moody men ill suit our quiet court.

50 The both of you I hold as rudesbys,[21] both:
Yes, king, who would o'erbear in his queen's name,
But doing so o'erbears that queen you serve.
Thy sonnet is become a plump ballade,[22]
Good earl, and scowls will yield thee yet more verse.

55 For peevish king, on thee falls heavy doom:
A masque[23] for Martinmas[24] upon the theme
Of queenly wisdom.

Enter Gloucester

---

13. **unmitigated** Shakespeare uses "mitigate" on a few occasions, but "unmitigated" only twice, here and in *Much Ado About Nothing*. Apparently it didn't catch on; it doesn't appear again in the OED until 1814, when Jane Austen picks up on it. [RV]

14. **two and dozen branches** A sonnet has fourteen lines.

15. **ban** condemn, rather than forbid.

16. **tick-tack** an early form of backgammon.

17. **tomboy** immodest woman; **geese** fools, but also slang for prostitute.

18. **empery** rule.

19. **sharp . . . neck . . . edge** "Keep talking like that and your tongue will get your head cut off."

20. **compulsatory** involuntary, required. [Another case where Shakespeare used a word twice and never again: here and in *Hamlet*. See "Have I Twice Said Well" by David Crystal in *Around the Globe* magazine, 23, p.11. —RV]

21. **rudesby** an insolent fellow.

22. **ballade** a poetic form of between twenty-five and thirty-five lines.

23. **masque** an elaborate music, dance, and verse entertainment.

24. **Martinmas** November 11.

	GLOUCESTER	King, the court must void
		And council sit at once to hear my news.
60	GUENHERA	My duke, why haste and noise in ladies' hour?
		This sorts[25] not with our majesty, dear friend.
	GLOUCESTER	My king, there is but now delivered word.
		Off Devon's Linmouth coast a forest sprouts,
		A wood at sea, but in its rise and fall
65		Distinct from landed trees that left and right
		Do rock. And from each countless, tow'ring mast
		Clap Saxon pennons: wolves and demi-fiends.
		Unfinished yet are that coast's daunting walls,
		And force more vast than any we have known
70		Now wets its tongue on English blood and tears.
	ARTHUR	We stand amazed at how it comes again,
		And summer blue grows black by Saxon clouds.
		Dear ladies, pray excuse our shifting key;
		We must unwilling now hear other tunes.
75	GUENHERA	An hour yet, King, to see our matter's end.
	ARTHUR	How sweet, my love, to count each grain of time
		Then turn th'hour-glass around again whilst thou
		Dost sift the virtues in thy manuals.[26]
		I feel remorse that we must turn to war
80		And bid you lead your ladies from the court.
	GUENHERA	Unhappily we yield, my fearful liege,
		But only if we may convene anon.
	ARTHUR	Enough! There can be no more talk. Now, go!

Exeunt all ladies

		Speak, Gloucester, Cumbria, all men of war:
85		What ready force might we in haste array?
	GLOUCESTER	King, we are taken tardy by a phoenix
		That we did reckon so much heaped-up ash.[27]
	ARTHUR	These conquered Saxons practiced sorcery
		That from their ruined state did plenish up[28]

---

25. *sorts* agrees, suits, conforms.
26. *manuals* books on etiquette and chivalric love, presumably.
27. *phoenix . . . ash* The mythical phoenix bird was thought to consume itself in flame and then be reborn from its own ashes.
28. *plenish up* replenish.

90 So titely[29] their annihilated strength.

CUMBRIA No sorcery but your soft mercy, king,
When for their scabby pagan vows at York
You set them back on sea to breed and then
At Bath did qualm to slay but half their ranks
95 And loosed their weeping bearing boys to fly.
At Linmouth they repay your gentleness
While you do wail of clouds and sorcery!

GLOUCESTER Withhold thine indignation, Cumbria,
And bow thy head in fear of thy king's rage.

100 ARTHUR Nay, nay, a king may rightly be rebuked.
'Twas youthful will to be unlike my sire
Provoked me to such bounty unadvised—
An Devon's bulwarks are imperfect still,
I fear to know our count of ready men.

105 GLOUCESTER Forsooth, scant thousand are trained up in arms.
To that add peasant ranks with knife and fork.[30]

CORNWALL My power, nearest Linmouth in its day,
Was all brought north to fortify the Tyne.

ARTHUR The Saxons find us lame, they will bestrut[31]
110 As far as London ere we give them fight.
What help can we account from northern lands?

CUMBRIA The Pict will lend sworn arms at your command
But only if he fears your swift reproof.

ARTHUR He knelt in Abbey's echoes, kissed my ring.
115 Sure I doubt nothing of his fast reply.
Send now to him. Command his every pick.[32]

CUMBRIA This reasons shallow, King. He bent his knees
When Arthur's power waxed, and Pictland's throne
Was filled as Arthur would.

120 ARTHUR   And now?

CUMBRIA   And now
Nor fear of you nor love for you hath he,
But grudgeful holds you Calvan's slaughterer,

---

29. *titely* quickly.
30. *knife and fork* hand knives and pitchforks. The dining fork did not appear in England for
    another decade. [RV]
31. *bestrut* to strut, walk pompously.
32. *pick* pike.

		And will no bloody aid deliver you
125		But smiling tarry as your England burns.
	ARTHUR	Though Britain joys first peace sith Roman days,
		And harvests more can feed each mewling babe,
		Though churches toll and tithe, and stalls[33] are full,
		Though our court's glories ring to Muscovy,
130		Barbarians flow across the land like rats,
		For Mordred, goat o'the moors, doth fear not me.
		I'll open up that cur from throat to paunch—
		Might we in France an ally find?
	GLOUCESTER	Sure not.
135		Not when their offered love was cast away
		And you must wed where no alliance was.
	ARTHUR	What game is this? Why come they yet again?
	CUMBRIA	Your prideful realm is built on women's dreams.
		Surprised are you this peace lasts but a day?
140		That on our shores again these devils wash?
		Beshrew[34] the tide that does not plaud[35] your court![36]
		There never will be day until the last,
		Without some foeman come t'unsheathe his sword.
		There's only war. 'Tis man's inheritance.
145		No peace, but now and then an instant's breath
		Made sweeter still by certain brevity.
		'Twas this your father Uter taught to me.
	ARTHUR	He taught me nought, nor this nor other words.
		As Mordred makes us beg that is our right,
150		What ransom must we pay the proditor?[37]
		What treasure yield to purchase love from him?
	GLOUCESTER	No golden-fingered Croesus[38] holds such sums.
	ARTHUR	Then what? Is't land he crave or privilege?
		I'll grant he is the Soldan of the Turks[39]

---

33. *stalls* market stands.
34. *beshrew* curse.
35. *plaud* applaud.
36. This may be a reference to the story of King Cnut, who demonstrated the limits of royal authority when he commanded the tide of a river to stop. [RV]
37. *proditor* traitor.
38. *Croesus* an ancient Lydian king renowned for wealth.
39. *Soldan* supreme medieval ruler of a Muslim power, though usually not the Turks. [RV]

155		Or Duke of Africa.
	CUMBRIA	Or Prince of Wales.
	ARTHUR	What sense is here?
	CUMBRIA	There is no prince, no heir.
	ARTHUR	The queen is bursting ripe with coming child.
160	CUMBRIA	The queen has lost two breathless bloody heirs,
		And may yet many false conceptions[40] shed.
		This Mordred knows. In change for his sworn arms,
		Entail[41] to him your throne upon your death,
		Conditionally[42] no natural heir is born
165		By this or any queen your highness takes.
	CORNWALL	Or any? Cumbria, I'll snap thy bones.
		Cod up thy will[43] and tame thy serpent's tongue.
	ARTHUR	Thy care of queen is brotherly, my earl,
		But hear with no more passion than a luce[44]
170		What wisdom here conceiveth: Mordred sure
		Doth take me as my family's dockèd tail.[45]
		If for some mouth-made[46] words he takes our part,
		And after is my heir safe-born, what harm?
		Thereafter I shall act my father's rate[47]
175		And ready me eternally for war.
		Go, smooth your sister's mind of what we do.
		It is a devil's chance to play a kingdom
		On th'unproofed vigor[48] of an unborn prince!
		Bold Cumbria, raise up what force we have,
180		And Gloucester, send our word to Mordred's court.
		Invite our momentary[49] son and heir
		To ride with us most lovingly to war. *Exeunt*

---

40. *false conceptions* miscarriages.
41. *entail* assign, as in a will.
42. *conditionally* on condition that.
43. **Cod up thy will** "Get hold of yourself." Literally, "Put your penis back in your pants." [RV]
44. *luce* a type of fish. [More precisely, a pike used in heraldry. —RV]
45. *docked tail* cut-off ending. [Also, slang for a circumcised penis. —RV]
46. *mouth-made* insincere.
47. *rate* manner, style, conduct.
48. *unproofed vigor* untested strength.
49. *momentary* temporary.

[ACT IV,] SCENE II

[Location: The Queen's Chamber, London]
Queen solus [very pregnant]

GUENHERA	Is no one waiting?
Enter Nurse	
NURSE	Majesty, you called?
GUENHERA	Is there no word from Linmouth? Of the king?
NURSE	There's nothing, madam. Have you any wish?

5
    The pain's come? Will you I should call the wife?[1]

GUENHERA I have no word of my own battleground,
No more than aught we learn of Saxon wars.
Come, press my back.

NURSE   Aye, sit.

10 GUENHERA   Nay, standing's best.

NURSE As comfort bids you, that's the way.

GUENHERA   O! O!
I cannot stand with ease.

NURSE   As lief[2] you'd sit.

15 GUENHERA Perhaps upon my side.

NURSE   So then, your side.

GUENHERA Is there then nothing for it?

NURSE   Nothing now.
You yielded comfort nine full moons ago.

20 There, there, sit quiet now. You jar[3] the prince.
But sit now! You do move and move, my queen,
As yet I washed your younger muddied cheeks.
Is't here you ache?

GUENHERA   Just there, that's well. Thou'rt kind.—

25 What ancient sage first wond'ring marked that line

---

1. *the wife* the midwife.
2. *as lief* I would prefer.
3. *jar* jostle.

Of moons 'twixt lover's smile and labor's cries?

NURSE 'Twas known when Adam first leered eyes at Eve.

GUENHERA The king did riddle me afore he rode

And put to me this question wrapped in smiles:

30 "What burden is't that cannot still be borne,

My queen, that day when it will no more bear?"

Quoth I, "My king, you riddle at your pleasure."

Came he, "Nay, at my burden." Mark'st thou, nurse?

It is a wife, a wife. He kissed me then,

35 And rode to war, and called me his own Guen.

NURSE And left your prince to start on his own ride.

Doth he yet kick and spur his heels at you?

GUENHERA He hath been still within an hour.[4]

As under-ocean spouts do lend their breath

40 To beasts below the waves,[5] find air, my prince,

Come out and fill my hungry ears and arms

And fill the king with pride of you.—No word?

How is't that we have nothing yet of him?

Would he not send to us? Not think on us,

45 Not wake[6] that we do think on him in broil?[7]

Conceiveth he that we have no concern

In victory or death? But who hath more?

NURSE Now back you go, my girl, sit still and calm.

GUENHERA If Arthur lives, he makes of me a bargain

50 With strange a king from strange a northern land.

They wrangle[8] over my own bursting womb!

The king has luck, my boy's in lusty health,

And cries out first for milk and then for scepter.

If th'child doth die, the other thanks his fortune.

55 Can such men be, that would raise kingdoms up

Upon a chrisom's[9] grave?

NURSE   Hush, hush, go to.

---

4. A short line. The queen begins to worry at her fetus's stillness? [RV]

5. Elizabethans believed that fish and other sea life were able to breathe underwater, thanks to spouts of fresh air that bubbled on the ocean's floor. [RV]

6. *wake* realize.

7. *in broil* in battle.

8. *wrangle* to dispute or contest.

9. *chrisom* a child dead within a month of birth, shrouded in its christening robes ("chrisom-cloth").

GUENHERA   If Arthur dies, then so too dies his heir,
             For Mordred will not stop at its small breaths
60   To puff him from the throne.[10]—I'll fly with him
             In peasant weeds[11] and kerchief.—Arthur lives,
             And child doth die, what then remains of me?
             For heirs must rise or kingdoms surely fall,
             And no king born can bear a barren queen.

65   NURSE You drop a case, my girl. I'll tutor you.
             If victory is won, the Saxons scourged,
             'Twas you who took the day, heroic queen!
             For by your lady's womb were allies found:
             Your king still lives, the child is born, and you
70   Are Linmouth's rescuer, bold Guenhera.

GUENHERA   I feel them both, those rival-friendly kings.
             They counter-strive[12] to read their fates in me,
             All futures vie in this discov'ry-space.[13]
             Wherefore he leaves me gnashing ignorant?
75   Is no one waiting there? Is no word come?
             O! O!

NURSE   There now it starts! So kings are born!
             Come walk a ways with me in th'lower hall
             And by that prompting urge our prince to fall. *Exeunt*

---

10. Mordred will not mind the infant's little cries, but will sweep him away to become king. [RV]
11. *peasant weeds* disguised as a peasant.
12. *counter-strive* strive against each other.
13. *discovery space* in Elizabethan theaters, a curtained area, also called an "inner stage." [Here, used metaphorically for womb. —RV]

[ACT IV,] SCENE III

[Location: The field of Linmouth]
[Enter] Mordred solus

MORDRED   And now does Arthur love me, says I am
          A steady friend he loves above his life,[1]
          Belovèd heir, his brother, almost son.
          When Saxon lance did fling me from my horse,
5   King Arthur charged, restored me to my feet,
          And shouted I was "Hector[2] born anew!"
          He lies, I know. He cannot think me so.
          He boasts more speed and brawn than I, and yet,
          Today, his words did something make it so,
10   And I did smite the Saxon with more strength
          For Arthur said I would, and so I did.
          At battle's end, whilst numbering the slain,
          I ought have plunged a blade into his back,
          But pleased was I to have his ear and eye,
15   To blush as he made me fair weather.[3]
          He seems to wish for nothing but that he
          Should breathe his last and I should warm his throne.
          I know he lies, and yet I thank his love.
          The Saxons vanquished, off he posts[4] to court
20   And thence to rebel-factious Ireland's shores,

---

1. Cf Christopher Marlowe's poem "Hero and Leander": "Above our life we love a steadfast friend." The poem was first published in 1598, but Shakespeare would likely have known of it before. As was often the case with these two men, it is nearly impossible to disentangle who was influencing whom. See *Rival Playwrights* by Professor James Shapiro. [RV]
2. *Hector* a Trojan hero.
3. *made me fair weather* feigned friendship to me.
4. *posts* rides with haste.

'Gainst death and all oblivious enmity.[5]
His kiss upon my cheek, I watch him fly,
And then do mind[6] his murder of my flesh.
Were I that king, I would send Mordred north
To wait his certain crown and wait and wait,
While queens do toil abed to thwart his rights.
By my assent he fashioneth complotment![7]
But I am I. I will not wait amort.[8]
I will to London, there to greet my queen.
I'll have her promise I am heir, and view
Her beauty, all renowned. Should Arthur die
In Ireland's wars, she could become my queen.
By reputation's whisper I have heard
That she is liberal[9] with gifts of love.
By Mordred's holy seed might not we soon
Implant a prince ourselves to hold our claim
And with her womb prove Mordred's right to rule.
Yes. Then will I obtain from England's lords,
And vulgar tribune sorts who must be paid,
Such love, subjection, dread that may be bought.
Success made sure, I'll turn resistant thought
To acting as a vengeful brother ought.   *Exit*

---

5. This line appears verbatim in Sonnet 55, line 9, published in 1609 but certainly written much
   earlier. A similar "pre-borrowing" from *The Sonnets* (or later recycling *for The Sonnets*) occurs in
   Edward III, approximately contemporaneous to *The Tragedy of Arthur*. [RV]
6. *do mind* recall.
7. Mordred is just realizing, in modern words, that he's been conned.
8. *amort* dejected.
9. *liberal* promiscuous, and here pronounced in three syllables. [RV]

[ACT IV,] SCENE IV

[*Location: The Royal Court, London*]
[*Enter Arthur*]

ARTHUR   There is, in truth, no urgency abroad
              But one must find a place to practice war,
              And Cumbria did touch me when quoth he,
              "Your father ne'er could subjugate the kern."[1]
5   So we shall capriole[2] o'er Irish bogs,
              And silence, for the now, rebellion's plaints.
              I say not "always": I am taught at last,
              Conceive no dream to peg[3] e'er-lasting peace,
              But slay an Irishman or two and breathe,
10   Fight Germans, rest, kill Picts, then infidels.
              A proper king am I and love my wars.
              I taste my peace in thimbles, drams, and grains,
              Not by the hogshead but the pennyworth,
              And count him glutton who would ask for more.

       Enter Gloucester

15   How fares the queen?
GLOUCESTER   She waits upon you, sire.
              The joyless Guenhera is grief's poor slave,
              But smiles and dries her cheeks to know you come.
ARTHUR   Anon. Is all afoot for our departure?
20 GLOUCESTER We stay but for the giddy[4] wind to choose.
              Yet, too: there's one would speak with you, my liege,
              Rode hard from Yorkshire for your ear, he says.
              He hath attended here for you these weeks,
              And hath refused to publish his desire

1. *kern* Irish foot soldier.
2. *capriole* leap, caper.
3. *peg* to fix, guarantee.
4. *giddy* indecisive.

25		To any but the king.
	ARTHUR	Bring him to us. *Exit Gloucester*
		My loving lovèd queen awaits her king
		And I would pass my hours of peace with her,
		Empillowed[5] on her breast before my ship,
30		Refresh all wearied ache within th'embrace,
		For she and I have duties to perform,
		Else we shall wake one morn and find us Picts.

Returns Gloucester with Philip

		A strong-limbed, comely youth, of noble face.
		What art thou, boy, and wherefore needs our ear?
35	PHILIP	God save you. I am Philip, come from York.
		And carry you remembrance from my mother,
		Who from her dying bed sends tender love
		To her one king and true.
	ARTHUR	Who is thy dam?
40	PHILIP	In York she sewed for the lord mayor's wife.
	ARTHUR	A lady of the wardrobe, yes—that's she?
		Elizabeth was that good lady's name.
		Thy mother is Elizabeth? Of York?
		But in her dying bed?
45	PHILIP	She is, my lord.
	ARTHUR	We sorrow at those words. What says she, child?
	PHILIP	She bids me kneel and love you as my father.[6]
	GLOUCESTER	Speak no word more of this deceit, queer[7] boy.
	ARTHUR	To love me as thou lovest thy own father?
50	PHILIP	To love you, father mine.
	GLOUCESTER	No more.
	ARTHUR	Is't so?[8]

---

5. **Empillowed** apparently a Shakespearean invention. [RV]

6. The episode of Philip of York is perhaps another clue to the disappearance of *The Tragedy of Arthur*. Queen Elizabeth's father, Henry VIII, similarly ennobled an illegitimate son, Henry FitzRoy. The boy died at age seventeen, but the king, having only daughters, had apparently considered making him his heir. As with the portrait scene in III.i, this scene may have been viewed as commentary on the queen's father and therefore more than sufficient to earn a banishment from the London stage. A further note: Henry VIII was the *younger* son of Henry VII, and would not have been king but for the premature death of his elder brother. His name? Arthur. [RV]

7. **queer** untrustworthy, suspicious.

8. Again, an opportunity for a director to decide precisely when Arthur believes Philip, if at all. [RV]

	PHILIP	In this alone do I claim more than kings,
		For I have known our truth since I could speak.
55		She sang to me of you and of her love,
		But said we must ne'er trouble you at court.
	GLOUCESTER	I am impatient for the swift and sure
		Conclusion of this show of cozenage,⁹
		So skip us quickly to your humble foist.¹⁰
60		Come, come, yield up your catalogue of boons.¹¹
	PHILIP	But nay, good lords, I hope of you no gift
		More than your royal hands upon my head,
		And you admit¹² my mother's dying love
		From her poor orphaned boy, then I'll to York.
65	ARTHUR	An if now orphaned, Philip, yet new-fathered,
		Or better far, restored to father true:
		I see in every sinew and thine eye
		Thy testimony's proof: thou art my print.¹³
		I know these lineaments¹⁴ as if I peered
70		Into a glass of other years, which guards
		In it past images long sith reflect.
		Come to my arms, my Philip, prince and heir.
		In court shalt thou adoptedly reside.
	GLOUCESTER	You course so speedily as this, my liege?
75		He came to London hoping for a coin,
		And you'll emboss his face on every one.
		'Tis not so plain to me the evidence
		You spy in this base sharker's¹⁵ reddening cheek.
		Nor is there policy in circumstance
80		Determining the fate of kings and realms.
		E'en it is true, are there not other such?
		Perchance this one hath not the claim of age.
	ARTHUR	'Tis so, all so, but this one came to me
		And this one has no parent now, but me.

---

9. *cozenage* fraud, deception.
10. *foist* roguery, trick.
11. *catalogue of boons* list of demands.
12. *admit* accept.
13. *print* copy, duplicate.
14. *lineaments* outlines, shapes.
15. *sharker* swindler.

85   I will not banish my own son by night
        Nor nurse my lineage in stranger's lands,
        But bind him to my side, to shape him king.
        Good Gloucester, call the queen to share our joy.
        Uprouse her from her weeping bed and we
90   Will consolate her in her grieving mood.
        For three small heirs she gains a prince today
        And must rejoice God's equability.[16]

GLOUCESTER   Your majesty, there is a haste in this
        That ill beseems[17] the matter and its cost.
95   This moment's consequence will echo long.

ARTHUR   Thou ne'er hadst son, old Gloucester, as I do,
        And in his eyes perceive our future strength.
        Now prithee cease to quirk[18] this case of truth[19]
        But lead my gloomy[20] queen to greet our son.

                                        Exit Gloucester

100   Young Philip, dost thou love to fish and hunt?
        And canst thou ride and thrust a keen-edged sword?

PHILIP   I have acquired skill in manly arts,
        And by my father's side, would prove my worth.

ARTHUR   'Tis spoke like any prince, my noble boy.
105   With pride we'll watch you stare into the sun[21]
        Then soar as Britain's eagle, Prince of Wales.

PHILIP   If I do stumble or speak slow, my lord,
        I am astonished that I orphaned woke,
        But will fall to my bed a son and prince.

110 ARTHUR   I too have supped on such perplexity.

        Returns Gloucester [leading] by arm Guenhera

        I am today the queen and you the king,
        Dear Guen, and here present to you an heir.

GUENHERA   You compassed[22] this rare feat as thund'ring Jove

---

16. *equability* evenhandedness.
17. *beseem* to suit, accord, fit.
18. *quirk* quibble with.
19. *case of truth* a legal question decidable on facts.
20. *gloomy* another clue to dating the play, *gloomy* appears only in Shakespeare's earliest plays. [RV]
21. Elizabethan zoology held that young eagles matured by staring at the sun. [RV]
22. *compass* devised, contrived.

Did pop Minerva from his splitting pate?[23]

115   Did not your skull protest at such invention?[24]

ARTHUR   New prince, embrace for me your mother-queen.

GUENHERA   And will his brother Mordred love him well?

ARTHUR   More dread have I of April rain and wind

Than of that flea-bit tench,[25] that ape, that patch,

120   The jordan-faced[26] and stinking Pictish scroyle.[27]

That league was pashed[28] in bits upon its terms.

GLOUCESTER   Shall we send word to him of his mischance?

ARTHUR   But wait for our return from Irish wars,

For he is one who poorly learns bad news.

125   GUENHERA   What further need have you of queen, my lord?

Have I not failed what you have asked of me?

ARTHUR   Hush, Guen! Thou must not speak such wretched
stuff!

We have made whole our question, only queen,

Be jovial now and kiss our son and heir.

130   GUENHERA   So as you bid, so shall I do. Come, Prince.

                                 [They embrace]

GLOUCESTER   What war will follow on from this fond kiss?

ARTHUR   Such war as would have followed all the same,

Such war as clouds the sky or dews the grass.

Our people ne'er would tolerate the Pict

135   And he had ruled 'gainst endless mutiny.

No English will abide a stranger-king

But offer up commotion without end.

We sealed that pact in other, different days;

He sure cannot conceive that it would hold.

140   Go see, my lord, that all is readiness,—

And, Prince, when I return, we shall converse.—

Come, Guen, a night of peace is granted us

---

23. *Jove . . . pate* In mythology, Minerva burst fully armed from Jupiter's forehead, where her mother had nurtured her.

24. "Didn't that hurt?" but also "Was it hard to think up this plan?" [RV]

25. *tench* a fish with red spots, giving it the appearance of being flea-bitten. [*Tinca vulgaris.* —RV]

26. *jordan-faced* resembling the contents of a chamber pot.

27. *scroyle* scoundrel, wretch. [Used again by Shakespeare in *King John.* —RV]

28. *pashed* smashed.

And savors it more nectared 'twixt two wars.

Exeunt [except Philip]

PHILIP   I have some royal heart, for this I met

145   And did not squeak. I have some royal gloss,

For that fair king doth see in me his twin.

If heart and gloss, though, yet I want the blood:

Elizabeth in truth did bear his son,

On selfsame day my own dam had a boy.[29]

150   My mother's son lives still, for years, I hope,

While th'other met his end some weeks ago.

I came in hope of some small token, aye,

And once or twice my fancy rode a gallop

'Til I was knighted or endowed with land.

155   But this mad whirling rush of fortune's wheel

Was all unlooked,[30] and frights me a wild duck.

My wings are bating;[31] I ought fly to York,

Afore they learn how small a wren am I,

Yet something is that mews me up[32] in court.

160   An I go now, all benefit is lost.

A day or two, perhaps, as Prince of Wales,

Whilst father is at war with duke beside,

Leaves vantage for good fortune to provide. *Exit*

---

29. In many ways, this is the least Shakespearean moment in the entire play, and, though Mr. Phillips did not note it, I will: the revelation to the audience here—that Philip is in fact a fraud—would normally occur *before* his acceptance by Arthur (if Arthur is sincere in believing the boy's story and is not simply accepting it as a useful lie to break his pact with Mordred). This particular dramatic effect occurs elsewhere in the canon—I am thinking of Iachimo and the trunk in *Cymbeline* and the statue of the "dead" Hermione in *The Winter's Tale*—but not in quite the same way. That having been said, the unique occurrence of an effect or word in one particular play by no means proves he didn't write it. There are canonical plays that include unique examples of vocabulary, for example, the technical term being *hapax legomenon*. That he did something only once does not prove he didn't do it. And, in this case, I am obviously not dissuaded of his authorship. Rather, I would consider this as an experiment he felt was not worth repeating, or an effect that audiences did not like. [RV]

30. *unlooked* unexpected.

31. *bating* beating impatiently, as if to take off.

32. *mews me up* Continuing the bird imagery, mewing a bird is to confine it or tie it down. [RV]

ACT V[, SCENE I]

[Location: The Royal Court, London]
Enter Mordred with personal attendants and colors, led by English servant

	MORDRED	How empty now great Arthur's halls do seem.
	SERVANT	The king is led his host to Ireland, lord.
	MORDRED	Where doth the queen reside in time of war?
	SERVANT	At court, with all her ladies and the guard,
5		And those that dance to fill her empty hours.
	MORDRED	Go greet her that her most well-willing friend,
		The King of Britain—but for one—awaits.

Exit servant

[Aside] And he would see her down before him kneel[1]
And pledge her weeping vow to her next lord.

Enter players[, including Player King and Queen,] and ladies of Arthur's court

10		What court is this? And with how many kings?
		Doth Arthur suffer them to share his throne?
	PLAYER KING	Here is no call, no space, no time for you,[2]
		But all is answered for by us, sirrah,
		And handsomely, and we will hold our place.
15		Off, off! The field's yet ours for many months,
		Commissions from the king to play for him
		Upon return from Irish wars no less
		Than comedy and tragedy, two each,
		And to invent a tale with all his knights
20		Displayed on stage as heroes in a quest.
		So, fly, avaunt,[3] ye paste-crowned, rat-robed king.
		Make haste or we will drop you from the walls.
		How bare, mechanical a king you make!

1. There is, perhaps, a sexual implication in this line. [RV]
2. Mordred mistakes the actors for foreign royalty. The actors, in turn, mistake Mordred for another actor, dressed, not very convincingly, as a king.
3. *avaunt* begone!

MORDRED	Art thou base interluder,[4] puffy[5] rogue?
25	Well, bow, O malapert,[6] to current[7] king.
PLAYER KING	Such currency is compassed[8] by the art,
	Not thine to claim by wishing, paper prince.
	Now I have in my days played Charlemagne
	And Caesar, David, Herod, Priam, Jove,[9]
30	And thou do aweless show thyself to me.
	But lift from here, and turn the head. Look tall.
	No, no, thou couldst be messenger, no more.
	Let drop thy hands: why press and pull them so?
	Thy manner calls to mind a washing fly.
35 MORDRED	I thank thee for this kingly lessoning,
	Though yet thy days in court are few remaining.—
	My lady, tell us what thou playest yet
	For Arthur should he safe return from war?
PLAYER QUEEN	We play the tale of flightful Icarus[10]
40	Who from ambition did destroy his life.
MORDRED	Too dark to play for joyful king, too dark.
PLAYER QUEEN	Too true, to speak more properly, too true.
MORDRED	La! Truth belongs in preachers' sermon texts;
	It ne'er yet paid a player's wage, nor will.

Enter Queen Guenhera, Philip, and attendants

45	But how? Are you more players yet or true?
GUENHERA	A gathering of kings o'erwhelms the court,
	But only gulls cannot distinguish blood
	From players' paints.[11]

---

4. *base interluder* a lowly actor.
5. *puffy* blustering, bombastic.
6. *malapert* presumptuous one.
7. *current* actual, real.
8. *compassed* built upon, contrived.
9. *Charlemagne . . . Jove* emperor of the Franks, Roman emperor, king of the Israelites, king of the Jews, king of Troy, Roman thunder god. [RV]
10. *Icarus* in Greek myth, the boy who with his wings of feathers and wax flew too near the sun and fell into the sea. [RV]
11. *gulls . . . paints* a virtuoso triple meaning (1) Only birds cannot distinguish makeup from real blood; (2) Only fools cannot distinguish kings from actors; and (3) Only a fool would mistake you, Mordred, for a king. One is reminded of the words of the Italian writer Cesare Pavese: "Shakespeare was conscious of a double or treble reality fused together into one line or a single word." [RV]

MORDRED	Great queen, I am unarmed.

50   Your beauty cuts—

GUENHERA	You carry yet a sword.
MORDRED	Your majesty?
GUENHERA	You said you are unarmed.
MORDRED	I meant to speak as poets do, O Queen,

55   Of beauty, love, and your most perfect self.

All Britain swells with pride and hies to tell

The world how Guenhera, in loveliness,

Is queen above all history's fairest names:

Nor Helen, Venus, nor Europa, none

60   May claim but meanest of similitude.

GUENHERA	We thank you, King of Picts, for these your words
	And ask of you what matter draws you south?
MORDRED	To fix between us the validity
	That comprehends our nations' league: that I

65   Am now your son, and you my loving dam,

And more, that should cruel war scythe Arthur down,

I will, made king, maintain you on your throne,

And take from "mother-queen" a needless word.[12]

PHILIP	Thou seemest to misconster[13] Arthur's will,

70   And place thyself, unasked, in other's seat.

Now who art thou that steals into our court

Demanding audience of my mother fair,

And crooning[14] words of love and legacy?

MORDRED	But who is this stands by in diadem?

75 PHILIP   'Tis Philip, Prince of Wales, no less than son

First-born to Arthur, heir to Britain's throne.

MORDRED	Another player and obscene to God?
	Is no one here who speaks God's holy truth?
GUENHERA	The comedy would have our exits now,

80   Each by our rightful doors, O King of Picts.

MORDRED	Unkind, madame, and unadvisèd pert.[15]

12. *needless word* remove "mother" from "mother-queen" and marry Guenhera as queen.
13. *misconster* misunderstand.
14. *crooning* bellowing, like a bull, especially Scottish dialect. [RV]
15. *pert* impertinent.

I came to offer you my loyalty
Until such time as God will have me king.
For God doth wish for my continuance:[16]
85   He speaks in omens, acts, and lineage,
His will is seen in your own barren womb,
The which when planted with my hallowed seed,
And not corrupted by the bastard's touch,
Will fruitfully bear forth a race of kings.
90   Yet kindness is not here with kindness met.
Instead, I find this painted treachery.
Your king, among his crimes, is now forsworn,
For he hath given that was never his.[17]
Perforce my message alters now, my queen,
95   And you will be my guest without delay,
And with false prince reside in Pictland's cold.
My men await: we leave at once. Make haste.

GUENHERA   Or no? You draw?

MORDRED   We will conduct you now.
100   Nor orphan boy of Wales nor kersey king[18]
Is like[19] to slow our swift velocity.

GUENHERA   With such celerity as altered thee
From stamm'ring suitor to a damnèd churl.
Was it but yesterday thou wert sweet child?

105   MORDRED   Most cruelly you misjudge me, Guenhera.
Budge on, and you will learn in Pictish court
How true and honest kings do fearsome reign.   *Exeunt*

---

16. *my continuance* "the continuation of my line."
17. I.e., the throne to Philip. [RV]
18. *kersey king* the player king, dressed in kersey, a coarse cloth.
19. *like* likely.

[ACT V,] SCENE II

[Location: Aboard an English ship]
Enter Denton, Sumner, and Bell. Thunder

SUMNER   The welkin[1] splits with shattering blue-gold fire,
              lashing our skin with cold-forged nails, hammered
              hard off heaven's anvils.

DENTON   It rains.

5   SUMNER   Aye, it rains.

DENTON   Aye, would you left it there. Better rain than we
              should see clear night and therein witness the comets,
              blots, and disordered heavens. The book of God is
              open for any who have eyes. Dark fires, fallen stars,
10   and bright midnights tell mischief.

BELL   Beshrew the sky. I would fain have some ground, e'en
              the most saggish[2] wet. I have sailed enough until I
              die. This ship seems fast to be my tomb. From out
              out Southampton, round Cornish tail to Ireland, but
15   do we walk on Irish sands? No sooner anchors drop
              than off the ocean floor rebound and we sail
              through Orkney ice thence round again to
              Yorkshire. Like Sisyphus, for all of time, we'll sail.[3]
              Is there no end? We sail and fight and sail again to
20   fight. I have no more stomach to fill of this.

DENTON   Be satisfied we did not fight. The Irishman will offer
              friendship, then turn and bite when back is shown.

SUMNER   We only show our back and leave the Irish standing,
              for the king did lose his errant queen meantime.
25   Inconsiderate, say I.

---

1. *welkin* sky.
2. *saggish* soggy.
3. *Sisyphus* a mistake on Bell's part, or my father's. In myth, Sisyphus was condemned by the gods to push a rock up a hill, never reaching the summit.

	DENTON	He had kept her clapped up close, she would not stray so.[4]
	BELL	D'ye think the sky is lit to warn us? Or tell we will be punished for his sins? His father was not wed to his
30		dam. Perhaps we cannot win more, whatever valor's shown. I would go home. I would be off this pitching boat!
	DENTON	I like thee now thy fire's cooled from time thou wert glory's bawcock.[5]
35	BELL	I am not afraid.
	DENTON	Then thou art no man. The noise is there to fear.
	BELL	I am not fearing. Not much. I only would stop. My guts do dance.
	SUMNER	And half the men's step live to dance with thine.
40		There's a devil's fever aboard our merry squiff,[6] and and we will set to land with fewer hands than took to took to Ireland.
	BELL	I will not number nor make plaint of the count nor any mischance yet to come, if we but greet the land.
45	[VOICES OFF]	Humber's mouth! Humber's mouth!—Strike her![7]
	DENTON	Then here is land for thee and I wish thee every joy awaiting, Bell. Here's land as thou wouldst wish, but thou'lt soon call back the ship, for up there is nought but the cannon's jaws set to prattling.
50	BELL	I'll up, beshrew the cannon, beshrew the rain.
	DENTON	The cold-forged nails.
	BELL	Aye, the nails, beshrew the nails, I'll be gladly wet in the first boat that drops and points toward the green.
	SUMNER	And we behind you, lad. Lead on. *Exeunt*

---

4. There is in this line an implication of Guenhera cuckolding Arthur. [RV]
5. *bawcock* from "beau coq"—fine fellow. [RV]
6. *squiff* skiff.
7. *Strike her* a command to lower sails.

ACT V, SCENE III

[*Location: The English camp on the Humber River*]
Enter Arthur

ARTHUR   Our backs are pressed to th'raging Humber's waves;
There is no way but forward, as in life.
Our feet are pulled into this water-turf,
So eager is some fate to see us earthed.
5   What chronicle will soon be writ of us
In this so yielding and unyielding ooze?
Is this the promised end to such a realm
As I had built upon my father's wars?
If Arthur's story ends in quaggy[1] field,
10   How will it play and how best fill a stage?
Some sermoner[2] for epilogue intones:
"Deserving nought of fortune's gifts to him,
He squandered them in rage and lust and haste."
It is not right for right:[3] the stain of birth
15   Was ne'er forgot nor ne'er forgave in me,
No matter I upraised a gloried realm.
No vantage e'er was granted me but I
Must front[4] battalions of others' wills:
The rival kings and discontented lords!
20   I could have fled to France, or shepherd's life,
And this gray night be lost with Guenhera.
'Twere offered me anew, I would abjure.
Abjuring, I would choose to live in peace.
In peace, I might escape this grip of shame,
25   A shame that I have failed to be myself,

1. *quaggy* boggy.
2. *sermoner* a preacher.
3. *right for right* fair.
4. *front* confront, oppose.

And yet that self can only be a king,
So abjuration is forbidden me.
I am no author of my history.
What man knows aught of his own chronicle?
30   Or kens[5] what ill tomorrow hides for him?
So let us greet headlong—if mud allows—
Such end as heaven will: I will not wait.

Enter Gloucester, Cumbria, Cornwall, etc.

My lords, well met this night for promenade!
I was but now considering my joy
35   To find myself again with you beside.
How shall we to the queen, by foot or boat,
Or dangling each from tercel-gentle's[6] talons?

CORNWALL   My king, our pikes stand recklessly enranked.
We yield all vantage an we fight from here.

40   GLOUCESTER   Nor hoof nor boot might hope to leave this field:
Advance in mud or else retire in waves.

CUMBRIA   We want for arrows and our carriages
Of culverin are sunken to their caps.[7]

ARTHUR   I would a fletcher[8] and a gardener,
45   Good friends, appear from air, or heaven's car[9]
Might tumble from above to scorch this mud.
But Constantine, my queen, thy sister, weeps
For thee and me an arrow's weak flight hence.
If any here do quail at mud, then go
50   With love and venge my death another day.
Come dawn—if sun can pierce these Yorkish clouds—
I will alone trudge through this birdlime muck,
Encouched up to the chest if God desire,
To fetch my queen and heir, and give the fico[10]
55   To these o'ertopping[11] dung-breathed caterans.[12]—

Enter Ambassadors

5. **kens** knows.
6. **tercel-gentle** male peregrine falcon.
7. **carriages . . . caps** The wheeled cannons are sunk to the axles. [Anachronism. —RV]
8. **fletcher** an arrow maker.
9. **heaven's car** the sun.
10. **give the fico** make an obscene gesture.
11. **o'ertopping** surpassingly arrogant.
12. **caterans** Scottish troops.

	Be brief, good men, you interrupt our work
	Wherein we plot your havoc and despair.
FIRST AMB.	You brave good humor, King, despite of war,
	And we from Mordred bring yet more relief.
60	Aware that you most dangerously are placed,
	And wishing in his love for you no ill,
	He offers you your bastard and your queen.
ARTHUR	'Tis well: he yields to us. We do accept.
	Go set them free and we will spare your lives.
65 SECOND AMB.	Nay: interchangeably, you abdicate.
	You must forsake your child, and he his rights,
	The queen forsake her rights, and any birth.
	All this does Mordred grant you in your peril.
FIRST AMB.	Else menaces most pitiless fell war,
70	The end of which you will not live to see,
	And ere the first blow's struck, the queen will die.
ARTHUR	I abdicate or Mordred slaughters her?
	Is't he who whets his blade against her throat?
	And you will gladly serve such king as this?
75	What men are you that speak a tyrant's words?
	You will pay forfeit of your embassy.
GLOUCESTER	But hesitate to anger, King, and know
	We are o'ermanned[13] and fever gnaws our ranks.
ARTHUR	Must I unqueen the queen to buy her life,
80	Unking the king, depose myself for Picts?
CUMBRIA	A kingdom for a queen? In chess perhaps.
	I give no faith in this that if we yield,
	The queen will live or we will leave this field.
	'Tis sure there be more queens to woo and wed
85	And other heirs that you can litter out.
CORNWALL	Nay, Mordred dare not spill such holy blood.—
	[*To Ambassadors*] Go tell your king I'll front him brow
	to brow
	And singly[14] fight with him by lance or sword,
	With queen and all this island at the prize.

---

13. *o'ermanned* outnumbered.
14. *singly* in single combat.

90	ARTHUR	Good Constantine, enough: we are engirt.[15]
		Content ourselves, my brothers, this must be.
		I would lose kingdoms, e'en my own, for her,
		And ne'er would kill her in my wilful pride.—
		[*To Ambassadors*] He must grant terms protecting all
		my men.
95	SECOND AMB.	To all who yield he swears his clemency.
	Enter scout	
	CUMBRIA	But, lo, here's panting word that wants for ear.
	SCOUT	Your Majesty, the enemy's abroach[16]
		In two large wings that hawk-like spread themselves
		And will in rapid minutes close us up.
100	ARTHUR	Speak that again: doth Mordred now attack
		While we do entertain his embassies?
	GLOUCESTER	The night's too black to see with certainty,
		And mud gives no preferment to the Pict.
		No stratagem of men can sweep with haste
105		Across this hellish fog and bubbling mire.
		Tell slower now what thine own eyes did spy.
	CUMBRIA	By dark night's coverture they creep at us
		While embassies do talk us to our beds!
		This crime doth disannul civility.
110	FIRST AMB.	Good king, I swear, we know of this no word.
		No action can begin ere we return.
	CUMBRIA	They lie. Within these bags of flesh and wind
		Intelligence does nook[17] and it must flow.
		Large secrets want large outlets to escape
115		So we must loosely pierce and vent their hides.
	SECOND AMB.	I vow, fair majesty, this cannot be.
	ARTHUR	I fain[18] had given kingdoms to the wolf,

---

15. **engirt** encircled.

16. **abroach** in motion. My father, I am reminded, told me that he once announced a University of Minnesota football game for the college radio station, KUOM. Among the reasons he was not asked back was his repeated color commentary that "the backfield is abroach."

17. **nook** to hide in a corner. [Interestingly, the next recorded usage of this rare verb (1611) is by a younger playwright, Thomas Middleton, who collaborated with Shakespeare on *Timon of Athens* around 1605. A case, perhaps, of being able to trace Shakespeare's direct influence—in one small way—on the generation after his. —RV]

18. **fain** gladly.

But now I'll send you on your way to hell.

[He kills Ambassadors]

FIRST AMB.   No! No! Unjust!

120   SECOND AMB.   O, villainy! I die!

GLOUCESTER   What crazèdness! In haste you slay the queen
                 And slay us all!

ARTHUR   You are a woman, Duke!
                 Now thundering into this mud and bog
125   We march ere Mordred's slavering jaws do lock.
                 To arms! To arms! And arm yourselves with hate!
                 Hot rage now wing us o'er this drowning field!
                 Let fly the mangonels![19] Swing, trebuchets![20]
                 Belch fire, cannon, lift us on your breath
130   And speed us to the queen or to our death!

                              Exeunt with charges

19. **mangonel** a catapult.
20. **trebuchet** a swinging catapult.

[ACT V,] SCENE IV

[Location: The Pictish camp]

Enter Mordred, Guenhera, Philip, Pictish soldiers

MORDRED   What noise is this? What motion is begun?
                 Wherefore are not my embassies sped home?

FIRST SOLDIER Th'usurper's massed battalia shoulder through
                 The swamp and murk of night with mighty speed.
5   Our wings are far advanced but close on air.[1]

MORDRED   He spurns our embassy and hies to fight?
                 He offers nothing for these ransomed lives
                 But values them beneath his throne and glory?—
                 [To Guen. or Philip] Your king doth sooner laugh and
                     greet your corpse

1. An interesting example of "the fog of war." It is not clear who has attacked first. Does Arthur lose
   control of his temper or has Mordred lost control of a subtle plan? [RV]

10		Than change his crown for safe exile with you.
		'Tis his command and he who chooseth now.—
		These two are proofed uncurrent gold today.²
		They serve no further use that I can see.
		Though sure I will require this day a queen
15		She'll not be this unstaid³ and misproud⁴ stale.⁵
		[*To Soldier*] I would thou trad'st⁶ upon them now. I go.
	FIRST SOLDIER	The child beside its mother dies the same?
	MORDRED	'Tis sure the poison's thickest in the young.⁷

Exit Mordred

	PHILIP	This cannot be. Call back these fearful words.
20	GUENHERA	What is your name, O gentle knight?
	FIRST SOLDIER	But choose.
	GUENHERA	I would choose one who's spoken of in verse,
		Whom poets praise for courtesy and grace,
		A name befitting one who nobly fights
25		And never would do harm to innocents.
	FIRST SOLDIER	Then choose such name for me. That is no matter.
		Prepare yourself howe'er you will: time's brief.
	GUENHERA	I am prepared. Art thou? Thine act's thine own.
	FIRST SOLDIER	I would not have it any other wise.
30	PHILIP	In killing me you disobey your king.
		Your king would have you cut off Arthur's line,
		But I am not of Arthur's blood or seed
		Nor am no heir nor can endanger you.
	GUENHERA	The boy speaks plainsong,⁸ sooth, and ought be freed.
35	FIRST SOLDIER	And you are not the queen, nor that the sky,
		For queens reside in London not in mud,
		The sky, being often blue, cannot be black,
		And all these things being other than they are,
		It's best we think no more, or never act.
40	GUENHERA	To slay anointed queen gives thee no pause,

2. **proofed uncurrent gold today** proven as worthless hostages.

3. **unstaid** uncontrollable.

4. **misproud** haughty, wrongly proud.

5. **stale** low-class prostitute.

6. **trad'st upon them** act upon them, deal with them.

7. Elizabethan zoology viewed young serpents as having concentrated venom, which diluted with maturity. [RV]

8. **plainsong** simple truth.

Then contemplate before this foolish boy:
His face and mad outrageous circumstance
Must pluck forth pity e'en from blackest heart.

FIRST SOLDIER How often do I hear of pity spake,
45   Yet glean no sense of what the word must be.
It seems a kind of shriek or bootless prayer.

GUENHERA Then God have mercy on thee.

FIRST SOLDIER   And on you.

PHILIP But, Queen, cannot you make this vision end?
50   I would awake from this and see my home.

GUENHERA Be brave, and thereby something of a prince.

FIRST SOLDIER You will awake right soon, they say, now come.

Stabs Philip

PHILIP But no, but no, this cannot be my end!   *Dies*

GUENHERA O, God be merciful and take me in!

[First Soldier] stabs Guenhera, she dies

55 FIRST SOLDIER [*To Second Soldier*] You stand as well as any man I
                   know.
But be now better used and give your hands.

SECOND SOLD. The king gave you the baseness, I the watch.

FIRST SOLDIER Well-watched, bold guard, now lift and to the bog.

Exeunt [with bodies]

[ACT V, SCENE V]

[*Location: Humberside battlefield*]

Alarum. Excursions. Enter Pictish and English soldiers fighting. Enter Mordred

MORDRED   King Arthur's dead! Fly, English! Arthur's slain!

ENG. SOLDIER The king is dead! The day is lost! Give back!

Exit Mordred

No king, no heir, no queen, but fly and live!

Alarums. Enter Arthur

ARTHUR   But see! From my uncovered face take heart
5   And we will push them to the drowning wash!

ENG. SOLDIER	King Arthur lives! He lives! Fight on! Fight on!	

Exeunt

Alarum. Enter Gloucester and Mordred. They fight

GLOUCESTER   I would spend all my breath in slaying thee,
Thou hag-born demon of the darkest pit.
Thou never wilt be Britain's king a day.

10   MORDRED   Old Gloucester, God doth wield my sword for me
To lead me to that throne and do His will,
And first of His designs must be your doom.

GLOUCESTER   No king art thou, bereft of Arthur's strain.[1]

MORDRED   Thou diest, poltroon![2] Now out upon it, die!

Gloucester is slain

15   The lord protector leads the way to hell.
The brat he taught will follow him apace,
Though I dare not dispatch him without aid.
To me! To me!

Enter Pictish soldiers

FIRST SOLDIER   My lord?

20   MORDRED   Thy work is done?

FIRST SOLDIER   My king, to its perfection.

MORDRED   Honored friend!
Then to my side until th'usurper falls.
The coward vowed to strike me from behind.

Exeunt

Alarums. Excursions. Enter Arthur

25   ARTHUR   Nay, Gloucester, nay! Still offer wisdom's words;
Thou wert my father, too, and I thy son.
Your worthless boy must lean on you today.

Enter Cumbria

CUMBRIA   O King! The frenzied Pict doth waste the field
And hazards with his soul to win a crown:

30   He murdered Philip and your Guenhera.

ARTHUR   Say no, say no! Can death so envy me?
Englutting[3] all my loves before my eyes
Yet scorning my own life, that I must stay

---

1. **bereft . . . strain** deprived of his lineage and quality.
2. **poltroon** coward, wretch.
3. **englutting** gulping, devouring.

To roam such hell as this, to flay my heart?
35   O, Father! Doth this end now prove my birth?
O, bloody ghost, I am become thee.
For this I hid those years in Gloucester's woods?
For this I lived my seasons all at war?
I rescued York and Lincoln in my youth[4]
40   And asked for my own pleasure not a whit
Save for a queen I loved beyond all else.
E'en this is more than any king deserve.

CUMBRIA   There is no flight, my king, but only on.
Red Humber washes off the country's sons,
45   And limbs like branches float upon its waves.
But crush the scattered foe! Now rise, my king!

Enter Cornwall

CORNWALL   Dear brother, friend, and Britain's hero, stand!
The day can yet be ours for all our grief!
                 Alarums. Exeunt [Cornwall and Cumbria]

ARTHUR   To be some other man than what I am!
50   O, God, but free me from this rising mud
And give me sign how this unworthy king
Can do your will.

Enter Mordred and Soldier

              I thank thee, God. Come, knave!

MORDRED   O, weeping king! Poor bastard boy, death's fool,
55   Lift up thy knitting-stick, thou sobbing dame,
And strike at me! [*To Soldier*] You cut him from
behind!
       They fight. Arthur is wounded then kills Mordred [and Soldier]

ARTHUR   May all my blood make rich this British soil
To strengthen it 'gainst pox of rival kings.

Alarum. Enter Constantine [Cornwall] and British nobility

CORNWALL   O King!

60 ARTHUR   Good Constantine, here cradle up
This frail and draining shape and from my head
Lift this oppressive weight to rest on thee.
                    [Cornwall takes crown]

---

4. In fact, Arthur was not at Lincoln (II.vii). [RV]

On rightful brow it shines and will but float.

CORNWALL Farewell, sweet king, sweet friend, my brother lost.

Arthur dies

65 Sound drum and trumpet up to heaven's ear
In intermingled notes of thanks and sorrow.
Full thirty thousand men did die today
To win our victory at Humberside,
With loving king who joined with them in death
70 To pledge with blood his kingdom's lasting peace.
Inter their mortal shapes as each deserves.
May Britain now and ever more be blessed,
And ne'er be torn asunder by such strife
As plagued this realm and stole from Arthur life.
75 May heaven grant this prayer and yield this gift:
That peace may buckle fast this island's rifts.
Raise sepulchres for both great queen and king
And for their souls, and ours, raise voice and sing.

Exeunt

THE TRAGEDY OF ARTHUR

Arthur Phillips

A Reader's Guide

FAMILIES, FICTION, LIES, AND LIVES

A Discussion Between Pat Conroy and Arthur Phillips

Arthur Phillips: Let's talk about families in literature. First of all, do we agree with Tolstoy that all happy ones are the same?

Pat Conroy: No. A friend of mine wrote about military brats, and she thought all unhappy families were the same.

AP: There are certainly patterns in literary family dysfunction: alcohol, adultery, abuse, alienation. The Four A's.

PC: But, you know, Tolstoy did something more with those. I simply revere him, almost above any other writer. And it amazes me how he touches the complete world. He can take you inside a Russian family, but by the time you have finished, you are replete. He gives you everything. How in the world does he do this? In *The Tragedy of Arthur*, you took this small family, this immensely complicated family, and you created a world out of it.

AP: Somebody on the web wrote of [Conroy's autobiographical novel] *The Great Santini* that it represented a time when people still understood that certain jobs required you to be an [expletive] and that brain surgeons and fighter pilots were basically allowed to beat their wives and kids if necessary because they do such important, egocentric work, and if you were the kind of guy to read a story to your kids, then you obviously weren't cut out to be a fighter pilot.

PC: It's hard to kill people, but my dad killed thousands. I interviewed him on his deathbed, and I'd had no idea. He once caught a battallion of North Koreans wading across a river, and he and his wingman slaughtered the battallion, two or three hundred men. I said, "How do you know you got 'em all?" He said, "I went down and checked. I counted arms and legs." He turned the river red. So I'd listen to this and I had to admit: what was I expecting for my childhood? Bill Cosby? This was not Bill Cosby. This was a guy whose job it was to kill people.

AP: So let's take that to writers, then. The poet Czesław Miłosz said, "When a writer is born into a family, the family is finished." I'm wondering if, to be a writer of a certain type, you basically have to be an [expletive], that a certain type of literature demands a certain type of writer. Writers who write about families and who use their own families as the material for their fiction: the first two names in American literature who come to mind are you and Philip Roth. Do you have to be an [expletive] to be that kind of a writer? The problem is, you don't seem like an [expletive]. Everyone says you're an incredibly sweet guy. I don't hear that said much about Roth. But to write that kind of book, does it demand the same kind of personality, in a way? Does it excuse certain behavior and impolitenesses? To write a book like *The Prince of Tides*, you are taking the interior life of your family members and turning it into art. And they must have some sense of ownership of their interior lives, which must require of you what Graham Greene called the sliver of ice in your heart, which he said every novelist has. There must be a sliver of ice in your heart to say, "Well, I'm taking your interior life and I'm going to use it."

PC: I think there is, there is. When I write, you know, you are entering a different realm. But, too, I love this father, this sister, this brother in *The Tragedy of Arthur*. They tickled the [expletive] out of me. And I'm reading this thinking, "Poor Arthur. I didn't know this about his dad! I had no idea." I told Marly [Rusoff, their shared agent], "My God, this is the most wonderful creation, but I didn't know Arthur had suffered so much growing up."

AP: Good! But, at least in this one case of you reading that book, my own life wasn't necessary to give you the feeling that it was my own life. When you read other family novels, can you tell, or do you think you can tell—or do you care—how much of it seems to be autobiographical?

PC: I don't care. I really do not care. If they grab me. When it happens to me, there is no more magical thing that can happen. I got through my childhood, Arthur, because my father thought I was studying when I was reading. I wasn't; I was escaping that terrible household he had created. That's where I went to hide from my father. I started falling in love with stories. But your father, that sister, that brother, in your book, they felt as real to me as my father, my sister, my brothers, in any of my books.

AP: And yet, there is a limit to autobiography once you set yourself to write fiction. It bends, it breaks, it turns into fragments or pieces you can reshape. Henry Wingo [from *The Prince of Tides*] and Bull Meecham [from *The Great Santini*] are different characters. So we have this hovering Colonel Donald Conroy [Conroy's father] who can become transmuted into different fictional forces.

PC: Dad considered himself a fictional creation by the end of his life.

AP: Because of your writing? He became the character you had written?

PC: Yeah. He said, "I made Duvall's career, son. I was the first part he ever had with any meat on it." [Robert Duvall played the lead in the film of *The Great Santini*.] I said, "Oh, yeah, Dad, not like *The Godfather*? *Apocalypse Now*?" A real movie buff, that guy. He said, "Nah, I'm the one that made him a leading man." But he had one pretty good literary criticism, for my father. After *The Prince of Tides*, he said, "You made me a mean shrimper in this one." Then *Beach Music* came out and he says, "Oh, now I'm a drunk judge in this one." He said, "Son, I was such a powerful influence in your life that you can't write the word *father* without me looming up behind you."

AP: That's extraordinary: your father became all fathers. In my own case, I don't want to portray my father in my books. He's my father and I don't want to share him, and so I'm free to invent new ones. Do you think your father ever felt injured, slain, put in his place, by any of your varied portrayals of him?

PC: That's funny, I'm writing now about when Mom and Dad were going through the most horrendous divorce you have ever seen, in which a copy of *The Great Santini* was submitted as evidence, where Dad comes into court and they haven't seen each other in a couple of years and my mother goes hysterical, saying he was going to kick the [expletive] out of her right there in front of the judge, and she's crying. And then Dad is so upset, he bursts into tears. No one had ever seen Dad cry.

AP: What about other members of your family? Are you in touch with Carol Ann still? [Conroy's sister, the poet Carol Ann Conroy, was a model for the schizophrenic poet sister Savannah in *The Prince of Tides*.]

PC: Oh, no, no, no, no. Another story. Carol's basically not talked to me for thirty years.

AP: Because of *Prince of Tides*?

PC: It started with *The Great Santini*. Carol is this great black hole in the family. My brother, Tom, committed suicide, jumped off a fourteen-story building in Columbia. So I look at us as a greatly wounded family. We did not all walk out of this. All of us have carried this like a tortoise shell on our back. Our family has been the central thing in our lives.

AP: In mine as well—of course, perhaps in everybody's life, but not tragically so. So naturally enough, when you decided to write, the engine behind everything, as your father sort of noted, was your family history. He famously once said, "If I'd beaten you more, you'd be a better writer." You felt when writing fiction that you were being driven by that family history and you were going to fictionalize it, but you had to keep working through this mass of pain. Have you tried other engines to write from?

PC: I think I write from one engine, and I think it's the great weakness of my art, but when I go down in there to write, that haunting always comes roaring up at me.

AP: Weakness? I don't know. Was it Proust's weakness?

PC: That boy didn't have no weaknesses.

AP: You know, I used to hate it when I learned my favorite writers sometimes did not admire one another. So why do you guess Tolstoy was so famously anti-Shakespeare?

PC: We are all writing after Shakespeare, and we all know where to genuflect in world literature. It seems to me Tolstoy was jealous, which I've seen in other writers. He too recognized the absolute greatness of Shakespeare, but it made him jealous. He couldn't quite do what Shakespeare did, but none of us can.

AP: People are desperate to find the autobiographical elements in Shakespeare, something I think is now literally impossible in most cases. I imagine him as a man who generally did not leave recognizable traces of his own life in his work, though of course I can't prove that. Let's look at the memoir genre as opposed to fiction, especially as opposed to autobiographical fiction. You've written both; I've written neither, and I'm very curious: how do you pick? What made you decide, on some occasions, to write the literal truth as opposed to a fictional "truth," such as it is?

PC: Well, you and I both know that the "truth" is a difficult little matter. When I wrote *My Losing Season*, I had eleven guys [Conroy's college basketball team], and they were driving me crazy, and their wives were terrified. I had to satisfy those guys, so anytime anybody said something or remembered something, I called all eleven, "Do you remember saying it like that? Do you remember it different?" And they would tell the story again. Finally, I had to choose which one. I just had to choose.

AP: The demands of honest memoirs are steep. On the other hand, Tolitha [the grandmother character in *The Prince of Tides*]: how close is she to your grandmother?

PC: Certainly the grandmother looms large: my grandmother had four children in the middle of the Depression. They were starving. My grandfather wasn't working. No money was coming in. And she hooks a ride on a mule wagon to Atlanta and deserts her children. My mother was eternally marked.

AP: Your mother's family? Because in *The Prince of Tides* that story is given to the father's mother. As a nuts-and-bolts matter of technique, why did you fictionalize that, for example?

PC: My family history is fluid, but I didn't know anything at all about my father's Chicago Irish history, so I moved that story across to the mother's side.

AP: That's funny. My mom really is from the Minnesota Iron Range. She has a cameo appearance in *The Tragedy of Arthur*, and loans her name to a bit character, but steps aside for my fictional mom. Something about her life in the Iron Range, though, appealed to me, seemed important to me to memorialize, in a way, to preserve for my story: my grandfather's clothing store. But I gave all of that to a fictional family, transformed it away from reality. I may lack that sliver of ice. . . . But why did you decide to write *My Losing Season* as a memoir? Why not a novel about a basketball team?

PC: I certainly thought of that, but I wanted those guys to know how much I cared for them, how much I loved them, how much they meant to me. It's worked out beautifully. Three of them were down in our house on Fripp Island and they were staying there last week. We've become friends again where we'd lost one another. But, yes, obviously there is a fusion between my fiction and my nonfiction. My wife likes to drive me crazy with it: she hears all these stories coming out of my brothers and sister and she'll say, "Isn't that in *The Prince of Tides*?" I'll say, "Uh, yeah, it's in some book." And she'll say, "Pat, you know, you ought to try and write fiction sometime."

AP: When you look at your five novels, do they seem like your life story?

PC: Yeah. Do your books?

AP: Only to me; no one else could find my life story in them. They're my life story in that I remember where I was in my life when I was writing them. They're souvenirs to me, but no one else can read me in them, except the development of me as a writer. Were you ever tempted to write a memoir about your family instead of one of your novels?

PC: Not early on, but I'm doing it now. My brothers are nervous; the wives hysterical.

AP: Are you going to use the same procedure you used with the basketball team? Of double-checking everyone's memories?

PC: I double-check everybody.

AP: That sounds like too much work to me. When you're finished, you're going to have a memoir of your family and five novels forming a sort of prismatic version of that family. How do you think those will compare? Are they six works? Or two works? Or one work?

PC: Here's what I plan for the rest of my life, if I live long enough. At the end of this memoir, I want to finally say, "Mom and Dad, I leave you now. I will not be coming again." This will be the end of one long work. Then, after this memoir, my next book is going to be a huge book about Beaufort, South Carolina.

AP: Do you feel influenced by other novels about cities?

PC: I love 'em. I love a sense of place. I've always loved books where someone makes me comfortable with a place. I've always loved *Augie March*. You and I were talking about *A Dance to the Music of Time*. In *The Alexandria Quartet*, the sense of place excited me. Because I had no home, a sense of place in books is very important to me. That's what I'm going to try with this novel about Beaufort. I've collected stories about this place for years and years. And you realize at the end of your life, you have a reservoir that you want to get out.

AP: And will your family be recognizable in this?

PC: Nope. That will be over.

AP: So it's never too late to get a new engine. That's inspirational, I must say.

QUESTIONS AND TOPICS FOR DISCUSSION

1. At one point Arthur reflects about his father, "His life was now beyond my comprehension and much of my sympathy—even if I had been a devoted visitor, a loving son, a concerned participant in his life. I was none of those." (page 82) How did you feel about Arthur's relationship with his father? Do you think his feelings were fair? Do you think he was a good judge of their relationship?

2. As Arthur writes, "So much of Shakespeare is about being at a loss for identity, being lost somewhere without the self-defining security of home and community, lost in a shipwreck, confused with a long-lost twin, stripped of familiar power, taken for a thief, taken for the opposite gender, taken for a pauper, believing oneself an orphan." (page 246) What role do you feel the theme of identity played in the novel?

3. How did you feel about Arthur's relationship with his twin sister, Dana? What did you think of the overall family alliances—Dana preferring their father to their mother, Arthur preferring Dana, et cetera? Do you have similar alliances in your family? Are they something people can control?

4. What do you think would happen if there really was a new Shakespeare play discovered? What would you have done in Arthur's position?

5. At what points do you suspect the character Arthur starts and the author Arthur ends? What did you feel that you knew for sure? Did the possible truth or falsehood of the "introduction" matter to you?

6. How did you feel about Petra and her relationships to the siblings? Overall, what role did the theme of twins play in the novel?

7. What did you think about Arthur's mother? Did you feel there was more to her than met the eye?

8. Overall, what did the novel bring to mind for you about family? What were some other important themes you came across?

9. What did you think about the play? Do you feel it enhanced your reading of the introduction? Was the feeling of reading it similar to any experience you may have with Shakespeare?

10. Did the book change how you thought about Shakespeare? About authors and stories?

ABOUT THE AUTHORS

WILLIAM SHAKESPEARE was born in Stratford-upon-Avon, England, in 1564, the son of a town official. Likely educated at the local grammar school, Shakespeare then traveled to London in the late 1580s, making his name as an actor, poet, playwright, and co-owner of theaters and theater companies. His career ended as a member and partner of the King's Men company serving King James I. His works include *Hamlet*, *Macbeth*, *King Lear*, and *The Tempest*. He is widely considered the greatest writer in the history of the English language. He died in 1616.

•

ARTHUR PHILLIPS was born in Minneapolis and educated at Harvard. He has been a child actor, a jazz musician, a speechwriter, a dismally failed entrepreneur, and a five-time *Jeopardy!* champion. He is the author of the novels *Prague*, *The Egyptologist*, *Angelica*, and *The Song Is You*. *The Washington Post* called him "one of the best writers in America," and *Kirkus Reviews* wrote, in 2009, "Phillips still looks like the best American novelist to have emerged in the present decade." He lives in New York with his wife and two sons.

Join the Random House Reader's Circle to enhance your book club or personal reading experience.

Our FREE monthly e-newsletter gives you:

• Sneak-peek excerpts from our newest titles

• Exclusive interviews with your favorite authors

• Special offers and promotions giving you access to advance copies of books, our free "Book Club Companion" quarterly magazine, and much more

• Fun ideas to spice up your book club meetings: creative activities, outings, and discussion topics

• Opportunities to invite an author to your next book club meeting

• Anecdotes and pearls of wisdom from other book group members . . . and the opportunity to share your own!

To sign up, visit our website at
www.randomhousereaderscircle.com

 When you see this seal on the outside, there's a great book club read inside.